"YES," HE SAID. "I WANT TO SLEEP WITH YOU."

He turned toward her with a sensual grace at once lethal and provocative. He purposely held her gaze and lifted the shirt he wore over his head and tossed it aside. "You want me," he said. "And I want you."

Naked to the waist, he stood honestly before her. His broad chest was clearly defined, every muscle outlined. His body was corded with a network of muscles placed like narrow stones, one atop the other and two, side-by-side. Rock hard biceps flexed naturally and easily with every movement and the strong, powerful legs sheathed in leggings and covered with a breach cloth only accentuated the masculine design of broad shoulders that narrowed toward a lean waist and long, powerfully built thighs and calves.

"Sleep with me and be my wife."

The intensity of the eyes gazing at her was frightening and unrepentant. Dark and dangerous, they flirted with her in a subtle, charismatic and nearly hypnotic way. Then he smiled softly, his expression yearning, sultry, earthy, clean and masculine. She was caught in the turbulent undertow of a maelstrom so powerful that she could not break free.

"Love me or reject me, Kathryn," he said defiantly, shaking his head. "I'll never be a beggar at your feet."

THE EAGLE
AND DOVE
THE

VICTORIA MORROW

LEISURE BOOKS NEW YORK CITY

A LEISURE BOOK®

September 2007

Dorchester Publishing Co., Inc.
200 Madison Avenue
New York, NY 10016

ISBN-10: 0-8439-5842-1
ISBN-13: 978-0-8439-5842-3

The name "Leisure Books" and the stylized "L" with design are
trademarks of Dorchester Publishing Co., Inc.

Printed in the United States of America.

Visit us on the web at www.dorchesterpub.com.

ACKNOWLEDGMENTS

The American Eagle Series is historical fiction. The period of American history represented in the trilogy spans an era from 1850 through the Reformation. The McCallums and Dorys are fictional characters whose lives were shaped by the times and events in which they lived.

The backdrop is historically accurate, including most of the events and some of the people whose lives led to the single greatest enterprise in American history—the building of the transcontinental railroad.

The history of the United States of America is brief; barely more than two-hundred years. It is with gratitude, that I, a citizen, humbly acknowledge those individuals whose lives were given in service toward building this great nation, the men and women of our armed forces and the legislative body. Without their strength, courage, and foresight, many of the events which shaped our country would have had vastly different consequences.

I would also like to recognize the leadership of the United States of America, the American President. Since I have been writing professionally, four presidents have served our nation to the best of their ability, guiding us through difficult times, shouldering massive responsibility, taking both credit and blame with humility as the leaders of one of the greatest nations in the world.

President Ronald Reagan and the First Lady,
Mrs. Nancy Reagan
President George H. W. Bush and the First Lady,
Mrs. Barbara Bush
President William J. Clinton and the First Lady,
Mrs. Hillary Rodham Clinton

In addition, I was given permission by the Media Office at the White House to include our standing President and the First Lady, "as long as it is respectful." It is. I mentioned that I believed they had suffered through more national hardships than many of their predecessors: everything from the attack on the World Trade Center to natural disasters and war, acting with dignity, courage and responsibility. It is with great honor and respect that I include them in *The Eagle and the Dove*.

Our President, George W. Bush and the First Lady,
Mrs. Laura Welch Bush

And lastly, in memory of President Gerald R. Ford, 1913-2006 and with sympathy for First Lady, Mrs. Betty Ford and her family.

May God bless the U.S.A.

DEDICATION

Please accept my heartfelt thanks and gratitude.
Alicia Condon, Erin Galloway, Renee Yewdaev, John Scognamiglio, Irene Goodman, Joan Diamond, Sherry Newman, Kathryn Falk, Carol Stacy, RWA, Kathy Roberts, Maggie Crawford, Brenda Chin, Steve Fallert.

Special Agent Mike Wagoner, F.B.I., Officer Russell Stanczyk, Nebraska Highway Patrol, Daniel R. Cronk, M.D., Giles Hedderich, M.D., Dan Stevens, M.D., Julie Stevens, M.D., C. E. Wilkinson, M.D., Kim Hilliard, PA-C.

The Scottish Rite of Freemasonry

University of Nebraska at Kearney

Chancellor Douglas Kristensen, Neva Klemme, Beverly Mathiesen, Chancellor Gladys Styles-Johnson, Dr. Richard L. Miller, Deanna Ellingson, Dr. William Wozniak, Dr. Joseph Benz, Dr.Wayne Briner, Dr. Krista Fritson, Dr. Jean Mandernach, Dr. Robert Rycek, Dr. Theresa Wadkins, Dr. Krista Forrest, Stacy Mostek, Dr. Mary Elizabeth Ailes, Dr. Roger P. Davis, Dr. Mark R. Ellis, Dr. Carol S. Lilly, Dr. Linda Van Ingen, Darby J. Carlson, M.A., Kim Gronewold, M.A., Dr. Julie Shaffer, Richard Simonson, M.A., Dr. Janet Steele, Donna Dudley, Ruth Ann Behlmann, Charles Fort, M.A., Dr. Susanne Bloomfield, Anita Lorentzen, M.A., Dr. Samuel J. Umland, Dr. Thomas Scott Martin, Dr. Stephen Glazier, Valerie Vierk, Dr. William Aviles, Dr. Peter J. Longo, Mary Ann Rittenhouse, M.A., Carleen Jurgensen, Mary Wrede, Mary Iten, Mary Sommers, Matt Johnson, Jacque Triplett, Dr. Dennis Potthoff, Dr. Dennis Brown, Dr. Joan Lewis, Dr. Glenn Tracy, Mary Frew, Geraldine Stirtz, Jan Kuebler, Len Fangmeyer, Ellen Dake, Dr. Paul Bishop, Dr. Lewis Snyder, Vicki Snyder, Dr. Abdouleahe Alavi-Behbahani, Carmen Brewer, Dr. Mathew Bokovoy,

Debby Maire, Todd Jensen, Dee Goedert, Audrey Caldwell, Pam Proskocil, Angela Lang, Aaryn Prochaska, Judy Kuebler, Dr. Stephen Branch.

Creighton University
Dr. Brent Spencer, Chair of the English Department

Central Nebraska Community College
Dr. James Kosmicki

Administration – the State of Nebraska at Lincoln
Commissioner Butch Lecuona, Phillip Baker, Administrator, Kay Marti, Deputy Commissioner, Kathy Copas, Mike Budler, Floyd Colon, Aurdra Kramer, Carrie Bellmore-Gaul, Becky Raymond, Dave Bauer, Charles and Jeanne Buswell, Nan Merrill.

Family and Friends
Gerald and Mary Louise Bydalek-Bates-Wilson, Michelle Ann Wilson, Dan and Kathy Bydalek, Bryan and Patty Bydalek, Jeff and Brenda Lindstrom, Chuck and Dorothy Pfeifer, Roger and Lynn Skorniak, Rob and Sheila Osborn, Rick and Kim Skorniak, Larry and Stacey Dirks, Claudie and Imelda Gressley, Alicia Gressley, Naftolie and Denise Kotler, John and Lanette Beck, Jr., John and Bonnie Beck, Sr., Pastor Earlin and Jeni Shanno, Nick and Angie Shanno, Rachel Shanno, Robert and Cleone Bates, Leonard and Doris Shanno, Clifford and Sara Warren-Bates, Kent and Joanne Lilly, Jared and Samantha Lilly, Helen Wilson-Nelson, Faye Rihanek, Eric Rihanek, Brett Rihanek, Ken Rihanek, James and Katharine Danklesen, Samantha Jo Danklesen, Adam Danklesen, Luke Danklesen, Elizabeth Bates, Cheryl Bates-Lawson, Lawrence and Margaret Palu, Jeffery and Suzzanne Palu, Connie Palu, Matthew Palu, Michael and Vicki Palu, Ken Guzinski, Stephen Guzinski, Leonard Shaffer, Jr., Vernon P. and Jan Miller, Kelly Nichols, Robert de Lozier, Jayme Maciejewski, Jason Maciejewski, Troy Eilenstine, Randy Maynard, Jason

Peck, Jeff and Brenda Lobner, Josh Button, Tishawna Isenbart-Sawyer, Jody Sweeney, Harry and Kathy Spotanski, Jerome and Marcene Kaslon, Clarence and Delta Placzyk, Randy and Julie Wilson, Ken and Lois Maschka, John and Jane Maschka, John and Theresa Hulinsky, Jim Maschka, Kirk and Lisa Harrington, Lance and Sue Kizer, Jim and Delores Stanczyk, Steve and Kathy Glinsmann, Mark and Becky Goerecki, Bryan and Joan Stanczyk, Cheryl Guggenmos, Waldo Smith, Peg Truby, Caroline Hurlbert, Carmen Ostrander, Tom Cooper, Katina Psota, Verna Woods, Leonard Petersen, Ron and Carol Cope, John Lillis, Nick and Jenifer Wicht-Franssen, Jaci Fletcher, Cindy McNiel, Brandy Hall, Ron and Deb Ridder, Cynthia Archwamety, Sheree Kelly, John Parella, Cindy Arnold, Kathie Bonnell, Cheryl Church, Connie Decker-Ullman, Brooke Dougherty, Barbara Einspahr, Marvin Fisher, Mary Foltz, Annette Goodner, Leslie B. Halley, Della Hambek, Melanie Houchin, Zibbey Kelly, Kevin Kula, Kathy Larson, Michael Lowe, Debra Maddox, Michelle Meyer, Melvin Munsinger, Karen Nixon, Richard Ossian, Laura Peterson, Myles Peterson, Eva Polanco, Kathleen Quail, Marlene Quinton, Jennifer Scarlett, Patty Schelling, Sherryl Stansberry, Sarah State, Deena Strieder, Latrice Stubbs, Bonnie Teel-Smith, Mike Vaughn Williams, Olga Vilalpando, Paulette Wagner, Chris and Jennifer White, Ginger Zahl, Fr. Matthew Koperski, Fr. Charles Torpey, Sr. Caroline, Sr. Pat, Sr. Mary, Jerry and Mollie Waller, Richard Holt, Tami Kohl, Bruce and Sandy Beatty, Randy and Annette Kearnes, Paul Mileris, M.D., Dennis Flows, M.D., Carmen Soltis, Jeralynn Rollins, Mary Howard, Judy Jensen, Allen Hall, Norma Jean Ringberg, Candace Schrader.

Pat Sajak, Vanna White and
David Letterman.
A fan.

Last but never least, my heroes,
Daniel Christopher Morrow, Heather Ann Lilly-
Morrow and Drew Ann Morrow.
I love you.

THE EAGLE

AND DOVE
THE

Chapter One

*May 1851—Sangre de Cristo Mountain Range, Colorado
Territory*

*H*e came from the high country where Old Man Winter
had a stranglehold on the land, and the world was blinding
white, and his traps were full. He rode hard through a
range of mountains that the setting sun turned the color of
blood, pushing his big, dun-colored stallion until its powerful body was bathed in lather and its once nimble legs
shook from exhaustion. Lying low over his horse, he thun-
dered down the mountain at breakneck speed.

Born in the dark of a November night twenty-four years
before, he was a Celt. His Scottish ancestry was apparent in
his pale skin, which contrasted sharply with his dark eyes
and hair. He wore soft fringed buckskins, threaded with
turquoise. In his long hair, an eagle feather was wound,
tied in place with a thin strip of hide. Towering over most
men, he spoke fluent Gaelic, the language of his father, as
well as a curious mixture of French, English and Pigeon

Blackfoot. He was a white man raised in a red world and comfortable in his skin.

Driven by obsession, he had covered some of the roughest country in Colorado at breakneck speed. He slept little and ate less. Pulling a piece of deer jerky from his pack every now and then, he would suck on it until it softened and the smoky juices ran down his parched throat. He was going toward the dunes at the base of the ridge, a mountain man covered in buckskins and fur with a shock of wild, midnight hair blowing in the wind and piercing, black eyes locked onto the horizon. And he wasn't alone.

Above him in the zinc-colored sky, an elegant falcon-hawk circled lazily, easily keeping pace with his relentless speed. Beside him loped a lean, slant-eyed wolf. The three were companions: a trinity of primitive power—beating wings, talons, fangs, sinew and cunning—bound together by the knowledge that they were of the same clan: predators. Yet, though all were formidable, the mountain man was, by far, the most dangerous of the three. He was as savage as the November storm that had spawned him twenty-four years ago with but one purpose in his mind.

Revenge.

Cresting a bald ridge of rock, he pulled back on the soaking reins, stopping abruptly in a shower of powder-red dust and fragments of nail-thin shale.

"Ease up, horse," he growled as he absently wiped the sweat from his upper lip. " 'Tis the blighted camp of the Philistines."

He had a commanding voice. Though companionably soft, it was filled with such unmistakable menace that his horse's ears came to attention. Narrowing his eyes, the man studied the scene below.

A sudden, sickening shock knifed through his groin, and his breath quickened in response.

Hatred.

There was hatred in every breath he took and in every

shuddering beat of his heart. Overwhelmed by the power of the emotion, he didn't turn away from it, but breathed it in, owned it. Other men might have walked away, trusting God or a badge to fight their battles for them, but not him. His blessing and his curse was the nobility of his soul. He knew right from wrong and took responsibility for every thought, word or deed, expecting others to do the same.

God might show mercy, but Jesse McCallum wouldn't.

Beneath him, nestled as contentedly near the root of the Sangre de Cristo Mountains as an infant to its mother's teat, was a crudely built cabin. Massive dunes of rolling sand surrounded it on three sides, and on the fourth, a vertical wall of granite effectively sealed the basin from the rest of the range. No one could approach the cabin from across the dunes without being seen for miles, and the vertical incline of the mountain on the fourth side of the cabin made it suicide for a man to try it on foot or horse.

Weighing his options, he studied the scene below. Behind the cabin stood a makeshift pen fashioned with posts of thorny mesquite and rails of frayed hemp, spliced now and then with bits of knotted rags that still hinted at some nearly forgotten color. Every few feet, empty cans that were once filled with succulent peaches, tangy stewed tomatoes and other such citified delicacies were tied to the uppermost rope, clanking noisily with each passing breeze.

The "gate"—and it was a charity to call it that—was nothing more than the remains of a buckboard bleached nearly white and laid on its side. Decorating its sagging top were stiff gray blankets, mile-worn saddles, tangled leather traces and rusty bits, one for each of the dozen horses and the odd assortment of New Mexico mules mingling in the little pen. Just outside the corral and within spitting distance of the front door was a pyramid of packs filled to overflowing with stolen booty.

"Something's not quite right," he said evenly.

He felt edgy and keyed up. He knew what to expect in a

man's camp, and something was awry here. No smoke in the chimney. No movement. Then he saw him.

"There you are," he said to himself.

His parched throat emitted whispered words that sounded strangely disconnected. He was exhausted. His handsome face was edged in lines, covered in trail dust, unshaven and unkempt. The soft words were a strange contrast to the frightening expression in his eyes. They spoke volumes, gleaming like black opals filled with infernal fire, hellish in intensity and intent.

Cursed.

He felt that his tortured soul was dying and that he was a prisoner of flesh and blood. Once a proud man with a quick smile and twinkling eyes, experience had changed him. The cold hand of guilt had ravaged his conscience until he felt that he was lost forever to the light of innocence, beyond forgiveness and dead to everything except pain.

"Here I am," he said at last.

He suffered in silence and he suffered alone. His journey was over and the circle was about to close. Impassive as stone, he sat on his horse and stared.

Guards.

Some twenty feet from the pen was a man posted in a sweetbriar thicket. He looked to be of average height and build and was resting his dusty buttocks on the scuffed back of his worn boots, digging feverishly in the sand with his knife. He was so preoccupied that he didn't notice the man on the ridge above him, or the patterned head of the rattlesnake poking out from beneath a rock directly behind him.

Jesse grinned. A thin tear fell unnoticed from his eye.

"Trapped," he said.

Turning his head to one side, he spat a stream of dark liquid onto the ground, narrowly missing the head of the wolf, who didn't take notice or offense.

"What do you think, Sammy?" he said. "Who's going to get the first bite? Me or Old Wiggly?"

The wolf cocked his rangy head to one side as if to say, *Who cares?*

"Aye," Jesse agreed. He interpreted the wolfish language as only an intimate could. "Either way, he's dead, right? But I'll wager a buffalo liver on this one, Sammy, that I'll nail that mangy pork eater before Old Wiggly does!"

The second guard was sleeping a few feet away from the front door.

"And that big bastard, too."

Then he spat again and wrinkled up his elegant nose.

"Store bought," he said in disgust, digging the plug of tobacco out from his lower lip and flinging it to the ground. "Ain't worth a damn."

A muffled scream pierced the afternoon stillness, and the cabin's door was tossed open. A thickset man shoved a girl roughly through the door, and she stumbled, falling to the ground, helpless. Her dark hair was caught in braids, and a thin sheath of doeskin covered her small form. Laughing, the man tossed a piece of rope to the guard sitting by the door and went back inside.

Jesse's anger built like fire doused with kerosene. With white-knuckled rage, he gripped his saddle horn and watched as the girl was bound and tied to the buckboard's wheel. He realized that another girl was sitting in the shade a few feet away.

"Prisoners," he said quietly. "I should've known."

His expression changed and the mask fell off. The face that appeared was utterly terrifying. No trace of humanity could be found in its hard, wind-burned lines or outraged eyes.

"Easy, Sammy," Jesse cautioned. He was desperately trying to control his breathing and not entirely sure which of them, himself or the wolf, he was attempting to calm. His entire body trembled like a thoroughbred about to run the toughest race of his life. "Those pilgrims will bolt, sure enough. Maybe kill those gals if we lose our heads."

Which was exactly what the mountain man wanted to do, bolt pell-mell into their midst, make them pay for their sins as he was paying for his. Oh, yes! Pay and pay until there was nothing left of them but dust.

He shuddered, and the wolf grew silent. Out of fear, Jesse did too, not because he valued his own life so highly, but out of the possibility that hot-blooded actions might cause him to make a mistake that might let even one of the villains live! So he became watchful. Then he sniffed, reading the scents mingled in the air as easily as another man might read a book. The wolf sniffed too.

Smoke. Roasting meat. Someone's started a fire inside the cabin . . .

Quietly he slipped from his horse. He could almost hear his father's soft voice whispering in his ear. *To everything there is a season,* he would say. *A time to be born and a time to die.*

"Ecclesiastes," Jesse said aloud as he dropped silently to one knee.

With righteous finality, he pulled an eight-inch boning knife from the scabbard laced across his broad chest. A sly voice whispered persistently in his mind that it could be *his* time as well, but he didn't care. Not anymore. Sick with experience and resigned to his fate, he was the deadliest beast on the face of the earth: a man who didn't care if he lived or died.

Tucking his tongue against his palate, he carefully placed the razor-sharp blade between his teeth. The feel of it was familiar and reassuring, and the taste metallic and bitter as wormwood. Fitting. Then he lay down on the hardness of the ground, pushing all thoughts from his mind, except one. Revenge.

"An eye for an eye," he said. His lips cracked and bled from thirst.

Grimacing, he pulled himself forward by digging his elbows into the grainy soil, snaking toward the man posted in the brush with only the whispering hiss of sand to mark his passage. His wolf followed, instinctively angling off toward the right, skirting the few scrub trees like a low, loping phantom, working with the man.

Hunting.

Above them, the hawk wheeled and turned slowly like a gliding black shadow.

Searching.

On a rock below the hawk, a huge diamond-backed rattler slithered languidly into the feeble light of day. Still dimwitted from its wintry nap, it didn't notice the hawk.

But the hawk noticed him.

The hunters had spotted their prey.

The guard in the thicket was still drawing pictures in the dirt with the sharp end of his knife. A half smile played across his grimy features, twitching merrily as the outline of a woman took shape. Round head. Squiggly, springy curls. Narrow shoulders and large, drooping breasts punctuated with staring nipples—a sagebrush Venus tempting the cowboy with vacant, oval eyes.

" 'Leave off'n the white gal,' " he mimicked petulantly. His smile disappeared and was replaced by an ugly sneer. Bending forward, he caressed the dusty nipples with the club-shaped tip of his finger, erasing the lines and snorting in disgust when he saw his work vanish. " 'She's our ticket to easy street. Take yourself one of them Rickarees if you got to have yourself a gal.'

"I'll give you a 'Ree,' Josiah," he threatened murderously under his breath as he forced the knifepoint viciously into the ground. "Right up your scraggly old arse!"

He never saw the man coming up behind him like a cloud of smoke. A powerful arm encircled his neck and pulled him backward so hard and fast that he was lifted off his feet.

"Hey!" he shouted. His knife flew into the air, whirled slowly like an awkward pinwheel, then fell to the ground with a muffled *thunk*. With his left hand, he worked to ease the pressure of the forearm braced against his neck, while his right hand instinctively scrambled for his gun. Fumbling, he tried to lift it free from its holster.

He never made it that far.

"One," rumbled the mountain man savagely. He clamped a hand over the guard's mouth and thrust the knife upward. There was a moment of resistance when flesh met steel and refused to give way—but just the briefest moment. Jesse's knife was sharp, and the power behind it formidable. He drove it in through fascia and tendon, ripping upward until the blade encountered bone and could go no further. Silence. Not even a scream.

"Who killed me?" said the guard.

His voice was choking with blood and confusion.

"You!" replied Jesse harshly. He lifted the man and turned him with one hand until their gazes met and locked. "The day you bastards set foot in my camp! That was the day you died!"

Recognition and resignation came.

Jesse nodded slowly. He saw it in the guard's eyes. Satisfied that the man knew the sin he was paying for with his life, he let go of his shirt. With a sigh, the guard slid to the ground. All thoughts of the dusky Arikara maidens and the white woman he wanted were driven forever from his mind.

A score was being kept. *Four murdering thieves for one innocent life*. No jury was needed. No judge required. Jesse had read their confessions in the dirt some seventy miles north. Their signatures were etched in the hooves of their horses and in the distinctive tread of the men's store-bought boots. He knew their sex, their size and their number—the way they smelled—and what they ate by the spore they left uncovered on the trail. And he knew they were going to die just as surely as he knew the sun would rise in the east. It was mountain justice and a righteous law, and the only truth Jesse ever cared to know. But the balance wasn't met yet; there were three more men who needed killing, *badly*.

Sheathing his knife, he paused and deliberately caught and held the gaze of the smaller girl. Her eyes were black, badly swollen and open barely a crack. He pressed a finger to his lips, telling her to be silent, and she nodded weakly. Then he raised his fist in a silent promise and placed it against his heart.

"You're safe," he said aloud.

Understanding came, and she closed her eyes slowly. Satisfied that she understood, he dropped down low and started toward the cabin with deadly intention and unshakable calm.

Chapter Two

*J*esse was as silent on his feet as the Indians who had helped raise him. He was careful to keep within the distorted shadows of the few scattered bushes so that his silhouette would not betray his movements. Within seconds, he was at the back of the house.

Calming his breathing, he flattened his tall frame against the horizontal slats, scanning the horizon for any sign of movement. *Nothing. Empty.* He was safe, at least for the moment. Quietly he reached across his right shoulder and grasped the cool metal barrel of his bear rifle. It was his pride and joy, a double-barreled 50-caliber Hawkins. He'd won it at the *boisson*—a bare-knuckle fight at the spring *rendezvous*. He valued the rifle more than the gold he earned from his pelts, or the masculine satisfaction that came from testing his strength and prowess against other men. The rifle was the prize he had given to his father, Tom McCallum, on his fiftieth birthday.

He remembered his father's birthday as if it were yesterday. It was August and Tom was sitting in the shade of a clump of newly budded birch trees, humming when Jesse strolled into camp with the rifle hidden behind his back. There were no words to his songs, just the remembered mountain melodies that the cleric could no longer see but still keenly felt. He sang songs of Scotland and of Amelia, his wife. Jesse knew about the Grampian Range, the lochs, glens, and straths; he could describe the ragged peaks by recounting what his father had told him. There were many similarities between the Highlands of Scotland and the Rocky Mountain Range. Steep inclines, moss-covered stones, the cool, crisp air and early morning mist.

And he knew about his mother, Amelia, because his father talked about her nearly every day. "I miss her, Jesse," he would confess. "It's not a weakness for a man to love a woman better than himself, and I loved your mother. Lord, but she loved you! Don't ever forget!" Jesse never did. His father's stories about her always started with an affirmation of how much she'd loved him, and Jesse would listen quietly with a tender ache in his heart for a woman he could barely remember but dearly loved. She had died when he was still an infant, and several years later Jesse's father was blinded in a mining accident. A subtle shift of power occurred that year: The seven-year-old youth who ran with the braves grew up, doing his best to care for the man who had taken care of him. His father.

Tom McCallum was disabled from the day they pulled him out of the mining shaft, unconscious and beaten. But on the road to recovery, he refused to let his disability make him helpless. Stubbornly, he fashioned an oaken staff when still confined to bed and then struggled daily, carrying water in buckets or finding his way to the cabin while holding an armful of firewood, counting his steps.

Jesse could still see him walking the lonely trails, no longer a visitor passing through the landscape but part of the world around him as though he were content to fade into the scenery. His constant humming was not just his music but also the voice of the mountain he had come to love. In the dark of the evening, surrounded by lamp or thin candlelight, he would still pull his books of law from the makeshift shelves and the Bible, touching lovingly what he could never hope to read again.

Silently, with his head held down, Jesse placed the barrel of the Hawkins close to his face and closed his eyes, remembering.

"Look, Pa," he had said proudly. He held out the rifle and guided the old man's fragile, white fingers along the bore and the smooth, elegantly scrolled stock. "A shooter that can stop a rampaging grizzly dead in its tracks!"

"You don't say?" said Tom. He was suitably impressed. His gnarled hands fluttered lovingly over the highly polished wood. "Go on, Jesse, paint me a picture!"

"It can turn a boulder into mush, or so I'm told, Pa," Jesse said.

And there was no doubt in his mind, then or now, what the Hawkins would do to a man.

He opened his eyes and summoned a grin so cold that the sight of it would freeze another man's spit. Then he gathered himself like a beast and brought the Hawkins out in front of him, holding it like a club with the butt end pointing south as he stepped around the corner of the house and looked down.

The second guard was unaware that he was being watched. He was sleeping, sprawled across two old crates, snoring loudly. His size startled Jesse. This was a huge man. He was taller than Jesse by nearly four inches and nearly three times as wide. A star-shaped scar ornamented his left cheek, testimony to an uninvited bullet and a considerable amount of luck—and a bottle of Taos Lightning lay drained at his feet. Thick-jawed, dark and heavily mustached, he wore a double set of crisscrossed bandoleers across his barrel chest. The Simpson rifle he obviously favored was clenched so tightly in his squat, square hands that his knuckles were white. The rifle was cocked and the safety off.

Jesse laughed quietly beneath his breath. It would have been kind to kill the man in his sleep and let him fall from one dark dream into another, but Jesse's pain left no room for compassion. "Wake up, Goliath," he said. " 'Tis Judgment Day and David's come to call."

He stepped nearer and kicked the stiff, booted foot with the toe of his moccasin. He wanted the man to see who was about to kill him.

"What?" mumbled the guard drunkenly. He was startled awake by the tall shadow that fell across him, blotting out the light. "Whattya want, mister?" he said gruffly. He brought one fist up to rub the thick sand from his bleary eyes. His right arm tensed as his index finger sought the trigger like a blind, white worm.

"We met before?" he questioned suspiciously, trying to buy a few seconds of precious time with conversation. "You look just like . . ." Then he stopped and stared.

"No," replied Jesse coldly. "If we had, you'd be dead."

A ghostly smile flickered briefly like heat lightning across Jesse's face. He waited with infinite patience for the sleep to leave the guard's eyes. Then he drove the stock end of his rifle down, hard.

CRACKKK!

The man's squat nose was destroyed in a single, hammer-like blow.

"Two," counted Jesse coolly. His hunter's eyes gleamed with a militant, triumphant light as he watched the man slide to the ground, taking the wooden crate with him. The trigger of his Simpson was still cocked and the safety jammed.

"Needs cleaning," Jesse said. He kicked the rifle into the dirt. Then he stepped across the fallen man and walked silently along the front of the house, stopping when he neared the door.

Chapter Three

*T*here was no turning back. What lay inside was his, and Jesse meant to take his hellish prize regardless of the cost. So he paused by the door and listened, letting the sounds wash over him, catching them in the web of his fine senses, identifying each with the quickness of his agile mind. He heard the shrill whistle of his hawk soaring overhead, the sudden rush of a breeze scooting aimlessly across the glittering, barren dunes. Closer to him was the gentle woofing breath of the horses collected in the pen, accompanied by the tinny clanking of empty cans scoured silver by endless seasons of wind and sand. Beneath those sounds was the quickening beat of his heart thundering madly in his ears.

A sudden movement in a clump of plum thickets to his right caused him to turn his head. The brush rustled slightly and bent forward, parting at the base, and a narrow, gray muzzle poked curiously through. Jesse wasn't surprised to see his wolf, Sammy, appear from beneath the scrub. His front legs were spread wide apart for balance and his bushy tail was twitching like a cat's.

Ready to run!

The wolf's narrow head was lowered and his silvered muzzle stretched upward so that its four-inch incisors were clearly visible.

Ready to bite!

The wolf's intelligent eyes were the color of antique gold and appeared to be filled with only one question.

When?

Jesse shook his head, and his unspoken command caused the wolf to lower his eyes and look away. Sammy understood and disappeared behind the house with the fluid grace of a black thread being pulled into a cloth of woven shadows. Still, no sound from inside the house.

Jesse had expected all hell to break loose when the guard on the front porch hit the ground. But there was no answering shuffle from inside the cabin. No alarm. No raised voices. Nothing. Yet he knew someone was inside because he could *feel* it. He had a hunter's intuition, which went beyond the realm of the five senses. It was a dangerous gift, with no visible proof except that in this wild land where nothing was certain, he was still alive.

Driven, he moved toward the door.

"Ain't one to disappoint," he said.

There was dark humor in his words and finality in his voice. He cushioned the butt of his rifle against his hip and leveled the bore at the center of the worn wooden door. Then he took a small, single breath, lifted his long, buckskin-clad leg, aimed for an imaginary spot at least four inches behind the door, and slammed his booted foot against it with all his might.

KA-BOOOM!

The door exploded inward, sending a cloud of choking dust swirling into the air. Calmly Jesse stepped inside. The interior of the cabin was dim and stank like cooking grease left to turn rancid in the summer sun. Light was scarce within the room, filtering sluggishly through the oiled skin of a lamb that hung over the solitary window. Flies buzzed. Cobwebs hung like tattered lace from the eaves, and the only furniture that Jesse could see was a small, black cook-stove with a crooked, rusted pipe that was leaking smoke, and the remnants of a table surrounded by three pressed-wood chairs, one of which was occupied.

"Well, boy, cat got your tongue?" growled the seated man. He tore a piece of venison from the thick chunk, dripping grease in his hand, and started to chew.

Jesse tensed and looked him slowly up and down. Though not nearly as big as the man on the porch, he was just as dark in color. But there the resemblance ended. This fellow was wiry and lean, with the perpetual right-eyed squint of a man who had peered too often down the narrow sight of a gun. The whites of his calculating eyes were unhealthy, red and runny as old sores, and whether it was from the smoke in the room or the contents of a bottle, Jesse didn't know and cared still less.

"My name is Jesse," said the mountain man bitterly. "Tom McCallum's son." There was loathing in his voice and eyes as they met and held the other man's muddy gaze.

"That a fact?" the man drawled as he continued to chew his meal. Then he paused and wiped the grease on the faded red plaid of his shirt. Appearing thoughtful, he tore another piece of meat from the bone with his teeth. "Well, Jesse McCallum, my name is Josiah Mott and I want to know what the hell are you waiting for? An invitation to dance?" Then he laughed, letting the bone drop to the floor. It was then that pretense ended.

"Pups and sons o' bitches!" snarled Mott suddenly. "Pups and sons o' bitches, the stinking lot of you mountain scabs!" He spat on the floor in contempt.

"I'd rather be a breathing son of a bitch," promised Jesse

softly, "than a dead bastard." He watched in satisfaction as a nerve jumped beside Mott's left eye.

Silence.

Then Mott's eyes flared slightly. It was nothing more than a small glance toward the far corner of the room. *Satisfaction. Hope. Triumph. Revenge.* Jesse read in an instant all that in the wordless glance.

A trap!

Instinctively Jesse turned and fired. The report from the Hawkins reverberated loudly, blowing a four-inch hole through a dirty wool blanket that partitioned off a portion of the narrow room. A second later, a man fell through, dragging the curtain down with a look of total surprise frozen on his rough-featured face. A bright red stain blossomed on his chest, and the hunting knife clenched in his hand fell to the floor.

"*Three!*" Jesse crowed in satisfaction. His momentary triumph was forgotten when he saw what was hidden behind the curtain—a woman, a very beautiful white woman with wild red hair and huge emerald-green eyes filled with tears. She was tied to the footboard of an old bed, and his shot had missed her by only inches. He was stunned speechless.

"Yeah, that's right, McCallum! Keep lookin' at her!" roared Josiah. He startled Jesse as he knocked the table over and sent his meal flying around the room. " 'Cause she's the last thing you're ever going to see!" Then he laughed as he held up his hand. In it was a shiny new Winchester—Tom McCallum's prize Winchester—one of the things Josiah and his boys had stolen from the McCallum camp nearly four weeks ago.

"We had us a time," he confessed with glee. He dove for cover behind the table as Jesse sprang for the shelter of the stove. "That blind old pappy of yours *invited* us into camp, offered us supper and preached to us about some damn 'gold rule' while he praised God for a burnt rabbit that weren't hardly fit to chew! Well, praise this, boy!" he bellowed, squeezing off a shot. The whining *pinnnnnggg* was proof that he had missed as the bullet ricocheted off the cast-iron stove and buried itself harmlessly into the wall.

Jesse answered the report with one of his own, which missed Josiah. He scrambled to reload as Josiah began his taunting once again.

"Say, now, McCallum," he sang, "can you hear me?" He wiped away the sweat that had trickled into his eyes. He had only one shot left. One. And the way he saw it, only one chance to bring Jesse out into the open for a clean kill. "I said, can you hear me, boy?"

Jesse didn't reply. Pinned down next to the stove, he waited for the next round of shots. He felt like a sitting duck with very little protection and only a slim chance of walking out of the cabin alive. But when Mott didn't fire, Jesse knew that he was either out of shells or fixing to lay a trap. Maybe both. But it really didn't matter, because he knew that Mott was going under, even if it cost Jesse his life. So he waited, letting the seconds nibble away at Mott's bravado, biting his lower lip to keep from crying out in pain as the stove branded his ribs.

"Are you deaf, McCallum?" shouted Josiah irritably. He was desperate to get under the boy's skin any way he could. "I want to know why a big, strapping pup like you left a blind old man all alone, unprotected, out in the middle of nowhere. Want to tell me why?

"Maybe . . ." Josiah offered slyly, trying to keep the note of uncertainty out of his voice as he fingered his rifle. His smile was beginning to fade along with his confidence the longer Jesse remained silent. "Maybe you left him all alone 'cause you wanted all that gold you were digging for yourself. Is that it? But you couldn't bring yourself to kill your old pap. Right?"

Uneasily Josiah licked the sweat from his upper lip as he strained his ears, listening for the faintest sign of movement. *Nothing.* The only sound he heard was the increased beating of his heart and the singing rush of blood pounding through his veins. His index finger, still slick with grease, slid off the trigger.

"Damn!" he muttered as he struggled to hold the gun steady. He was desperate. He felt like a man trapped in a burning house by a patient mountain lion, the lion knowing sooner or later that the man would have to come out into the open. He shuddered at the thought. Then he said almost coyly, as though talking with Jesse over a friendly beer, "Probably just tired of taking care of that sick old man with his queer, Bible-thumping ways. Believe me, son," he continued with a chuckle, trying his best to lure the big cat into the flames, "I can understand that. Hell, I shot my old man for a plug of tobacco and two old horses! But, Jesse," he added, trying to put a smile into his voice, "if that's the lay of things—"

Time to play . . .

"you should be *thanking* me for what I done—"

. . . his trump card.

"when I cut that old man's throat!"

The cabin was filled with a low, anguished moan. It took a moment for Jesse to realize that the sound came from himself. A blood-red haze enveloped his mind, terrifying in its intensity. He began to shake as he realized that the man hiding behind the table was the one who had killed his father, slit his throat and left him to die like a pig in a pool of blood.

And he hadn't been there to protect him.

"You bastard!" Jesse roared as he lunged forward.

All power.

Blood-red.

Pure hate.

"You're going under!" he promised. "I give you my word! You're going to pay for what you done to my pa!"

Ignoring his rifle, Jesse reached for the table and grabbed the broken leg, flinging it across the little room with one mighty heave.

"I don't hardly think so," snickered Mott wickedly. The barrel of the Winchester was pointed at Jesse's head, the greasy finger poised near the trigger. "Say hello to yer daddy, boy!" Then Josiah laughed, hoping that Jesse would faint or plead for mercy. But he did neither. He just stood completely still. His icy fearlessness was eerie, and the contempt in his eyes tangible. Then he whistled—a short, sharp burst, high and slightly warbling, like the cry of a hawk as it plummets to the ground, sure of its prey.

Josiah blinked and grunted in surprise.

"What—?" he started to say, and then he appeared to reconsider, thinking it best if his surprise didn't show. "Mountain tricks, eh, boy? Well, they ain't gonna do you a bit o' good here!" Then he wiped a hand across his mouth, and the trigger began to move.

Suddenly a new sound filled the room. It was the sound of tearing lambskin followed by a low, menacing growl.

"What the hell?" Josiah muttered. As he turned toward the sound, his eyes widened in fright. A wolf, a large male wolf with his fangs bared and his head lowered, was only a heartbeat away. "Chrr-issttt!" Josiah stammered, nearly falling as he pulled the rifle around. Then Jesse was on him, driving him to the floor with two hundred and thirty pounds of pure hatred.

Whooommm!

The rifle jerked sideways and the barrel spun as the shot slammed harmlessly into the ceiling, sending down a shower of dust and debris over the struggling pair.

"Let me go!" wailed Josiah. "Don't kill me! Have mercy, boy!"

"Don't kill you?" Jesse stopped and stared. "Did my pa ask you not to kill him? Did he beg for mercy after he invited you into camp, fed you and prayed with you? Did he ask you not to kill him?"

"It weren't me, boy," Josiah lied.

"Funny thing. A minute ago you were just bragging how you killed a poor, helpless, old blind man, and now you tell me it weren't you."

Josiah glared at him. He was losing, and he knew it. Using one hand, he pushed against the broad chest that forced him to the ground as his other hand fumbled for the Bowie knife in his belt.

"For God's sake, boy," he whined as he pulled the knife free and whipped it upward, viciously slashing the hard muscle of Jesse's shoulder and drawing a fair amount of blood.

"God," Jesse hissed, "don't have nothin' to do with this!"

Jesse grabbed the hand that held the blade and twisted it until the wrist cracked and the unforgiving point was directly above Josiah's heart.

"Noo-oo-o!" wailed Josiah. "Don't do it! I was just funning you!"

Josiah watched in mounting horror as the steel guided by Jesse's powerful hand began to move downward, drawing fire from a stray burst of sunlight that fell through the broken window until it seemed to be a ball of moving light, flashing through the air like Gideon's avenging sword. Then it stopped. A half-inch above Josiah's heaving chest, it stopped. And Jesse said in a voice that rang in the little room with the crystal clarity of the final trumpet, "Since you don't like rabbit, you murderin' bastard . . ."

The blade quivered . . .

". . . *eat* . . ."

. . . moved . . .

". . . *this!*"

. . . and *slammed* home.

Josiah grunted. His eyes flew open as though yanked by a string. Stark terror settled on his face, twisting the jaded features into a grimace. One last sucking breath and he lay still.

"Four," Jesse said quietly. Breathing hard, he rolled away from the body.

It was done.

Like a vessel emptied, Jesse lay on his back and stared at the pockmarked blue sky through the shattered ceiling. The hatred that had possessed and sustained him these past weeks was gone. Now sorrow trickled in, and he felt a lump grow in his throat. His father was avenged. He had seen to that. Yet he knew that if he had the power to resurrect Josiah and his men and spill their blood a thousand times over, it would never make up for his loss.

"Sammy," he called hoarsely, "where are you?"

Rolling to one side, he tried to stand. The world, once steady and sure as a rock, became quicksand beneath his feet. Dizziness filled him, causing the room to spin and his vision to waver, double, then blur until his surroundings grew dim. It was an effort to breathe.

The wolf, as though sensing his distress, trotted to his side. Whining deep in his throat, he gently nosed Jesse's burly hand, letting his pink, sandpaper tongue lick the callused palm. It was as close to a consoling kiss and a reassuring hug that the canny wolf could muster.

"Good laddy," Jesse murmured. Awkwardly he stroked the narrow head, feeling the deep jagged scar on his muzzle . . .

Sammy's fight with the badger.

He willed himself to breathe as he touched the ragged left ear, half eaten by frost.

The night on the mountain when he had broken his leg and Sammy refused to find cover, lying beside him through the maddening hours of black, howling cold until help came.

To remember.

Memories.

Each memory tying him to the present and reminding him of a past he would just as soon forget. Then, as though he remembered a little detail he had forgotten, he pulled his knife from its sheath and turned his attention to the woman in tattered mauve silk huddled on the dirt floor.

"Now," he said with a tired sigh as he wiped the blood on his leggings, "what've we got here?"

Chapter Four

*D*amien North III pushed back the thick waves of his lustrous, wheat-colored hair with the heels of his trembling hands. "Perhaps," he said, "I'm not making myself understood."

His voice was like water dripping off an icicle, frigid and clear. It was a cultured voice with a hint of arrogance that matched his deceptive beauty. He looked like a Renaissance painting of an angel, otherworldly and exquisite, his coloring as pure as if a master had infused each hue with light. There were no hard angles or lines to mar his pale complexion, and no dark stubble to conceal the perfect bow of his sensual lips. His nose was ideally straight and finely drawn; surrounding his oval face like a gilded Baroque frame were waves of shining, flaxen hair. He left his hair slightly longer then convention deemed proper. But Damien never gave a damn about convention, except when it served his purpose. He was a law unto himself, a sleek jungle cat prowling through a herd of unsuspecting sheep.

Yet he was able to conceal his predatory nature well, burying a mean spirit beneath his wit, hiding his avarice within the grip of a firm handshake, and cloaking his envy behind the blinding glitter of a dashing smile. He was an ambitious man who courted the favor of only those elite souls who would add to his prestige, plotting and scheming to fulfill the drives and urges of his never-satisfied flesh, which tortured him relentlessly. *Do what thou wilt* was his creed, and he acted upon it with surprising, oftentimes subtle and insidious force until he got exactly what he wanted, regardless of what he had to do or whom he had to hurt.

"I want to know if there is any word about Katharine Dory from your scouts."

He was in love with her. They'd grown up in Boston together and he had courted her for years, showering her with praise and expensive gifts, and always careful not to touch her except tenderly—to brush his lips across her forehead, to lightly squeeze her hand—to be the epitome of a gentleman in her company. They were of the same social class, and their families had known each other for years. He refused to entertain the notion that she was out of his reach for even a moment.

"No, Mr. North. I'm sorry."

Slowly he turned until his gaze was level with the duty officer seated behind the polished oak desk. He laughed softly, sick inside. Placing his gloved hands on the officer's desk, he leaned forward.

"Ironic. My fiancée has been kidnapped," Damien said. "*Kidnapped*. Do you understand? A lady has been forcibly abducted not thirty miles from this godforsaken post by a pack of border ruffians, and you aren't doing a damned thing about it. Why is that?"

Lieutenant McGuire stopped drumming his short, capable fingers on top of the desk and looked long and hard at North. He didn't like the man. Not one bit.

"Sit down, Mr. North," he said stonily. "As I told you before, I cannot call a rescue mission without a direct order from Captain Atkinson, and he will not be back until late afternoon tomorrow."

"*Tomorrow!*" shouted Damien, slamming his fist on the desk. "It's been two weeks since she was taken from her bed! Two weeks! *Yesterday* was too late!"

McGuire looked down and shook his head. He said nothing. The gloomy little room with its dark oak furnishings seemed to grow smaller as the two men eyed one another.

"Please do something to help us," Damien pleaded softly.

McGuire looked up and finally gave voice to what he had been thinking all afternoon.

"You should have thought of doing something before you 'gentlemen' ever brought that young lady into the Kansas Territory. This isn't some expanded version of a Wild West show!

"*You* risked her life," he added quickly. "I didn't." He picked up the small portrait the girl's father had given him. "And I can tell you that for a woman—especially one as beautiful as this"—he thrust the cameo within an inch of Damien's furious face—"her chances of surviving are very slim, let alone the chances of finding her *unharmed.*"

Damien stared blindly at the portrait. He was haunted by her image. Enraged, he took the cameo out of McGuire's hand.

"You're the law here! I pay your salary. I demand that you do something to help me find my fiancée!"

His voice was tight and controlled, his color high, and his eyes feverish with emotion. He wanted to hit McGuire for sitting there in his safe office while Katharine was in danger or possibly dead. He hated him at that moment, but instead of hitting him, he took a deep breath.

"Please help me find my fiancée. Money is no object."

"There isn't a damned thing I can do," said McGuire tiredly. "Now, will you gentlemen kindly leave?"

"Leave?"

Damien exploded. Lunging across the desk, he grabbed the lieutenant by the collar. "You can shoot a gun, can't you?" he demanded.

A single-shot Remington was pointed at Damien's head by the guard who had been posted by the door. He heard the loud *click* of the hammer being pulled back, and he tightened his grip on the lieutenant.

"Lieutenant, get your man off me," he warned, "or I'll break your bloody neck."

"Let me loose," said McGuire, "or you'll find yourself in the stockade and there will be no one to help your fiancée. I mean it, Mr. North. I won't tell you a second time."

Damien reluctantly let McGuire go, turned and batted the rifle out of the guard's hand. He thrust his finger in the air.

"Stay away from me," he said evenly. His blue eyes glittered, and the lieutenant knew at that moment that North was a very dangerous man. He knew better than to show any fear or give him an edge, because he would take advantage of it instantly.

Behind Damien's head on a small shelf, a nearly new pillar-and-scroll clock prepared to chime the supper hour. In the pregnant silence of the little room, each *tick-tock* sounded like a giant's muffled heartbeat.

Damien calmed down slightly and studied McGuire's face. He could read people with an uncanny ease, and this one, he knew, was a man who couldn't be budged or bribed. He had *principles*. Damien snorted, and his breath quickened. The pupils of his eyes were dilated and fixed, and his jaw worked back and forth as though he counted the seconds while he waited for a dent in McGuire's steel-plated composure. None came. A rifle was again pointed at Damien's head, and McGuire had a cavalry-issue handgun in his hand, cocked and pointed at his chest.

"Oh, you're good," Damien breathed softly. He raised his hands in mock surrender. Only after he backed away from the desk did the lieutenant speak again. He kept his gun in his hand.

"As I said before, I sympathize with you, Mr. North . . . and you, Mr. Dory," he added hesitantly. "It is an extremely difficult situation. I would help you if I could." He looked from North to the soft-spoken gentleman slumped in a chair. It was easy to forget that he was in the room. With his haunted eyes, Edwin Dory seemed to fade into the shadows as though he was nearly one himself.

McGuire turned and directed his speech and attention to the elderly man, trusting his guard to keep Damien under control.

"Mr. Dory, let me explain. Ever since President Taylor died of cholera last July and Fillmore's taken his place in Washington, we've had nothing but chaos in the Territory! Between the influx of miners heading for Oregon or California and the bounty hunters looking for anyone who'll pass for black, Fort Larned doesn't have a man to spare.

"And as you are probably aware, there isn't another regiment within a hundred miles."

The lieutenant's voice drifted off as the clock began to chime. Six o'clock on the dot. The bugler was announcing supper and the sun was preparing to set, leaning its golden head further and further west. Time to rest. But not for Damien. He could neither sleep nor eat.

"I'll be your regiment, then," Damien said desperately. He stared at the grotesque caricature of his shadow lengthening slowly on the wall. For one brief, dizzying moment, he had the peculiar sensation that *he* was the shadow.

A monster.

"Is there no sympathy for the devil?" he said mockingly.

"I beg your pardon?" said McGuire.

Damien turned slowly like an automaton activated by the surprise in the lieutenant's voice.

"Give me a hundred rounds of ammunition, then," he said. "Some fresh horses and some supplies, whatever you can spare. As I told you, money is no object. I'll find her myself, even if I have to search every blade of grass between here and the Pacific!"

McGuire noted the dark circles beneath the younger man's red-rimmed eyes. A stab of guilt hit him. Perhaps he had misjudged North and he was no more than a distraught and persistent lover. But McGuire didn't think so. Not with eyes like that.

"None to spare," McGuire said bluntly. "Not a bullet or a bean." He put the gun on top of some papers in his desk and slammed the drawer shut. The threat was over.

"There must be a way," Damien said. He knew he would never give up until he found her. Never. Suddenly, like a lion ready to pounce, he turned and looked at her father.

"If it weren't for you, Edwin, and your stupid dreams of building a railroad through this hellhole, Katharine would be safe in Boston, where she belongs!"

The older man looked up. His once handsome face was carved in wrinkles, and his vague, seascape-blue eyes were shaded to tombstone gray and bleak as a February morning.

"Please, Damien," Edwin begged. He was choking back tears. "Don't you think I know that? She is my *daughter!*"

"Fine father you've turned out to be," scoffed Damien. He reached for the bottle of laudanum in the inside pocket of his topcoat. It was only half full, and the pain in his head was getting worse. Flecks of light were dancing at the corners of his eyes, and his stomach felt twisted into one gigantic knot. *Suicide headaches*, his father called them. *Another of your mother's weaknesses.* Clusters of pain exploded in the side of his head, and he pressed the bottle as hard against his temple as he could, in danger of shattering the glass.

"My father was right about you!" he said. His voice was

tight and controlled. "Nothing more than an eccentric fool who plays with tracks and trains like a boy still in knee britches! Bah!"

Taking a breath, he twisted the bottle in his hands.

"But that isn't the worst of it, is it?" he went on. "You used your daughter, Edwin, your very own flesh and blood, to induce me into taking this ridiculous expedition! You knew my feelings for her and used her to persuade me to lend money to you so that you can shovel it like sand down your rathole railway with no bloody end in sight!"

The building of the transcontinental railroad would bring untold wealth to investors, enough to interest Vanderbilt, Gould, Carnegie and John Rockefeller. Damien knew that. He had the prospectus and had calculated the figures. He knew the shipping magnates were interested, as were most of the industrial financiers here and abroad. But all he could think of was his kidnapped fiancée. Popping the cork, he rolled a few of the powdery tablets onto his sweating palm and swallowed them with brandy from a half-filled old-fashioned glass on the edge of McGuire's desk.

He closed his eyes. The opium tasted bitter, but the rush of pleasure was orgasmic. The pain receded, pulling back gently like a red-tinged wave. He looked at Edwin with wide, glassy eyes.

"If anything has happened to Katharine," he said, pointing his finger at the older man's face, "I'll hold *you* entirely responsible for her *murder!*"

Edwin winced as though he had been struck, covered his face with shaking hands and wept.

Chapter Five

*H*er eyes glittered like emeralds through the watery veil of her tears. In the oppressive gloom of the little room, she glowed like a firebrand.

Jesse was stunned.

Beautiful, he thought. *Too beautiful.*

Instinctively he drew back from her with the distrustful wariness of a tiger confronted by a flame. He knew her face, as all men did. It was the face of Helen, who had launched a thousand ships; the face that set Anthony against Caesar. The face that seduced Adam into taking that first, luscious bite.

It was the face of a legend.

She was a summer rose so perfect, a man would be willing to bleed on her thorns simply for a chance to touch her, look at her, breathe her perfume. A fragrance so intoxicating and rare, she courted disaster by her very sweetness. He had seen her kind once or twice before in his twenty-four years and had always had the good sense to avoid them like a plague.

Until now.

He was caught on the sharp edge of her beauty, his heart pierced by her tears.

Taking several steps, he closed the distance between them rapidly and hunkered down, resting on his massive haunches. His face was within inches of hers, his humid breath mingling with her breath, his brawny arms within inches of her heaving breasts. Her reaction was instantaneous and fierce. She pulled her legs in and began to worry the ropes holding her to the bed, pulling so hard that a thin ribbon of red trickled down her fair skin.

"Stop!" he shouted in exasperation. He straightened and shook the footboard above her head for effect, snapping a worm-eaten spindle in half. "There is no one in this room *alive* except me!" He pointed to his burly chest, now black with ash from the stove. "I have a gun and a knife, and I've been known to hunt bear with no more than a stick and my bad temper. So it seems to me that unless you're packing more than a fine pair of tits, there's not a whole hell of a lot you can do, now, is there?"

Quietly he stepped forward and knelt beside the bed. His knife was unsheathed, and with great care he moved his hand up her leg, pushing aside her dress. In fear, she kicked him, and with infinite patience, he gently deflected the blow.

"Don't you dare touch me, you filthy beast!" she cried. Her voice had risen to nearly a hysterical pitch.

"Filthy beast, is it? Look, you infernal heifer," he said, patience evaporating, "I'm not going to hurt you. All I want to do is cut you loose and ride. Understand?" He was mad as hell, hurting where his chest had been burned and his patience had worn thin. A sheen of sweat developed on his forehead, and he felt close to passing out. "Now hold still so I can get my knife in between your damn skinny legs."

Her eyes widened in shock as she stared at the huge man with the leathers across his chest still smoking and a cut along his shoulder bleeding so badly that his hand was crimson and a puddle had begun to form on the hard dirt floor near her leg.

"Don't touch me," she hissed. Unable to stop herself, she flinched when she felt his hand on her leg. "I'll kill myself if you do! I swear I will if you touch me."

Something in the eerily quiet tone of her voice and her shallow breathing told him better than any words that she was serious. He looked at her, understanding.

"Dying is easy," he said slowly, remembering. "Like falling off a log." His baleful eyes fixed on her. The halo of his night-black hair moved fitfully in the intermittent breeze, shadowing his craggy features like a dark angel's outstretched wings. He looked like the Grim Reaper with his crescent scythe replaced by a hunting knife spattered with gore.

"Look at him," he said harshly, pointing his knife in Josiah's direction. "Like sleep, it appears." His voice was low and hypnotic. "Who can say if the dead dream? Now, living is damnably hard. It takes sand, it does, real grit."

He wasn't sure what had happened in this cabin but he had a good guess. Silent, he studied her, and the quiet surrounding him seemed to expand, encircling them in bands of cold steel, locking them together. His strength radiated in waves from eyes as magnetic as lodestones.

Katharine shuddered, unable to look away.

"I don't know what those men did to you. More to the point, I don't care. But dying is a coward's way out. I figured you had more sand than that."

Hope. Something in the calm tone of his voice reached across her fear.

"I tried to run away," she said. Her voice was the trembling song of a child, and her startling green eyes were wide and filled with tears. Her expression filled him with pity.

"Did you now?" he said politely. "Didn't get too far though, I guess."

She was gratified to hear the unexpected kindness in his voice.

"No," she admitted. "I took his gun and tried to escape, but they caught me and took my shoes. He hit me. And I . . ." She couldn't speak, falling back into silence. She had never been beaten by a man before.

"So they tied you to the bed to keep you from running away," he concluded. Taking his knife by the hilt, he carefully cut the rope holding her hands to the bed, calmly noting the abrasions on her wrists, the broken nails and the tender-looking bruise on her cheek. She was leaking tears; her nose was running. She was as disheveled and pathetic-looking as a drowned kitten.

"Yes," she said through her tears. "Otherwise I would have run away again to be free from those horrid men and this awful place!"

"Then it's good they tied you," he said. He was briskly rubbing her arms. "You would never have survived the desert."

She pulled away, stunned by what he'd said.

"Good that they tied me? You have no idea what you're saying. No one should be treated as cruelly as we have been!"

Jesse stared at her and in that moment knew they were worlds apart. She was new to suffering, and he was not. It still had the power to fill her with righteous wrath and disbelief. He was not so naive.

"What seems cruel to one," he said through gritted teeth, "is no more than a small vexation to another. Beat a dog three times a day and he will think you kind the day you beat him only once. I know men who lost a toe and their will to live within the same hour, and others who lost everything and still bless the sunrise.

"Considering the company you were keeping," he said, "I'd say you're lucky to be alive."

With that, he made short work of the ropes holding her legs, ignoring the pained expression on her face. "We'll make camp here tonight," he said evenly. "It'll give you a few days to recover."

Without saying another word, he turned and left the

room. Once outside, he allowed himself the luxury of breathing. He felt an instantaneous and powerful masculine attraction to the woman. It wasn't love, but it was definitely desire.

He shook his head as though warding off a blow. He had never seen a woman as beautiful as she was. Never. Somehow, he knew just by looking at her how she would move and how she would feel beneath him. It might take time to make a friend a lover, but desire happened in an instant, a blinding, dizzying rush as old as the earth and as relentless as the sun chasing the moon.

Sexual heat.

Jesse craved the woman like a fallen angel craves the light. Yet, there was something about her that bothered him, a half-buried recollection that her image stirred. Suddenly it dawned on him with a visceral awareness as acute as a blow to the stomach.

"Deirdre of Sorrows, that's who you are," he whispered beneath his breath.

He named the puzzle before him, relying on his memory to supply lines from the *Exile of the Sons of Uisiliu*. As adept at the Irish epics as an ancient *ollave*, he was able to recite over three hundred tales, thanks to his father's teaching. And he was wise enough to understand that history repeats itself, seeing proof of it in the woman before him.

His brow furrowed in concentration as he conjured the words from the hazy corners of his sleep-deprived mind, and his dark eyes narrowed with effort. Leaning against the outside of the house, he ignored the oppressive heat. He ignored the howling wind that could not cool his inner fire. He ignored everything around him, even the blood dripping from his aching shoulder as he thought about her.

"Wise Cathub said to the mother, 'In the cradle of your womb there cried out a woman with twisted red hair and beautiful sea-green eyes. Foxglove her purple-pink cheeks, the color of snow her flawless teeth, brilliant her Parthianred lips. Though you may have fame and beauty, Deirdre, you will destroy much.' "

He described her flawlessly, using the ancient verse. He prophesied without malice, without emotion of any kind. He simply said aloud what his heart knew to be true, as though he had a premonition of things to come. At that fleeting moment when dreams merged with reality, Jesse rejected the perfect rose and her deadly crown of thorns.

He had suffered enough.

"I want to hire several able-bodied men!" shouted Damien North over the din of the crowded saloon. "I'll pay each one ten dollars a day plus a hundred-dollar bonus to the man who finds my fiancée!"

"You got that much money on you, mister?" asked a man. He looked every part a rascal. Turning toward Damien from his place at the center of the wide, crowded bar, he smiled. His gnarled thumbs were hooked in his belt, and his wide-brimmed hat was shoved arrogantly high on his forehead.

"What do you take me for?" said Damien quietly. "A fool?"

Edwin Dory stood silently behind Damien, holding a telegram from his son John.

"Well, no, not exactly." The man appeared to study the bottom of his glass with great interest. "I'd say any man willing to pay that kind of money for a woman probably ain't half as much a fool as he is a pussy-whipped fop." Grinning insolently, he looked Damien slowly up and down, noticing the stylishly tailored cut of his suit, his clean-shaven face and the sweep of his shining, gold hair. "Pretty good in bed, was she?"

All of his friends laughed.

"Hell," he said. "If you're willing to pay that kind of money for a little twist o' tail, she must be damned good! Maybe I'll just keep her for myself if I find her."

"I'd reconsider," Damien said calmly. His eyes glittered like a snake scenting prey. "And while I was doing that, I'd practice keeping my mouth shut if I were you."

"Well, you ain't me, pretty boy!" snarled the man viciously. He reached for his gun, tied low on his hip in the fashion of a gunslinger. "And I'm thinking that it's *you* who ought to keep his damn mouth shut!"

"Is that a fact?"

Damien's Colt appeared from his shoulder harness and fired so rapidly that the movement was a blur. No trace of emotion, not even anger, showed on his face as the man fell to the floor in a heap. Placing the gun back into its harness, Damien carefully smoothed the lapels of his coat. No one in the room spoke a single word. Only the faint squeak of the roulette wheel turning idly marred the uneasy silence.

"Damien?"

He turned at the sound of Edwin's voice.

"John just wired me. He is in President Fillmore's entourage. The rail lines have made it to the Great Lakes."

"Yes?" Damien said, clearly irritated.

"I sent a reply and told him about Katharine. He's coming. He'll let his brothers know."

"Well, that's good. But I'll wager that by the time John makes it to the Colorado Territory, I will have found Katharine myself. Now, are you coming, Edwin? Or do you have better things to do with your time?"

Edwin's pale cheeks colored deeply. "Of course I'm coming," he said. "Damien, I've had about enough!"

"So have I," said North quietly. He stared at the men in the saloon. "Anyone else care to throw down?" he asked softly. He was begging for a fight.

No one said a word. No one dared.

"I didn't think so. As I was saying before I was so rudely interrupted, I need several good men who know the area north of the Santa Fe Trail, the Sangre de Cristo range."

"Spanish territory? How far north you talking, mister?" asked one of the fallen man's comrades. He had been to the gorge before. Walls of sheer granite a mile deep, not fit for man or mountain goat. Still, the money interested him and he was wiser than his friend had been; he treated Damien with a lot more respect.

Damien considered his question thoughtfully and closed his eyes. He knew the Sangre de Cristos encompassed 14,000-foot-high peaks, impassable in the winter and barely passable in spring because the snow never melted.

"Until we meet the rising sun or fall off the top of the world. In other words, gentlemen," he said as he opened his eyes, "we will go just as far as we have to."

Without a backward glance, he pushed through the double doors.

Chapter Six

*I*n the shadow of the wagon, the two young women remained bound and gagged. The sight of them sickened Jesse, and his unspoken promise to the young woman whose silence had saved him was about to be fulfilled.

"Here," he murmured softly. "Don't be afraid." She nodded, but her fear became apparent when his arms moved too quickly and she flinched. With a quick stroke, he loosened her legs and then her arms, which were bound above her head. The ropes were as vicious as the men who had tied them. Scratches and cuts were embedded deep in her skin, and the bruises on her legs and arms told a story of torture and rape. As soon as she was free, she ran off a little distance and hid herself in some bushes.

Quietly and with deep humility, he moved to the other girl. Her condition was even worse. Her face had been beaten, and her eyes were swollen nearly shut. He knew she wasn't more than twelve. She was barely conscious, her breathing deep and sonorous as though she found it difficult to draw air into her lungs. When he moved toward her, she started to cry and then pulled her legs close to her body, trembling violently. The sheath she wore was ruined, cut in places and torn. She had no leggings or moccasins. Her feet bore the marks of ropes and walking on desert sand without protection.

Reaching out, he thought to reassure her by stroking her hair gently. He spoke to her in every Native language he knew and still received no recognition or response. "I'm not going to hurt you," he started to say very gently, but the moment his hand touched her hair, she screamed.

"I'm trying to help you."

His words were interrupted by a touch on his shoulder almost as gentle as the feeling of a small bird alighting there. When he turned, the white woman in the tattered mauve silks was standing behind him. Her magnificent mane of red hair was loose about her face like a fiery halo, and her green eyes sparkled with unchecked tears. Though no one touched her, she trembled. He thought of a fawn in the deep woods or a willow swaying in the breeze, yet all that stood before him was a fragile woman, weeping.

"Let me try," she said. "You've no idea what she's been through."

"And you?" he said quickly. "What about what you've been through?"

"It's not important," she said numbly. "Please, let me try to help her."

Jesse didn't argue; he simply moved back.

Unsteadily, like a reed wavering gently in the wind, she walked toward the girl, who was now sobbing incoherently with her face pressed against the wagon wheel. Her beautiful black hair was free of braids and leather and covered her small body like an angel's broken wings.

Timidly Katharine knelt beside her and touched her gently. The girl cried aloud as though she had been scalded.

"Here," Katharine said, insistent and gentle. She was crying as well, though she didn't know it. "Let me . . . let me help you! You poor girl! Let me help you!"

Half turning in fear, the girl struggled against her bonds. Her dark eyes watched every move that Jesse made, widening in fright when he handed the knife to Katharine.

"He won't hurt you," Katharine said, pointing to Jesse. "He's not like the others. He's helping us."

The girl became silent and watchful.

Hoping that she understood they were trying to help, Katharine began with unpracticed skill to cut the girl's bonds with the huge knife. Meanwhile, the mountain man had gone back into the cabin; he returned a few minutes later with a canteen of water.

It took longer for Katharine to release the girl than it would have for the man, but her soothing voice and appearance had a calming effect on the child. Once freed, though, the girl stumbled quickly to her feet and ran like a trapped animal seeking shelter with no particular direction or plan, just the desperate need to get away. But her injuries wouldn't allow it. Every few steps she took ended with a stumbling fall to the ground and one more feeble attempt to rise and run again.

"Stop," Katharine pleaded, watching the girl's every move. "Please! You're only hurting yourself!" She held the girl's arms and the girl fought back, loosening the hold long enough to run again, stumble and fall. Whatever strength she possessed was exhausted. She tried to crawl away. Finally giving up, she rolled onto her back, staring at the sky above with her hands held together as though pleading for mercy.

Katharine dropped to her knees beside the child.

"I won't hurt you," Katharine said. "I would never hurt you! Shhhh . . . you're all right, child. I won't hurt you! Water, look." She poured some on the ground and then held the flask to the girl's lips as she slipped her arm about her back and helped her to sit. The water touching her dry mouth reawakened her thirst, and she grabbed the canteen and drank deeply.

"Just a little," cautioned the mountain man in the background. "Otherwise she'll get sick." His voice was soft and reassuring.

Katharine heard him and without turning around, nodded her head. She pulled the canteen away, feeling physically ill at the sight of the young girl; so much so, in fact, that the hand that held the flask was shaking uncontrollably and the water splashed onto the girl's sheath.

"I'm sorry for spilling the water," Katharine said, shivering as she tried to wipe up the spill. "So sorry." It was the child's face that arrested her attention, and those deep, haunted eyes, which gazed at her from beneath shadowed lashes. Katharine was trembling so violently that her teeth were chattering.

"Here," the man said. Gently he took the canteen from her. "There is plenty more water."

Katharine barely heard him. She touched the girl's cheek, shocked by the blood flowing from her lips; the skin above her right eye was so badly swollen that it had begun to ooze. She had no bandages and no clean cloth. With nothing to reach for except the garments she wore, Katharine lifted the girl with one arm and tore a row of cloth from her undergarment. She held it out to the mountain man, and he soaked the cloth until it was dripping wet. Then gently, with infinite tenderness, she began to clean the girl's wounds, washing her skin with the tattered remnants of her petticoat.

"I'm so sorry," Katharine repeated. "I know you can't understand me—but I'm sorry." Their eyes met and held in that peculiar communion of survivors. Their fragility was their bond and the knowledge of a history that neither could escape from. "I'm so very sorry."

Unexpectedly, the little girl reached for her and wrapped

her arms securely about her middle. Burying her small, bruised face against Katherine's breast, she sobbed openly and desperately. The child's pain was like a blow to her middle, and Katharine felt as though she couldn't breathe. Desperate, she pulled her closer, listening to her ragged breath. "I won't hurt you," she whispered. "You are safe, child. Safe."

Instinctively she began to rock softly, holding the girl as tenderly as possible until the horrid sobs had subsided into exhausted whimpers. Slowly, the other girl crept out of her hiding place and joined them.

The mountain man stood behind them, watching, impassive as stone. Above them, the sun in the sky had begun to set as the winds that had howled all day became silent and twilight descended on the dunes.

Damien had had no difficulty assembling a crew. Now, two days after his recruiting speech in the saloon, the search party was ready to depart.

Edwin stood silently beside the horses, watching quietly as North spoke to a couple of men some distance away. They were not anyone he knew, but he assumed they had been hired to help find his daughter. They were an odd group, some men with faces like fresh-faced choirboys and others whose gaze would curdle milk.

Saddling up, North spotted Edwin and rode toward him. "Coming?" he said tersely.

Edwin nodded. "John is on his way from Michigan. He's wired his mother and brothers and I've hired a couple of wagons. They're being filled with provisions." His shock was wearing off, and he was angry now.

"You're traveling too heavy," warned Damien. "I'm not waiting for you, a wagon train or anyone."

"You won't have to wait for me," Edwin said pointedly. "Or the surveyors. The wagons are going to follow." Appearing calmer than he felt, Edwin mounted his horse. "All that matters to me, Damien, is that we find Katharine! You do not have a monopoly on her affections or feelings toward her. I will pay whatever ransom necessary, but I swear, whoever is responsible is going to pay with his life sooner or later!"

Damien nodded. "And I know just where to look."

"What?" Edwin turned in the saddle and eyed him suspiciously. "What did you say?"

"Nothing," replied Damien sharply. He looked down, then gazed toward the western horizon. "Let's ride."

With a wide sweep of his arm he kicked the flanks of his horse and started to move out, followed by the men. The surveying team from Boston that Edwin had hired would follow with the additional provisions they were bound to need. Precious maps and photographs that documented the areas already explored were rolled and placed in waterproof canisters. He had hired some of the greatest surveyors of the century, all in debt to men like John Charles Fremont and explorers who had not set out simply to catalogue a passable route but to tame a land.

In the distance, McGuire stood outside the officers' quarters. He was leaning against a pillar that supported the roof and watching with a mixture of anger and embarrassment as the men made ready to ride out of the fort, led by North. "I don't know how he did it," he said to his aide as he ground a cigar into the planks beneath his feet. "But he did." Somehow, within forty-eight short hours, North had assembled enough provisions and ammunition to last a winter.

"Money," the aide replied. He rubbed his fingers together. "Bites, doesn't it? We can't even requisition shoes, and that bastard snaps his finger and he has an army overnight. Hell, some of my men were tempted to go AWOL because they are damn sick of living on nothing but promises and half-baked beans."

McGuire nodded. It was time for reveille and to hoist Old

Glory. He was proud of that flag, but human enough to wonder what it was like to have so much money you could buy your way into and out of everything.

"Assemble roll call," he said. "I have a feeling that isn't the last we'll be seeing of Damien North." The aide nodded, and both men stood quietly watching until the riders were out of sight.

Chapter Seven

*T*he tracks have made it to the Great Lakes!" shouted a ruddy-faced youth as he ran and skipped across the railroad ties of Peru, Illinois. "Mr. Dodge, I've a telegram from New York City for you! And Adam Dory, I've got one here from your brother John all the way from Michigan!" The boy knew the importance of the telegrams and ran along the new line that had just connected the terminal in Peru to the East Coast. Branches of the railroad were beginning to grow in all possible directions. Every compass point was represented in the web of rail yards—north, south, east, and now, west.

G.M. Dodge laid aside his level. This internship with the Central Pacific Railroad had come upon graduation from college. It was his first chance to work with the engineers and put his education to the test. Briefly he glanced at the relief maps spread out on the makeshift table and took the telegram from the boy, tossing a nickel high in the air.

"Heads!" said the boy. Tipping his hat, he caught the coin

in it and squinted briefly at the man in front of him. "Double or nothing?" He cupped his hand over the coin. Dodge laughed, knowing he had already seen which way the coin landed.

"Nothing, you scamp! Now get along with you, I've got work to do."

The boy smiled. "Your turn," he said to Adam Dory. He held up the nickel and grinned. With a couple of missing teeth, freckles on his face and bright red hair, he made quite a picture.

Adam came from a large, well-established family in Boston. He was one of ten children and the second to his eldest brother, John. Well-groomed and soft-spoken like his father, he'd graduated from Captain Alden Partridge's private engineering school in Vermont, where he'd met Dodge. Then they'd attended university together.

"Let's just cut to the chase," Adam said with a laugh. "Here's a silver dime, now get on with you!"

"Whoa!" the boy whooped in delight.

"You'd better pocket that coin," warned Dodge. He was a handsome man with dark brown hair and eyes, short of stature, energetic and charismatic. "Or I'll arm-wrestle it away from you!"

"Not likely," said the boy, laughing as he picked up his bundle of papers and started down the length of track. "Papers!" he yelled. "Posts! Papers! All the news what's fit to read! Hot off the press!"

The men laughed as they were joined by Fremont, known as the Pathfinder because of his many expeditions into the wilderness.

"He'll make it someday," said Dodge confidently.

Adam agreed. "I can't imagine what it's like being that poor."

Dodge smiled thinly. "It's a wretched life, Adam. A boy like him is nothing but a guttersnipe, hundreds of them around. They break their backs working from the moment they can walk, a bunch of young Arabs with no home or family to call their own. I know what it's like."

"How so?" said Adam. He was a kind, good man. Engineering came naturally to him, but his real interest was in divinity school.

"Because I was that poor," Dodge admitted. "He is like me. Only I was lucky. I had folks who cared. Back in Massachusetts I grew up shoveling coal and laying lines for the Eastern railroad before I was fourteen. I stood in line for hours, ready and willing to do any honest work they gave me. I know what it's like being that poor because I had to fight for everything I've ever won. I learned firsthand what a man can do if he's willing to work hard."

Dodge was English, a descendant of the respectable and highly ambitious Grenville family. Though small, he was a capable man with a horse, gun, level or book. "I got into Norwich University based on merit, not money, and I'm grateful for every chance I've been given since."

Adam nodded quietly. The telegram from his brother lay idle in his hands.

"Don't condemn a man who has money, Dodge," he said softly. "Sometimes the good Lord gives to those men the means to help others to succeed."

"I know," admitted Dodge.

"Still, fifteen cents for a couple of telegrams," said Fremont. "Don't you think that is a mite generous for such a youngster?"

Dodge reached upward and squinted into the early morning sun. The air was gray and already thick with smoke from the factories roaring into life and the locomotives resting on the lines, being loaded with firewood, coal and water from the towers. He had been born at the advent of the industrial revolution, and everywhere he looked its effects could be seen. The locomotive's motors idling always reminded Dodge of a great cat purring. As he turned to Fremont, his dark eyes became hard, filled with the knowledge of experience.

"Do you really think that boy'll spend the money on himself?" Dodge said.

Fremont was a tall man, son-in-law of the prominent Senator Benton from Missouri. He was known for being quick-tempered and warm-hearted, a brilliant engineer with a firm conviction about the best route for the transcontinental railroad. He thought a second about what Dodge had said and shook his head. He knew, too. Dodge had simply said aloud what they both understood as the reality of life on the frontier. It was hard.

Fremont had made three expeditions across the Continental Divide; the last had nearly cost him his life. Frozen, bitter winds, blocked passes, hostile Indians and starvation had greeted his survey crew. He still hadn't recovered from the last expedition in the San Juan Mountains of Colorado. They had nearly starved to death, and he'd made his men promise that under no circumstances would they touch a fallen comrade. He did not want a repeat of Donner Pass.

"No," Fremont said pensively, remembering. "He's probably got a pack of brothers and sisters waiting at home, folks who need whatever he can bring in, just to keep them going."

"Right," said Dodge. "If I could, I'd give him more than a nickel. I'd give him a job and a chance to break out of the poverty he is in."

Fremont nodded and Adam Dory agreed.

"What's in your telegram?" said Adam.

Dodge tore it open. "Like the boy said, the railroad's made it from Dunkirk to Lake Erie in Michigan. Theodore Judah has joined the Corps of Engineers."

"Who?"

"Crazy Judah," said Dodge. "I hear tell he is one of the best engineers they've got. He's pushing to extend the lines for the transcontinental, but the best route hasn't been decided yet; some are talking Santa Fe, others the Oregon Trail. From what I hear, Commodore Vanderbilt, Jay Gould, Rockefeller, Morgan Pierpont and Carnegie are some of the interested investors. They need Congress to give them right-of-way through the Territory, though; otherwise they're done. So they've hired some lobbyists."

"Like Whitney?" asked Adam. He had been in session listening the day Asa Whitney asked Congress to sell him a sixty-mile-wide strip of land, mostly wilderness that ran from Michigan to the Pacific Ocean. He outbid nearly every contractor present, offering ten cents per acre, claiming all he needed to do was build the first ten miles of railroad and settlers would start buying the land adjoining the tracks, making the project self-sustaining.

Dodge nodded. "He was nearly sandbagged when he went into the lobby. Tell a man he can't do something and some men are determined to prove otherwise. Add money to the mix and you have a riot."

Fremont grinned and slapped Adam Dory on the back. "They'll take the Old Spanish Trail," he said cheerfully. "Through the San Luis Valley."

Fremont remembered the Sierra Nevadas and the Rocky Mountain peaks, so steep that not even a goat could climb above the tree line, with air so thin you gasped as though drowning while you scaled the range. The Chinese were coming with gunpowder and blasting caps, but it would take an engineering genius to blow a hole in the Sierra Nevadas big enough for a locomotive to push through.

"Why the Spanish trail?" Adam asked.

"The mountains," Fremont said knowledgeably. "It'll take thunder and lightning to make those mountains passable in the winter, or a boatload of dynamite."

"Never met a rock I couldn't break or a woman I couldn't tame." Dodge was thinking about the gun-toting, bareback-riding Ruth Ann Brown. She looked soft as a goose-down pillow, but he knew she was made of cords of steel and stronger stuff. He loved the change in her eyes.

Comrades, the three men grinned. The world was theirs to conquer. The railway was beginning to take shape. Their dreams were coming true, and somehow they knew there would come a day when the lines would connect East to West, unite neighbor to neighbor, state to state, opening the Territories and bridging the distance between farmers and markets. And it was through the hands that held the maps, compasses, picks and shovels that destiny would manifest itself.

"We'd better get going," Fremont said. "Me and my boys are heading west tomorrow, toward California through St. Louis. Since they found gold at Sutter's Mill and admitted California to the union, Congress is damn sure it wants a way to bring all those riches back East."

He was thoughtful, haunted by that last winter in the mountains.

"Just one more expedition for me," Fremont said intuitively.

Dodge, on the other hand, had been given orders to go north. His task was to find a way to bridge the distance between the United States and Canada. Still, travel whatever distance he might, he knew a part of him would be in Illinois, in the peacock-blue eyes and green silks of a woman he couldn't get off his mind.

"I'm going north, Fremont," Dodge said. "I'm supposed to hook up with Peter Dey. The Central Pacific has hired him to survey the trans-Iowa route for the Mississippi and Missouri route. But not tonight."

Dodge thought of impassable mountains and unconquerable lands.

"Tonight I'm going over to Miss Ruth Ann Brown's to pay a social call and maybe play some pinochle, too." Smiling, he remembered meeting Ruth Ann. She played the piano, rode a horse better than any woman he had ever met and could even shoot a gun. Blue eyes, dark hair and a trim figure.

"Old stock," Fremont said, referring to Ruth Ann's family.

"Old stock," agreed Dodge. "Miss Ruth Ann is Plymouth Rock, a descendant of Governor William Bradford and General Simon Spaulding, I'm proud to say." Then he winked. "Besides, she is damn good-looking, too!"

"You're too young to get serious about a woman," said Adam. His eyes were twinkling. Seminary school was very different from Friday nights and hell-on-wheels rail towns, but he felt it was his calling. "Wait until you get a little older."

"Hell, next April I'll be twenty-two," said Dodge. "I think it's time I got a little serious. Besides, Ruth Ann has good taste."

"Yeah?" said Adam.

"Yeah," said Dodge. "She picked me!"

Fremont laughed. "You are an arrogant little cuss."

"Arrogant?" retorted Dodge. "Naw, just confident, and I'm as big as I need to be in all the important places," he said.

"Well, I've got a woman to boast about, too," said Fremont. "Jessica Benton. She is far too good for me," he admitted ruefully, thinking of her loyalty and his long absences from home and the warm welcome he always received. "But I'm proud and humble enough to say she chose me anyway." They had eloped, and it had been a while before her father, Senator Benton, had accepted him. "I married up," he said quietly. "And she married right."

Adam remained silent. He had his eye set on a woman back East, but as yet, the way to make her acquaintance had eluded him. He had been smitten the moment he first saw her at the opera. As an engineer, he could calculate the shortest distance between two points, but the quickest route to her heart still eluded him. Frowning, he toyed with the telegram in his hands.

"There's time enough for love," Adam said quickly. With his characteristic understatement and nonchalance, he opened the telegram and started to read. The smile he wore started to fade as all the color drained from his face. He looked as though he had been struck a blow to the stomach.

"What's wrong?" asked Dodge.

"It's my sister, Katharine," said Adam. "She's been kidnapped."

"What?" said Fremont.

Adam nodded, stunned.

"John says she traveled with the surveying party and her fiancé to lend support. Father was against it. He wants me to hire a crew and head to Colorado Territory. I'm to meet up with them near Dodge City as quickly as possible."

"Kidnapped? You're joking," said Fremont, trying to understand how a woman could have been kidnapped with a full guard and crew. It didn't make sense.

"No, I'm not joking!" Adam said. He was in a state of shock. "John said they were working with a group of surveyors and some investors. Damien North, her fiancé, was there, and evidently someone took her from the wagon in the middle of the night. Now there is talk of ransom."

"That's good," said Dodge.

"What?" said Adam.

"It means she's still alive," said Dodge.

The impact of his words hit Adam like a blow.

"I've got to go," said Adam. "If anyone has hurt my little sister, I swear I'll kill them with my bare hands!" Seminary school was forgotten. Grabbing his maps, he headed off at a sprint toward his horse. Dodge and Fremont watched him soberly.

"I wouldn't blame him if he did," said Fremont grimly.

"Do you know her? His sister, Katharine, I mean?"

"No. But I know his father, Edwin. The Dorys are good

people. They're involved with Congress and the investors looking into the transcontinental rail route. I heard tell about her, though. Men who have seen her are struck by her beauty."

"Blond, like Adam?"

"No. I hear that she has hair the color of flames and eyes as green as emeralds, fair skin so pale it looks like new snow, and a laugh that rivals church bells on Sunday morning."

Chapter Eight

*T*hey had stayed at the cabin at the base of the Sangre de Cristo Mountains for two days. They were silent days when the heat of the sun beat down intently on the three females and the tall, quiet man who had set them free.

They slept outside beneath a makeshift lean-to, fed lavishly on simple foods that the mountain man caught or trapped. Their wounds were cleaned and dressed in bandages cut from the undergarments of a Boston debutante. Though fragile, she tended the younger girl with the help of the older one. Poultices were made from cactus plants that oozed a thick, viscous fluid, applied to sunburned skin and open wounds. Pain was remedied by a flask of brandy, sipped until merciful sleep overwhelmed them, and hunger was instantly answered by pemmican, dried meats or fresh kills.

The nights among the dunes came suddenly, characterized by skies teeming with brilliant stars and freezing temperatures. They kept warm with blankets, pelts of buffalo skins and the civilized glow of a fire burning brightly. There was comfort in the night-light of the campfire's glow. Not once, even during the earliest part of morning, had the fire been allowed to die. For Katharine, the fire was a Promethean gift, and she cherished the cheerful blaze, moving as close to it as possible.

The third day when she awoke, she noticed that the pack animals were standing beside the fence. Water had been taken from the single well near the cabin, drawn up by a rope tied to a simple bucket. The mountain man was filling the pouches, but instead of bringing them to the cooking fire, he was lacing them to the backs of the pack animals. Nearly every animal, whether mule or horse, was tethered and loaded with goods.

He was preparing to leave.

During the past few days, he had barely spoken. And when he did, it was words like "Yes," "No," or "Why?" which were responses he gave only after she spoke first; otherwise, he never spoke at all.

He reminded her of a hunting hound her father had, Blue. He was a silver Irish wolfhound, huge and rangy, intelligent, who had a habit of bringing everything he caught to her father and dropping it at his feet. Satisfied that he had done his job, Blue would go silently to the hearth, circle his rug three times, lie down and curl his wiry tail around his snout before falling asleep. He expected nothing for his effort, not even a pat on the head. Her father loved that hound, even though Katharine, with her clownish and energetic Irish setter, Molly, which constantly dug holes in their lawn, thought him the most standoffish animal she had ever encountered. Her father said he was "dignified and honorable," to which Katharine replied, he was a "stick-in-the-mud."

Predawn had left a thin frost on the sand and the buffalo robe that covered her. More lucid than she had been a few days before, she noticed how sore she was. Her body ached. She reached up to feel the thin chain of her cameo necklace and was upset when she found that it no longer circled her neck. A miniature of her family was fixed inside. She hated the thought of going back into the cabin, but she needed the reassurance of her family and their faces to give her the courage to continue.

Quietly, so he wouldn't notice, she slipped from beneath the robe and crept to the cabin. Early morning light had barely entered the oiled lambskin, and the door was ajar. She hated the idea of going inside, know what was within, but if there was a chance that her locket was still beside the old bed, she wanted to find it before they left.

Inside the cabin she skirted the edges of the room, shuddering. What was left of Mott lay where the mountain man had left him. Nearing the bed, she saw a glimmer of gold and reached down to pick it up.

"What the hell are you doing in here?"

Startled, Katharine turned, staring mutely as he stood in the doorway. Her mouth had suddenly gone dry. "My locket," she said. "I dropped it. I wanted to find it before we left."

"We?" he said. One beetle-black brow rose cynically above his left eye.

"You're packing the animals," she said. "You're leaving."

He nodded his head slowly.

Yesterday, what looked like a German Shepherd had come into camp. He had given the dog meat and patted its head and it had lain down beside him all night. She learned that it was a wolf, and the next thing to the mountain man's shadow.

"I'm going home," he said. His face was in shadow. "North. Into the mountains. Listen to what I have to say. Stay with the two girls. They know this area, leastways the older one does. Follow the creeks south along the Santa Fe.

Half the animals are loaded with fresh meat, food and gold from my mine; enough gold to buy you passage back East or wherever you're from, lady.

"The pack mules are surefooted—just follow the waters; the trail's well marked and it'll lead you to Old Bent's Fort. Usually there are a few soldiers around.

"Can you shoot a gun?" he asked.

"Yes," she said, barely breathing.

"There's a couple of rifles, plenty of ammunition. Don't hesitate to use 'em. Steer clear of the Comanches and head for the fort. Let the soldiers take care of you and get you home."

He turned and started to walk away, stopping suddenly when he noticed the two girls he had freed standing in the doorway. They were in silhouette, outlined by the early morning light, and their hands were linked. Exhaling slowly, he stared, slightly amazed as they looked at him, the body on the floor and then the young woman. The next instant they ran toward her, and the younger one buried her face against her breast and wrapped her arms tightly about her.

"Wait!" Katharine said sharply to the man. Instinctively she wrapped her arm around the older girl and pressed the younger one closer to her. It was a protective, motherly gesture that came quite naturally when she realized that he intended to leave her in this place, alone and unprotected, to strike out with two girls in a hostile country to find a place she had never heard of.

Boston was her home. A sheltered world where winter opera gave way to discussions of spring gloxinia, yachting at Cowes and shooting in Transylvania. She lacked for nothing in Boston. Her sleep was regular, her bed clean and soft. She ate routinely and modestly, keeping her refined palate in exquisite working order by dining on canvasback duck and vintage wines, Veuve Cliquot and warmed croquettes from Philadelphia.

She was only eighteen, capricious and naturally as warm

as a southerly wind. Fearless, too, of that she was certain, since she had refused to wear a tucker in the crevice of her bodice during her "coming out" ball two years ago and nearly had come out in front of the scandalized eyes of every society matron on the East Coast. Her innocence was the uniform of youth, and her smugness a paper shield; bravado was her sword of straw, and her armor was formed from the glass of innocence, destined to break on the first hard fall.

She had fallen. Life had changed, and she was barred from the garden of naiveté. It had been easy to be fearless when there wasn't anything to fear except a little gossip.

Katharine stared at the mountain man, unbelieving. Her orderly world had turned upside down as though she had stepped backward through the looking glass of sanity and entered a land of madness, where giants with waist-length hair and bloodied shoulders killed men as easily as swatting flies, and devilish dogs were wolves who stared at you with lantern-yellow eyes so intelligent that they appeared human, while hawks perched above your head and cooed like contented pigeons.

"*Kismet!*" she heard a huckster say in her mind, and she was transported back to Boston, wandering along the carnival booths with Damien's hand tucked securely beneath her elbow. "*Fi'-penny bit for a shot at a ten-dollar Gold Eagle!*" *the barker cried.* She remembered stopping at his booth and smiling in delight at his gaudy dress of scarlet kerseymere pantaloons and garters, Hessian boots and garibaldi shirt of bright yellow.

"*How 'bout you?*" *he asked as he held out a pair of freckled dice.* "*Fortunato's my name,*" *he said with a grand smile, and she recalled gray-green eyes that twinkled like Fourth-of-July sparklers in his ruddy, jack-o'-lantern face as he held out the dice.* "*We got it all!*" *he boasted, waving his magician's hand at the array of games displayed in his booth.* "*Craps! Faro! Three-card monte! But just remember, miss,*" *he warned with a mischievous wink as he handed her the dice, still warm from his hands. "Fate plays hard and fast! No favorites! Toss the dice! Take your chance! Only the tough and the lucky survive! What will it be, m'pretty? Will you give Fate a little push?"*

"Yes," she said softly, brought back to the present by the sound of a chair being kicked out of the mountain man's way. "Wait! You!" she cried, frantically waving her hand in his general direction as though hailing a carriage.

He stopped. He didn't turn around. He just stopped, deadly quiet.

And Katharine Dory picked up the dice, squaring off against Fate, taking control . . .

"Please," she said with effort, rending the cocoon supplied by wealth with a scalpel-thin cut of her newly discovered will. "I need you," she confessed, recognizing that her only chance to survive lay in the strength of this man. "What," she asked, "are we to do?"

He kept his broad back to her; his shoulders and his entire body were rigid.

"What you do," he replied tightly, "ain't my business."

"Snake eyes, miss!" sang Fortunato as he gathered the dice and tossed them back to her. "Roll 'em again!"

"Please," Katharine begged. *She stubbornly picked up the bits of ivory.* "I'm sorry for being rude and I didn't mean to call you a filthy beast, although you're in such need of a bath you do bring tears to my eyes! And I'm sorry for being an imposition." Tears returned. She was struggling to understand and to survive. The younger girl was holding her so tightly that she could barely breathe. "I didn't plan to be kidnapped or interrupt your life." She started to shake, praying for the right words. "I know you want to go home, and so do we, but we cannot do that on our own. We are not prepared for these mountains, or the desert. We need you. As you can see for yourself, these girls are just children who have been horribly used. They are weak, still sick and hurt. You're right, I can shoot and ride, but I am not prepared to challenge this country on my own."

He didn't move. She knew he was breathing because she could see the leathers he wore move, but he was as immobile as stone. Perversely she felt both angry and desperate, remembering his fight with the man on the floor, the rage on his face as his hand had arched downward, and his mention of his father. Something awful had caused that pain and rage, of that she was sure.

"Blow your sweet angel breath on 'em for luck, miss!" Fortunato urged with a smile.

"If you want me to beg, I will," she said softly.

She blew across the spotted ivory and . . .

"Not for myself, I ask nothing for myself, but be decent to us as you were the day you freed us. I don't know what brought you to this place any more than I can understand how I was brought here, and I'm not trying to blame you or prevent you from returning home, wherever that may be— but I am begging you because I have no pride left inside of me. So, please, for the love of God, help us!"

He exhaled slowly, balled his hands into fists and turned around. "You don't know what you're asking."

"Oh, but I do!" she replied in a rush, eager because at least he was listening. "You must help us!" She was crying so hard that her lips trembled.

"Why?"

"Because," she said, "I know we'll be murdered in this horrid place if you don't!"

The full reality of the situation took hold of her, and the grimness of her future became apparent.

. . . tossed the dice as hard as she could.

"And it will be all *your* fault for having left us!"

Chapter Nine

*M*urder! Now you're blaming me for your murder, even though it hasn't happened yet?" said McCallum.

"Yes," she said. "*Yet.* It hasn't happened *yet.* I am firmly convinced that we will be murdered in this place if you leave, and knowing that it is *likely* to happen and doing nothing to prevent it makes *you* responsible for our deaths!"

"Me? Responsible?" Jesse stopped breathing. He stared hard at the woman standing before him. He couldn't believe what he had heard. Didn't want to believe it.

"Yes," she said, gathering steam. "You could've prevented our murder, and that makes you an accomplice!" Her brother John's law-school training was coming in quite handy.

"An accomplice?"

"Accomplice! It's the law and a matter of habeas corpus and burden of proof!"

It sounded silly to her ears the moment she said it, but

desperation gave voice to what otherwise would have remained silent.

"Habeas what?"

"Corpus. Bodies, here are three bodies, sir, alive still and well. But I know with fair certainty that if you leave, we will not make it. We will be killed!"

"You're still breathing, miss," he said through gritted teeth. "Though I will admit, you are pushing your luck."

"I'd wager not for long," she argued boldly. "You see that man on the floor? How many more men like that are there in the wilderness? Chances are considerable. If you won't protect us from them, you're no better than him!"

"What? Me? Like him?" he said, enraged. *Now she went too far!*

Turning, he slammed his fist into the nearest wall and right through it. Now the shabby little room had *two* irregular windows.

"That man lying on the floor murdered my father!" he said hotly, pointing. "Murdered him! And he probably would have murdered you, too! He beat and raped those children, and you have the audacity to say that I'm like him?

"Lady, I am the man who set you free, stayed three days longer than I needed to playing wet nurse, and you have the nerve to say that *I'm* like *him*?"

"I need your help," she said simply. "I'm ashamed," she admitted, "to need you so badly, sir, but I do. Please help us."

He had reached his limit. He shut his eyes, but could not shut out her plea for help, her face, her tears, the silent, wounded children. He could not in good conscience walk away.

"Christ!" he admitted. "I'm doing this to myself! Can you believe this?"

All he had to do was leave. Close his ears to her plea, set his heart in stone and forget he ever knew her. But he couldn't. Every time he closed his eyes, he saw her face.

The hawk was settled comfortably out of harm's way on the rafters above his head, peering at him curiously. She was used to his calmness, strength and his comfortable silence.

"Can you, Hawk?" Jesse demanded.

The hawk answered by fluffing her feathers until she resembled a huge pinecone before settling them securely around herself like a cape.

Hiding.

Irritated by Hawk's apparent indifference, he turned his attention to his wolf, Sammy, who just looked confused. *Bite*? his tawny eyes asked as he drew back his muzzle and growled at the shadow of the stove, gazing furtively at Jesse to see if that was what he wanted. No, that didn't seem to be the answer. *Run?* he quizzed, and he picked up a fair amount of speed, loping around the room before finally settling down on the floor as close to the open door as he could. *Hide?* he finally inquired with a timid look. Now, *that* seemed like a very good suggestion indeed! So he covered his silvery muzzle with his tail and peeped uneasily through the bushy fur, waiting.

All was still in the little room. The spider stopped spinning her web. The dust forgot to fall. The wind ceased to blow. All things, it seemed, including a thoroughly terrified Katharine, were waiting and watching as Jesse paced the little room, struggling with his conscience.

"I'm not like him," he said evenly. His voice was deadly quiet. "I'm nothing like that man. I'll never be like that man."

He looked at the girls and felt sympathy stirring within, but paired with his compassion was a smoldering anger driven by resentment. He would never forgive the red-haired girl for comparing him to a man like Mott. *Never.*

"Don't you dare blame me for what might happen to you or them!" he shouted. He pointed a rock-hard finger at her, unsure of whom he was trying to convince. "I'm not your father, your husband, your brother, kin nor keeper, and I don't want the responsibility of your lives!"

Angry, he shoved his hands roughly through the tangle of his dark hair and looked up at the hole in the shattered ceiling.

"I've had enough!" he shouted. "Enough!"

He appeared to be talking to a cloud that just happened to be drifting by.

"I don't want the responsibility of their lives," he said to the cloud. "It would do no good anyway. I can't help her. I can't help them," he said, jerking his head in the direction of the young girls. "Other than setting them free, which I was happy to do. But nothing else! No more!"

He stopped breathing. He looked at her again. What he saw was a wealth of brilliant red hair framing a small, desperately pale face and huge green eyes upswept with deep black lashes beaded with tears. He had made up his mind to turn away from desire. She would bring him nothing but sorrow.

"I know," she said, trembling, "that I don't have the right to ask more from you, but I'm not brave enough to face this wilderness without you. I don't even know your name."

A momentary truce had been reached.

"McCallum," he said pointedly. "Jesse James McCallum. The man *he* murdered was my father, Tom McCallum. He was a cleric, miss, a preacher and a damn good man."

"I'm sure he was, Mr. McCallum."

Guilt was eating him alive. Swallowing, he closed his eyes seeking the High Places that called to him in the infinite boundaries of his mind. He hadn't slept in three days. In his mind he sought refuge in the distant peaks cloaked with ice-blue snow. And he saw his father, tall and proud, turning his face like a flower following the warmth of the sun. " *The Lord your God puts you to proof,*" he heard him say sternly in his musical Highland voice. "*To know whether 'tis ye do love the Lord yer God with all yer heart and with all yer soul. Your strength is great, Jesse, me son, and 'tis a gift, to be sure. But the greater the gift, the greater the burden to do right by it. Freedom isn't running away.*"

Never could, Jesse admitted to himself with humility. *Never would*, because he knew that the price for walking away and leaving the helpless females would be the loss of a part of his soul. At that moment he stopped struggling, ripping away the weeds of selfishness and self-pity that he had allowed to take root in his heart.

It was decided.

He faced the trembling young woman, resisting the urge to touch her. Instead, his hard, hostile eyes sought her tearful green gaze.

"I'm going north, but I'll take you and the girls as far as the trading post over at Canon City, near the Gorge. It's a meeting place for all kinds of folks. The best place to get news of your whereabouts to your father," he said. "It's rough going, lady. In this school, you don't get good marks on a paper; you get a chance to live another day."

"We'll make it," she said, staring at him defiantly. "With your help."

He nodded. "All right, then."

He had done it.

He had taken a vow and sealed a pact.

"You'll have to keep up," he warned. He didn't think they could.

"We will!" she said.

"No arguing," he said, pointing a finger at her.

"None," she said quickly.

"You'll do exactly as I say?"

"Yes," she said. "I promise."

Satisfied, he nodded his head.

"Follow me, then," he said, "if you're able."

He turned abruptly on one worn, moccasined heel and headed straight for the door. Behind him, Katharine stood absolutely still, gaping incredulously at the man who was walking away from her. He was scowling and nearly snarling at everything in his path like a grizzly bear with its tail caught in a steel trap.

The next instant, Jesse was gone, the curious dog fast on his heels and the hawk exiting with a great flutter of glossy wings through the open window, as though it, too, was afraid of being left behind.

"Is he mad?" Katharine whispered. "Or am I?"

The echo of her voice was the only reply, and a soft tug at her skirt. Looking down, she gazed into the face of the littler girl. Her cuts and bruises were healing, but the haunted expression in her eyes was numbing.

She had to trust this man with more than just keeping his hands in the proper place for a dance, or to bring her a glass of punch and not spill half along the way. *Trust* was the wager, and she would have to bet her life and the lives of these two girls on the game.

Her decision was made.

"We'll follow you," she said to the absent man, inexplicably relieved.

Smiling and determined, she grasped both girls' hands and hurried through the room, stopping hesitantly at the open door as though it were a passage from one life to another.

"Kismet," she said suddenly, startling herself as her view of the world changed and she realized that life had always been a gamble, a constant challenge. She was finally ready to take the risk. "I've won an Eagle," she told herself, ready to give Fate a mighty push.

"Come on, girls," she said. She felt that Boston was right around the next bend. "We mustn't argue, and we have to keep up and do exactly what he says."

Chapter Ten

*T*he mountain man rode his horse like one possessed.

He ate the daylight and seized the night with each relentless step his stallion took, bleeding the light from the waning moon until nothing was left after the sun sank on the twelfth day but a cavernous chest of darkness filled with glittering diamonds of fire and ice. By the thirteenth day, the air had become thin. The altitude was so high that even a simple thought became an effort, and by the fourteenth day, Katharine was sure she was hallucinating when she heard him say they could go no higher, at least not in the dark.

Or did she imagine the words? The truth was she really couldn't tell anymore. The world she traveled in was a blurred and warped image of remembered reality.

She could not focus. What sprouted from her neck and used to be her head was nothing more than a dull ache between her shoulders, incapable of making sense out of the kaleidoscope of images flooding her tired brain.

Through weary eyes she watched indifferently as the mountain man reined his horse in beside a shallow stream that sparkled like champagne in the deepening twilight.

She felt intoxicated, giddy and light-headed, though she hadn't drunk a drop of wine or spirits. The world she had grown up in was filled with pleasant smells, courteous men, and days and nights regulated by a clock that ticked off the seconds of her life with structured precision and comforting monotony.

The chaos of the mountains was maddening. There were no rules and no need for white gloves. She loved her white gloves, her damask tablecloths and polished silver.

On the mountain when she was thirsty, she knelt like an animal and drank water from the cup of her chilled, frost-bitten hands. When she needed privacy, she crept behind a curtain of pine needles instead of lace and relieved herself while an ever-curious, cold north wind touched her intimately between her thighs as urine ran yellow and hot down her legs. She was disgusted by the primitiveness of the world, which reduced her to a station no greater than a lynx or timid deer, leaving her scent in the snow and modestly covering her excrement in an icy cairn of white.

Monosyllabic sentences were the norm; speaking flowery phrases was a useless waste of time and energy. At night, she heard Jesse's wolf howl. She understood his lament in a visceral way; its tone described the world of his feelings more eloquently than prose.

He scratched and rolled in the snow, nipped at his hindquarters and licked his fur clean. She watched him with envy, thinking of her scented tub with its steaming water, oils and perfumes. She was used to bathing daily and sometimes twice or more if occasion demanded. Lotions, perfume and soft, expensive clothes had covered her body more artistically but less practically than the adaptable fur of the wolf. With revulsion, she realized how long it had been since she'd bathed. She knew she stank, and yet was powerless to provide the necessities she required to change her peculiar and loathsome state. She tried, though, scrubbing her skin with snow, combing her hair with a brush made of evergreen needles and then braiding it simply.

"Life is so dull and monotonous," she had often been heard to lament to the cook, maid, a jealous friend or an amorous, gleaming-eyed gentleman. "I just wish, oh, I just wish something exciting would happen!"

The mischievous gods must have listened. Excitement had come, with chaos fast on its heels. The change had been like an earthquake, changing her perception of reality forever. She couldn't help it.

Now, during one perilous trek up a steep-sided mountain with the valley floor nearly twelve thousand feet below, she suddenly remembered her Sunday-school teacher telling her to be optimistic and see life as a glass half full instead of half empty. Full? Her glass had shattered and the contents had long since spilled. She was drained dry.

So she simply followed McCallum's lead, looking for signs of a settlement and praying that Canon City was just beyond the next defile or peak. No one said a word, not when camp was set or the evening meal was warmed. Privacy was maintained, not by distance but by the courteous lowering of eyes, which was more effective than brick walls.

It was an alien existence to Katharine, who was used to the pleasant buzzing of inane conversation and the constant diversion of music. The civilized noises dulled the senses and filled the mind. Yet when removed, they left a huge, yawning chasm that echoed with the utterly foreign sounds of wind, icy rain, river, hoof and howl—each one a barometer, alerting her to subtle changes that had lately become so important. A whistle in a twisting wind meant moisture, and she automatically adjusted the skins around her to deflect the inevitable sleet and snow. The sound of a trickling stream or the roar of a rushing waterfall found her fumbling for her canteen, shaking it to see if it needed to be refilled. Slowly, inevitably, she was adjusting to the new tempo, growing more in harmony with the natural world than she had ever been in her life.

They were near the summit of the Sangre de Cristo, nine thousand feet above sea level, a curious caravan of three females linked by pack lines to a man who appeared to pick his way along the roof of a world with the same leisurely familiarity that Katharine had felt when she strolled through Liberty Square. But there were no vendors peddling their wares, or the customary Sunday afternoon fashion parade performed by her neighbors and friends.

This was the real world, not a picture postcard. The complexion of the terrain had altered subtly the higher they climbed. Salt-white sand became sepia-toned stone and rubble dotted with patches of sugar-glazed snow; mesquites gave way to dwarfed pinyon pines that grew out from the weathered old face of the mountain instead of upward, resembling the scratchy stubble of a coarse beard. And the clouds, which had seemed as solid as cotton wadding at the base of the ridge, lost their clear edges and became a pale gray dress worn by a phantom wind that never stopped dancing to the sad song it sang in this stony cathedral of tears.

Lost, it seemed to sigh. *Lost . . so lost . . .*

What would she have heard in a happier time? Did the wind's song depend on the listener, mirroring feelings as mournful as those she carried inside? The winds sang to her, piercing her very soul like the first poignant breath of life and the last sighing gasp of death.

She cried, aware as never before of her own insignificance.

Shuddering, she closed her tired, burning eyes and tried to hide for a brief second in the illusion of safety and the womb of darkness.

"Look, you," Jesse growled. "Did you hear me?" He had barely spoken a civil word to her since leaving the cabin. "I said we'll camp here for the night. Now get your bonny ass off that horse and be quick about it!"

"How can you be so cruel to me?" Katharine said. She was convinced that he hated her for practically forcing him to take them to Canon City, and for comparing him to a murderer. She was thoroughly ashamed of herself and had tried to tell him so, but he wouldn't listen, shutting her out time and time again. Still, she admitted, when she held the two girls close to her at night, she would do it again, for them if not for herself.

"Cruel to you? How do you figure that I've been cruel to you?"

There was a thinness to his voice. He had already dismounted and built a fire. His face, shaded by the hood of a buffalo robe, was half in shadow and half in light. A beard covered his cheeks and chin, and in the muted light of the evening, he seemed as rough and rugged as the mountains framing him. "I don't have to be cruel to you," he said arrogantly. "You're doing a fine job all by yourself."

"Cruel to myself?"

He nodded his head.

"Look at them," he said, pointing to the girls, who were setting up camp. "You've been so worried about them the past few days, hovering over them like a peahen tending chicks, that you have hardly slept."

His detachment had been a sham. She had held the younger girl all night long, soothing her beside the fire and wrapping her arm reassuringly about the older one. They didn't understand each other's language, but there was a bond between them that was growing stronger every day.

"You don't eat enough to keep a bird alive, let alone a woman," he went on. "And I'll just bet you're running a fever, too. You're wasted so thin that your ribs show, and your cheeks are flushed. A few more days and I'll be burying you on this mountain. Is that what you want? Do you think those two young ones want to bury you?"

His sharp words were intended to shock her, to reach her through the walls built by exhaustion and confusion. Against his better judgment, he had started to care. There was something gentle about her that permeated every word she spoke. Unsure of herself and timid at times, she had a veiled shyness that he found as inviting as spring wildflowers. He had seen her gazing in rapture at the torrential flow of the waterfall and caught a surreptitious smile, sweet and hesitant, as she looked out over the vast labyrinth of mountains, defiles and valleys. Heartsick, she had wept silently. He had heard her cry once and turned to look at her. For some reason, he never heard her weeping after that, just saw the captured tears scrubbed away by small, chapped hands placed guiltily against her mouth, shamed by her fear and pain. She was obediently impassive and impressively strong, working and taking care of the others while never asking anything for herself, because he knew she felt she had asked so much already.

"So like a child," he whispered aloud before he could catch himself.

"You don't understand," she said, startled when he pulled the mitt off his hand and reached over to her, placing his palm against her cheek.

"Fever, like I said."

The girls were busy picking up pieces of dry wood, and the moment was as intimate as any she had ever experienced. He was a contrast to everything she knew. Their gazes met and locked, and she couldn't help comparing him to the men she had known with their clean, bright faces and thin, bookish looks, their carefully cultivated manners and charm, their pleasant conversations and unspoken rules of etiquette.

He was a pagan prince, who held his head as high and proud as a king. There was a ruthless arrogance about him that she was certain would bow to no one. If there was an architect of humanity, the embodiment of masculinity stood before her.

"What don't I understand?" Jesse asked coolly, interrupting her thoughts. "That you're alive?"

He dismounted and, without warning, reached up and lifted her from her horse. Her buffalo robe hood fell from her face as he lowered her to the ground in front of him. His breath caught at the sight of her weakened condition.

Standing very close to him, she felt safe, sheltered. Her gaze was drawn to his face; the eyes above her were now heavy-lidded, filled with a peculiar light and appraisal.

He tried to shake off the effect of holding her, remembering her first delicate touch on his shoulder and the impression of a tiny bird alighting there for the briefest time. Fragile, her body weak and ill from weeks of suffering, she was giving in to the specter of death.

"You have to want to live," he said. "You're giving up, and I won't let you do that."

"Why?" she asked quickly. "I've called you a loathsome name, insulted you, and badgered you to help us. My father will never find me here. Never. It's hopeless! This place is so vast, I am but a speck of dust in infinity!"

Jesse was quiet. He could feel the soft rising and falling of her breasts beneath the robe. Her hair was loose and unbound and rivaled the setting sun in brilliance and fire. The mountains of the Sangre de Cristo were covered in a blanket of snow that glowed scarlet red in the sunset, like her hair. Her emerald eyes held the languor of fever, burning brilliantly in a face too thin, yet as haunting as the most beautiful landscape he had ever seen.

"Your father was murdered," she said softly, condemning herself, "and you would be home if it weren't for me."

He nodded. His hands still held her close and he resisted the urge to pull her closer. She was as intoxicating to be near as any strong drink, and as hypnotizing as a thousand and one starlit nights. A month ago, he had surrendered his soul to darkness, praying only for oblivion like an avenging angel whose vision of the future was dark and obscure. That timid touch and those gentle eyes and her need had drawn him reluctantly back to the present.

"You saved me," he said quietly. The wisdom in his eyes softened the raw power radiating from them. He had been on the brink of the abyss.

"How?" she said.

He pressed his hand gently against the softness of her lips and shook his head slowly. He smiled, and she was startled at the contrast of the hard whiteness of his teeth against his lips. Time had ceased to pass, and the world around them began to fade as his presence filled her completely. "What's your name?" he asked.

"Katharine," she said. "Katharine Dory of Boston, Massachusetts."

"Well, Katharine Dory of Boston, Massachusetts, I've shot a couple of rabbits, and when they're cooked, I want you to eat enough to put some color back into that wasted cheek."

He released her, and the loss of the strong arms holding her was somehow disappointing. She looked at him, trying to understand the strange feelings he stirred in her, and why it was that in a wilderness where bighorn sheep outnumbered humans, she should find a man who overwhelmed her senses with a simple, single touch and one searing, unforgettable glance.

"We need to talk."

Bart Cobb stood in the darkness just outside the surveyors' camp, nervously waiting for Damien North. It was past midnight, the real witching hour, but Damien wanted no witnesses to this meeting.

Damien smiled with smooth sophistication as the man struck a match, illuminating his face in the shadows. Bart Cobb, the gunslinger he had engaged in the saloon at Fort Larned, *knew* things and had the uncanny ability to ferret out leads that seemed to escape everyone else. *Ratlike*, Damien thought, chuckling dimly as he imagined Cobb slinking through smoke-filled back rooms, nose twitching and his overly large ears straining for any snatch of conversation that might earn him a few extra dollars and an edge against his competitors.

My kind of man, Damien thought darkly.

"I'll give you a name," Damien had told Cobb as they stood together outside the saloon. Cobb's face and dark eyes had lit up when Damien promised him "plenty of money if you find my Katharine," adding somewhat cryptically that he would give him a lead. Then he told Cobb the name that was the key to finding his fiancée. Cobb had grinned in recognition. He knew the man that Damien had named.

"I know just where they'd be holed up," he'd said. Then he'd left. Now it was time to see exactly what Bart Cobb had sniffed out.

"I'm listening," Damien said calmly. "What do you want?"

"Money."

"What do you have for me?" Damien asked quietly.

Bart knew that he would be useless to Damien if he gave him the names and the information. "I'm not sayin' 'til I get my money."

Damien nodded and shrugged his shoulders, then produced several large bills. "Here's your money, but if you think you're going to do what I suspect Mott already has done, the chances of your waking up in the morning, no matter where or how far you run, are slim to none."

"They double-crossed you, didn't they?" said Bart. "C'mon, you can trust me."

"I don't trust anyone," said Damien meaningfully. "Yes, they double-crossed me. They have been acting as my agents on the frontier for the past year. And were well paid, I might add."

"It's about the railroad, ain't it?"

"Yes," said North. "It's about the railroad. They were my runners—my jackals, so to speak—keeping me informed. I also used them for other things," he admitted. "Strictly business, you understand?"

Bart nodded. He did.

"How's this play with your fiancée, though?" said Bart.

A momentary stab of what could have been guilt or pain flickered briefly in Damien's light, predatory eyes.

"It didn't play well at all," he admitted. "Her father, you see, and his family have controlling shares in the Central Pacific and most of the major shipping lines. They import a lot of goods from the Orient. I tried to buy them out repeatedly, but they wouldn't sell, so I decided to create some financial pressure."

"How?" Cobb asked.

"Look!" said Damien dangerously. "You don't need to know all of that. I'll bring you in, but if you cross me, you are a dead man. Got it?"

Bart nodded, feeling important. He knew he could handle the job. "I'm your man," he said. "I don't do the double-cross or double-deal. You pay me good, I keep my mouth shut. You pay me better than good and I'll do anything you ask."

Damien looked at him and made a decision, nodding. He knew he could have Cobb eliminated any time he wanted, and he needed another runner. Besides, something else, something slightly perverse, was stirring in him: a need to confess. He was almost overpowered by it, as though he was trying to find some way to alleviate the guilt he was feeling over Katharine's kidnapping.

"I know Edwin's business better than he does, and I do not buy into his and Whitney's idealistic mumbo-jumbo about the railroad and the greater good of all humanity. I feared he would never sell his shares in the Central Pacific, even though I told him it was a fool's project. The government contracts will be up for bidding soon. The Army Corps of Engineers has been using Fremont and Dey to map the Territories, and interest is peaking with a lot of foreign investors and some very well-heeled industrial magnates who are interested in investing in the lines, too, like Vanderbilt, Rockefeller and Gould. I was being outgunned and phased out. So I knew I had to move quickly.

"And I wanted to be first. I wanted control. I realized Mott knew this area like the back of his hand, so I had him follow our group with his brother and a couple of his men. I let them know when it would be safe to take Katharine. They were just supposed to hold her for a couple of days."

Perspiration caused Damien's handsome face to shine in the eerie starlit night with a nearly preternatural glow. His normally alert eyes shifted as though looking for a way to escape and, unable to find one, closed briefly.

"You kidnapped her for the ransom?" supplied Bart quietly.

Damien's eyes snapped open. "No, not for the money!" he said quickly. "To pressure her father into selling me controlling shares in the Central Pacific!"

"But when Mott heard about the million-dollar bounty and saw that pretty little twist o' tail, he and his brother decided to keep it all for themselves, probably head south of the border, right?"

"Right," said North with finality. "Now you know! So where are they?"

"I got a job, right? And money?" repeated Bart. He was in need of a drink.

"More than you'll ever spend," said Damien lightly, the hidden meaning lost on Cobb.

"Mott's holed up in a place down by the dunes. It's a far ride from here, and he has been riding in circles, covering his tracks, but I heard tell that the girl is okay."

"And Mott?" asked North carefully. His voice was so pleasant. He asked after the outlaw as though they were the best of friends. But the voice did not match the deadly gleam in his eyes.

For a moment, Bart felt sorry for Josiah Mott, and wondered about a man who could have his fiancée kidnapped by the likes of him. Bart wasn't necessarily a principled man, but he couldn't imagine himself ever doing anything like that.

"I hear tell he's fine, far as I know, anyway."

"Anyone else with my fiancée?" Damien demanded.

"I reckon that gal has all the company she'll ever need or want," Bart said easily. He wouldn't want any woman he knew to be alone with that gang. They were the worst lot.

"Be ready to ride at first light, and make sure you stay at least a day ahead of the main surveying party. And if you want a job with me for longer than you can hold your breath, don't talk to me when others are around, is that clear?"

"Well, sure."

Turning, Damien headed for his horse. His own wagon was with Edwin's, several hours' ride ahead of the surveyors' camp. He hadn't wanted to risk being seen talking with Bart there.

"Hey, Mister North!"

Stopping in mid-stride, he turned and looked at Cobb.

"I hear tell she's real purty, that woman you're looking for. Ain't that right?"

"Yes, that's right," said Damien. "Real 'purty.' "

A quick step toward his horse caused him to pull up

short. Standing near the leeward side of the nearest Conestoga wagon was a man with a familiar face, outlined in the remote light for a few brief seconds before ducking back behind the ribbing.

"Hugh," murmured North, shaking his head. How much had he heard? His lower lip curled in distaste, and he began to shake. Reaching quickly into his breast pocket, he pulled out his laudanum and popped the cork, rolling a few of the powdery tablets into his sweating palm.

Hugh de Angelucci was one of the surveyors he and Edwin had hired. Damien could do nothing more tonight, but he would be paying Hugh a visit soon. Very soon.

Chapter Eleven

June 1851—Colorado Territory

*T*wo nights ago, they'd had deer meat roasted above the flames. Tonight it was rabbit, caught by Jesse's hawk. A subtle truce and compromise had been reached and a companionable silence settled among the travelers.

As Jesse ate, he tore into the juicy meat with gusto, wiping his mouth on his leathers. He caught Katharine looking at him in surprise, and his eyes twinkled merrily. Confused, she looked away and blushed, then heard him laugh very softly. It was an unnerving laugh, low and wicked. He made her nervous, yet, strangely enough, he made her feel safe. One moment he would be near the campfire, lounging as comfortably as in a drawing room, and the next, vanish like the undulating smoke from the fire.

He had a curious way of walking silently, always ready to spring into action like a mountain lion she had observed at the Boston Zoo. There was something calculating, feral and regal in his gaze. She had watched him hunt the rabbit with his hawk, releasing the bird to arch up and soar high into the cold, thin air before plummeting to the ground like a thunderbolt with talons open and ready. Finally the bird had returned to the man, satisfied to be petted, preening contentedly while she nestled securely on his large, muscular arm. Katharine envied the hawk. Jesse whispered to the bird in loving words, making her wonder what he said. She was unable to control the images parading unceasingly through her mind of what it would be like to have his hands touch her that softly. She blushed at the thought and the heat that arose spontaneously within her.

She was fascinated by the man. She was hypnotized by his movements, the combination of subtlety and rugged strength working together. Rippling muscles moved beneath his skin, and his quick, agile hands were rough to the touch yet surprisingly gentle. She liked the rough feel of his hands.

Katharine had seen a few mountain men and knew he was different. The fur traders she'd met in Independence had been pointed out to her from a safe difference. They were a rowdy troop of men dressed in loose leggings and a mix of skins, cloth and animal-teeth jewelry, with a rifle always at hand. Jesse looked more like an Indian. He was sheathed in soft, camel-color buckskins, sewn together with sinew and edged with a fringe that ran the length of his shirt. A bit of color hung about his neck in a turquoise eagle rubbed smooth and set in old Spanish silver.

So intensely was she watching him that he raised his head and looked at her. Fierce winds from the valleys below rushed up the mountain and sent the flames from the campfire soaring; the biting cold caused her to pull her buffalo robe high about her neck and face, shivering, and she caught a glimmer of blinding white teeth in a thin, amused smile. In that moment, immune to the weather and winds, he seemed as savage and elemental as the world he called home.

He raised one black brow above his eye as though he couldn't quite understand the part she was to play in that world.

"You oughta start cooking our meals," he said, gesturing at the remains of the rabbit on the spit.

"I would," she replied honestly, "but I'm not sure how."

"You're not too educated," he said condescendingly, "are you?"

"No," she said wryly. "I'm absolutely ignorant."

He nodded in agreement. "What do they teach you women in Boston?" he asked.

"Evidently nothing you would find of value," she replied.

His dark eyes settled familiarly on her lips. "I wouldn't say that. Not entirely."

With unnerving insolence, he studied her face, and his warm gaze trailed to the hills and valleys below. Chewing on a piece of meat, he lounged back, satisfied. Evidently he liked what he saw. A slow, steady, appreciative smile replaced the roughness of his husky voice. Sexual heat radiated off him.

For Katharine it was safe to admire virile masculinity in the drawing rooms of Boston, but here with no chaperone, she admitted to herself, it was just plain *dangerous*. Flirting was an art form and a favorite pastime of her feminine peers, but she realized it could have unforeseen effects. Taking in a steadying breath, she pretended a calmness she didn't feel, knowing her cheeks were blushing scarlet. She wondered if he knew the effect he had on her and prayed that he didn't.

"I could school you," he offered, his husky voice dropping nearly an octave.

"I imagine you think you can," she said evenly. Her heart was beating in a taccato fashion.

"You kinda like me, don't you?" he said, baiting her.

"Not one bit," she lied primly, holding her breath. Confession could wait.

He laughed aloud, stretched his well-muscled arms above his head and lay down, pulling the hood across his eyes, smiling.

"Oh," he said evasively as he closed his eyes, peeking at her out of one, "I think you do."

Chapter Twelve

*T*he following night, Katharine tried her hand at cooking the rabbit Jesse caught. At first, the carcass looked like nothing but a pelt and long ears to her, but the Indian girls came to her rescue, showing her how to prepare it.

Silently they ate the cooked rabbit, and afterward they fell automatically to their tasks, gathering wood, banking the fire, covering the food and laying out robes for sleep. Another day would come too early, seemingly moments after her eyes closed, and the hopeful thoughts of being closer to home would tantalize her again, making her strain to see around each bend along the winding, narrow trails, looking for any sign of civilization.

Ready to seek oblivion in sleep, to narrow the distance between the world she traveled in and the one she sought, she was surprised to find Jesse looking at her from across the fire. There seemed to be a question or appraisal in his gaze. He watched her unroll her robes, his eyes lingering on the fiery strands of her hair. Then on her eyes. Just as quickly, he pulled away from the intimate connection, as though scalded. Without a word he left camp.

"When I was a boy," she remembered her father saying, *"I used to think that monsters lived beneath my bed. But now that I'm older, I know they are in my head, and when I whimper at night, it isn't because I'm dreaming of monsters, but because I know that evil is real in the world and more hideous than anything I could possibly imagine."*

Katharine stared moodily into the flames, wrapped in robes, thinking of her family. The night was numbingly cold, the sort of cold that creeps beneath your skin, settles in your bones and makes you believe you'll never be warm again. But the emotional numbness that had shielded her was thawing. Flashbacks and images of the past few weeks were creeping into her dreams, and from her dreams into conscious thought. She couldn't avoid them. They ran riot in her mind and startled her from sleep. She would awaken to find tears on her cheeks and her body shivering uncontrollably as she gulped for air.

During the day, fragments of conversations and images she tried to crowd out of her mind reasserted themselves. She was not brave enough to walk through that vale of tears. Whenever she looked at the two girls riding beside her, the pain was real enough to drop her to her knees, sobbing.

"Monsters are real, Father," she whispered aloud. "We just don't recognize them because they look like us."

"Monsters?" said a deep voice behind her, and she jumped, brushing away a tear.

"How many monsters have you seen of late?" Jesse asked. He dumped an armful of firewood next to the campfire.

"Too many," she confessed. He noticed she was crying.

Awkwardly, when normally his movements were so fluid, he sat down next to her, clearing his throat as he brought his knees up and rested his forearms on them. The camp was quiet; both girls were sleeping. The two had endured so much. The farther they traveled from the cabin, the lighter their spirits became. The older one had introduced herself as Little Fox. She was from a tribe that wintered on the Great Plains, traveling the route of the Arkansas River and sometimes camping in the Platte Valley. She was Cheyenne, tall and lithe of form, with a high forehead and cheekbones, and an aquiline nose. She and the other girl had been stolen during a Shoshone Rendezvous when they went for water, she explained. The Nez Perce, Crow, Ute, Cheyenne and several other tribes had come together to trade. She did not know the men who'd taken them. She did not know who the little girl was.

As far as Jesse could tell from her dress, the little girl was Nez Perce. But she never spoke. He signed to her, but she would not acknowledge the hand signals, or French, English or any other language he spoke. She did not startle or run away, but stood mutely, staring at him as though she couldn't see him, lost somewhere deep inside, in a place that no one could touch. She walked in Katharine's shadow and whimpered in her sleep, crying inside where no one could see, beyond consolation. Katharine and Little Fox knew why. They often looked at each other in a tragic conspiracy of silence, pulling the little girl as close as possible and holding her hand continuously. They refused to let go.

Jesse tried to be kind. He made her a doll out of husks and pinecones, handing it to her as she clung to Katharine, managing to comfort her a little with a brief pat on her head. He spoke to her in Nez Perce, and a flicker of recognition lit her eyes, then died. They all tried their best to bring some measure of comfort and safety to the child but were inadequate to the task.

"Why are you weeping?" he asked Katharine. "Is it monsters you've been seeing, or only the darker side of some men you've come to know?"

"It's the children," she answered. "The little girl. I can't stop thinking about her, and I don't know how to help."

She stared at his face set against the shadows, and an involuntary shiver coursed up her spine.

"Sometimes," he said, "things are better left alone."

"You have no idea what those men did to her!" she said in an unusual moment of rage.

"I don't?" he responded tersely, angry, not with her but at what had been done. "Don't look at me like a child with your thumb in your mouth! I got a pretty good idea what they did to her. Killing was too good for them!" The heat in his gaze was hotter than the campfire. "But I can't change what happened, and don't go getting a big head thinking you could have done more."

"I tried," she admitted. The tears in her eyes scalded her cheeks. "But he beat me—"

"Beat you?" It was Jesse's turn to lose what composure he had. He knew the men had been slavers, and he knew the price of human flesh in these parts. Women were labor and comfort, sometimes swapped or stolen, other times sold by their families to gain wealth.

Katharine looked into the fire and remembered rushing forward, grabbing Josiah's arm, begging him to stop, and then he had struck her repeatedly as he warned her never to interfere again. He had slapped her senseless because she had tried to save the little girl's life.

"I hit him," she said quietly. "I took his gun and tried to shoot him. As you can probably tell, it had little effect."

Jesse shook his head, furious. "Lady, you're lucky you're alive." The image of the fragile bird came to Jesse's mind, and the memory of the soft, gentle touch on his shoulder. He could not imagine Katharine jumping between Josiah and the little girl, or shooting a gun. He was amazed by her courage, and his heart was touched.

"My pa," he said, "taught me that hitting a woman or child was about the most cowardly thing a man could ever do. He said it was *unmanly* because the stronger a man is, the gentler he can afford to be. He wouldn't stand for it. Being a cleric, he would preach about it."

"Did anyone listen?" she asked quietly.

"I did," he said. "I listened to every word that blind old man ever said." Jesse didn't mention that he couldn't read. The mining accident that had taken his father's sight had made it impossible for him to teach his son to read.

"What those men did was wrong," he said. "It wasn't your fault, and it wasn't those girls' fault. Mott got his just rewards, and you weren't to blame, understand?"

She tried to move past the pain and suffering. "I'll never forget," she said.

"I know," he said. The image of his father arose spectrally in his mind, and his nostrils flared briefly. "Some things stay with a person, but just remember, most men aren't like those men."

"True," she said. She recalled images of her brothers, John, Adam, Luke, Dan and Nick, her father and family, friends and people she knew. "If I could only make sense out of it."

"Don't try," Jesse warned quickly. "Let God separate the chaff from the wheat, that's His job. Those men could've done different." There was a hardness in his expression. Surprising her, he stood up and walked to his pack. Reaching inside, he pulled out a small sack and went to the fire. There was melted snow in a pot, nearly boiling. Carefully he measured coffee into the small pot, and the scent filled the clearing. "Special stock," he said proudly. "I've got some sugar, too." He placed a little sugar on the tip of his finger and smiled. He loved the taste. Within a few minutes, he brought her a tin cup filled with the strong, sweet brew and settled in next to her. There was no awkwardness in his movements this time, just a comfortable familiarity. "Now," he said. "Tell me, what in the hell are you doing here?"

Katharine almost laughed. She thought of her home and the elaborate silver service, the carts loaded with pastries, the lace and damask tablecloths. At this moment, all that finery couldn't compare to the tin cup with the little handle and the strong black, sweetened coffee offered to her by this good, honest man. He held out the bag of sugar and she pulled her mitt off and dipped her fingers inside, then tasted the sweetness.

Satisfied, he closed the bag and tucked it beneath his robe. "I've got some whiskey stowed away, if you'd care for a nip."

She laughed, and he produced a seldom-touched flask from his pack and poured a draft in her mug and one in his. "Coffee's always better Irish."

"I quite agree," she murmured, taking a sip and delighting at the warmth that coursed through her.

"Now," he said, settling back with his hands wrapped around the mug. "Why are you here?"

"To make history," she said.

"Ambitious goal. Just how do you propose to do that?" His tone was casual and amused; his brogue thick. His black eyebrows arched quizzically above his eyes, making her wonder if there was anything that frightened him, and seriously doubting that anything ever did or could.

"The railroad," she said, taking another sip. It was the most delicious coffee she had ever drunk. Suddenly the night didn't seem so cold and the stars not quite as distant.

"The railroad?"

"Yes."

It was the simplest and most complicated phrase she had ever uttered. In her mind she could see the study where the gentlemen had gathered all winter long, talking animatedly about a project they believed in with so much fervor they were willing to risk more than money on the venture.

"My father and some of his friends have a dream. They see this entire continent as a 'New Atlantis,' a democracy so just that its light will shine into the darkest corners of the world, freeing all people from oppression."

Jesse nodded slowly. "Go on," he said. His father had told him of Parliament and Scotland. "I'm not a man ignorant of government."

"Father said that people are lining up to buy tickets on steamships, harnessing carts or heading on horseback, wagon or on foot for the Territories, just waiting for permission from Congress to settle. In fact, Congress is being petitioned daily to make it official. The railroad makes sense. It would provide a way across lands where no waterways exist.

"Senators Douglas and Richardson are attempting to organize the Nebraska Territory and bring it under civil law with the help of the Department of War. There are many issues being discussed, and it is a difficult situation they face."

"Issues like the Indian tribes and slavery?"

Katharine nodded.

"Congress is trying to maintain the balance of slave and nonslave states while permitting new territories to be accepted into the union."

"Balance slavery?" Jesse mused. His eyes narrowed. "The missionaries say it's a plague on this nation." He thought of Isaiah Briand, his friend and a black man. He remembered the day Isaiah had stumbled into camp, just a youth. His clothing was in rags, and his hands and feet had to be bandaged for weeks to save them from frostbite. He spoke French and English fluently, murmuring in his delirium that his father was a judge. Jesse's family had taken him in and never regretted it. Like brothers, Jesse and Isaiah had grown up together. "I tend to agree with the missionaries about it being a plague on any nation."

There was something in the firm set of his jaw and tone that would brook no argument on the subject.

"I do too," Katharine said. "So do my father and the majority of the legislative body. It's more economics than morality with some men."

Jesse shook his head slowly.

"Those men who took you were slavers. Here, you're worth about as much as a New Mexico mule and a few packhorses. I've seen them chain men and women of all colors and barter for their flesh like trading livestock. I got no use for slavers."

"Neither does my father, or I," Katharine said. "Everyone is fighting over the issue, and there is talk of civil war, which they are trying to prevent. The railroad will open up the Territories and allow settlement, but there isn't agreement on what route to take. That's why I came here, to encourage my fiancé to invest in the transcontinental railroad."

He heard only one word: fiancé. His expression became guarded once again.

"Fiancé," he said. The railroad was forgotten. He took a long pull directly from the flask of whiskey.

"My father encouraged me to study his law books and took me to Capitol Hill, along with my brothers. We heard the senators debate, Jesse, and sometimes they became so heated that a shouting match ended in blows," she said. "Whenever a bill passed and the gavel struck the podium, it sent a thrill right through me and I just wanted to stand up and shout 'Hooray!' "

"Did you now?"

"Yes," she said. "Could I have some more of that Irish? My coffee is cold." As she reached past him for the flask, her hair trailed across his face, the sweet scent of her overwhelming.

"Lady, you can have anything you want," he said.

He poured the last of the whiskey into her waiting cup, which was now more Irish than coffee. They were seated side by side, shoulders touching, and he was fascinated by the way the buffalo robe rose and fell over her breasts.

"Oh, blast," she whispered. "Is it all gone?" He loved the

look of her when she pouted. She had the biggest, most beautiful eyes he had ever seen. He shook the flask and looked thoroughly disappointed when nothing came out.

"I reckon so."

"What was I talking about?"

"The fiancé?"

"No," she said, concealing a small hiccup. "Law."

"Oh, that."

"I slept with my law books."

He nodded. He was glad she didn't say the fiancé; however, he could think of a lot more interesting things to sleep with than a book.

"I hid them beneath my pillow next to my popular romances so my mother wouldn't see."

"Wise decision," he said, turning more fully toward her. *Fiancés and romances.* The talk was getting interesting.

"Someday I hope to vote," she said with a smile.

"Someday I hope you get to vote," he said. She was so damn cute!

It seemed that quixotic, enlightened windmill-tipping ran in her family.

He watched the firelight illuminate the beauty of her face, laughing beneath his breath every time she hiccupped. *Damn cute.*

"Father said there are vast resources in this region, land, wood, gold. It won't take much enticement to get settlers to come, because there are so many people who would love to have land of their own, a home, a place to worship as they please, as well as a chance to live together in peace and harmony. Surely for blessings like that they would be willing to brave the discomforts of the frontier. What an adventure!"

Jesse suddenly felt as though he had been drenched with a bucket. Trapping was becoming scarce. The bison were disappearing. "Paradise? Is that what you found on your little *adventure,* lady?"

His tone of voice had gone from amused to mocking. Traders coming upriver had told him about the talking wire, the steam engine with the whistle that traveled faster than a man on horseback. Some said it was bad medicine, and others called it progress. All he knew was that wherever the white men came, disease, whiskey and sickness followed.

The missionaries brought solace and something he could understand: faith. He never questioned God. His father was a cleric and knew the Bible chapter and verse, but his son's heart was untamed. Jesse admitted to himself that he had gone Indian from the moment of his birth, running with the braves, hunting with his wolf pup, trapping and living free and unhindered. He ignored the missionary schools and chafed when they gave him knee britches and stretched a tie around his neck. It wasn't for him. Still, he knew civilization was coming, changing the landscape for better or worse.

"Paradise?" Jesse repeated. "Do you imagine your messiah to be molten iron?"

"A messiah? Of course not," Katharine said indignantly. "The railroad will connect the East with the West and open a gateway to the Orient for trade. Its merit has already been proven. Wherever the tracks go down, towns spring up virtually overnight. Men once isolated from fellowship with their brothers and markets in towns will no longer be alone."

"They might be better off alone." Jesse laughed quietly and stared at some distant point over her head. His eyes were hard. "The traders up and down the Missouri and Arkansas talk about the settlers' progress from the East Coast across the plains. The traders laugh sometimes, watching them stumble across ground that has been used for generations by Indians, thinking them foolhardy for risking their necks when the snow starts to fly and there is no grass to winter their horses on. Mostly they shun them, though, out of good sense."

"Good sense?"

Jesse nodded. The quiet of the camp settled around them, and the elevation of the mountains caused a faint, dry brush of snow to start falling from the heavens. Down below, flowers might be blooming, but near the summit of the Sangre de Cristo, winter held court. Clouds came quickly, danced softly and departed with subtlety, leaving traces of their passage across the landscape. Snow dusted Katharine's fiery hair, and large, dry flakes lay gentle on her lashes and rosy cheeks. The whiskey had done her some good, he noted. Her lips' natural rouge had been intensified by the cold, and the contrast with her milky skin was like strawberries in a cloud of cream. Frowning, she turned to face him, impaling him with the startling clarity of green eyes that galvanized him on the spot.

"Lady, don't look at me that way," he warned. The whiskey made him less cautious, and his guard was down. Stunned, he shook his head as though warding off a blow and tried to look anywhere but at her. His efforts failed. A powerful arousal took hold of him, intensified by her nearness. He felt as though he had looked into those eyes a million times before. He wanted to tangle his hand in her hair, loosen the braids and feel his rough hands mold her soft breasts, kiss lips cooled by frost to blazing warmth and feel her beneath him.

"What is it about you?" he said aloud, frustrated. He'd had his share of women but had never met one that affected his senses as she did. "Is the railroad the reason you came here, or just to raise hell with a man's sensibilities?"

He remembered the gentle touch on his shoulder and her soft feminine voice.

He wanted to kiss her. The receptive, yielding look on her face said he might have a chance. More out of compulsion than common sense, he gently traced the edge of her chin with his hand. The touch of her skin, the delicacy of her features, drew him like a beacon. Her soft, full lips partially opened, ripe as cherries in spring.

He couldn't look away or deny that he wanted her, badly; otherwise, his body would make him a blatant liar.

"I'm not here to cause you a problem, Mr. McCallum," she offered, apologetic and shy once again.

"Glad to hear that," he said, settling in a little closer. Angling his face, he noticed the long sweep of her lashes and could feel the brush of her breath on the skin of his lips. They were so close.

"We needed you," she admitted. Turning, she sat up on her knees, facing him a scant few inches from his arms. "It was just the most practical thing to do."

The touch of his hand sweeping gently across the curve of her jaw and the light pressure of his thumb caused her to close her eyes, breathless. She was used to having him reach for her in the saddle and guide her gently to the ground; his touch then offered the comfort of a friend. This feeling was like a slow burn on a hot night. It was a carnal touch with carnal intent. She opened her eyes, and his dark gaze eclipsed her senses as he peered at her from beneath his lashes. She noticed the texture of his skin, the movement of his tongue between the perfect whiteness of his teeth. The feeling frightened and excited her, made her dizzier than the momentary languor of the liquor. "I think of you almost like a brother, and I trust your honor."

His hand drifted quickly away, followed by a deep exhalation of breath.

"If it's my honor you're banking on," he said cynically, "you're in more trouble than you know. You should have stayed in Boston."

With that said, he pushed himself up and walked quickly to the other side of the fire, breathing hard. *A man could only take so much.*

"Brother?" he muttered beneath his breath. It was nearly a growl, and he headed off at a trot like a scalded wolf.

"Where are you going?" Katharine called.

"More firewood!" he shouted back, adding ruefully beneath his breath, "With temptation like this, I'm never going to make it past the Pearly Gates."

John, the eldest of Edwin Dory's sons, sat quietly in a saloon in Independence, Missouri. Adam, Dan, Luke and Nick were on their way and ought to arrive any time in the next few days. They would set out immediately to join their father.

John's doubts about finding his sister increased every time he looked at a map. The last message he'd received from his father was that the search party was heading toward Canon City with a caravan of engineers trailing behind. There was word that Katharine had been sighted near the Sand Dunes, a vast wasteland at the foot of the Sangre de Cristo Mountains.

"It's going to be like finding a needle in a haystack," John whispered to himself, his blue eyes showing his exhaustion. He was sick at the thought of what had happened to his little sister, praying they would find her in time. In his valise, he had the ransom money, a fortune that had been earmarked for investment in the railroad. The sum was now noted in the ledgers under the heading *Miscellaneous Expenses*.

John knew that Edwin didn't care about the money.

There was no price on earth he wouldn't pay for the safe return of his daughter.

Chapter Thirteen

*D*amien North III moved silently through the darkened camp. Once again, he had slipped away to ride back to the surveyors' camp. Pausing for a second, he glanced around to make certain he was alone. Then he entered the wagon of Edwin Dory's surveyor, Hugh de Angelucci. He'd expected to find Hugh inside, but the wagon was empty.

"The Skeptical Chemist," Damien said, reading the faded gold title on the worn spine of an ancient and valuable volume he held in his elegant hands. His blue eyes twinkled with malice and irony. "How amusing you are, Hugh," he murmured. "How patently predictable and abysmally boring all of you are with your altruistic motives, as if I believe them for a minute." He tossed the book carelessly onto a pile of painstakingly folded clothes. "Now, what other treasures do you hoard in your sanctum sanctorum?"

The large Conestoga wagon was bathed in the dim glow of a single candle. Perhaps its owner had left to answer a call of nature. "This here prairie schooner is nineteen feet long and capable of carrying ten tons of cargo!" the wheelwright had boasted when he'd sold the expedition six of the brightly colored red and blue wagons in St. Joseph, Missouri.

Hugh de Angelucci, the resident surveyor and engineer, and a distant cousin of the New York Hamiltons, had been intrigued by the claim and was determined to test its validity. He treated the wagon like an engineering project, and by the time he was done loading the Conestoga, there was not one inch of space that his clever mind hadn't put to good use. The wooden ribs supporting the canvas were higher at the front and back. Near the center of the rear support hung his transits and levels. He kept the fragile telescopes stationary by stringing supporting horizontal ropes every six inches. The vertical rods that he used to calibrate the distance in elevation were carefully numbered and set within a deep, narrow pot that resembled an umbrella stand. And the rulers and tapes, which measured the horizontal linear distance between any two given points, were carefully hung according to their length on a large board affixed to the starboard side of the wagon.

Along the aft wall, Hugh had built a draftsman's table, complete in every detail. Yet the most striking feature of the interior of the schooner was the abundance of books. There were literally hundreds of them stacked in piles according to subject and alphabetized in each stack according to the author. The range of subjects was astounding. There were dozens of books on geometry and trigonometry. These Damien understood because they pertained to Hugh's profession, but mathematics was only a fraction of the intellectual wealth contained in the wagon. There were thick volumes dealing with alchemy written in German, Italian, Latin and Greek, books on philosophy, mysticism, physics, poetry and the natural sciences.

"Such intellectual conceit," Damien scoffed. He never read anything unless it pertained to business or finance.

He did not read for pleasure, finding watching a fierce bout in the boxing ring more entertaining.

Toppling a pile of books with the solid gold tip of his cane, he laughed at the sudden mental image he had of handsome young Hugh down on his knees, straightening each pile fastidiously every night when they stopped. Holding his cane like a billiard cue, he toppled a few more books and laughed again. "As if any man would actually read such drivel. Eh, what's this?"

His attention was diverted by a thin, white apron hanging above Hugh's narrow berth. With a flick of his cane, he ripped it from the wall and found the objects Hugh valued most—a simple twenty-four-inch metal ruler and an archaic crest. It was a striking emblem. A single gold letter "G" was enclosed from above by an open compass and from below by a stonemason's square with its apex resting firmly on the ground and its legs pointed upward in the shape of a V.

Damien choked.

"Freemason," he muttered in disgust. "I should have known. You haven't changed one whit since Harvard, Hugh. A Constitutionalist, a Democrat, and now what? A devout believer in a 'Supreme Being'?"

Damien hated all Freemasons. It was true that he belonged to the brotherhood, but only because he believed it furthered his ambition, not because he agreed with the tenets of the order. He was also a member of the faltering Whig Party and an Episcopalian who bent his knee regularly and received the sacraments with such devotion and solemnity that he had earned the reputation as a devout and good man. Yet faith eluded him. It was irrational and preposterous. He believed that God was dead, because his father had told him so the night his mother died.

"Is she in heaven with the angels, Father?" he had asked. That was so long ago! His voice was soft, the tremulous voice of an eight-year-old boy choking with tears and burdened by unfathomable grief.

He knelt beside his mother's bed that evening on thin, spindly legs with his elegantly tapered fingers clasped so hard that his knuckles were white; his eyes were wet, wide and starkly blue in his pale face. "Consumption," the doctor had said with his hat in his hand and his black bag closed. "Nothing I can do. It affects the lungs. She can't breathe."

Damien didn't know what that word meant, not exactly. He stood in the shadow of his father, fully expecting the doctor to produce a cure, but none came. The bag remained closed, and the only explanation offered was a word, *consumption*. He supposed that consumption was a robber of sorts, a clever thief of life who stole his mother from him bit by bit, day by day, until all that was left was a wax image stretched out in front of him on damask sheets. She seemed like a reclining statue in the weak, guttering light, without even the strength to draw a breath.

Dead. Nothing he could do. Consumption.

But perhaps, thought the boy, there were other places where *consumption* could not creep and glide, and steal the life from his mother's smile and the tenderness from her blue eyes.

"She's in heaven," he said. He hoped.

"Heaven?" repeated his father harshly. He was the mature image of his son. There was sarcasm in his voice and no tears in his eyes. If he had felt tenderness for the woman, it did not show. He stood at the foot of his wife's bed and did not weep.

"Yes, Father," Damien whispered. "Th-there are streets of gold."

He imagined his mother in an angel's dress of white.

". . . and there are many fine houses . . ."

He imagined his mother in a crystal palace.

". . . and there will be no sickness . . ."

He imagined his mother vibrant and alive.

". . . and w-we'll all be together a-again . . ."
He imagined himself with her.
". . . forever and ever."
"You stupid pup," snarled his father.

He brushed past the doctor and rounded the corner of the bed. He grabbed the kneeling boy by his shoulder and hauled him roughly to his feet.

"Heaven?" His voice boomed, reverberating starkly in the high-ceilinged room. "God and angels? Your head is full of your mother's nonsense!

"Dead, my son, is dead! And just to make an impression on you that you'll never forget, because I love you, I'll show you exactly what I mean!"

Damien was stunned, confused and frightened. He longed to remain by his mother's side, but his father wouldn't allow it. He pulled him from the room into a hall filled with twilight shadows and the homey smells of beeswax, pot roast and gravy, wood smoke from the countless blazing hearths, and literally pushed him down two flights of stairs and out the back door. Damien would have fallen had it not been for his father's hand holding him by the scruff of his neck.

The light was going from the yard behind the stable, and the little boy had the crazy feeling that *consumption* had stolen that as well. He shook with February cold and burned with fever. In despair he looked upward, searching for solace in a sky that held no comfort, only the leprous scabs of darting gray clouds. He waited for a revelation, but none came.

"Look!" commanded his father.
And he did.

Like a puppet with no will, he followed the line of his father's arm to a pile of rubbish. A black web of sticks and withered gray leaves bled of all color was all that he saw until his father kicked aside a few twigs.

Yellow.

Like the sun, gold as daffodils and the bright, burnished tresses of his mother's hair. The color caught his eyes. Like a magnet his gaze was drawn and held, watching spellbound as his father kicked away the dull top layer to reveal what lay beneath.

Goldie. His pony. Weeks ago, he'd been told Goldie was being sent to the country.

With questioning eyes scrubbed dry by more misery than a boy could stand, he looked at his father.

"Dead," his father said. "A mass of hair and muscle and bone that will rot and be nothing more than fodder for worms."

"Like your mother" was the implication.

"There's a lesson to be learned from death, and I'm going to tell you about it, my son."

"Because I love you," his father had said. This was love, then? What was all that softness from his mother, those smiles, hugs and kisses?

"All human beings are *not* created equal. The weak ones will tell you that 'the meek will inherit the earth' because they do not possess the strength and ability to acquire it on their own! That is why they believe in a 'God' who will ultimately balance the scales and set things right, so their advice to you is to 'turn the other cheek,' but I tell you that God is as dead as this horse and that angels do not exist and the only 'higher power' on this earth is *you!* So make your own commandments, my son, and mold the earth into your heaven, because this"—and he kicked the lifeless pony with the golden mane the color of his mother's hair—is the end of the game and no one is keeping score!

"Do you understand why I'm telling you this?"

"B-because you love me?" Damien stammered. He repeated dully what he didn't understand. The light was gone from the sky and the darkness in the yard was absolute; so deep that he could not make out a single feature of his father's face. His voice seemed to come at him from all sides, then inside, as though it resonated from within his own head. His father possessed him, sucked away his innocent soul, leaving a vacuum of misery.

He had taken away his hope.

"That's right, Damien," he said as he reached for the shivering boy's hand. "Because I love you. Now, repeat after me. 'I'm strong and I will not cry.' "

A dog started to bark somewhere in the distance. Damien heard it in a vague, disjointed way as though he were submerged in water and the sounds were muffled. Then the dog started to howl, a high, keening, wailing sound filled with grief and the night and the cold wind and bitter, bitter tears.

"Stop that!" he heard his father say.

The darkness grabbed him by the shoulders, shook him until his teeth rattled, and slapped him so hard that a sun exploded in a ball of white light behind his eyes, rocketing his head backward.

The dog stopped howling. It was then that he realized the animal sound was coming from him. His head began to hurt from the blow. The sun was gone from behind his eyes, and all that was left was black shadows robed in pain. Sobbing, he reached up and began to rub his aching temple. The watery world surrounding him was getting thick, viscous and muddy.

"No son of mine," his father said, "will be a crybaby full of humbug and nonsense! You will be a rational man, Damien, a successful man! And if the only way I can ensure that you will not grow up tipping at imaginary windmills, waiting for some pie-in-the-sky reward for letting other people walk all over you, is by being cruel to you now, *then I will be cruel to you now.*

"Goldie is dead and you will never ride on his back

again. Your mother is dead and you will never see her again. Heaven and angels do not exist! They are the drug of the weak-willed and simple-minded. All there is, is *this!*"

Darkness? Damien wondered. The water surrounding him was black as sin and very, very cold.

"God is dead," his father said, "and dead is dead."

"Dead," Damien repeated.

He understood.

Soberly he reached for his father's hand and started to walk back to the house, knowing that he would stand in his father's shadow at the foot of his mother's bed and not weep.

"Dead is dead," Damien said. Remembering.

His voice was soft and distant. He stared blankly at the Masonic symbol, trying to remember what he had been thinking. His head was pounding. Absently he reached up and began to rub his aching temple, wondering if he had brought his laudanum with him.

It didn't matter; he was used to the pain of his migraines. Besides, he would be finished in a few minutes and then he could return to the search party and wait for more news of Katharine.

"Soon," Damien whispered as he rehung the white apron over the emblem and went to the drafting table to study the latest maps. Once they'd ascertained the best route, the building of the transcontinental could begin in earnest. "Soon I will have everything I want!"

"And just what might that be?"

Damien froze.

"Well, good evening, Hugh. I wasn't expecting you back quite so soon."

"Obviously," said Hugh coldly.

"Obviously," repeated Damien. "Ironic, isn't it? I was so preoccupied that I didn't hear you sneak in." He dropped his hands slowly from the table and turned around. He smiled, and his right hand went for his lion-headed cane. The cane was weighted, and the lion, like his ring and cuff links, was formed from solid gold. They were family heirlooms and priceless antiques.

"I don't think I have to remind you that I don't need to sneak into my own wagon, Damien," Hugh said. "Nor do I remember inviting you in or giving you permission to go through my private papers. Considering your negative attitude toward the project, I really don't understand why you would be interested in my maps in the first place. It just doesn't make sense!"

Damien's hand tightened around the cane.

"Of course it does," he replied lightly. "I lied, Hugh. I believe that a transcontinental railroad is the greatest project of this century, and certainly one guaranteed to gross millions."

Hugh was flabbergasted by Damien's admission.

"Then why the pretense?" he said. "Why the constant disparaging remarks and the lack of support?"

"Because," Damien said coldly, "I don't want a *share* in the project, I want it all."

With that admission he flipped up the cane with practiced ease. He swung it as hard as he could, hitting Hugh in the forehead. The sound of the cane striking bone was as harsh as the groan that escaped Hugh's mouth. His eyes went wide in shock and disbelief and excruciating pain, and he reached out to grab Damien's arm. But his expression had no effect on Damien. He simply hit him again and again until he was sure he was dead.

With a slight moue of distaste, Damien wiped the gold head of his cane on the blankets covering Hugh's berth. He was splattered with gore and mentally rehearsed the steps he would need to take to cover his tracks. The body didn't matter. But the maps did.

Damien would no longer have to fear that Hugh would reveal his part in Katharine's kidnapping. And he would have the added bonus of stealing the maps the talented surveyor had been working on.

He walked back to the drafting table.

The maps.

The papers were the key, showing accurately and in clear detail how to link the Eastern United States with the frontier West. His engineers would get the jump on the other teams searching for the best route west. A greedy gleam lit his eyes. In his hands he knew he held not paper but power.

"Seventy-seven million acres of land for sixteen cents an acre. You overpaid, Asa, by a good six cents, I'd wager. But then, what price a kingdom? And yes, one man can rule it and own it."

He laughed softly.

"Perhaps Milton said it best . . . 'Better to reign in hell than serve in heaven.' And with these, I'll be able to build a paradise even Old Nick would envy!"

Satisfied, he stepped over Hugh without so much as a downward glance or a pang of guilt. "I need a bath," he muttered. He left the wagon, mounted his horse and rode back to his own camp at a gallop, thoroughly upset over having ruined a nearly new suit of clothes.

Chapter Fourteen

Savage beauty.

Colorado is the land of the soaring eagle and the wily snake. Heaven and hell meet and merge in her cathedral peaks and sweltering dunes, creating a mythic landscape where anything is possible.

Even dragons, mused Katharine. She let her eyelids open just a fraction, feeling an absurd pleasure as droplets of morning mist clung to her lashes, the light refracting through the prisms of water and turning the clouds into jeweled fantasies and the dawn into a rosy blaze so brilliant that it set the cloud-dragon's cotton wings aflame.

Wistful, she watched as powerful shoulders took shape above her in the sky, melded to the wings, and then the neck thickened. Where once a narrow, reptilian head appeared with wise yellow eyes of sunrise fire, there appeared the face of a man too beautiful to be a mere mortal; he had the power of a thunderclap in his voice and the brilliance of lightning in his dark eyes. "Born of a dragon," she sighed wistfully. "I wonder what it would feel like to be loved by a legend."

"Katharine Dory! You! Miss! Roll your lazy self out of that sack! You've slept half the day away, and we've many a mile yet to ride!"

Groaning, she rolled her eyes in irritation. There were no rest days. Just hard days riding narrow trails in unpredictable weather and nights of exhaustion. The Irish coffee had sent her tumbling into a deep, hypnotic sleep so that now, waking, the edges of fantasy and dreams blurred, leaving a mental dullness that rivaled her muscular aches and pain. She longed for a bath in thick, soapy, fragrant water, clean clothes and fresh linens, hot coffee and croissants.

"Lazy?" she said, offended. "I'm up at sunrise, riding until dark, hauling water and wood, cooking hard corn cakes on flat rocks, finding forage for horses beneath snow, and you have the audacity to call me lazy!"

Turning over, she placed her chin on her hands, preparing to tell Jesse McCallum just what she thought of his less than civilized morning greeting, but her words caught in her throat along with her breath.

He was standing in the small stream that wound along the boundaries of their makeshift camp. No leather covered his body, and no matted animal fur concealed his magnificent strength. He stood in the stark morning light in icy water to his knees, naked except for a small breechcloth draped carelessly around his waist. In his hand, he held his knife and methodically scraped his face, which now was quite bare, free of any hint of his blue-black beard.

Her heart skipped a beat and picked up speed. Unable to stop herself, she stared at him. Worldly and sophisticated though she might be, having traveled the globe and enjoyed the company of many men, she was confident that he was the handsomest man she had ever seen. Stunned, she noticed the dark, romantic waves of his hair moving in the wind against his wide shoulders and trailing seductively down the expanse of his muscular chest. Every movement he made caused his muscles to ripple beneath his skin, and she felt a responsive heat rise within. She blushed, unable to stop herself from stealing glances. A lady would surely look away! She tried, but no matter how much she chastised herself, she could not.

He was so tall. And his face was such an arresting contrast of light skin and dark hair. There was fierceness in the set of his brow, and pride in the aristocratic lines of his high, wide forehead. His lips were generous and sensual, framing startlingly white teeth.

Desire, like winter giving way to spring thaw, rose inside her the more she stared. She was not a novice to these feelings; indeed, she had been dubbed "flirtatious" by her Grandfather Dory, who would frown and scold her for the unabashed admiration she'd shown for the males in her company. But those lean, sinewy youths could not compare with the masculine beauty before her silhouetted against wood and mountain. Jesse McCallum was a confident hunter who moved with easy manly grace.

Try as she might to remember the rules she had been taught since birth about how proper young ladies should act, she could not pull her gaze away from Jesse's muscular form. His dark hair and light skin. His impenetrable eyes and wide shoulders, narrow waist, rippling, thick thighs and wide, rough hands sporting long, agile fingers. Sinful images arose, unbidden and startling, of his rough hands tangled in her hair. She could not control her thoughts or the feeling of her lips swelling as her eyes were drawn irresistibly to his mouth. Shocked, she turned her head to one side so he would not see the effect he was having on her. *Too late*, she feared!

Hot blood pounded in her temples and filled her with a delicious, sweet ache. Her body, it seemed, had a mind of its own. She reacted to him like fire to tinder, each glance acting as kindling, stoking the flames. She sought his eyes, trying to understand the forces raging inside of her.

They connected.

A slow half smile turned the edges of his lips up, and she could read masculine wisdom in his natural, challenging gaze. *Some things were meant to be.*

Quite unexpectedly, Jesse pegged his knife into the frozen ground, shook back his still damp hair and started to walk toward her, sporting a lazy grin. Somewhere between the creek and the few steps he'd taken, she had forgotten to breathe. He bent down, and the dark river of his hair whispered across her face, causing a shiver so delicious to rush up her spine that she closed her eyes against the sensation. She tingled and sighed.

"Lady," he said softly. He squatted down in front of her a hairsbreadth away, resting his powerful forearms on his knees. He was naked except for the breechcloth hanging down between his legs like a tradesman's apron. She could see the curve of every muscle in his calves and thighs, the slender, powerful ankles, the corded muscles of his stomach whispering in and out with each breath, and the hard, rounded muscles of his chest with its dusting of black hair.

"Yes," she said. She wasn't sure what exactly was happening to her. *He was such a splendid savage!*

"I'll go upstream," he offered, jerking his hand in a northerly direction. The silver eagle on his chest caught the morning light and shone bright blue. "If you'd like to bathe, that is."

"Bathe?" she mumbled, tangling her hand in her hair, bewildered. She hadn't combed her hair in days, and soap almost sounded like a foreign word.

"Uh-huh," he said. "Bathe. I don't mean to insult you by calling you a filthy beast, but I must confess you do bring tears to my eyes." He gave a little moue of distaste and fluffed his hair, imitating her.

"Why, I never!" Katharine said, shocked at his impertinence. Her romantic fantasy was all but forgotten. Embarrassed, she impulsively pushed him over on his back as she scrambled from under the buffalo robes and headed toward the stream.

Jesse tumbled over backwards, laughing as he fell.

Looking at the sky, he stretched out in her still warm bedroll and sighed at the feeling of her warmth against his skin. Folding his hands beneath his head, he gazed upward. The birds were singing as he closed his eyes, dreaming.

It was a sweet, beautiful morning after all!

The Senate chambers were filled to overflowing with thick-waisted politicians and eager lobbyists. The noise was deafening. Acoustically perfect, the second-floor room with its plain white walls and domed ceiling reverberated with masculine voices raised in heated debate.

"Private ownership versus government control. Isn't that what this debate is really about, Mr. Whitney?" asked Missouri Senator Thomas Hart Benton. He stood behind the podium and looked down disapprovingly at the gentleman who had the floor and had lately become his greatest adversary.

"A certain amount of government control is necessary," responded Whitney dryly. "Or is your promotion of St. Louis as the hub of the railroad for the good of all the people, eh, Senator?"

Asa Whitney wished he were with his friend and business partner, Edwin Dory, at this moment, trudging over the mountains or on one of his ships, heading for China, instead of confined to the second floor of the Capitol Building, debating sectionalism, westward expansion and the railroad.

"Do you think," Whitney added dryly, "that there is not one man in this room who isn't concerned about his profit margin in this game? The question isn't who will profit from the railroad, because we will all profit. The question is who will build it, the best route to take and who will *own* it." Asa cut to the chase and spoke plainly. The word *own* hung heavily on the air within the room.

"The goal of the transcontinental route is to connect the East Coast with the West Coast and provide a terminus for shipping lines to the Orient via the Pacific coastline," he went on. "The only logical way to connect the East with the West Coast is the railroad. We must have a consensus of approval, and then apply our combined energies toward its completion in a practical manner, which is what I am attempting to do."

He held up a portfolio, which he had copied and distributed to every member of the Senate.

"I've been criticized rather heavily by the author of the *American Railroad Journal* for—how did he put it?—a 'hearty contempt for the whole engineering process.' It isn't true. My partner and I have hired the best engineers in the country, including Mr. John O'Sullivan. Right now, these gentlemen are out mapping the territory west of the Divide. I have no doubt that they will find the most economical southern route."

"The government has commissioned my son-in-law for a fourth expedition," Benton put in. "Fremont will winter again in the Rockies and along the Sierra Nevadas, though God knows, I'm glad it's not me. It may well be that the South Pass will provide a route through the Divide."

"Gentlemen, investors are lining up," Whitney concluded, "not only nationally but abroad as well. If you don't take advantage of this opportunity, someone else will. Remember, I'm not your adversary, nor am I in competition with the United States Government for control of the railway. I am simply a rational man who is interested not only in my welfare but the welfare of this nation." Whitney was a patriot. He made no bones about that, and he was an advocate of capitalism and democracy.

"Well put," said the senator, acquiescing with a thin smile. "For an opportunist." Benton was well aware of the potential of the transcontinental railroad. He was lobbying hard for the overland route to begin in St. Louis. He wasn't about to allow Territories further north to take the terminus away from Missouri. Economically it would be a windfall. Water stations, by necessity, would be built every few miles, and he knew from observation and experience that towns would follow.

The two men looked at each other and a moment of silent truce was reached.

"A man who doesn't take advantage of an opportunity of this magnitude is a fool," said Whitney pointedly as he arched one graying eyebrow. "And you are not a fool, Senator."

They understood each other.

The senator nodded as Asa turned and started to walk toward the double doors.

"Mr. Whitney!" said the presiding senator. "You haven't been excused! If you don't stop and turn around, I'll have no recourse but to hold you in contempt."

"That's fine," Asa responded casually. "Because I am—in contempt of this entire legislative process. Molasses running uphill in winter is speedier than the Senate. If you gentlemen would look at this as a business transaction and nothing more, it would be done within a fortnight. I'm not a social worker."

"The people come first, Whitney," said the presiding senator.

"Exactly, Senator. That is why you are a politician and I'm an opportunist. The transcontinental railroad is the single most potentially profitable enterprise that the United States Government will venture into, at least in my lifetime. If you doubt my words, then look at the results. Wherever the tracks go, wealth follows. I want to be part of that at a grass-roots level. I think the rest of America does, too."

Chapter Fifteen

*J*esse had led his little group over the summit, and they were picking their way down the east side of the mountain toward the Arkansas River and the trading post at Florence, stopping late in the afternoon to rest. A clump of birch trees near Hayden Creek provided firewood, and the females started a campfire while Jesse left to hunt.

"Like this," said Little Fox. She knew some English, and what she didn't know she signed, piling wood above thin bits of dried grass and wood shavings and blowing on it gently until a blaze started. Katharine was grateful for the warmth and smiled. She picked up the tin kettle and walked to the creek to fetch water with the smaller girl holding tightly to her skirt.

"It's alright," she soothed, disengaging her hand long enough to stoop and fill the kettle with water.

A sudden movement had her looking up in horror as three men on horseback trotted to the stream. Their horses were painted with bright colors on their rumps and foreheads, and their manes were braided tightly. The men sitting astride them were dressed in leggings and buckskin shirts and wore braids in their hair.

The young Indian in the lead lifted his leg over his horse's head and dropped easily to the ground. He went up to Katharine and greeted her, smiling. He lifted her hair with a familiarity that sent a shiver through her.

"I don't understand," she said woodenly, absolutely terrified.

"I do," came a familiar voice behind her. With a whoop and a holler he was running full speed toward the men, pulling down the first one and wrestling him to the ground, laughing.

Jesse. She exhaled in relief.

The next moment she heard a loud shout, and the other two men joined in until all four were a jumble of arms, elbows, legs and backsides, tumbling into the creek until they had had enough.

"Friends," Jesse said easily, smiling broadly and slapping the first man on the back as he helped him to his feet. He invited the men to join them for a meal.

When they reached the campfire, he found a small deer, cleaned and ready to cook. "You gonna cook that?" he asked Katharine with a grin.

"Yes," she replied. "I'm an *educated* woman, after all." Then she laughed as they all pitched in to prepare the venison. Conversation came easily. The men were Blackfoot and knew Jesse. They were traveling to the Rendezvous with their pelts to trade.

Talk of Canon City, trading and gossip amongst the tribes peppered the meal with anecdotes, tall tales and speculation about next year's trapping. The females for the most part were silent, eating together and waiting on the men. Katharine was secretly relieved that they were so close to the trading post. She began to entertain hopes of home.

Little Fox talked with one of the young men after supper and told Katharine she was going home with him to rejoin her tribe. Katharine watched with tears in her eyes as he prepared to leave. Mounted, he offered Little Fox his arm, and she swung up behind him onto the Appaloosa's back, waving good-bye with a smile. Katharine would never forget her.

The littler girl clung to her, hanging on to Jesse's pinecone doll and hiding behind her skirts. "It's alright," Katharine whispered, bending down. "I'll call you Emily from now on. You can stay with me."

They were at eye level and the warmth that radiated from Katharine to the child was returned with a breath-stealing hug. Katharine tickled the girl and Emily laughed, the sound startling her so much that her hand flew to her mouth in surprise.

"Looks like you've found a friend," Jesse said softly. Every night he'd watched Katharine cuddle the girl by the fire, pulling a robe around her and rocking her until she fell asleep. They were practically joined at the hip. Katharine always sang to her softly when she lay next to her by the fire with her arm wound tight about her middle, holding her close. Jesse had watched them and found himself listening to her sweet soprano voice and thinking that it matched her personality. His gaze never left her face long after she had closed her eyes and sleep had claimed her.

"I just love her," Katharine admitted. "I know my parents won't mind one more child. They already have eight."

"What about her family?"

"When I make it back to Boston," she said wistfully, "I know my family will make every effort to help her. I can't leave her here alone, Jesse. I just can't."

He stared at her for a moment. "Borrowed," he said with a nod. Her face was upturned as she held the girl in her arms. The tumble of Katharine's red hair, her green eyes, her lovely skin and her voice meshed like facets of a gem. Once, he had found a fawn in a thicket, nearly starved. He wanted to find a way to help her, so he'd lugged her back to his cabin. Milk-soaked bread and finally a bit of grain had brought the fawn back to health. One day she was old enough to be released, and he had watched her bound away into the forest. She stopped once before she disappeared into the thicket, looked at him and then was lost in the dense green foliage. He still remembered those long, gangly legs, big eyes and upturned lashes. *Beauty*. A quality that was more than physical.

"Borrowed?" Katharine repeated, bewildered.

"You," he whispered, suddenly overwhelmed by his feelings for her.

The next morning they continued on down the mountain. They traveled slower together than Jesse would have alone. He didn't push his charges, letting them rest when they needed to and sleep as much as possible.

Some nights he would awaken to the sound of Katharine crying, still asleep, dreaming. One evening when the sudden heat of the day called the rain to the parched earth below, sleet coated her buffalo robe, and with a start she awoke, gasping for breath.

"Here," he said quickly. With practiced ease, he formed a quick lean-to out of a few boughs, shielding Katharine and Emily near the fire. The rain had coated the robe with ice, and the fire burned blue and hot with dry wood topping the kindling.

With teeth chattering, Katharine covered Emily and, unable to fall back to sleep, drew her knees up and stared into the flames, haunted. Her long red hair was unbound, and droplets of water trailed down her face.

"You were dreaming," he said.

"Yes," she said. "A nightmare." She stole a furtive glance at Emily, and he knew instinctively what she was thinking.

He blurted out the question he had wanted to ask for days.

"Why didn't they rape you?"

She gasped at the sheer brutality of the words. She felt as though she had been struck.

Somehow he knew.

"I don't know," she said, shivering.

Jesse was feeding the flames of the fire, his black hair unfettered and the wind lifting it away from his rugged face. The dark beard had returned, but it could not hide what she felt was the harsh line of his lips and the occasional flash of brilliant teeth that seemed almost too white.

There was an arrogance about him that dominated and unnerved her, but it was his eyes that terrified her tonight; not as Josiah Mott's had with their rheumy orbs swimming in alcohol, but because Jesse's eyes held a glimpse of true power.

Like a magician, he seemed to be delving deep into her soul, searching with his eyes and piercing her as he brought back the nights of absolute, mind-breaking terror with his questioning gaze. She could still hear the screams of the two girls and see the greed in the men's eyes whenever she closed her eyes.

Like some dark magic, Jesse pulled the memories up from deep inside just by looking at her. Possessed by memories, she forgot the cold. Without saying a word, he willed her to remember. She was caught in the circle of his power.

"They took me from my wagon," she said in the voice of a sleepwalker. She stared at the flames, hypnotized.

"Go on," he urged.

"It was night and we had made camp. My wagon was parked between my father's and my fiancé's." She gave a short, sharp laugh. "Ironic, isn't it? For safety's sake I was flanked by the two men I love the most, and yet even they could not prevent me from being taken."

The raindrops on her face were now mixed with the warmth of salt-water tears.

"Everyone was gathered around the campfire, and I'd gone back to my wagon to retire for the night. I didn't hear

Josiah come up behind me. I tried to scream for my father and Damien to come and save me, but Josiah was quicker. He placed his hand over my mouth, gagged me and wound a sheet around my face, hands and legs. I couldn't see him or the men with him, but I could hear them . . . their breathing.

"They tossed me over the back of a horse and walked the animal for a while. When we stopped, they pulled me off from behind and took the cloth away from my eyes. I saw them then, Josiah and his brother, the large man with the scar on his cheek."

Jesse nodded, remembering the guard he had disposed of on the porch.

"So they were brothers, then?" he asked.

"Yes, at least I think so," replied Katharine. "The other two were just"—she swallowed, seeing their images in the flames—"their men."

Jesse was silent. Something didn't make sense. She had been protected by her father and her fiancé and still Josiah was able to get to her and kidnap her.

"Did they rape you?" he said.

She sucked in her breath and closed her eyes.

"No," she said emphatically, shaking her head. "Not me." A tremulous sob escaped her and she placed her head against her knees, weeping. Jesse moved quickly to comfort her, pulling her robe up and holding it tightly about her as he held her against him, feeling her wracking sobs and trembling at his inability to help her.

"The girls," she whispered. "They already had the two girls with them, Little Fox and Emily." She shuddered. "I thought one of the men was going to rape me, but Josiah stopped him. He told him to take one of the 'Ree's' if he had to have a girl. He said I was their ticket to easy street."

"Ransom," Jesse said grimly. He knew that was the only reason she was alive and unharmed. It was starting to make sense. "Did you know them? Ever see them before?"

Katharine shook her head. "Not that I remember. Josiah tried to make me watch. Grabbed my face and said, 'Scared, ain't ya!' I was! I was so scared, Jesse, I started to pray and said aloud, 'I will fear no evil.' I kept repeating those words, hoping I could turn him to dust before my eyes. But it didn't work. He just laughed and said, 'Fear me, Miss Dory, because I *am* evil. Truly evil.'"

Jesse pressed her head against his chest, holding her tight. "You were taken for ransom money. He knew your name, Katharine. He knew everything about you, even where you were sleeping. But it doesn't make sense. You came with a whole expedition of men. Someone should have heard something. Was anyone else in camp harmed? Did you hear a shot, shouts, anything?"

"Nothing," she said. Her trembling increased the more she remembered. "But I was wrapped tightly in a sheet, and he whispered for me to be still or he'd slit my throat. There were a lot of men in the camp, Jesse, hired ones, men I'd never seen before."

"You were set up," he said. "Mott had an inside man, someone who knew you and your father, and who told him where you were and when to take you."

The reality of what he was saying started to sink in. "Who would do such a thing?"

"Money'll make fools out of sensible men. You get a man like Mott and he'll do anything, including murder, to line his pockets."

Jesse knew Katharine was still in danger. He couldn't just leave her at the trading post. It was no simple matter to abduct a girl of money and pedigree from a camp full of men. The person behind the abduction had to be someone very close to her.

"I'll take you to your father," he promised suddenly. Somehow he would keep her and Emily safe. Someone was after her, and money was the reason; someone she knew, or who at least knew her. "You have my word."

She looked up into his face, feeling safe in his arms. "I'm tired of being brave," she admitted. "I'm tired of imagining myself adequate to the task."

His sympathy for her momentarily eclipsed the pain of remembering his father's murder. He couldn't stand the thought of anything happening to Katharine.

"You're exhausted," he said. One arm was wound tightly about her middle and the other softly stroked her wet hair. The rain had left her skin moist to the touch, and a tear merged with the storm as he bent his face and gently kissed her lips.

She felt the tenderness and comfort, the heat of his lips against her cool mouth, the gentle parting of his mouth and his humid breath mingling with her own, melting resistance. There was no pressure or demand, just power restrained and comfort given.

His eyes were open, and she looked deeply into them, searching.

"I won't let anything happen to you," he said. She believed him. Somehow the poison of fear had been drawn out of her, leaving nothing inside but a sense of emptiness as she rested against him, stunned and confused, yet strangely feeling safe. She was certain that neither wind, storm nor men like Josiah would have a chance against Jesse McCallum.

Unexpectedly, he lifted her and laid her in a nest of sweet furs, dried from the fire, and covered her to her chin with furs. "I'll sleep right here," he indicated. There was a spot less than half a foot away. Jesse saw nothing odd about a Boston debutante lying at a mountain man's feet; it was, after all, the safest spot around.

Sleep without dreams or demons; sleep with him resting close by. She surrendered to a sweet languor. She could still feel the touch of his mouth on her lips, the taste of his skin, the humid muskiness of his warm breath, and remember the strength of his arms around her.

"The goblin king," she said in her half sleep.

Jesse was kneeling by the fire. "Goblin king, is it?" he said.

"Pluto carried Persephone to his kingdom beneath the ground," she whispered. "A dark prince, powerful, ruling realms below . . ." Her soft eyes gazed at him languidly.

"How do you know which kingdom I rule and whose master holds the marker to my captive soul?" An edge of guilt colored his words, which waxed eloquent in his unguarded moments. The wind moved fitfully, lifting his hair like fingers, and the fire outlined his ferocious, handsome features starkly against the night.

With his characteristic intensity, he held her gaze until her eyes fluttered shut.

Troubled, he turned from her now sleeping form and rummaged in his buffalo robe where his tattered Bible had been placed. Quietly, he opened the book and moved his hands across a page, touching words he could not read, reciting softly, "In the beginning, God created the heaven and the earth and the earth was without form and void; darkness was on the face of the deep. And God said, 'Let there be light,' and there was light. . . ."

Brokenhearted, he saw his father shattered on the ground and felt guilt consume him at the sight of his father's handsome face with his Titian red hair kept short as a schoolboy's, well-groomed even in a wilderness; and those sightless gray eyes that now could not even feel the warmth of the sun, let alone follow its course through the skies. Never again would he talk about Scotland or the love of his life, Amelia.

"Let there be light where you are, Pa," he whispered, letting go. "Let there be light."

Then Jesse McCallum bowed his head and cried very softly so no one would hear.

Chapter Sixteen

We'll reach the river tomorrow," Jesse said. He worked quietly beside the fire, stitching his buckskin leggings together using a large porcupine quill with a hole bored into one end, working it like a needle through the soft leather. The skins had been sewn so many times that patches overlaid one another.

There was something about him that filled Katharine with a sweet ache.

"You need new clothes," she said self-consciously. Her own clothes were worse than beggar's rags. He looked up at her with his beautifully rugged face and smiled, grasped a sinew and pulled it through the leather with his teeth, tied it off and cut it with his knife.

"Why?" he said. Uncomfortable, he knew the image he presented to her; like an exile of war, destitute of family and comfort, alone in a world she would never understand. Now that they were close to the Rendezvous, he allowed himself the luxury of looking at her, holding her image in his mind whenever he closed his eyes because he knew he was losing her, too. His promise to keep her safe was nearly kept; their time together almost at an end. He would find her father and turn her over to him. But the burden he didn't want had become the cornerstone that had anchored him to a world he'd almost renounced. He was reluctant now to let her go, even though he knew he must.

"Your clothes are rags," she said awkwardly.

"Yours haven't fared much better," he said. His eyes were twinkling. Emily was firmly rooted beside her like a graft on a tree, and the sight satisfied Jesse.

"True," Katharine said with a laugh. Her mauve riding suit was in tatters; her crinolines, used as bandages and shredded along the edges, crusted with earth and cockleburs, were irreparable. Her expression changed when she thought of Boston. Soon she would be home, surrounded by her possessions, family, in a normal, sane and orderly world. And she owed it all to a man who owned less than a single suit of clothes. "But wouldn't you like some nice new clothes and a fine home to live in with shining windows and many comforts? Aren't you tired of sleeping on the cold, hard ground?"

Jesse smiled. He couldn't imagine the world she lived in, and she disdained his. The remnants of her gown felt like the leaves of a lily between his fingers when he touched it, the stitches so fine he could scarcely see the tiny spaces between them. The locket around her neck was worth a fortune, and the jewels encrusting it would have set more than one man at war with another; yet he knew that what mattered to her was the picture within, not the ornate covering.

"Clothes," he said. "How can I explain? I grew up with the Blackfoot, a warrior and a brave. We have societies. Our clothes are like a"—he paused and reached for his father's worn King James Bible—"like a book. They speak of who we are, the battles we've fought, our medicine." He lifted the shirt he was now mending and showed her the beaded breastplate. "Counted coup many times," he said proudly. "Why would a man like me care what a peacock wears when I can turn and see a plain wren and listen to her sweet song in the morning? What does it matter if the houses where white men live are whitewashed when I can sit beneath a roof of lilacs blooming on a fragrant spring afternoon?

"You've never seen my cabin, Katharine. It's made of timbers cut and fitted together and topped by wooden shingles." He looked into the distance with his hands resting on his knees. Emily had found a place, nested in Katharine's lap, and for a few minutes Jesse felt peaceful.

"My pa came from Scotland. He crafted furniture so fine that the edges are smooth as store-bought glass. I'm not the savage you think," he said, raising one eyebrow. "Maybe rough, by your standards, but your comforts don't matter to me." Impulse made him wish he could show her his home, the tartans on the walls that spoke of Scotland, his father's books, the desk and the oil lamps; the fireplace that spanned the entire length of one wall, its stones made smooth by the flow of water across their surface for centuries. Sturdy and masculine, his bedroom also had a fireplace, a large bed with a mattress stuffed with feathers, quilts and woven blankets. The earthen floor was overlaid with wooden planks, rubbed until the light filtering through the opened door set them to gleaming. Beaver pelts had been traded for iron pots and a copper teakettle, which graced the mantel. He knew his home was dark today, empty and echoing without the red-haired missionary whose warmth welcomed even the wickedest sinner to his table and gave a warm night's rest to the weariest traveler. He lay at rest now beside his Amelia. *"Kin you hear the wind singing, Jesse, my son? Wist, wist, goes the wind."* Jesse could hear the wind, and mingled with it was his father's beautiful voice.

"Then what does matter to you?" she asked. Her arm was wound around Emily's waist and she instinctively rocked gently, holding the girl.

Jesse became thoughtful, paused and turned to look at Katharine, studying her face.

"You," he said candidly. "You matter to me. And Emily." It had been about a month since the first day he'd seen her and been badgered into acting as guide and protector. Now he couldn't imagine a day without seeing that beautiful face, hearing that low, self-conscious laugh or watching the way she would drop her head to one side, smiling until the dimples in her cheeks showed. "I'll take you swimming when we get to the springs," he told her. "The waters are dark and warm there. They bubble straight up from the heart of the mountains, and when you get tired, Katharine, we'll chase butterflies with a pack of wolves and eat ripe blueberries until the juices run down our arms. Stay with me here," he said spontaneously.

Katharine smiled. "I want to go home, Jesse," she said.

He nodded his head, accepting her refusal.

"I've seen things since I have been here that I wish I could forget."

"You've seen the worst, not the best."

"You would have a better life in Boston," she said.

"I would? What could Boston offer me compared to what I have?"

"My father would give you a job to repay you for your kindness."

Jesse looked off into the distance, and his voice became impossibly soft. "There is mystery here," he said. "Once, after a summer storm when the clouds were racing westward and the last few drops of rain hung like jewels from the leaves of every tree, I walked with my father into a rainbow. We stood like kings crowned in jeweled lights and laughed." He remembered the day and how in the distance they could hear the echo of the thunder, which seemed to chase the clouds away from the edges of a shy, new moon barely visible in the eastern sky.

Jesse suddenly became quiet. His smile vanished, and his thoughtful eyes sought her soft ones. "I belong here." Above them the hawk soared and the wind whispered through the pines; nature was as intimate as a friend, not distanced by mitered walls and smooth plaster. "For all your high words," he said coolly, "in your world I would just be another *boy*, worth less than a mule. Would those senators you're always talking about hear my words, or would they just show me the front door?

"I've seen men and women sold, bound and of less value than the rope that held them. Will this New Atlantis you talk about break the chains of all men or only a select few?"

Katharine looked at him silently and suddenly understood. Here, he was free. Her eyes grew sad as she recognized the gulf between them. "You're rich in experience," she said. In the distance, she could see an antelope with a full set of horns; she seemed to see wisdom in the eyes that looked straight at her. Quietly she pointed, and Jesse followed the line of her hand.

"Old buck," he said quickly. The next instant, the antelope bounded away, white tail flaring like a flag of warning as it vanished into the forest.

"You can go," Katharine said, feeling guilty for making him help her. She vowed silently to be brave; unable to look at him, she bit down hard on her lower lip. "I can't stay here with you, Jesse." He was primal energy, wild and pure; he would feel caged in Boston's manicured world. "And you can't go with me. You said the river was just around the next bend."

"You'll never make it," he said, shaking his head. "I promised to take you to your pa."

"You said there are soldiers at Canon City, Jesse, and it's just a day's ride. If you lend me money, I'll see that you get it back. My father will pay you for taking care of me all this time. You've done enough." She thought of the antelope, eagles, his canny wolf and the wilderness he fit into so well. "I'll take Emily, and we won't be a bother anymore."

"Did I say you were a bother?" he asked edgily.

"Yes, you did," she replied, drawing on all her training as a lady to distance herself from him. "Many times, and I thank you for everything you've done for me. For us, boy." Deliberately, she added a supercilious note to her voice. "But we don't need you now, so you can go."

Jesse's left eyebrow rose a fraction.

"*Boy? Boy*, is it?"

There was a subtle change in his facial features. The soft lines of his smile hardened and his eyes glittered. He brushed a little snow from his leggings. Without a word, he rose to his feet and walked to the tethered horses. He saddled the black mare and the tamest paint, filled the packs with as much food as they would hold, then dropped the lines on the ground and walked away without looking at her. A yawning chasm opened up between them.

"I don't need you," she said. *What have I done?*

Jesse nodded silently. He was letting her go. Katharine looked at the horses, then she looked at the mountain, and then she looked at him. Protectively she gathered Emily in her arms. "I don't need you," she repeated, her lips trembling. "Neither does Emily. We'll be fine."

"East is that way," he said calmly, jerking his head in the direction of Canon City. Crossing his arms over his burly chest, he looked at her coldly, dismissing her when he looked away. "You look a fool," he said bitingly.

"I do?" she said, suddenly angry. "Perhaps I'm not as helpless as I appear!"

"Hurry home, Katharine," he said. "Your mother's waiting to tuck you in."

All the color drained out of her face, and with more anger than common sense, she bent down and picked up the reins. She was aware of only three things at that moment: she was angry, she must go east, and she must get down the mountain in one piece with Emily.

"Gladly!" she said.

"Well, good riddance to you, then!"

"I'll see you at the bottom of the mountain!"

"Aye!" he predicted. "That you will! And probably in a dozen pieces too!" In frustration, Jesse scooped up a handful of snow and threw it in her general direction. "Christ!" he shouted, clenching his hands into fists. "You could drive a saint to the bottle, and probably have!"

La Junta, Colorado Territory

Damien North, Edwin Dory, and his friend John O'Sullivan were traveling with a small group of men, riding hard with bedrolls laced to their saddles and modest provisions, heading toward Canon City, where a Rendezvous was being held for the fur traders. Katharine had last been seen riding toward the Sand Dunes, and the best place to obtain information about her should be the Rendezvous, where so many of the Territory's inhabitants would be gathering.

Along the way the men had filled their canteens from streams so alkaline that the taste was metallic and coppery, and they had traveled across grasslands so flat that a minor hillock became a marker. Mileposts and an occasional notation on maps were the only directions they had. O'Sullivan had been here several times, and he loped along confidently at a steady pace as the earth changed from loamy, arable ground to the red clay of the Southwestern desert.

Renowned for his strength and endurance, O'Sullivan was unwilling to admit to anyone except himself that this trip was sapping his strength. The only thing that kept him moving against seemingly impossible odds was his belief in what they were attempting to accomplish. But he had had enough for one day. "Let's make camp," he suggested. "I'm starved."

Concealing a yawn behind a burly hand, he reined his horse in and dismounted, and the men made a quick camp. In the strong afternoon light, he pulled a map out of its canister and smoothed it out across the ground in front of the campfire so that Edwin and Damien could see the problems more clearly. "Since prospectors have found gold in the Rockies, it'll be just a matter of time before a fast, reliable means of transport will be needed in the higher elevations—a branch of transcontinental."

Edwin and Damien moved closer to examine the maps.

"Is there no other way across the Divide?" Edwin asked.

"Of course," replied O'Sullivan. "There are many, but the scouts I've sent out in every possible direction run into impassable canyons and physical obstacles that would take an engineering miracle to surmount. South Pass in Wyoming Territory is different, though. It's wide open, flat, and has been used by the tribes for centuries. It is the only logical choice through the Sierras. It's even passable in winter."

"That's what we need," said Damien. He sipped a cup of coffee made possible by a campfire that O'Sullivan considered a frivolous waste of time in the middle of the day. Calmly Damien chewed a biscuit from the diminishing store of his knapsack. "According to the engineers' reports I've read and the surveying maps, we're better off using one of the two main routes for the railroad. Both begin in Missouri, so that is the logical place for a terminus. But there the similarity ends. The Oregon Trail veers sharply northwest and the other branches south."

"The old cattle route? The Santa Fe?" Edwin asked.

"Yes," said O'Sullivan. Damien nodded. "Congress wants California. Go south with the tracks, you get desert, no water or grass. Locomotives need to take on water every few miles. But through the Rockies the rail is going to come to a dead stop, because no matter what route you take across the Divide, we're talking walls of sheer granite and inclines so steep they've been estimated at over 14,000 feet above sea level in some places. It's so cold up there, the snow never melts, except through South Pass.

"The only way a train could get through the mountains is on a narrow-gauge track. It uses a toothlike mechanism that pulls the train up one track at a time and has a brake on it that gives it traction on the downward grade," said O'Sullivan.

Edwin nodded. "I've seen a few of those in the Alps. But is it possible here?"

"Of course. Anything is possible," said O'Sullivan with a shrug. "But is it feasible? The trains need to take on water and wood, so stations would need to be built. The draw in Colorado is gold and timber, but right now all Congress wants is a fast, cheap and direct route to California."

"The Oregon Trail," said Damien. There was a note of finality in his voice.

O'Sullivan nodded. "All we need is for Congress to pass a bill that will give us the legal right-of-way."

"Gentlemen," said Edwin softly as he peered up into the milky sky. "I don't mean to be a tyrant, but there are a few more hours of daylight and I am for pressing on." It had taken a month to get across Kansas Territory traveling a modest twenty miles per day. "Every time the sun sets, I think of my darling Katharine," he admitted quietly. Pausing, he looked at Damien, who nodded in agreement. "You're sure that man you hired told you the truth about Katharine being sighted near the Sand Dunes?"

"Yes," said Damien. He looked up and speared Edwin with a coldly calculating gaze. "Traveling northeast, according to some Comanches who saw them. He said she appeared to be alright."

"For now," said Edwin.

"I'm for riding tonight and taking advantage of whatever

light we can milk from the moon," Damien said. "I'm not tired."

The men stood up and had started walking to their horses, tethered nearby, when they were startled by the sight of a solitary rider giving hell to his mount, shouting, "Dory! Edwin Dory!"

"What's he saying?" asked O'Sullivan.

"My name," said Edwin, allowing himself a surge of hope. Damien must have felt the same way; both men hurried toward the man, Damien at a run.

"Here!" shouted Edwin. Waving his hands, he moved toward the rider, who dismounted before his horse had come to a full stop.

"Got news for you, Dory! Urgent!"

"My daughter?" asked Edwin. "They've found my daughter?"

The man paused and took a deep breath. His anger was apparent in his narrowed eyes.

"No," he said. "Hugh's been murdered!"

Chapter Seventeen

*K*atharine's world was frozen in time. The little hand that held hers confidently and the trusting dark eyes that looked at her gave Katharine a courage that she hadn't known she possessed. "We'll make it," she whispered so Jesse wouldn't hear. "You'll see."

Emily's nose was running with a cold she hadn't quite gotten over, and her eyes were filled with something like yesterday's tears—not quite new enough to drift down her round cheeks but old enough to make the chocolate orbs shimmer in pools of water. Katharine wiped Emily's nose and said cheerfully, "Blow," placing a small bit of her torn gown against the girl's face. Emily looked at her and blew—two short little puffs followed by a weak smile.

"You're coming home with me, Emily," Katharine said. "You'll love Boston."

Emily nodded, and Katharine hugged her and lifted her up onto the paint.

"Let me know if you need me," said Jesse.

Katharine turned around and glared at him. Then she

mounted up with the lead line in her hand and looked at the winding trail, which now meandered down the southeast side of the Sangre de Cristo. It was less than a goat path, but she was determined to make short work of it.

"There's gold in the packs," Jesse said loudly. "Find a soldier!" He shook his head. "You are a damn fool, Katharine Dory. This isn't Boston." He wanted to remind her of what had happened just a few short weeks ago, but against his better judgment, he was silent. "A damn fool."

"My father will repay you," she said. "When I get home, he'll send money to Canon City for you. A lot of money."

"I don't want your money," Jesse said, frustrated. "Keep your rifle loaded and make sure the safety's on." He looked at her sitting on the black with her long red hair atumble about her face, her fair porcelain skin, emerald eyes and deep, rose-red lips. She looked like a child sitting in a saddle bigger than she was, holding reins with hands wound in cloths to keep them warm, leading a girl who cried in her sleep and clung like a vine to her every movement.

"I will," Katharine said. She remembered the antelope bounding in the woods and the hawk soaring above Jesse's head, the wolf loping beside him and that distant, yearning look in his eyes. She ached whenever their gazes met and touched intimately. It was almost as if she could read his mind. "Keep running, Jesse," she said softly. "You're free. Thank you for what you've done for us. I'll never forget."

Stoic, she turned the head of her mare, pointing her down the trail, making sure Emily was following behind. The path down the mountain was steep and winding. The trail before her was not broken, and the snow and ice had been brushed smooth by the wind and polished by the subdued heat of the sun that melted the crystals and created a waxed landscape of indescribable beauty. Rounding a bend, she turned and gazed surreptitiously behind her, half in hope and half in fear. Where once McCallum had been, solid as granite, only an empty clearing appeared. Whirling snow and the soft, sibilant sigh of winds sent ghostly fingers of white reaching gently toward her. With tears in her eyes, she whispered, "He's free." Closing her eyes briefly, she heard the sound of the hawk overhead, hunting. "Free."

Satisfied that she had repaid his kindness nobly by removing herself from his care, she pushed her mare along the trail, heading for Canon City. Red squirrels scampered in the lush, green pines. A cardinal, as fiery red as the heart of a ruby, darted through the air, which was crisp, clean and fragrant. She was no longer afraid.

The mare was surefooted and seemed to sense the trail with such an unwavering accuracy that she allowed herself to relax and not be fearful of the approaching night. With a sense of wonder, she realized that she was looking forward to the burning stars and the warm fire she had learned to build on her own. There was food in her packs, water and a warm buffalo robe, a loaded rifle that she knew how to shoot.

The temperature on the mountain was climbing. She could hear the cracking of ice as the ground began to thaw beneath the warm air currents flowing over the peaks. *Chinook*, Jesse had called the dry wind. She had liked the sound of that name, saying it repeatedly several times in a row. It had made Jesse laugh, and the thought of his laughter made her smile.

The day was slipping toward sunset, and the hues of approaching night blossomed in deep purple shadows across the frozen earth. She pointed out a pheasant to Emily, laughed at the scampering quickness of small deer, surprised as they nosed gently into the thawing earth for green lichens.

"Emily, it's time to make camp. Whoa," she said, pulling back gently on the reins. Stiff from a day's ride, she dismounted gingerly. The mare shook back her head and snorted, stomping her hooves impatiently in the snow.

"Hungry?" Katharine led and tethered the mare to a low-hanging birch branch near the clearing she had chosen for camp. It was protected on three sides by thick evergreens and an outcropping of gray granite that formed a natural roof. She thought it looked somewhat comfortable, and smiled at how different her ideas of comfort had become within the last few weeks. The packs were overfilled with food, grain and raw gold.

She went to Emily and helped her down, giving her a comforting hug. "I think we're almost there," she said, pushing the black strands gently back from the girl's beautiful little face. Emily nodded silently. "Let's make camp, Emily."

Working together, they pulled the knapsacks from the horses and filled a small pouch with grain for each horse. Then they set to work to build a fire. The canteens were filled with water and ice.

"We need wood," Katharine said once the fire was blazing bright. Supper would be dried meats and berries. At the bottom of the knapsack, she felt a round, sealed tin and lifted it free. "Coffee." Next to it was Jesse's prized possession, sugar. He had given her all of his coffee and sugar. Katharine smiled. "But no Irish," she said nostalgically, laughing softly under her breath. Turning with a smile on her face, she knelt down and put her hands on Emily's shoulders. "You stay here by the fire," she said. She did her best to look firm, until Emily nodded. "I'm going to get firewood, Em. Stay put."

The terrain was steep, sloping sharply downward the farther she walked from camp. Her foot caught on a rock and she fell forward into the snow, knocking the wind from her lungs. Irritated at her clumsiness, the dug her fingers into the snow and started to push herself up when she slipped, belatedly realizing that beneath the snow was a layer of ice. She became acutely aware of her pounding heartbeat and fast breathing. She could feel the cold, glasslike surface and instinctively pushed with the heels of her hands against it. The moment she transferred her weight to her arms, she heard a sharp popping sound like the staccato firing of a rifle as the ice began to crack.

Startled, she looked down, watching in horror as thin black lines radiated outward from beneath her palms in all directions. It looked like chain lightning etched in jet against the silvery sheet of frozen water. Then she saw the blackness bubbling like boiling oil beneath the surface and felt the first touch of frigid water against her hands.

Terrified, she looked toward her camp. Standing on the bank, silhouetted in orange light from the campfire, was Emily, looking at her with a horrified expression on her face, her hands covering her mouth as though she was trying to prevent herself from screaming.

"Go back, Em!" Katharine cried. "Go back!" She was afraid to breathe. Afraid of what might happen to Emily. Even the smallest movement increased the pressure and the break in the ice. She didn't know how deep the water was beneath.

She had no idea where land began and water ended. Calming herself, she looked at the child on the bank and inched backward, cringing each time she heard the thin, ripping sound following her every movement, like the low-throated growling of a predatory beast. Her dress was wet, and the thin cloth wound around her hands was soaked.

"Please, God," she whispered. The buffalo robe that Jesse had given her was becoming saturated and she felt the increasing weight settle ominously over her shoulders. She began to shiver. Closing her eyes, she shifted her weight, increasing pressure slightly on her right knee. Then it happened.

Cra-ckKK!

The ice gave way beneath her in a tremendous explosion of sound. Geysers of frigid water shot up.

"Ohhh . . . my . . . God!" she shrieked as she fell into the water. Her clothes were so heavy that they felt like hands pulling her down. Panicking, she found that the water was deeper than she'd thought. *It must be a lake,* she realized. She just kept sinking lower and lower, with the weight pressing around her as she kicked her feet, searching for something solid to step on.

On the bank of the lake, Emily was crying, "Kat! Kat!" She took a timid step toward the water.

"No, Emily! Stay away!" Katharine shouted. The cold water was so intense it felt like fire creeping along her limbs. The layers of clothes, which had kept her warm in the winter snows of the summit, were now lead weights dragging her down.

Desperate, she tried to shake free of the buffalo robe, but it was tied securely around her middle, and no matter how hard she tried, she could not work the knot free with her cold and clumsy hands.

Starving for air when her head went beneath the surface, she felt a great pressure in her lungs, like a balloon ready to burst. She kept her lips shut tightly against the water, but her lungs were beginning to hurt with the effort of holding in what little air she had. Soon, she knew, soon she would open her mouth and the frigid water would come pouring in, forcing her to breathe liquid.

The thought of dying terrified her.

Frantically she tore at the robe; the pressure in her lungs was unbearable. Her limbs had grown numb, and she could no longer feel the rough pelt beneath her hands.

She had the irrational urge to lie down and sleep. Her mouth opened a bit as she exhaled the stagnant breath from her lungs and by reflex inhaled. Water entered her lungs, her nose. Liquid ice burned its way down her throat while pinpoints of light exploded behind her eyes. Suffocating, she began to lose consciousness, still kicking weakly and reaching upward.

Her last thought was of McCallum, the hawk soaring high above in the pure sky, his haunted eyes and her whispered words, releasing him from a forced promise. *You're free*, she thought a moment before she stopped struggling and surrendered, unconscious, to the water.

"Ashes to ashes and dust to dust," said Edwin softly. Bending down, he placed a blanket gently over Hugh's still face. They would place him to rest in a cairn of stone and mark the grave in such a manner that it could be found again. Yet Edwin knew that the young surveyor deserved so much more.

O'Sullivan drew a small red cross on the map. Even without it, he knew that they would never forget their friend. Hugh de Angelucci had been so much a part of the project. He never tired of speaking of the days to come when the track would be completely laid and the entire country would be open and accessible to everyone. He believed in the United States of America and everything the nation stood for and was yet to become. He was a practical idealist, implementing his dreams and determined to make them real despite the daunting odds.

"I believe in what we are trying to accomplish," he'd said countless times. He'd staked his life on his belief and lost— a martyr to idealism.

The men stood together, bound by shared principles, integrity and conviction. It was a picture of solidarity and sorrow, men standing in the deepening twilight, mourning the loss of their friend.

All but Damien. He stood apart, contemplative and quiet, seemingly bored.

"I'm cold," he said abruptly.

Edwin looked at him sharply. "Yes," he said softly, "you are that." They had ridden hard back to the surveyors' wagons, going in the opposite direction from Canon City.

Damien arched his eyebrow. "Well, Edwin," he said slowly, "I'm a practical man, you see. If we must mourn, can't we mourn in comfort? Or is there some unspoken ritual that requires suffering?"

"I don't think you are capable of that, Damien," said Edwin quietly.

"Agreed," said O'Sullivan in disgust. He and Edwin began to place white rocks over Hugh's prone body. The others joined in, working silently side by side. They would make the monument as tall and as majestic as they could. They would work through the dark hours to see that Hugh was laid to rest in a tomb of granite that neither the elements, animals nor time could destroy.

"Sentimental fools," muttered Damien. He turned toward the gathering nighttime shadows.

All that this represented to Damien was an inconvenience and a total waste of time.

Chapter Eighteen

*B*reathe, you infernal heifer!" shouted Jesse.

A sharp pain exploded between Katharine's shoulder blades. She gagged and vomited water and bile. She was in agony. Her head was pounding and she was shivering, lying naked on her belly in the snow. She felt rough hands pushing against her back, pushing the water out of her lungs and stomach. It hurt to breathe. She would rather not, so she simply refused to draw air into her lungs. It hurt to open her eyes, so she kept them closed. She wanted to go back to sleep. It was warm there and didn't hurt at all, but Jesse wouldn't allow her to fall back into the abyss. Insistently he reached for her, pulling her back to the present.

He wouldn't let go.

"Open your eyes, damn you! Do you think I've brought you this far to let you slip away now?"

His hands worked over her body. He pushed against the small of her back, forcing every ounce of stale water out of her lungs. It hurt when he touched her. A pain radiated from the base of her skull to her frigid toes. She had no choice. She *had* to breathe because he wouldn't let her stop.

"No," she murmured. "Please, Jesse, it hurts."

"It hurts, does it? Well, good! I'm glad you're alive enough to feel pain. Five more minutes under water and I'd be burying you!"

He was still shouting and still rubbing her down with the rough palms of his hands.

"I hope it hurts like hell, you spoiled child!"

The next instant, he turned her over toward him, winding her within robes of fur. It took a moment for her to realize she had no clothing on, blushing even now at the thought of him seeing her naked. Weak and shivering, she lay helplessly in his arms, drifting in and out of consciousness, disoriented and coughing. Day had fled and darkness ruled so completely that she could barely make out his face, except for the handsome profile ringed in firelight.

He was enraged. And she was so disconnected from her surroundings that she didn't understand it was fear, not anger, that lit his dark eyes. "I'm sorry," she whispered.

"Sorry?" The word was disjointed, muffled by emotion, low and anguished. Her breathing steadied as her heart began beating once again on its own. Life, warmth and pain flowed through every limb. Pulling the robes tightly around her, he lifted her as he stood up, crushing her against his massive chest.

His heart beat next to her ear, comforting, loud, steady and a little too fast. She felt his warm breath on her face, and now, in the deepening night sky lit by the fingernail crescent of a new moon and a billion twinkling lights, the dimness that clouded her vision began to lift like a veil.

She saw dark, beautiful hair and his eyes bright and shining, wet with tears. *Tears?* she wondered vaguely. "Are they for me?" she asked aloud. Someplace in her troubled, painful mind, a connection was made; she drew the elements together—his words, his hands, his anguished eyes.

He loves me, she thought in wonder, and never questioned why. She just enjoyed the security of his arms, the comfort of his warmth, and then finally the feel of gentle, trembling lips touching her forehead. She sighed and accepted his kiss. "I'm tired," she murmured against his chest.

"Sleep," he said. "I'm here and I'm not leaving." She felt the rumble of his words against her forehead, the accelerated beat of his heart and ragged, indrawn breath.

Sleeping in his arms was easy.

Like a child, she pressed her face close to his chest. She heard his heart, and it comforted her. She felt his warmth, and it saved her. She looked up into his face, and he kissed her mouth gently. His lips were trembling, the taste of salt tears and the soft pressure mingling with his breath.

As she gazed at him in wonder, her attention was drawn by a gentle tug. Looking down, she saw Emily. The girl's face was streaked with tears as well and she was shaking her head saying, "Oh, no, Kat! Oh, no!"

"Now, Em, don't you go scolding me, too," Katharine said sweetly. "I'm alright," she whispered, slipping into unconsciousness, barely alive.

Chapter Nineteen

*C*anon City mimicked the moon: it waxed full during Rendezvous and waned when the traders and soldiers departed with their pockets full of gold and their heads heavy from too much ale. The post was situated in the eastern valley alongside the turbulent Arkansas River.

It was the beginning of a town with a few skeletal wooden frames dotting a wide central path that ran east and west. In the middle of the settlement was a great tent, supported on three sides by the limbs of strong trees and stout ropes. Kegs of ale and beer were stacked on the north side, serving as the fourth wall. Slabs of unfinished wood lay on crates and made a makeshift bar, littered with tin cups, bottles and the residue of last night's meal.

Beside the large tent was a smaller one with the word *BATH* etched in charcoal black along a whitewashed plank. The words *Hot Water Extra!* were stenciled neatly beneath. Threadbare towels were piled to one side on a stand next to thick bars of lye soap and a rare rack of ready-made, Eastern-style shirts with real buttons. A rough bench wobbled in the steady south wind, where a polished bit of copper serving as a mirror, a collection of combs and a store-bought pair of scissors completed the barber's tools.

Life was rude, rough and simple. Katharine, Jesse and Emily walked the last few yards into the camp leading their horses and pack animals.

It had taken three days for Jesse to nurse Katharine back to health. He'd been most solicitous, tending to her with a rich meat broth soup and strong coffee laced with sugar. She'd caught him looking at her anxiously. Waking in the middle of the night, frightened, she would see him looking at her with his hands cupped beneath his chin; his face thoughtful and guarded, silent and withdrawn. Seeing her awake, he would cross the few feet separating them, bring water to her lips, pull her robes up securely around her and then settle back on his haunches like a massive sphinx, enigmatic and brooding, staring intently as if he could somehow will energy into her from his vast, unlimited reserve. The emotion he'd shown at the lake was gone as if he had brutally severed a connection too painful to continue.

Emily empathetically had dived beneath the robes, wrapping her arms about Katharine's neck like an anchor, snuggling against her and falling asleep, relieved, almost immediately. By the second day, Katharine had been sitting up and taking timid steps, and by the third, the weather had grown warmer and she'd pulled on the clothes that Jesse had washed in the lake and dried on the rocks in the strengthening rays of the sun.

The fourth day, her eyes had opened naturally, replete with sleep. The first face Katharine had seen was Jesse's. He lay opposite her, with his head resting on his arm, gazing softly at her. Then he'd smiled. "Time to go," he'd said. It was. And by mutual agreement, the three had saddled up to make the last of the journey.

Going down the mountain had been infinitely faster than climbing up. The rocky bluffs and granite walls were free of snow and ice, and the weather was warmer. It seemed to Katharine that spring had finally arrived. Sometimes, in her private moments, she would find herself gazing at Jesse's broad back as he led the way, or study his handsome profile, remembering his kiss—which was something he never acknowledged, making her wonder if it had happened at all.

"Look!" he said. Jesse pointed to rows of tents and tepees dotting a clearing, the only stationary objects in the valley, which was a kaleidoscope of shifting shapes, movement, oxen, horses, men and women. A carnival atmosphere fairly pulsed in the early spring air.

"Jesse, there are thousands of people here!" Katharine said.

"Once, twice a year," he said. "Welcome, Miss Dory, to a Rocky Mountain Rendezvous.

"Baths," he said emphatically, and Katharine and Emily followed him to the tent. "Hot baths," he said to the attendant, a young Chinese girl, who smiled in reply. "As much soap as they want."

Bowing, the young woman went to work, speaking Chinese as she ushered Katharine and Emily behind the flaps of the tent into a steam-filled room where a fire burned and three cast-iron, porcelain-lined tubs waited with elegant claw feet.

"I'll be back for my bath in a bit," he called out to Katharine. Halting a couple of young men, he asked them in Cree to stand guard at the tent and not let anyone enter. Then he paid them well in nuggets of solid gold. "No peeking!" he ordered when he saw them grin.

Then he went in search of the most beautiful clothes he could find for two of the most beautiful females he knew.

As he rolled out of his bedroll, Damien found the camp already astir with men ready to make the last leg of their journey to Canon City. The town of Florence had provided wagons, a measure of provisions, and a trade of two trail-weary men for new men eager for a wage.

Damien's mind was not on the railroad. It was on Katharine. For the past two months, it was always "one more night," and the frustration was weighing heavily on him. Talk of catching Hugh's murderer was escalating, and Damien was unable to escape conversations about what "a good man" Hugh had been, or how they "couldn't believe anyone would murder poor Hugh," and what a "tragedy" and "heinous crime" it was. Damien could hardly suppress a yawn at their constant insipid and useless chatter.

"Go catch your killer," he muttered beneath his breath as he pushed back his hair. "I prefer to tend the living, not the dead." Of course, when he reminded them, "We still have Mr. O'Sullivan, so the project shouldn't run into too many delays," everyone became silent, stared at him and seemed shocked by his cool attitude. Sighing, he would excuse himself, leaving them to their perpetual mourning. "You cannot resurrect the dead," he said, "but you can perhaps save the living. Katharine Dory, my scouts have said, is alive, and you sit like old men in the sun recounting the gory details of an event that may never have a satisfactory ending. But you could still make a difference to a young lady!"

"I have cried for you, my Katharine." But his confession was uttered alone. The closer to Canon City, the more urgent was his need to close the distance.

Chapter Twenty

*W*ho's man enough to take me on?" bellowed Tete Rouge. He was one of the rankest keelboat men around. "Whoever's left standing gets my gun and my woman! Whaddya say, McCallum?"

"I'd leave that one be," said a tall black man seated next to a beautiful Creole-Comanche woman in her early twenties. "He got the hair o' the grizzly in him."

Jesse turned around at the sound of the familiar French-Canadian voice and smiled broadly. In a group of people who were eating and drinking was a black man with a fine, aristocratic face, high cheekbones and forehead, an expressive mouth and wide shoulders, dressed as a Blackfoot warrior. He smiled warmly.

"Isaiah," said Jesse with a grin. "I knew I'd run into you sooner or later."

"Where there are wine and women, that is where Isaiah will be. Who is the beauty?" he asked, looking up from his feasting long enough to study the woman in the ivory-colored sheath made of the finest doeskin, fringed and beaded with turquoise and amethyst. Her face, framed by masses of red hair glittering in the afternoon sun, was pale in comparison to the emerald of her soft eyes and the rose red of her lips. Her skin was so fair that it seemed to glow porcelain-white from within.

"Leave me be?" snorted Tete Rouge, interrupting and ignoring Isaiah's warning. He swaggered toward Jesse and stopped directly in front of Katharine, looking her appreciatively up and down. "This puppy," he spat in a voice filled with contempt. "He ain't worth a pimple on a grown man's ass! Hey, little woman, why don't you come be with a real man tonight, huh? I show you a good time."

Isaiah Briand saw the look on Jesse's face and stretched back, pillowing his head on the ample breasts of the woman seated contentedly behind him. "Ah, Tete," he said, clearly amused. "You are about to get the shit kicked out of your sorry ass, and I'm going to enjoy every minute."

Tete Rouge forgot about Jesse and the woman for a minute and turned around, glaring at Isaiah. Embarrassment and anger caused his entire face to blaze outward; fire poured from his eyes as he pointed at Jesse, whose posture changed subtly, becoming more electric and intense, matching the expression on his face.

"*That?*" Tete Rouge exclaimed. "He couldn't whip his way out of a wet newspaper! You think I'm afraid of *that?*"

"No," said Isaiah. "You aren't smart enough to be."

"He is just worthless mountain trash!" Everyone was silent. Rouge started to smile, and the stubs of his brown teeth seemed black in the light of day. Then someone laughed, bruising Rouge's fragile ego, and he turned to face Jesse with an aggressive stare and stance.

"You hate him," said Isaiah, "because he is free, like me, and you are no more than a slave to your boat and greed." Isaiah hated Rouge. He was a slaver. Taking the half-empty bottle from his woman with a playful tug, Isaiah took a long pull and kissed the woman behind him, now tasting of the sweet, intoxicating fruit of the vine. "You sign one pledge after another, you *voyageurs*, you river men." He said the word "*voyageurs*" as contemptuously as Rouge had said "mountain trash." "Then you find yourself caged on a narrow little boat, pissing over the side and pounding on your chest, praying for the day you'll be free. That's not the worst of it, though, is it? You sell men and women, put them in chains!" Isaiah's voice rose passionately as he dropped his woman's hand and held up his arm to show the white, knotted scars left by shackles that he had worn night and day until he killed the slavers who had taken him; taken and beat him until he killed them one night when the moon was slim. Then he ran north, following an elusive star to freedom. "You're a rich man," he said, "but all your money can't buy back your soul. You're a slave to your wickedness and greed."

"You th-think I'm a slave?" Rouge stuttered, reaching for the knife lodged in his belt.

"I know you are!" said Isaiah savagely. "That's why you hate him, that white boy, because he is more than you will ever be! Much more! He has power!"

"Power?" shouted Rouge. He unwisely moved closer to McCallum, blowing rudely across the top of his head, lifting a snow-white strand of hair that had marked Jesse since his youth. "You think he's got power because of this little strip of white?"

A soft murmur of agreement rose and fell uneasily around the camp. Some said McCallum talked with wolves, found game where none existed, challenged the old gods, talked with spirit winds and changed beneath the light of a full moon. A man with fire in his eyes and medicine in his heart.

"That white streak of hair means nothing!" shouted Rouge. He didn't like being challenged by anyone, especially a long-legged mountain man and a runaway black slave.

"You right, Tete," agreed one young laborer. His traps were still shiny and unused, his trousers made of store-bought cloth instead of skins. His round face was clean-shaven, and his wiry hair as short as a choirboy's. "He ain't nothing but a thick-chested mountain man, probably got no hair on his ass."

Rouge smiled. "Like I said, a little puppy." Behind him Jesse was barely breathing. His eyes had narrowed to mere slits, and a thin smile began to grow on his face.

"Ah," grumbled a grizzled old-timer as he eyed Rouge and the youth suspiciously. "You're both so full of shit your eyes is mud brown."

"Am not!" said the youth. He was deeply embarrassed and nearly turned purple.

"Are too!" said the seasoned trapper. He was a "hivernan"—a trapper who'd survived forty of the meanest winters anyone could remember and was respected by nearly everyone, not only for his endurance, but also for his fearlessness and blunt honesty.

"Am not! Am not! Am not!" shouted the boy. He looked for backing from Rouge, who, like the trickster he was, glanced away. Starting trouble was his forte, but picking a fight with a hivernan like Judah, who had so many friends, was just not a sensible thing to do. The young laborer was on his own.

The old man stretched his feet out until his toes nearly roasted in the fire. "You," he said tiredly, "couldn't find your narrow ass with both hands if I gave you directions."

Everyone laughed, including Isaiah.

"You tell him, Judah!" hooted one veteran mountain man, who had been busy parlaying four horses, a bolt of red cloth and an iron pot for a wife.

"Sure," laughed another as he held up five fingers, indicating that one more horse was in order for such a beautiful woman. "Set that lowlander straight!"

"Of course I will," agreed Judah confidently. Not taking his eyes from the fire for even a second, he said, "I saw you come from the flats way down yonder one day about a half a moon ago, boy, and I said to my mule, 'Mule, here comes walking buzzard bait with a whole lot of necessaries he ain't never gonna use unless he wise up powerful quick!' You *do* get my drift, son, don't you?" His words, though pointed, were not unkind. Thoughtfully he pulled a butcher's knife from beneath his tunic with subtle grace and placed it calmly on his bony knees. It was sharp, in good repair and had been used, often. The boy, blushing furiously, looked around. There was no help in sight, so he wisely kept quiet and quickly sat down.

"Well," sighed Judah as he picked his teeth with the blade and flicked out an offending particle of meat with his tongue. "Reckon there's hope for at least one pork eater yet."

Everyone laughed; everyone except Tete Rouge.

"McCallum's a little girl," Rouge said. He poked Jesse in the shoulder. "A scared little motherless cub. You too pretty for the likes of him," he said to Katharine and reached for her arm. "Maybe you'll be my squaw for a time. What do you say to that, white girl?"

The camp became eerily quiet except for the barking of the dogs and the "pop" of fat falling from sizzling deer, moose and prized buffalo meat spitted over the bonfire.

"Ah, Tete Rouge," Isaiah said with a sigh as he tore into a leg of venison, "you are one great fool." He looked down just as Jesse looked up, locking eyes with Rouge. Jesse's dark, predatory eyes were on fire. "Here it's coming now," Isaiah predicted.

Tete Rouge froze. His blood cooled in his veins and felt like sluggish ice beneath his skin. His scalp tingled, and the fine hairs on his neck stood on end. Used to seeing fear in another man's eyes, he was unprepared for the cool confidence that greeted him, or the low, deep-throated laugh.

"Get your filthy hands off of her," McCallum said. He was

sober as a saint; a strange, icy smile settled on his face, and a wild, primitive light danced in the reflected firelight of his eyes. "I said, get your fucking hands off of her, now!"

That did it.

"You curse at me, boy?" shouted Rouge. "No one curse at Tete. No one!"

Not even a man with the eyes of a beast.

"I just did. And so you don't misunderstand this mountain trash," Jesse said, "you touch her again"—his hand went to Rouge's arm—"and I'll kill you." He lifted Rouge's fingers with a force almost inhuman, one hand peeling them from Katharine's arm and the other hand holding the forearm stationary, calm and deadly as the eye of a hurricane. Small beads of sweat had collected on McCallum's forehead.

Rouge winced in pain, releasing his hold, and Jesse moved Katharine and Emily quickly back, gesturing for Isaiah, who went to the women quickly. Then Jesse turned back to Rouge and smiled.

"You bastard!" shouted Rouge, rubbing his wrist. McCallum could've snapped it, but for some reason he hadn't. "I'll teach you to make a joke out of me!"

"Too late," said McCallum. "You're already the biggest joke on the mountain." Then his smile faded and all color drained out of his face. "Where are your friends now, boatman?"

Blind with fury, Rouge rushed him. "You'll eat those words, McCallum!"

"I don't think so," said Jesse evenly. He grasped the other man's shoulders and dropped to the ground. He rolled over backward, taking Rouge with him, and ended up astraddle his chest, pinning him to the ground. Rouge twisted his body to one side but didn't move quickly enough to prevent a well-aimed knee from connecting with his groin with a breath-stealing *WHOMP!*

"Oh-hh-h!" wailed Rouge. "This one is killing me! You!" he said, seeking the eyes of the young laborer who had sided with him earlier. "Help Tete!"

The boy turned away just as Rouge had done to him. Jesse laughed, gripping his opponent's wide, round shoulders and pressing his fingers mercilessly into the joint of the collarbone and arm, squeezing until Rouge winced.

"Help!" cried Rouge, coloring green when Jesse's knee connected for a second and third time.

"What'd you say, you little puppy?" McCallum asked as he rolled him back. "Speak up, boatman! I ain't got all night to fool with your sorry ass!" Then the lethal hands pistoned, working rapidly over Rouge's face, leaving reddened welts as if by magic.

"Assez!" Tete Rouge choked as his body began to swell. The blood began to flow like a scarlet river from his nose and mouth. "Enough!" he begged and began to vomit.

Jesse looked at the circle of people surrounding them and saw the woman that Tete had wagered on the fight. "You're free," he said grimly. The woman smiled gratefully as she backed away, glad to be rid of the cantankerous Tete Rouge, fading like smoke into the yawning cavity of the forest, determined to return to her people from whom she was stolen long ago.

"Who," Jesse said as he bent forward, grabbing the beaded medicine bag that hung around Rouge's neck and wrenching it free, "has the medicine now?"

Tete Rouge didn't answer. He was beaten, and he knew it. Beaten by a man without a scratch on him; a man who showed no respect for the King of the River, defied the spirits of a man's medicine pouch. A man with the "hair o' the grizzly" in him, surely destined to be a legend.

A man of power.

"Stay away from my woman," Jesse warned ominously. He turned to look at Katharine, breathing hard, and she gasped, startled by the searing passion in his dark eyes. Raking back his long hair, he pointed at the men in camp. "Stay away from her."

He meant it.

Chapter Twenty-one

*Y*ou can't fight every man in camp over her, Jesse," said Isaiah softly.

Jesse was pacing like a caged tiger in a little clearing some distance from the main camp. "You got all the answers, then? What should I do until we get word to her pa?"

Katharine had put Emily to bed in the back of a Conestoga wagon guarded by some matronly Cree women. There was something fragile and beautiful about the girl who couldn't speak but a few words. She touched a person's heart. One of the older women said Emily had the Gift and walked in two worlds; that her sight went beyond the physical and that her mysterious silence was her magic. Sleeping soundly, she seemed to know she was safe now; no whimper or tear belied the fear she'd felt for so long.

Katharine stood close to Isaiah, who had given her a glass of warm wine. Her nerves, which had been frayed, were beginning to calm.

"You could marry her," Isaiah said with a smile.

"Marry!" both exclaimed in unison.

Isaiah shrugged. "I'll marry her, then. There is always room in Isaiah's tepee for one more woman."

"Last count you had three," said Jesse.

"I stopped counting after two," Isaiah admitted. "Another wife would be no trouble at all." Smiling, he flashed a brilliantly suggestive look in Katharine's direction. "Isaiah would treat you good."

"Over my dead body," muttered Jesse beneath his breath.

"Over it, around it," Isaiah said calmly, his eyes twinkling as he took another swallow of wine, "Isaiah don't care." He stopped long enough to kiss the woman with him, and then laughed at the irony of the situation. He knew Jesse better than he knew himself. Jesse was trying to convince himself that marrying Katharine would be a charitable act, when the motive was actually selfish need.

"Alright," said Jesse. "I'll do it."

"Do it?" said Katharine nervously. She was nursing her second glass of wine. "Do what?"

"Marry you. First, Isaiah, you gotta find a Holy Man," said Jesse.

"Which one?" asked Isaiah.

"Whichever's got the most medicine, I reckon," Jesse said with a shrug. "I saw Father de Smet over by the buffalo roast, and some of those Jehovah Wigglers by the gospel tent. Rope me one of 'em, will you? We got to make this stick."

"Stick?" said Katharine, a little tipsy. "To what?"

"Each other," said Jesse. He shot her a look that made her knees weak, his gaze lingering too long on her lips. Closing his eyes, he looked away. "You got one chance around here. There are about four thousand men in camp tonight, drinking, gambling and carousing. Isaiah's right. If one of the missionaries marries us, they'll leave you alone, for the most part. The other part I'll take care of," he said dangerously.

Katharine nodded. "What do I have to do?" she asked, earnest as a schoolgirl.

Jesse was quiet. "Pretend you love me."

Katharine's eyes widened. Her hesitancy caused him to close his eyes against the magnetic pull she had on him. *Lady,* he thought, *if you knew what I wanted to do with you right now . . .*

"Look," he said. "We have to stay here long enough to get word to your father. Tonight was just a taste of what happens here."

Isaiah wisely walked away, leading his woman behind him. He had never seen his friend so enamored of any female.

Jesse didn't notice Isaiah leave the clearing. His eyes were focused solely on the diminutive woman who had suffered so much in the last few weeks. He was desperate to protect her, yet didn't know if he had the right to interfere. "Katharine," he said. "I won't pretend I don't have feelings for you." In fact, he liked everything about her—the way she looked, her genuine compassion, her mothering instinct, the laugh that caused dimples to appear and her eyes to crinkle at the corners. The confidence she had in him made him feel good about himself. "I'll do whatever you want," he said. "But Isaiah is right; I can't fight all of them off, and they'll keep trying."

"Alright," Katharine agreed. Tipsy from the wine, she assumed the wedding would be just for show. He wanted her to pretend to be married, that was all. He was trying to protect her. Dutifully she looked at him and said seriously, "I'll pretend I love you, then."

Something like pain flitted across Jesse's eyes, followed by a flash of anger. Her response felt like a slap in the face. A sardonic smile, bitingly white as lightning, lit his features, and he laughed.

"You do that," he said harshly, "and I'll pretend I care."

They stood two feet apart, both poised on the brink, ready to pretend to fall in love. There was a subtle harmony, tension and beauty in their posture. His stance dominated the night, and her pose, accompanied by the soft inhale of quickened breath and the rise and fall of her shapely breasts, aroused him to the point that passion wasn't the distraction but the purpose.

He couldn't deny his attraction. He wanted her, badly.

"Isaiah!" he shouted. "We're getting married tonight!"

Isaiah stopped and looked back at his friend, silhouetted in firelight with his hands resting on his hips, glaring at the woman who stood defiantly opposite him with her head up, large eyes wide and somewhat fearful, like those of a deer ready to take flight.

"A *pretend* wedding?" Isaiah asked.

"Anything the lady wants," Jesse replied, but his dark, brooding stare said otherwise.

Chapter Twenty-two

*A*re either of you Catholic?"

Father Pierre-Jean de Smet was a Jesuit and one of the first missionaries in the central United States. Years ago, the Nez Perce and Flathead had gone to the mission in Saint Louis to ask for a "black-robe" with a Bible. On his way to Creek Valley near Fort Laramie, he'd stopped at the Rendezvous for fellowship, to celebrate Mass and to convert heathens to the gospel.

"We got a man in need of marrying," Isaiah had announced to him. And without a word of dissent, unmindful of weariness if he had any, and not annoyed at the interruption, Father de Smet had risen to his feet and calmly followed Isaiah to the clearing with his Bible in hand and his rosary belted about his waist.

He'd been surprised, however, when he entered the clearing. The couple stood more like adversaries than lovers. The priest frowned a little and rephrased his question. "Have you been baptized?"

"Presbyterian," said Jesse. "A Scot."

"Protestant," said Katharine automatically. "English. Church of England," she said primly.

"I didn't know you were English," Jesse said.

"You never asked me," she replied.

"True," he said.

Father de Smet interrupted them. "It is you two who want to be married?"

"I've nothing better to do tonight. Do you, Katharine?" Jesse asked innocently.

"I can think of several things I'd rather do."

"How do you know? As far as I can tell, you have no basis for comparison." He looked at her with the innocent face of a choirboy and the sultry, wicked eyes of a sinner.

"This can't be happening," she said.

"You can either be wedded and bedded," said Jesse easily, "or bedded without the wedded. You decide."

He was enjoying this, but if truth were known, he wanted desperately to keep her safe; his sanity depended on it. Isaiah laughed, and Father de Smet looked a trifle suspiciously at the pair.

"Are you tipsy, miss?" he asked.

"Thoroughly," Katharine admitted. "And scared." She looked at him nervously, made a quick sign of the cross and curtsied, not sure if she was doing it correctly. She looked at Isaiah for reassurance; he nodded, and she felt a little relieved.

"A drunk bride. McCallum, you have all the luck," said Isaiah enviously.

Jesse laughed. "Willing and ripe," he said.

"It's normal to be scared," Father de Smet said sympathetically to Katharine, ignoring the men. "Maidens usually are. Now let's get started."

Katharine's mouth dropped open! How did he know she was a virgin? she wondered.

"Does it show?" she asked nervously.

Father de Smet nodded. "Now, do you *both* willingly consent to this marriage?"

Katharine nodded without looking at the man beside her. "Yes," she said, wondering if her willingness was a by-product of the wine, fear for her own safety in this male bastion, or the fact that Jesse was the most amazing human being she had ever known. "Probably a combination," she murmured to herself beneath her breath.

Jesse nodded and said, "Yes." A sweet, warm feeling began to fill him when he looked at her, trembling, small and trusting beside him. Unexpectedly, she reached for his hand with both of hers and held it tightly. He almost laughed. She looked terrified.

I love her, he admitted to himself, looking up at the stars beginning to shine brightly, unaware that those soft lights now lit his eyes as well. He had saved her life, protected her, cared for her, and he felt inexplicably proud at this moment.

"Jesse! I'm not experienced!" she interrupted anxiously.

"I am," he said easily. Then he looked at her, and the heat of his eyes would have melted an iceberg. "I'll teach you everything you need to know." He smiled in a slow, sexy way that made her weak in the knees. *"Pretend,"* he added with a twinkle in his eyes that said otherwise.

"Pretend," Katharine repeated.

"Your names?" interrupted the priest. There were other people in need of his care.

"Jesse McCallum."

"Katharine Dory."

"Jesse, wilt thou take Katharine for thy lawful wife, according to the rite of our Holy Mother the Church?"

"I will," he said clearly, sure of his decision.

Father de Smet turned to Katharine, who was visibly shaken.

"Katharine, wilt thou take Jesse for thy lawful husband, according to the rite of our Holy Mother the Church?"

Silence. Katharine turned slightly and looked at Jesse. He felt her eyes on him, desperate and searching, the word *pretend* hanging unspoken on the air between them. She was beginning to think she should have gotten it in writing before the ceremony. Part of her knew with perfect clarity that if she asked, Father de Smet would allow her to accompany him back to civilization. Yet the fabric of the last few weeks had woven a subtle enchantment around her, which some might have termed a crush and others infatuation or first love. Katharine refused to acknowledge the meaning of her hesitancy or the reason why she held so tightly to Jesse's hand. In the morning she might deny what her heart knew tonight, but it was trust that made her entwine her fingers in his and gaze at him with a certain hesitancy and challenge.

"Katharine?" It was the priest's soft voice, prompting. She had to decide.

It was trust and love that won over doubt and uncertainty. *Some things are meant to be.*

"I will," she said finally, her voice like a sigh and her words a whisper. She wasn't just tipsy, she was besotted. She began to wonder what had happened to her feet and why the clearing was starting to roll along the edges. Her only recourse was to hold tightly to McCallum.

Grasping his arm, she hung on for dear life. He looked at her curiously and frowned, steadied her with his arm and turned his attention to the priest. The rest of the ceremony was a blur. Katharine responded when she was asked, and allowed Jesse to place a blessed wedding band on her finger. She barely noticed that it was a piece of raw gold, beaten into a Celtic braid with a knot in the center. It was something he had carried with him for quite some time. His mother's wedding band. When she felt it slide over her skin, she swallowed hard, wondering how something so small and cool could feel as though it had wrapped itself around her heart and soul with such finality and grace.

"I now pronounce you man and wife," Father de Smet said with authority.

There was a moment of incredibly heavy silence as though the very breath of God were still. Katharine held tightly to Jesse, whose arm had found its way around her small waist, holding her next to him. She could feel the beating of his heart next to her heart, and the gentle warmth of his arms, holding her and shielding her.

"You may kiss the bride, Jesse," said Father de Smet with a warm smile.

Katharine remembered the kiss by the lake, the warm pressure of his lips, his humid, hot breath. His lips felt like silk now, cool against her flushed skin. The sensation of their first touch was like a drift of cherry blossoms covering her with delicate, open petals.

She dared to look at him. The expression on his face was soft, thoughtful. A look of infinite peace permeated his eyes. Where once searing passion had burnt like a flame, scalding her with earthy light, now there was a guarded glow like a candle welcoming the weary traveler home. He smiled softly, and she noticed that the corners of his eyes held tears.

With his free hand, he gently cupped her chin and tilted her face upwards, toward him. Then he kissed her oh, so sweetly full on her mouth! His lips felt like the brush of a soft feather against hers, and he allowed her to melt against him, moving his hands down the length of her back, his hands touching and tangling in her long red hair. He refused to let go. The wind that sighed through the clearing moved through his hair, and she thought of an angel's wings beating slowly, almost magically, about them.

Pulling away, she looked at him and whispered, "Did it stick?"

"I'll be damned if I know," he whispered back, exhaling slowly, "but I'm bound to find out." A hunger that was more than passing fancy possessed him, and his lips sought hers in a deeper kiss. The arm that wound about her middle pulled her closer until it seemed there was not one inch of her that didn't touch him. Her breasts strained against the soft sheath and her belly touched him in the most intimate, masculine places, and it was without fear that she felt the hard, hot length of him. His powerful thighs pressed against her legs, and his arms made hard as steel brought her closer to the tiger's flame. Inhaling deeply, she felt precocious desire move through her, like a rolling wave unfolding from an infinite ocean within, welcoming his tender touch.

"Congratulations, Jesse and Katharine McCallum," said Father de Smet with a smile.

Like a man roused from a pleasant, hypnotic dream, Jesse looked at him, his eyes heavy with languor and awakened passion. "Thanks, Padre," Jesse said quietly. He was peaceful inside.

"You're welcome," said the priest. "May your life be rich with love, long and filled with the gift of children." Then he bent and kissed Katharine on the cheek. "You are a beautiful girl," he said. "Be a good wife. I have a feeling McCallum will make you proud someday."

Katharine looked at him in a slightly bewildered way. "Today is someday, Father. I am proud of him. He saved my life more than once."

"God works in mysterious ways, daughter," said Father de Smet. "We are the hands and feet of our Maker, and oftentimes, when we least expect it, there are angels amongst us."

Jesse smiled, holding Katharine tightly as Father de Smet walked toward Isaiah, his eyes twinkling. "We need to talk, Isaiah. It's time I heard your confession."

Isaiah threw Jesse a baleful look. "How far back, Father?"

"Grade school?" Father de Smet prodded. "I have plenty of time, Isaiah."

"I was afraid you were going to say that," he admitted. "Father?"

"Yes, Isaiah?"

"How many Hail Mary's can you say in one night?"

"As many as it takes, my son. We have to make it stick, and a five-dollar minimum donation will gladly be accepted, gold or currency. You choose."

Jesse laughed, watching them walk away together, and so did Katharine, inexplicably blushing when she realized that they were alone in the secluded clearing.

Damien studied the bottom of his empty glass. The Scotch hadn't lasted very long. The bottle was empty and lay on the floor of his new wagon amidst a pile of papers that he had told himself he was going to go through that night. The papers hadn't moved, and neither had he.

He lay in his berth with the portal open, staring at the gathering darkness and watching as Venus winked into view. He was somber, and the night had left a bitter feeling in his mind, just beneath the surface.

Ironically, the darker the night grew, the stronger the feeling.

He shut his eyes and let the glass fall to the floor.

"Sleep," he whispered. It was a command of sorts. He was tired of thinking about maps, railroads and mountains that would take more dynamite to tame than he had access to now. Money. He knew how to make money on the railroad. Simple economics and advertising. And of course, the farmers would need a way to transport their grain to the cities.

"Free land," he said flatly. "For a price, of course."

Because Damien knew there was a price for everything.

Everything, even love.

And the last thought that crossed his mind before he fell asleep was of titian hair and green eyes, and laughter that never seemed to have an end. But it was expensive, this gentle, confusing feeling. It was costing him what was left of his sanity. He ran after her even in his dreams, afraid that he would never see her again—more afraid that he would.

She made him feel.

She made him long to be gentle.

She made him want to remember what it had been like to love and not care who was keeping score. She drove the devil out of him and made him feel once again like that vulnerable boy so many years ago standing at the foot of his mother's bed.

Need.

To be able to lean on someone for once in his life and find more than empty air. He knew that as gentle as she seemed, there were reservoirs of strength beneath the surface. Strength.

She was as dangerous as she was desirable, as unpredictable as she was sweet. In desperation, he ran after her, and somewhere in the land of sleep, he found her . . . and he groaned aloud in his sleep because his deepest fears had come true.

She wasn't alone.

Chapter Twenty-three

*D*on't hurt me just because you can," Katharine whispered.

She trembled like a leaf in the wind, impossibly white and fragile-looking in the pale moonlight; her ruby-red hair atumble about her face shimmered like a halo of fire. Instinctively she took a step away from him, poised like a dancer, ready to run. Her trust was disintegrating as the full impact of this moment became apparent on her beautiful face.

"I would never hurt you," Jesse said.

There was uncertainty in her eyes, which matched her self-conscious laughter. The awareness of her fragility and the precariousness of her situation caused her to hold her breath.

"Never is a long time," she said. She felt suddenly cold, vulnerable, transparent and alone, as if the shock of the last few weeks was wearing away like a thin, protective veneer and reality was settling uncomfortably around her. *Is it merely gratitude or love I feel for him?*

"We don't know the number of our days," Jesse said quietly, looking up quickly. "But if I had only one day left to live, I would want to spend that day with you."

The distance between them could be measured in mere feet, yet a wide cultural abyss separated them. He had been her knight, saving her life countless times, asking for nothing in return. His strong arms had supported her, covered her, healed her and held her, pulling her from a watery grave. But she was promised to another man. The image of Damien intruded into her thoughts, and her conscience fought with her newly awakened passion; her desire for Jesse was pitted against years of friendship. Her feelings for the two men were incredibly different. Friendship could not compete with this consuming passion. Never in her life had she been so powerfully attracted to a man. *Never.*

She looked at Jesse as if seeing him for the first time.

Is this love? she wondered again.

The light from the fire set his form in stark relief. His wealth of blue-black hair, loose and unfettered, his handsome face and fluid grace made her weak with want. Desire, sharp and sweet as sin, made her tremble. An unspoken question hung heavy in the air. "You want to sleep with me," she said. The thought arose spontaneously, the words tumbling out like inspiration dropped into a deep well inside, echoing *pretend, pretend, pretend.* Yet it wasn't pretend. Her words were like a mirror, reflecting her powerful feelings for him. She wanted to sleep with him. She wanted him to touch her, tease her, hold her, kiss her lips and lie beside her. She wanted him.

Mortification blossomed crimson on cheeks that matched the scarlet flush of lips, swollen, warm and hot, and her hand went to her mouth.

Jesse nodded his head slowly.

A heavy silence followed. Her laughter, trust and sweetness, which usually blossomed naturally, withered in fear.

"Yes," he said. "I want to sleep with you." He turned toward her with a sensual grace at once lethal and provocative. He held her gaze and lifted his shirt over his head and tossed it aside. "You want me," he said. "And I want you."

Naked to the waist, he stood honestly before her. His broad chest was clearly defined, every muscle outlined. His trim waist was corded with a network of muscles placed like narrow stones, one atop the other. Rock-hard biceps flexed easily with every movement, and strong legs sheathed in leggings only accentuated the powerful masculine design.

"Sleep with me and be my wife."

The intensity of the eyes gazing at her was frightening. Dark and dangerous, they flirted with her in a subtle, charismatic and nearly hypnotic way. Then he smiled softly, his hard white teeth reflecting the moonlight; the smile was whimsical in comparison to the strength of his movements. His expression was yearning and sultry, earthy, clean and masculine.

"Love me or reject me, Kathryn," he said, shaking his head. "I'll never be a beggar at your feet."

In Boston, her life had been preordained and carefully orchestrated. The gallant gentlemen knew their roles clearly. They dipped, bowed, touched hands, flirted. Dangerous games of touching and pretense. There was no pretense in McCallum. None at all.

He was raw, naturally elegant, and honest as the first kiss of spring, icy and biting as a northwestern wind. He refused to play games.

Trembling, Katharine felt tears in her eyes, a painful ache in her heart, and desire fighting with maidenly fear. She swept her hair back from her face. No artifice existed between them; no lies or half-truths, buried memories or history. All he had to offer was himself. All she had to offer was herself. All that existed on this warm Colorado night was the two of them, a man and a woman alone, as if creation had just been formed and this forest was their garden.

Falling, falling, falling in love. . . .

Shyly she looked away; a blush the color of roses painted her cheeks. Her lips' natural rouge deepened, and her soft, gentle breaths increased until she could not look at him or find another breath to quell her fear. Yet, perversely, she could not look away, and when she dared to catch his gaze, she felt as if she had been hit by lightning.

"Love me," he said, "or reject me. Decide."

He was standing barely an arm's length away. Worlds existed in his eyes. *Lifetimes?* she wondered dizzily. She had the feeling that those same eyes had gazed into hers a million times before. Magic man, traveling the silver threads of time. Eternity existed in those eyes. A humid, wet ache replaced the heat.

She stood on a precipice of ice and fire, mesmerized by his soft, lazy smile, the sexy, enigmatic touch that hit her like a lightning bolt between her thighs, making her blush, stare at him with wonder and look away, bewildered by her intense feelings.

Then he reached out one hand, silent, beckoning. Timidly she touched the edges of his fingers, accepting. The rough texture grazed her fingers, and she felt a shiver roll outward from her hand like the ripples of a lake, sweeping up her arm and through the length of her body. A step was all she took and those strong arms of steel opened for her and then locked around her waist. "I'll never let you go," he said.

Gently he pulled her to him like the first movement of a dance.

One hand reached upward, and Kathryn saw an expression of peace in his eyes.

He touched her rose-red hair and held her close to his heart. Pressing her small face to his chest, he kissed the top of her head. She could feel her hair move beneath his breath. Tenderly he moved his hand up and down the small curve of her back, molding her to him like potter's clay, warming her with hands already startlingly hot. Her years of restraint brought an enchantment that excited her. One night or a million lifetimes? He made her feel as if time did not exist.

Gazing down at her, he lowered his face until his mouth met her forehead, his firm lips barely touching her skin. Then he kissed her nose, her cheeks, raining tender touches across her face, teasing a little and laughing softly when he felt her sigh in his arms and melt against him. He loved the way she fit so neatly and the soft undulations of her flesh pressed against his hard length.

Brushing back her hair, he kissed her mouth. "I love you," he said. "I don't know why or how it happened, but I love you." His mouth was close to her lips when he said the words, and he could feel her warm breath coursing across his skin. Silk. Her lips touching his. He kissed her deeply, increasing the pressure until her lips, which resisted subtly, gave way, opening for him. He wanted her to reply in kind; to say that she felt the same about him. He needed to hear it.

Do you feel the same? he wanted to ask, but was silent, knowing he would accept her with or without a declaration of love. He needed her.

"I—" she began to say, hesitating when he kissed her lips softly. She closed her eyes against a strong, languorous pull, acutely aware of the reaction of her body. "You make me feel as though I should be in confession," she said, a schoolgirl once again. Exhaling slowly, she was aroused and unsure, excited and frightened all at once.

"I'll be your sin," he said boldly, kissing her on the lips. His hand fanned out against her cheek, pushing her hair away and tangling his strong fingers in the thick tresses. The savage light in his eyes scalded her. He lifted her easily, and her eyes opened wide, languorous and heavy-lidded with passion. "I'll be whatever you want me to be," he said as he claimed her lips again with his, walking a few steps with his mouth covering hers. Then he laid her down on a bed of sweet pine boughs and robes of soft fur beneath a naked sky, shining with starlight. "Blame me for tonight," he challenged. "But love me as I am."

He knelt beside her as calm and natural as the night itself. Her fear of him had been eclipsed by his touch. Trust caused a small smile to make the beauty of her face radiant. She remembered his bemused smile in the firelight and the Irish coffee; his ferocity and unwillingness to back down to any man; his tenderness as he brought broth to her lips; his fear when he pulled her from the lake and the urgent, frightened kiss that had followed; the pinecone doll he had whittled for Emily, and mornings watching him in his solitude with his hawk, hunting.

"I love you," she admitted quietly. The words were a revelation of sorts. "I don't know how it happened either, or when, but I love you." One small, fragile hand reached trustingly for him and he bent forward, kissing the fingertips gently, holding her hand against his cheek as he moved closer. She linked her hands around his neck, tangling them in the wealth of black hair, which fell about them like a shower of dark rain. His lips found her lips, and she felt the hard, hot length of him as he lay down beside her, liking the way he touched her body, feeling no fear of his hands, his strong arms or powerful legs. He showered her with kisses, claiming her with unrestrained passion. The gentleness of his touch was beginning to give way to a noticeable pressure and urgency that caused a sympathetic tension to build inside her. The waves increased in intensity, expanding outward as though a distant storm were fast approaching and the lightning strikes were increasing in strength and frequency.

This sweet, delicious ache seemed to hold a promise, leading her on and carrying her with it, swelling, building toward an ecstasy she had never experienced. She would be led by him; she would willingly follow the trail of his hands, eyes, sweet kisses and the joy of his warm body into the crucible of earthly delights.

Alchemy, where the base instincts of two are dissolved into the shining gold of one. It was the first heaven and the closest to paradise a man and woman might climb without an angel's wings. *Desire*. She knew how to give him pleasure by the fire building in his eyes. His art lay in experience; her delight was in his touch, and she gave back to him with ease and vigor, surrendering her self-consciousness on an altar of passion. Her long legs moved apart for him. She burned for him. His hands guided her gently, teaching her as he loved her.

"I'll never hurt you," he whispered again, kissing her ear, tugging gently on the lobe, his mouth sliding down her neck to the hollow, moving toward the tower of her perfect breast, holding the nipple between his teeth. His hand moved gently between her thighs until he heard one sigh after another escape her partially opened mouth.

Unable to restrain himself any longer, he moved between her legs. Capturing her face in his rough hands, he looked at her, entered her, and saw acceptance and want; in one fluid movement, he claimed his bride.

For Katharine, the sensation was painful at first, followed by a rush of pleasure, swelling outward, deepening and increasing in pressure and intensity. He moved hard against her, and she arched her back, accepting him completely, matching his rhythm with her own. They climbed the ladder together and found paradise in each other's arms and ecstasy in each other's touch.

"I love you, Katharine McCallum, and I will always keep you safe," he vowed.

"I believe you," she whispered. "I believe you." Tangling her hands in his hair, she pulled him to her with a soft, surrendering, feminine moan of pleasure.

He looked at her in wonder.

He was lost, he was lost in making love to her, finding in himself a tenderness of feelings that he hadn't known he possessed. She made him want to be gentle. She made him want to be the best man he could be. She made him want to love, trust and hold her for more than a night. Eternity would never satisfy his feelings for her.

"You satisfy me," he confessed. Pulling her close, he buried his face in the wealth of her red hair and whispered, "I will love you forever. Forever."

Damien opened his eyes as the Conestoga lurched along. His head was pounding. He had been dreaming, but he couldn't remember what it was about, only that he woke with an incredible feeling of loss.

Swallowing, he looked around for something to drink. "Where is that bottle?" he muttered as he tried to sit up. The wagon was spinning, and he felt sick to his stomach. "What time is it?" He started to reach for his watch when Bart Cobb's face appeared in the portal. "Christ!" Damien muttered. "What the hell are you doing here?"

"I'm supposed to be here," said Bart sullenly. "This is where you told me to be. 'Meet me in Florence,' you said. You ain't trying to back out on me now, are you?"

"No, you fool, get in here."

Bart pulled himself up into the wagon. He was elated and thirsty.

"Well?" Damien asked testily. He reached beneath his berth and pulled out a fresh bottle of Scotch, opened it and poured a glass for himself and one for Cobb. "Did you find her?"

"Sure did," Bart said and took the offered drink. He grinned and looked at Damien, pausing for effect, expecting some show of emotion—something. After all, the man had paid a considerable amount of money. Yet nothing was registering on his face. He sat composed and sipped his drink. He looked sleep-tousled and as elegant and handsome as always, even in his wrinkled white shirt and black trousers.

"Either tell me or let me sleep," Damien said. "And if you choose to let me sleep without telling me what I paid you to find out, you would have been better off if you had forked that bronc and headed in the opposite direction, because I assure you, you'll never finish your drink." He didn't bother to tell Cobb that he intended to kill him anyway. Damien couldn't afford the risk of betrayal. Cobb knew too much to live once his usefulness was ended.

Damien stared.

The grin faded from Cobb's face. "I was gonna tell you straightaway," he said nervously.

"Then please do. I'm not in the habit of repeating myself, nor asking twice for something I want."

Cobb gazed uneasily at Damien. The silence and the absolute coldness of the man were unnerving. Cobb had been in Mexico a long time ago and seen a shark some fishermen had strung up to gut. He'd never seen such stone-cold eyes again, until now. True, Damien's were agate blue. Nevertheless, the expression was the same because there wasn't any expression at all. It was as if the man were already dead and someone had simply forgotten to extinguish the candle.

"You're in the right place. Tomorrow's ride'll bring you to Canon City," Cobb said soberly. "I seen her myself at the Rendezvous. But . . ." He suddenly remembered a story his mother had told him about an hombre who had bumped into Death one day and beat hell trying to outrun him, only to find him waiting at the end of the road. Cobb swallowed, waiting for Damien's reaction.

Damien did not breathe for a moment. Then he asked softly, "How is Miss Katharine?"

"Beautiful, like you said. A real head-turner. Every man in camp was in love with her." Bart stopped himself. Something akin to intuition told him the man before him was not as calm as he appeared. At first, upon seeing the woman, he could understand Damien's near insanity in trying to find her, and he admitted that when he saw whom she was with, he couldn't suppress the glee he felt or wait to tell Damien the news. Now, he wasn't sure that telling him was such a good idea after all.

"But what?" said Damien testily.

"She ain't alone."

"Did you think she would be, you imbecile? Now fill in the blanks. Who is she with? Josiah Mott, right?"

"Well, no, not exactly."

"Not exactly?"

"No. She's with a different fella altogether. She looked alright, though. Matter of fact, she looked pretty darn good."

"Did she now? And this other fella, does he have a name?"

"Sure does. He is sorta famous in these parts."

"*Is he?* Well, just what is this gentleman famous *for?*"

"Hell of a man. Outshoots, outrides, outhunts anyone in these parts."

"Got a name?"

Cobb nodded. "McCallum, a Scot from up around the Canadian border. He and his pa mined in the Colorado Territory. Been around for a long time."

"Indeed?" Damien was thinking that he might not be around too much longer.

"Yep."

"And how was Miss Katharine reacting to her *captivity* with McCallum?"

"Well, she was smiling, I can tell you that. She wouldn't be the first woman to go for him, just one of many around these parts." Cobb laughed a little self-consciously, wondering if he had said too much.

He had. It didn't take intuition to clue him in. He knew the moment the words spilled out of his mouth and the glass shattered in Damien's clenched fist.

Chapter Twenty-four

To awaken in Eden . . .

Paradise existed in McCallum's strong arms.

The clearing they'd chosen for their campsite was beside a lake that stretched to the horizon. Mist rising from it was being blown across its surface by a southerly breeze that blurred the edges of Jesse's private world until the water, wind and moisture became little more than variegated ribbons of pearl gray in the muted morning light; haunting. The air was damp and cool against his fever-hot skin. He had not slept all night; neither had Katharine.

He rose above her like a nighttime shadow, eclipsing the rising sun and refusing to give way to the day. "I'll never let go," he said. He wanted their wedding night to last forever.

"I'm not asking you to," she said.

Katharine's ivory skin was taut; her breasts rose to meet him, and the scent of her was humid in the morning mist, sweet as honey and enticingly warm. The column of her neck carried rivulets of sweat that wound down to the valley between her breasts, collected in the swell of her rounded belly, and trailed moist and salty between her thighs. Her hair was unbound, and the thick tresses reached well past her waist. Jesse kissed her, ran his hands from her temples to the small of her back, cupped her bottom and brought her closer until not an inch of him was parted from the warmth of her. Her vibrant hair was like a shower of red, flowing over the bed of pine boughs, shocking in its intensity.

The walls of McCallum's world had come tumbling down; the sound of her moans and tender urgings crumbled the enigmatic reserve of his solitary life.

"More," she whispered. Her eyes closed and she bit her lower lip. Katharine could not get enough of his lovemaking.

Jesse laughed at her ardent intensity. His broad shoulders were shiny with sweat, and his raven hair was pushed back from his face. A slow, sexy smile turned the corners of his lips upward.

"I've never . . ." she breathed with a trembling sigh as she grasped him about his waist.

"I know," he said. He moved his hands behind her head and lifted her closer, deepening his kiss. He was so in love with her that he couldn't breathe; whenever he looked in her eyes he felt a keen, shuddering sense of a man falling into unfathomable and mysterious waters, drowning, with no way back.

There was no room for middling gray in his life; his emotions were so polarized, he could not live without diving deeply into every experience. Making love to her each time was like diving for pearls in subterranean caverns. He was submerged so deeply in the sensations of his body that he was learning to breathe water, suffocate in sensuality. He inhaled slowly and closed his eyes, feeling a sensual warmth envelope him in waves of ecstasy. The bright sunlight of morning was pushing back the enchanted world of last night and the starlit memory of loving her for the first time.

Katharine looked up into the face of a man whose physical splendor enchanted her. His perfection was not the idealized beauty of art, but warm to the touch, and human. McCallum was a Scot, not a stone statue, though his resemblance to Michelangelo's David was notable. With the slightest movement, every muscle in his body was outlined in stark relief. Beneath the robe that covered them, his body was bare and magnificent. She looked at him in wonder.

"You frighten me a little," she admitted quietly. Touching him was like petting a black panther and hearing him purr; she was fully aware of his power, speed and lethal attraction, yet unable to restrain her desire.

"I need," he said simply. His arms held his body poised above her like a dancer, leaving a respectable space between them, teasing her. She'd surprised him with her heat and responsiveness—so keen to please and so willing to be pleased. He bent his head, and the rain of his silky, black hair whispered across her cheek making her close her eyes. "I want," he said. His face was a scant few inches above her, and he kissed her forehead chastely, acknowledging the respect he felt for her. Lips, which hid a secret smile, touched her nose, then moved to her eyes, brushing gently across the lids. He closed his eyes as he felt the brush of her long, black lashes against his mouth. "I hunger," he said. In the early morning light he revealed his nakedness, pushing the robe away from his body, hot with emotion and need.

The tiger touched the flame and how fiercely it did burn!

He looked into her eyes and claimed her lips with his softly parted mouth. The kiss was sweet! With difficulty he restrained himself, taking his pleasure slowly and appreciatively, building the fire within her until she would reach for him. "I'm a patient man," he said. He rolled off her to his side, and the roughness of his hands gently touched her legs, feeling silken skin against his hard hand. He moved it over the soft, velvety warmth of her thighs and her femininity. "But I always get what I want."

Softly as a sigh, she moaned at the touch of his hand, her eyes opening in surprise and delight. McCallum laughed. "Always."

He moved over her again, and her arms went about his neck. "Magician or man?" she asked with a warm, winning smile. "Angel or devil, which are you?"

A tenseness permeated every muscle in his body, rigid and controlled above her. "I'll be whatever you want me to be," he said seriously. "Some people swim in a teaspoon of water and think they are wet. I prefer to dive deep, feel intensely."

He rolled over on his back and took her with him. On their natural bed of pine boughs and furs, he held her protectively against his chest. His arms tightened around her middle, and he closed his eyes when the fiery rain of her hair cascaded around his face as she pressed her warm breasts against his hard chest.

"I won't ask permission to touch you, Katharine," he warned. "Or wait like a lapdog for scraps of affection thrown at me when I'm hungry for your touch." He didn't know much about her fiancé or what she was used to, accurately believing that he and that other man were radically different people.

She lowered her head and kissed him softly on the lips. "I love your mouth," he said. "The way you kiss, taste, your scent. I won't dab my lips and pretend I do not love the taste of your skin, the heat of your breath on my face, the feel of your tongue against mine." With a boyish light in his eyes, he held the back of her head and pulled her closer, kissing her with gentlemanly restraint and tracing the curve of her lips with his tongue. "I don't kiss primly with my mouth melded shut."

She blushed at the memory of last night. "It is your openness," she confessed. "Your boldness. You think, say and do what you feel, like a . . ." She wanted to say *a child*; his honesty was so much a part of who he was. In her circles, it would be considered a lack of sophistication.

"I don't lie," he said. "I don't think of myself as separate from my feelings."

"Your body would betray you anyway," she said with a mischievous smile.

"Is that a complaint?" he teased. His eyebrow shot up and she felt a blush rise from deep within at the intensity of his stare. Unable to hold his gaze, in maidenly fashion she looked away.

Gently he cupped her face and turned her to look at him. "I won't lie to you, Katharine. Ever. You'll never find me sleeping farther than an arm's reach away; at least, not by choice."

Naked to the morning sun, she felt free in his arms. The heat of the day beat down against every part of her in this private world he had made for them. His legs moved, and he rubbed against her gently. "You are a hot, beautiful, passionate woman," he said, thoroughly satisfied and more deeply in love than he could admit. His face moved against her silken breast, and his lips parted, tugging gently, eliciting a deep-throated moan. "Dive deep, Katharine, and when you do," he whispered, rolling her over on her back, "take me with you."

Father de Smet walked into the clearing with his fingers fervently working his beads and his lips repeating the rosary. He pretended not to notice the couple, keeping his head bent so they could not see his face, or the canny gleam in his dark eyes that knew exactly what they were looking for and missed nothing.

"Good morning," said Jesse easily. One hand reached out and pulled the robe across them while his other hand wound itself possessively around Katharine's waist. He was smiling lazily. "Fine morning to be out for a stroll, isn't it, Father?"

Father de Smet didn't answer. He nodded and kept mouthing the words to his morning prayers as he continued walking through the clearing, the canny gleam in his eyes blossoming into twinkling, knowing lights. His faith in McCallum was justified. He knew their love was consummated, their marriage solid as the rock upon which it was founded.

Katharine timidly peeked out from under the robe and Jesse's protective arm. She looked in alarm at the strolling priest. "What is he doing?"

Jesse yawned. "Checking."

"What?" Katharine said, exasperated.

"To make sure the marriage was consummated," Jesse replied. "That's the custom in these parts."

"That is barbaric!" she said. She sat up abruptly, pleasing Jesse no end with the sight of her perfect bared breasts.

"No," he said in a matter-of-fact tone. "It's just common sense around here. Padre will spread the word around camp, and the other men will leave you alone. You're my wife now, and these men, rough as they are, respect what belongs to another man. And you," he said, "belong to me."

The word *wife* caused a slight tremor to pass through Katharine, and Jesse laughed in delight at the distressed expression on her face. She remembered the word *pretend*, and the thought haunted her as she struggled with the reality of what she was doing.

"Oh, my God," she whispered.

"We'd better get dressed," Jesse said, his smile fading when he noticed her face. He feigned indifference. "I imagine they'll have a fine breakfast for us this morning. Probably figure we've worked up a healthy appetite."

"I am hungry," Katharine admitted with a shrug of her shoulders as she plucked at the hairs on the buffalo robe, causing her breasts to bounce slightly.

"So am I," he said roughly, mesmerized by the movement. "But not for breakfast. I'm never going to make it off this robe today or get enough of you," he said. Gently he pushed her back down.

Suddenly feeling extremely possessive, he vowed that he would ruthlessly stop anyone who tried to take Katharine from him. Capturing her face within his hands, he kissed her passionately, pulling away slightly and laughing when she blushed; he marveled at the sound of his own joyous laugh as he pulled the buffalo skin away from the rest of her body and took her in his warm arms again.

"Breakfast can wait," she said.

And it did. For hours.

"Get up, you fools!" shouted Damien. "My man has found her! My man has found Katharine!"

North was standing in the middle of camp beside the blackened fire, backlit eerily by the dim morning light. His white shirt was loose and open to the waist like fractured white wings billowing in the cool air, and his hair, so stylishly kept and combed each morning, was as wild as his bloodshot eyes. He seemed feverish, blazing with some infernal heat consuming him from inside. He had waited hours for first light, pacing.

Edwin Dory was the first to stumble from the new wagons that had been purchased in Florence. O'Sullivan followed, and then the rest of the men. The sight that greeted them was startling.

Damien stood silhouetted against the rising sun with his arms lifted high as though in the throes of some obscene, drug-induced ecstasy. His face was livid, and his voice repeated the same words: "He found her! He found my Katharine! He found her. My man found Katharine."

They didn't notice the dark spots of blood that stained his trousers, or see the empty bottle of laudanum in his wagon that had helped him to find the logic in killing yet another man.

A shudder passed through Edwin, and he looked at O'Sullivan.

"That man's insane," said O'Sullivan flatly. "An addict." He'd seen many like him in opium dens, addicted to a drug that left them mere shells of men.

Edwin agreed but said nothing. He had long suspected Damien's addiction to laudanum, and his bizarre behavior seemed to confirm his suspicions.

"This is the man affianced to your daughter? God help her," O'Sullivan said.

"No. I'll not let him marry Katharine," said Edwin. It wasn't a defensive statement, but a truth that had been taking shape in his mind for quite some time and one he was finally able to admit aloud. His dislike of Damien had been growing stronger daily. There was something about breaking bread with a man, sleeping next to him, sharing his thoughts, that either brought a closeness or created a rift. In this case, Edwin felt only revulsion for Damien, and a growing fear for his daughter.

Both men turned to look at the richest man in Boston with his arms raised like a Messiah above his head, paying homage to his dark passion. Neither man would have traded his sanity for one penny of Damien's wealth.

"Somehow," said Edwin, "I'll make sure he never gets his hands on Katharine. In fact, I regret ever offering him a partnership in anything. I'm beginning to believe it was the biggest mistake I've ever made."

O'Sullivan heartily agreed.

Edwin did not care what it would take to keep Damien away from Katharine. He had no idea what she had endured in the past few weeks, yet he vowed that even if Damien drove him out of business and took everything he had, the one treasure he would never get his hands on would be his daughter.

In the distance, riders were approaching from the east with their elbows up and their heads down. Squinting, Edwin couldn't quite make them out. Then he exhaled in relief. "It's my sons," he said. "Thank God."

Chapter Twenty-five

*D*amien North sat in the shade of an ancient pine tree on a chair that had seen better days. The legs were uneven and the seat was devoid of fabric, but it provided more comfort than the ground and hinted at a certain shabby elegance reminiscent of Louis XV. It made him wonder whose wagon had carried the chair, possibly a family heirloom, and where the owners were now. *Ghosts*. Faded, like the afternoon light slanting through the branches above his head, casting stark, sinuous shadows over his wide shoulders and narrow hips, delineating in graphic detail the hungry look on his face and his brutally aggressive posture. He looked like a cat on the hunt. *Feral*.

"Will I fade, too?" he wondered, thinking that his image would imprint itself on the landscape like a negative and a hundred years from now some travel-weary person would happen upon this spot and feel him as keenly as he felt every memory of his Katharine. He could see her face every time he closed his eyes, hear her laughter and even recall the scent she wore. He laughed beneath his breath, looking at the backwater trading post and feeling oddly detached from his surroundings.

Canon City was not much different from Florence, and he was bored with it. A residue of laudanum caused a staccato trembling in his limbs that made him want to run the excess energy off, but he must wait here instead.

"Patience," he reminded himself. They had arrived scarcely an hour ago. Edwin's sons, John, Luke, Adam, Nick and Dan, had come trooping to their father's rescue in Florence. John carried the ransom in his valise, and each man wore his sidearms, tied low on his hips. Every business and enterprise had been mortgaged in Boston, including their home and their shares in the railroad, to buy Katharine's freedom, and not one man amongst them regretted the bargain.

Edwin, bolder and braver now with the ransom in tow, rode in the lead, confident that he could buy his daughter's freedom. Relief was apparent on his face.

Damien, on the other hand, felt more tense than ever. She was here, close by. He knew it. He could feel it, searching every face that passed for the woman he had traveled two thousand miles to find.

Mountaineers and cavalry men moved around the perimeter of his vision. Some spoke to him, but he did not reply; he simply sat and waited and watched.

"Damien," said Edwin insistently. "I need to talk to you."

"What is it?" he asked impatiently. He turned and looked at Edwin, who was approaching with a cup of coffee in one hand and a plate of food in the other.

"You haven't eaten since yesterday," said Edwin. Their families had been friends for years. He'd known Damien since he was a child. Despite his earlier tirade, he felt sorry for the man. In the early light of day, dark circles ringed his eyes; he scarcely slept, and he drank far too much and probably relied on laudanum to mitigate the pain of his migraines when sleep would have been a better answer. Edwin remembered O'Sullivan's words, and his lips thinned in disapproval of the course Damien's life was taking. He honestly did not want him as a son-in-law.

"Breakfast? I'm not hungry," Damien said. The sight of food made him nauseous. "How is it that you know she is here, in Canon City, somewhere in this pandemonium, and yet you can remain so calm?" He took Edwin's composure for lack of caring, when nothing could have been further from the truth.

"My sons are out looking for her right now," replied Edwin. "*Your man,* Cobb, said she was fine, did he not? I have the ransom, and there is nothing I can do until someone spots her and whoever she is with. All we can do, Damien, is wait. Making yourself sick will not help matters."

For a moment the intensity in Damien's hard, agate-blue eyes softened. He was not used to being treated with compassion. Stirred by a rumbling empty stomach, he reached for the offered plate with the same practiced disdain that he used with his servants. Then his hand stopped in midair, trembled slightly, never touching the plate as his eyes caught a flash of brilliant, titian red hair and he heard a laugh that rivaled the sound of church bells at Vespers.

"Katharine," he murmured. Two months of pain and suffering ended in one single word. Quietly he stood up. His face had softened, and Edwin swore that tears formed in the corners of his eyes.

At that moment the sea of trappers and traders parted, allowing a small white woman with startling red hair and a tall, dark-haired man to pass through. Both were smiling.

Edwin recognized his daughter instantly. She was laughing and holding the hand of a little girl with a sweep of beautiful black hair, caramel skin, dark, brilliantly shining eyes and a wonderful smile. The girl seemed to be singing, "Oh, Kat, Kat, oh!" while looking at Katharine's face and holding tightly a doll made of pinecones.

"Katharine. Katharine!" her father shouted. "Oh, my God! Katharine!" Dropping the plate, he ran toward her with his arms opened wide.

"Father?" Hearing her name, Katharine frowned and turned toward the sound. "It is!" she said joyfully. Her hand flew to her mouth and she ran toward him, crying in relief.

"It is you," Edwin said as he gathered her into his arms. "My dear girl, I've been so worried! So worried!"

The next moment Katharine was surrounded by her brothers, laughing, playfully tugging at her hair, teasing her and hugging her by turns. There was no mistaking the joy on their faces at seeing her again, alive, unharmed.

"John, Dan, Luke, Nick, Adam . . ." Her voice was incredibly soft as she wept. "I am so glad to see you. How did you find me?"

John stepped forward. "Tracked you," he said simply. "We were worried sick about you."

"Yes," said Damien softly. "We were." Katharine pulled back a little from her father, her eyes widening and crinkling at the corners, and she smiled sweetly at Damien.

With speed and elegance, he quickly closed the distance between them and, uncaring of all present, pulled her from her father and held her close. "Darling girl," he whispered. "I have been sick with worry."

She could feel the hammering of his heart. And she smiled at the familiar feel of his arms around her. The last time he had looked so worried was when they were children and she had fallen into a well while recklessly walking along the top stones. Luckily, it was old and dry, filled with rubble, and he'd had no trouble pulling her out with a rope and bucket, chastising her for her foolhardy behavior. He'd looked so stern, like an old gentleman in a young man's skin.

"I'm sorry, Damien. Truly, I would never want to be a moment of trouble to anyone."

The look on Damien's face shocked her. Katharine had never seen him cry, not when he had fallen and broken his arm or even when his parents died; yet he was crying now, unashamed of tears in front of a thousand men.

"I thought I'd lost you," he admitted ruefully. "I would rather lose my life, Katharine, than to ever lose you."

A sense of pity and compassion, years of memories, rose up in her. "You didn't lose me, Damien," she said gently. "I'm fine."

The next instant Damien caught hold of her again and hung on as if for dear life.

Among the rough and rowdy trappers witnessing the reunion, a lone Scotsman, holding the hand of a little girl, looked on awkwardly. Edwin noticed him. "Who might this gentleman be, Katharine?" he asked. Katharine let go of Damien and smiled brightly.

"My protector," she said proudly. "My knight in shining armor, Father." Her praise had a slight tonic effect on Jesse, who glanced quickly at her and nodded. Rushing to him, she took his hand and Emily's and brought them forward to meet her father. Off to her right, Damien was glowering possessively.

"Yes," said Damien icily, "who is he, Katharine?"

Katharine noted the warning lights in Damien's glittering eyes.

"This gentleman," she said brightly, "is Jesse McCallum. He saved my life, not once but several times, and has been my protector, vowing to find my family and make sure that I was returned safely to all of you!"

Edwin smiled. "Thank you, Jesse," he said earnestly. "I will never forget what you've done."

"Nor I," said Damien grudgingly.

"And this young lady," said Katharine, gathering Emily to her with a hug, "is Emily. Father, Emily is coming home with me. I hope you won't mind. She is alone, and you already have eight children. I doubt you'll even notice one more."

Edwin noted the concerned light in his daughter's eyes

and looked from her to the child. Then he knelt down, looked into Emily's fey, beautiful face, and said, "Of course you may come and live with us, Emily, for as long as you like."

Unable to understand, she turned her face upward. "Kat?" she said questioningly.

Katharine hugged her tightly. "With me, Emily; you're coming home with me. I'll not let any more harm come to you, and neither will my father or brothers."

"No family, then?" her father asked.

Katharine sighed. "I don't know," she admitted. "But I cannot leave her here, Father."

"Then you won't," he said generously. "We won't." And so it was done. The Dorys had another daughter and sister.

Alone, Jesse stood on the perimeter, looking at the happy group. The burden he hadn't wanted was now the treasure he cherished most. He wouldn't allow Katharine and Emily to see how their leaving was affecting him.

"Borrowed," he said so softly that only the wind heard the word that was breaking his noble heart. He loved everything about Katharine. Everything. And because he loved her and had so little to offer her, he prepared to let her go and ride north into the mountains.

"So you're leaving, then?" he said to her carefully. It sounded absurd when he said it. He looked at her brothers' clothes and at Damien; their wealth was worn as casually as their education, manners and elegance. Wild as a wolf, warrior-proud, he was a part of the mountains.

She's so beautiful, my Rose of Sharon. Let go, he told himself silently. *Let go.* The thought broke his heart.

He took a step backward, his bow on his shoulder, his bowie knife in his scabbard, his rifle ready in his left hand. He started to smile a little, gazing at Katharine, memorizing every feature, imprinting her image on his heart, something he could take out occasionally to warm him on the long winter nights; a memory so sweet that it would last a lifetime. *Was I,* he wondered, *only husband for one night?* His thoughts were broken when Edwin stepped forward and gripped his arm, shaking his hand.

"Thank you, Mr. McCallum, for what you've done. You have no idea how much this means to us. If there is ever anything I can do for you, anything at all, please don't hesitate to ask." Edwin reached into his coat and fumbled in the hidden pockets, pulling out an ornately gilded card with his name and address. "Take this," he urged, placing it in Jesse's rough hand. "If you ever need us, come to Boston and look us up. I will do everything in my power to help you."

Jesse nodded, taking the card. "Thank you," he said politely. He looked at the card, and a twinge crossed his handsome features as his thumb grazed the raised gold letters of words he couldn't read. He looked frankly into Edwin's eyes and found a friend; unspoken warmth and a generous spirit gazed back at him.

"No. Thank *you,* Jesse," said Edwin. There was something about the rugged young man, his dark, intelligent eyes, his noble carriage that touched Edwin deeply. "If you ever need anything . . . anything . . ."

"I don't need nothing," Jesse said quietly. There was an earnestness and sincerity about Edwin that Jesse immediately liked.

Damien snorted a little beneath his breath. He knew what McCallum wanted. "Here you go, boy," he said, flipping a few five-dollar gold pieces into the air toward Jesse. The coins flew up, cartwheeled and fell to the ground, a shower of gold. "For your trouble."

"Trouble?" Jesse looked at the coins littering the ground and then at Katharine and Emily. He frowned and then squinted at Damien from beneath his lashes. "They weren't no trouble," he said. "No trouble at all." He ignored the gold, almost laughing when he thought of his father's mine and the McCallum deed filed at the assayer's office.

Stunned by Damien's callousness, Edwin looked quickly

at Jesse, ashamed at what he considered an insult to a noble man. "This," said Edwin, taking the valise from John, "is the ransom Josiah Mott demanded for my daughter." Inside the bag were new bills mixed with old ones. "A million dollars," he said, confident that his family would regain its fortune and grateful for the return of his daughter. He believed the money could change McCallum's life. "For saving my daughter's life! Thank you."

"I don't want your money," Jesse said. He shook his head and looked at Katharine. Emily was holding fast to her hand. Her pinecone doll had dropped to the ground. Katharine looked back at him as though peering through a keyhole into a world she barely saw from one she could not escape.

"Let's get out of here," Damien said icily. He was beginning to feel like a fool. Whipping off his topcoat, he placed it proprietarily around Katharine's shoulders and then turned her toward the waiting wagon, preparing to navigate her through the mountain men, Indians and assembled engineers. He had only one thought: returning her to Boston as quickly as possible.

Lifting her up, he placed her on the wagon's seat. The canvas tarp had not been pulled over the back ribs of the Conestoga and the contents were clearly visible. Even the shabby old Louis XV was in tow; Damien's decision to renovate the relic had cost him a dollar. Glancing back at McCallum, he lifted the little girl and placed her next to Katharine on the seat. "Thank you," he said to Jesse bitingly, "for taking care of my fiancée."

"Fiancée?" said Jesse. "Fiancée? The hell you say," he said quietly beneath his breath. He was looking down at the ground, choking back anger, hurt and humiliation. Bending over, he picked up Emily's pinecone doll from the dirt.

"Wait," he said.

Katharine turned in her seat to gaze at him with the oddest expression on her face, watching and holding her breath as he walked toward them. Jesse stood next to the seat, looked up at her and smiled wistfully. He would never forget her face: *Deirdre of Sorrows*. He had lifted her up, placed the thorny crown on his head, fallen in love and touched the flame. Amethysts, roses, emeralds, agates and ivory—a man's treasure, warm, loving and good. "Borrowed," he said softly. He saw tears collect in the corner of her eyes. *For me?* he wondered. *Let go,* he told himself.

"You forgot your doll, Em," he said. The little girl smiled and took her makeshift toy with its sinew braid, prairie-grass skirt and pinecone face. "Take care of Kat for me, will you?"

She nodded seriously, and Jesse let go, stepping backward, remembering hair bright as red roses and a laugh that rivaled an angel's song. He was no angel. He was a man who loved a woman he couldn't have, and he knew it.

"So you're going, then?" asked Katharine. Tears streamed from her eyes, mixing with her smile and trembling lips as she bravely looked into a face she would never see again.

"You don't belong here. All I want to do is ride into the mountains," said McCallum, "and forget everything." It was a noble gesture. He knew he had to leave now or he would never let her go. Never.

"Even me?" said Katharine very, very softly. Somewhere beneath her ribs, her heart had stopped beating. She felt something tear and knew that inside she was bleeding for what she was losing. *He was pushing her away*.

McCallum nodded, moving backward slowly, looking at her like a drowning man caught in an undertow as he began to fade into the mix of men and beasts until he vanished from sight.

"Jesse!" Katharine cried. One hand reached toward the crowd of milling, jostling men, then drifted slowly to her lap. Around the wagon, the men began to mount their horses. Silence hovered in the air as the men looked at her weeping for a mountain man in buckskins and fur who refused a million-dollar ransom for a woman he claimed "weren't no trouble at all."

"We ought to get going," said John quickly. He reached up and hugged his little sister, giving her a kiss. "You scared the hell out of us. We're going home."

Edwin reached up and took his daughter's hand, noting her tears. "He is a good man, isn't he, Katharine?"

"Yes," she said. "A very good man."

Beside her on the bench, biting back his words, Damien released the brakes on the wagon and checked the reins. "He's a damn fool," he muttered beneath his breath. He watched with disgust as Edwin picked up a million-dollar ransom left in the dirt by a mountain man, more beggar than noble. *Into the mountains*, he had said. Damien was grateful he would never see McCallum again. He had what he wanted beside him, and he wasn't about to risk losing her a second time.

His thoughts were interrupted when the little girl moved away from him and as close to Katharine as possible.

"Kat?" said Emily. Her face was anxious.

Katharine looked down. "It's alright, Emily," she said, biting down on her trembling lip. Unable to restrain herself, she looked back one last time. *Gone*. And Katharine knew she would never see Jesse McCallum again.

Chapter Twenty-six

*T*wilight had fallen and royal purple wings hung over the mountains. Midnight-blue shadows sculpted deep lines into the surrounding flint-edged ridges, and all around it seemed as if night were overtaking the land, blotting out the light.

Around the campfire the wagons were drawn in a circle of protection. The horses were tethered to a string line, and the blankets, packs and "necessaries" were placed within easy reach. The rifles were loaded and the ammunition kept dry in leather pouches.

An uneasy feeling permeated the camp as the men milled about, eating and talking in low voices. They glanced furtively at the small group sitting around the campfire in their elaborate chairs, sipping tea from their silver tea service. They studied the woman who held a cup demurely on her lap and looked at no one and nothing except the dancing flames. Emily was sleeping in her bed.

Katharine's skin was pale as moonlight, a stark contrast

of white porcelain against a sapphire-blue gown that was artfully draped about her legs so that the prescribed inch of cream-colored ruffle and just the tips of her slippers could be seen. She made herself a work of art, wanting to please those around her and grateful for the beauty and familiarity of her gown. The doeskin dress she had worn at the Rendezvous had been folded and tucked into a cedar chest. "Why don't you burn that?" Damien had remarked.

She had looked at the intricate work. "Keepsake," she replied. "All memories of the mountain aren't bad, Damien."

He hadn't liked the closed look of her face. "Secrets?" he'd said acidly.

Katharine had told them over supper the events of her kidnapping, while her brothers exchanged angry looks. Her words had made her father weep. "It's alright, Father," she'd reassured him, patting his dear hand. "Jesse saved us."

She'd forced herself not to think about McCallum, but found her thoughts moving to him more and more the closer to twilight the day drifted. It was as if a numbness were slowly wearing off. She had slept very hard for a few hours, not dreaming as far as she could recall, but she was still tired when she awoke.

This evening when Damien had offered her his arm, she'd taken it willingly, unable to admit how exhausted she was.

Now the horizon held the last bit of the amber wine of daylight, sparkling like firelight in her green eyes. The speculative gleam in Damien's eyes went unnoticed. Edwin, filled with guilt, looked sadly at his daughter. Gone was the child who had cajoled and wheedled her way into taking this adventure.

"If I could only turn back the clock," Edwin said. He was filled with guilt, unable to undo the last few months. His daughter had suffered. He looked at her gazing out toward the deepening purple of the snow-capped mountains. "There will be armed guards posted around your wagon tonight and every night, Katharine. I've hired guards who are of good character. You can sleep peacefully. You are safe."

"I don't think I will ever feel safe again," she admitted. Ironically, the first measure of peace she had felt was the night she had lain near Jesse. She remembered closing her eyes and knowing without any doubt that she was safe. Yet she knew she could not have stayed with him in the mountains. A pang of guilt as she remembered their wedding night caused her to glance at Damien.

Damien was dressed in black silk trousers and a matching cravat. He watched her face and made conversation that she answered in few words and brief nods, which made his eyes grow sharp, hard and angry as she continued to shut him out.

He could not draw her back to him. The strings that had been so artfully and strategically attached through years of careful cultivation and friendship could no longer turn her head as they had a few short months ago.

"What are you thinking?" Damien prodded.

Katharine gazed at him and then quickly looked away. "Mountains and moonlight," she said quickly, and then laughed in her self-conscious way. Tonight she would not walk with her dark-haired love in the forest, except perhaps in her dreams. Though the campfire was bright and homey and the wagons placed to keep her hemmed in tightly, she was not really with her companions but free and laughing with Jesse, unable to forget him.

"You've not eaten," Edwin said gently.

Her father touched her knee and handed her a plate.

"No, Father," she said with a sigh. "I'm not hungry. Just very tired."

"You need to eat," Damien said impatiently. "You look ill. And you're entirely too pale." He took the plate from Edwin with one hand and removed her teacup and saucer with the other. "I know you've been through a great deal, Katharine," he said sternly, "but you must forget about it and eat."

For the first time that evening, Katharine turned fully

around to face Damien. Her eyes flashed dangerously. But it was brief, that heat lightning, brief as a clap of thunder on a distant peak, gone within a single breath. "You're right," she said obediently. She took the plate and balanced it on her knee, ate a few bites and handed it back to him.

He couldn't reach her across whatever abyss now separated them. He followed the line of her gaze and saw only darkness, ridges of snow-capped peaks, starlight and emptiness so vast that their firelight was less than the light of a firefly.

"What dark enchantment has cast a spell over you, Katharine?" he asked. He fully expected her to be in shock after what she had experienced, and he was dismayed by her cool reaction to her rescue.

With a trembling hand, Damien laid her plate aside, stood up and walked toward his wagon, shaking his head.

Katharine watched him walk away. She loved him, too, in a way. She wanted to tell him she admired him for his fashionable dress, mannerly gestures, the calm demeanor that weathered any storm with little or no indication of what was going on inside. Yet her awareness of him had changed, and she knew that within him was an abysmal wound—a place where no one was allowed; a room that he would never allow her to enter. How often had she knocked on that door? How often had she smiled and teased him and tried to become close to him, and how often had she been denied? The watchtowers were always up and armed around Damien; no one entered his secret kingdom and his private hell. "Not even you, my angel," he had said one night as they'd walked in the Boston Common. Her light mood had caused him to laugh more than once as he proclaimed her "such a child!"

Now as she watched him walk away with his jaw working and his fists clenched tightly, she knew she was powerless to stop him, because she was hurting inside as much as he was.

A cool wind drifted teasingly across her face, and she shivered. She wrapped her arms tightly around her middle, unmindful of the cashmere shawl that her worried father draped around her shoulders. Edwin sat down beside her and struck a match to his pipe. He noticed the tears on her cheeks. "It'll take time, Katharine, to heal," he said. He refused to leave her side.

"Does it show, Father?" she said, hurriedly brushing a tear away.

"Yes," he admitted. "You're in love with that young man, aren't you?"

"I—" she began. "I don't know. He saved my life so many times. Is it gratitude or love, Father, and are they the same thing?"

"I can't answer that, Katharine," Edwin said. "That is something you are going to have to decide." Then he sank into silence beside her as a spark exploded in the flames like a meteor shooting across a miniature inferno, drawing Katharine's attention once again into the heart of the fire. The wind stirred the flames and the flames began to dance. . . .

Jesse wandered into the forest.

He was gorgeously drunk and nearly naked. His body gleamed in the fading light of the moon. He was sweat-darkened and scarred, beautiful, powerful and masculine and filled with unfulfilled desire for his wife.

"Katharine," he whispered.

He stood within a clearing. In his hands he held a nearly empty bottle of brandy and the stub of a cigar, chewed to the quick, gifts that Edwin had left behind; gifts that could not replace what Edwin had taken away. Wounded and sick, he turned slowly, searching for someone he knew he would never see again. "Katharine."

Night, the stark mistress of the errant day, had fallen, pressing her skin of black velvet across the still warm earth while her breath rose like mist into the open mouth of an infinite sky, like a lover's seductive kiss.

The night was so cold. So alone. He was so alone.

Then the caress of the winds returned. Sounds like fitful sighs filled the air as though twilight wings began to beat and the heat in the darkness began to rise.

Magic . . .

"What did you say, Father?" Katharine said, startled.

"I didn't say anything, Katharine. Why?"

"I thought I heard my name," she whispered. The haunted look in her eyes intensified as the sounds beneath the whispering winds increased. *The winds.* She felt touches like soft kisses on her fevered skin, against her cheeks and ears, in the hollow of her throat.

"I heard my name, Father. I heard my name."

Her eyes were wide and feverish, glittering with tears.

"No, Katharine," Edwin soothed. "You're just imagining it." He leaned forward and placed a comforting hand on her knee. "It was only the wind."

"Katharine . . ."

Jesse turned again in his primitive circle, remembering. He could hear the drums beating. Like a heartbeat. Pounding drums. His arms outstretched, he reached for her. He could see her as clearly as if she stood before him, her white skin and ruby-red hair, her emerald eyes, her arms open, yielding and feminine. He could feel her against him; the subtle pressure of her thighs touching his as she rose and arched her back with each powerful thrust, the remembered softness of her belly touching, moving against his hard length. He couldn't dive deep enough to satisfy his desire. Closing his eyes, he shuddered at her remembered sweetness, the maidenly way she turned her head to one side, unable to meet his gaze, the blush of her cheek, the warm, humid scent of her skin, shining with sweat, opening to him like a moonflower in the heat of the night when he cupped her small bottom and brought her closer to him, deepening his reach.

"Katharine!" He was going insane with want.

His voice shouted, ripped through the veil of night, tearing into the darkness like a bolt of jagged lightning against a stormy sky in a whirlwind of sound. The warrior danced . . .

The yellow flames of the campfire reached upward, twisting higher, fed by the rising wind that circled, moaned, bent the trees, and pushed demandingly against her skin.

"I can hear him," Katharine said, convinced, not questioning how or why. She stood up, still staring into the flames, which now seemed to hold more than dancing fire; an image was slowly coming into view. Her heart was beating wildly in her breast, like a caged bird wanting to take flight.

"Who?" said her father. Deeply concerned, he moved toward his daughter, who appeared to be hallucinating or under a spell. She stood near the fire in her sapphire gown, searching the darkness that refused to let her see who it was she sought.

Who had called her . . .

"Jesse," she said, mystified. "I hear him!"

"There is nothing there, Katharine! Nothing!"

"No!" she insisted, pushing her father's arm away when he tried to pull her close. "I can hear him," she insisted. Turning, she looked behind her, expecting to see her shadow transform itself into McCallum. "He's calling me, Father! I can hear him!"

The bowie knife flashed in the darkness.

A dark handful of raven-black hair was cut and thrown to the ground. Black rain. A part of Jesse that had died. Still, he knew that should he cut every inch of his body, drink his soul into hell, howl madly at the moon and damn the gods for denying him what he knew was his—still, in that dark cave of night, surrounded by nothing save the maddening wind, he knew he could not replace her.

"I cannot live without her," he admitted. Unable to breathe, he could still hear the drums pounding, their night medicine like thunder, evoking feelings of intense pleasure so closely linked to pain that they made him want to weep for his loss. In desperation, he sank to his knees, pleading softly, sacrificing the one thing that he'd believed he would never give again for anyone—his tears.

"I can't live without you!" he said helplessly. "Katharine!"

The wind took pity on him, kneeling all alone in a cathedral of darkness that threatened to consume him, and lifted his cry one last time into the bejeweled night while the stars stared down impersonally, uncaring of his plight. . . .

"Katharine."

"There!" she said, triumphant. A trembling smile appeared on her lips, which were now wet with salt tears. "It is him, Father! He is calling me! Father, I can hear him! Jesse! Wait! I'm coming, Jesse! Wait for me!"

She turned to run into the night and into the mountains. No food. No drink. Nothing, but the will to go to him and the desire to be held within the safety of those sturdy arms once again, to look into his eyes, to love him once more.

It was like hitting an invisible wall.

The mountain was unforgiving. There was no place to run to. The mountains greeted her with stone walls, keeping her out and shutting her away from her heart's desire.

"I've lost him," she said. There was no going back. The doors to the magic kingdom were closed and bolted.

I could have stayed. Better still, she could have brought him with her; showed him the world that she lived in, given his fine, intelligent mind a chance to share the wonders that she had taken for granted. But he didn't fit. His clothes were rags. He was not on the Social Register. He was brutally honest and had no need for social deceit. He covered nothing with artifice, not even the needs of his own body. He loved as he lived, fully and ardently, with passion and fire. She had never met a nobler soul. She had never met a man with a finer mind or more integrity. Never. And she'd lost him. The realization made her weak.

Her knees buckled and she sank to the ground.

"What have I done?" she cried in agony as the full realization hit her. "Oh, dear God! What have I done?" Covering her face with her hands, she wept while her father stood awkwardly beside the fire, not knowing how to help his hallucinating child. And in the darkness, concealed by the fabric of the night, Damien watched his fiancée with glittering, jealous eyes.

Chapter Twenty-seven

May 1852—Boston, Massachusetts

*N*early a year had passed since he had seen her, yet it seemed like only yesterday that Katharine Dory was in his arms. Dressed in buckskins, Jesse McCallum was well armed, with a caribou-handled knife sheathed in a wide, hand-tooled, turquoise-beaded belt, a polished Winchester at his side and a showy, Army-issue Colt Dragoon tucked into the leather of his waistband. He loped arrogantly along, mounted astride a dun-colored stallion like a heathen prince with his back straight and his noble face set toward the rising sun.

"I clean up pretty good, wouldn't you say, Isaiah?" he asked self-consciously with a laugh when he noticed all the people staring at him. His horse reared back a little, and he gentled him with one hand as he pushed his hair back from his handsome face, letting it trail down his wide shoulders in rivulets of thick, blue-black rain. He was not ostentatious by nature, and the attention he was drawing made him a little uncomfortable.

"We look like fools," said Isaiah.

"Uh-huh," agreed Jesse. His intelligent eyes narrowed. "The bad boys are back in town."

"Just keep smiling, McCallum. Act like you don't give a rat's ass what anyone thinks," Isaiah said, grinning politely at everyone who stared at him, even managing a wave or two.

"I don't," McCallum said matter-of-factly with a shrug. "Say, you think my hair's too long, Isaiah? I ain't ever seen so many ears."

"You had to come all the way to Boston to figure that out?" said Isaiah, shaking his head.

"Don't start with me," McCallum said, and then laughed, his dark eyes twinkling good-naturedly like sparklers in a Fourth of July parade as his pony pranced down the street.

Jesse was thinking about Katharine. He didn't care about the startled eyes, the changing scenery, the hard-edged words filtering through the cacophony of noise that grew ever louder the further east he rode. One image was on his mind. One purpose. Every other scene was but a shadow, pale in comparison.

Tucked into his wide belt was a worn card with the address of Edwin Dory etched in faded, raised gold letters. The edges of the card were dog-eared and dingy from trail dust and his all too frequent touching. Jesse brought the card out to show to any passerby in the hope that someone could read it, because he could not.

"Are we heading right?" Jesse asked in his rolling, melodic Scottish brogue. The replies were as varied as the surprised expressions of the people he stopped. Usually he would get a cordial nod and some reassurance that, "If you keep your noses pointed toward the rising sun and your back to the Rockies, most likely you'll run into the Dorys sooner or later. There are a lot of 'em in Beantown."

Jesse touched the card, rubbing the embossed gold lettering like a talisman. *Directions*. That was what the card represented. And a lifeline that he knew would lead him to his wife—whether she wanted him there or not! He had resolved to become a part of her world since she had refused to stay in his.

"Damn woman," he said savagely, his dark eyes glittering. It had taken him months to get over the shock of losing her, and just as many to realize that she was the one person he could not forget or replace in his life, no matter how hard he tried.

Behind them, they brought a treasure. A string of packhorses—three speckled paint geldings and a couple of Missouri mules—were loaded down with saddlebags of gold. It was his legacy—a gift from his father, who wanted him to be a gentleman.

"Get up, Jesse," he would say. "To the mine today. Someday you'll be as rich as the Laird of Aberdeen and a . . ."

"Whoa, Pa," Jesse would say, holding up his hands. Then he would spring onto his feet, stretching. "I know, Pa. I know. 'As rich as the Laird of Aberdeen and a *gentleman*, too.' " Then he would roll his eyes and his father would laugh, picking up kerosene lights, picks and shovels before first light of morning.

Jesse hadn't cared about being groomed into his father's idea of a gentleman. He lived his life as fast and recklessly as possible. He loved danger, testing himself and challenging himself. He enjoyed the heart-pounding sensation, as well as the increased confidence when he succeeded.

"Pa," he would say, "I'd rather wrestle my weight in wildcats than balance a teacup on me knee."

Then his father would roll his eyes and Jesse would laugh.

Jesse's world. Before Katharine Dory, it was trapping, hunting, fighting and loving as many women as possible. Raw and intense, he lived every second as if it were his last, challenging death more than once because it was his very nature to compete and his desire to win whatever he set his mind and heart on, regardless of the cost.

Driven by obsession, Jesse McCallum came to Boston to claim what his heart desired: Katharine Dory. He wouldn't take no for an answer because he loved her more than any woman he had ever known.

She was his greatest danger, because he loved her too much. She was a woman a man would desire too much, love too much, want too much and need too much. In losing her, he'd lost a part of himself, and neither time nor distance had healed the pain or lessened the desire.

There were mornings when he awoke and simply stared into the rising sun or sat and didn't move. He didn't notice the hours flying by or the wind in his hair or the ache of an empty stomach. All too soon a razor became a foreign object as his anger intensified; it was the only feeling he allowed full rein. It was a mask. Anger covered the fear he felt at the possibility that he would never see her again. Silence was his wall. Whiskey was the medicine that burned through his veins late in the night as he courted sleep. But even then he was unable to forget, surrendering in his dreams to an exquisite passion that he could not touch upon awakening. *Obsession.*

There were afternoons when he worked the gold mine his father had left for him until every muscle in his body screamed and he couldn't see for the sweat blinding his eyes or haul another rock from the wall. Single-minded, slamming the painful thoughts away with each thrust of his powerful arms, he dug into the hard bedrock for the gold that everyone prized. He was rich. He could learn to be a gentleman.

There were times when he almost forgave her for leaving him, for denying her feelings. He knew that she was no more than a child, needing those things that gave her comfort and made her feel safe.

But, he thought angrily, *didn't I protect her? Keep her safe*

and warm? Didn't I vow to love and cherish her all my life?
Would I not have moved the earth and strung the sun and
moon on a thread, handed her the crystal stars if she had
asked and I could? Yes, I would.

The thought of her made him long for her with every indrawn breath.

There was no second-guessing the morning he packed
his saddlebags, filled his canteens with water and whistled
for Sammy. He purposely ignored the hawk, who was
pointedly ignoring him. Isaiah hadn't questioned his motives. He didn't need to. He knew. He had simply shown up
that morning and found Jesse eating corn dodgers and
drinking coffee laced with sugar.

"The girl?" Isaiah had asked.

Jesse had looked up, chewing. "Hell of a situation, isn't
it?" said Jesse. Then he'd tossed the coffee into the fire and
stood up. "I can't get her off my mind." Pacing, Jesse had
kicked the packs lying on the ground, sending them flying.

"Boston," said Isaiah. It wasn't a question, it was a statement.

"Uh-huh," said Jesse, looking up.

The two men had mounted their horses and headed
east. With their elbows up and their heads down, they rode
into the rising sun, eating the ground with every forward
stride until the distance between the Great Divide and the
East Coast dissolved and they were riding down the streets
of Boston.

Jesse looked around coolly. They were heading down
Boylston Street, coming from the west into the very heart of
the city. The streets were polished cobblestone and neat as
a pin. When they reached the end of the Commons, they
turned on Bowden Street and made their way west to Wal-
nut and then north to Chestnut. They stopped to talk to
anyone along the way who was brave enough to answer
Jesse's question, "How do we get to Edwin Dory's home?"

A hurried nod and a pointing finger were the usual

replies, and the pair would set off again, trotting down the center of the busy streets as if they owned them. The colors of Boston were gay caramel reds, colonial blues and dark forest greens, lush and solid, like the sprawling city itself.

Without hesitation, Jesse drew his horse up short in front of Thirteen Chestnut Lane and dismounted, letting the reins drag on the ground. Turning, he pulled a single saddlebag from his horse and then looked critically at Katharine's town house. It was built of red brick and stood three stories tall with three elaborate dormer windows jutting handsomely from the dark, lap-shingled roof.

The house was elegant, welcoming and warm. On the step was a large, black iron urn with patterned flowers pressed on the side and filled to overflowing with bright yellow flowers that trailed over the side and spilled onto the raised step.

"Do you know where you are, young man?"

Jesse turned to see an elderly couple standing a few feet away. Both were dressed in the colors of spring showers and muted daffodils. Both stared disapprovingly at Jesse and Isaiah and their attire. Jesse said nothing. He was painfully aware of his leather skins and raw appearance. On the mountain, it was his Sunday finest, but in the city, he looked like a sideshow. He was too proud to show that it mattered, but it did.

"Well, this is Boston, young man!" the elderly gentleman said. "Have a care how you conduct yourself in these streets!"

"Boston? The hell you say?" said Jesse, trying to cover his embarrassment with a jokey attitude. "Isaiah, did you know we're in Boston now?"

"Boston? I had no idea. Can't say that I'm surprised," said Isaiah. He lifted his leg and cleared the sorrel's head, leaping easily to the ground. By that time, Jesse had made it to the front of the house, landing several sharp blows on the front door with his fist.

* * *

"Tighter, Emiline," breathed Katharine. Her hands were placed against the wall of her bedroom on the second floor. Her room was decorated in pale mauve, pristine blue and silvery green. A double door of French white edged in gold with brass handles and ornate hinges opened onto an opulent sitting room with two large windows draped in white lace curtains.

The walls were hung with white silk and furnished in the style of Louis XV. All the chairs were covered in mauve velvet and edged in twisted gold braid. The floor was covered with Aubusson rugs in elaborate patterns of navy blue, taupe and maroon.

"It must be thirteen inches, Emiline!" Katharine insisted. "That is the style, you know!"

"You're close to suffocating now," scolded Emiline. "There isn't a thing wrong with a sixteen-inch waist!"

"Kat, Kat," scolded Emily, playing in the window seat with her pinecone doll and a nearly new china one. She wore a white ruffled dress, her hair beautifully coiffed and tied with pink silk bows.

"Oh, now, Em," said Katharine, laughing so hard her dimples showed. "Don't you scold me, too!" The little girl giggled, smiled and ran to her, burying her face in her skirts. Since coming to Boston, she had slept in the same room as Katharine, following her about like a quiet shadow. She smiled often now, and the rowdy Dory household with its myriad children and lively conversations accepted her with open arms.

"Em," Katharine said, giving her a hug, "you're supposed to take my side no matter what!"

Emily nodded and scowled dutifully at Emiline, making such a face that both women burst into laugher. Their jovial conversation stopped in mid sentence when a thunderous *ka-booom! Ka-BOOM! Ka-boom!* echoed through the mansion. Emily's eyes grew to the size of silver dollars and she grabbed Katharine.

"Who in the world is that?" said Katharine.

Running to the window, she was followed by Emily. They pulled the curtains back and peeked down into the street. One glance at the figure below and she stopped breathing. The man's arrogant stance and noble features told her who it was in an instant.

"Jesse."

There was a finality to that word. His name was like a charm bringing closure to fitful nightmares and inescapable longings that plagued her from morning until night. She was haunted by the memory of him disappearing into the forest. Seeing him standing at her doorstep with his face turned upward filled her with indescribable joy.

It was all she could do to keep from running to him.

"Damn woman," muttered Jesse.

"Hit it again," suggested Isaiah, lounging against the wooden frame, and Jesse did.

Ka-BOOOMMM!

"Think they heard that?" Jesse asked.

Isaiah nodded. "Probably all the way to China."

Satisfied that they must have gotten someone's attention, both men leaned against the door, listening and impatient, until they finally heard footsteps approaching in a hurried, staccato rhythm. The door opened a crack and a wizen-faced man peeked out.

He looked at the men from head to foot, then said in a voice as starched as the white shirt he wore, "The servants' entrance is at the back, boy."

Jesse cringed. "I hate that word," he said beneath his breath. Looking up, he stared the butler down. "I'm no servant," he said.

"Vagrants are not allowed," the butler said with a sniff. "The city mission is down the street!"

"I'm no vagrant." The truth was, Jesse was worth millions. "I've got business to attend to with Edwin Dory. We're friends."

"Oh, really? Mr. Dory, a friend of yours? I hardly think so, and I really have no time for this."

The butler placed both his hands on the door to close it, and Jesse placed one broad hand on the door so that it wouldn't.

"I'm coming in," he warned.

"You most certainly are not!"

"I am," he insisted. Then he pushed the door, hard.

"No!" shouted the butler. Too late. He flew across the room and landed in an embarrassing position splayed across the black and white marbled foyer.

"You look a fool," Jesse said calmly as he walked inside.

"What on earth are you doing?"

Jesse glanced up at the sound of the indignant feminine voice and saw a beautiful mature woman standing against the elaborately scrolled white banister. Her dress was of yellow silk and cut low in the bodice, highlighting a full, womanly figure. But it was her face that arrested his attention. It was the face of his Katharine, only changed by time and infinitely harder. The softness he prized in his wife had been all but erased in this woman's eyes, replaced by a haughty arrogance that was cold and distant.

"Ma'am," said Jesse politely, bowing slightly at the waist.

Meanwhile the butler was scrambling to his feet. "Somerset!" he butler shouted. "Somerset!" He called for the gardener at the top of his lungs. "Oh, you ruffian! You'll get your just rewards for knocking me over when Somerset gets here!"

"Not likely, you little pissant. You fell," said Jesse. "I didn't push you."

"You did, a little," said Isaiah, contradicting him.

"Don't start with me," said Jesse.

Just then, Sammy loped through the door and knocked the butler to the floor a second time, sending him stumbling into a pillar that supported a Ming vase and sending it crashing to the floor, shattering it to pieces.

"My Ming vase!" gasped the woman just as Jesse's hawk swooped through the front door and landed on the chandelier. "Ohhh . . ." moaned the woman as she sank to the floor in a dead faint.

"What did you do to her?" Isaiah asked.

"Evidently I made one hell of an impression," Jesse said. "Whattaya reckon that jar cost?"

"More than money," said Isaiah seriously, and then he burst out laughing as the wolf settled down on the terrified butler's chest with his tongue lolling to one side and his hot breath in the man's face, while the hawk rocked gently back and forth on the crystal chandelier, preening its lustrous golden-brown feathers.

Chapter Twenty-eight

*E*dwin ran through the study and opened the door into the foyer. He was dressed in dark gray trousers and a maroon smoking jacket. In his hand he held his cold pipe with its chewed and familiar mouthpiece. The tang of sweet-smelling tobacco lingered on his clothes, mixing pleasantly with his cologne.

He was an elegant gentleman.

"What the devil is all the commotion?" he shouted over the din. His angry expression gave way to surprise and then elation when he recognized the tall figure hauling the shaggy brown and gray wolf off his terrified butler's chest.

"I don't believe it," Edwin breathed and then grinned. "It is *the* Jesse McCallum, isn't it?"

"The very one," Jesse said.

Edwin walked over and grasped Jesse's arm warmly while pointedly ignoring his butler and his wife, who, though not entirely unconscious, still maintained her pose on the floor, sighing melodramatically as she lifted her hand, then let it flutter to the floor. From time to time she would open one eye to see if anyone was watching and her sighs would grow louder. Edwin was used to it.

"Good to see you," Jesse said earnestly as a feather floated down from the chandelier, landing on the woman's silks. She screamed when she saw it, and this time when she fainted, it was real.

Edwin glanced up to see the hawk preening itself.

"I hope," said Jesse uncertainly as he glanced from Edwin to his wife, "that I'm not interrupting anything. Is she alright?"

"Oh, don't worry about my wife. Etta faints at least once a fortnight, and twice on Sundays if I fail to notice her new gown." He paused and studied her. "She's really quite good at it, isn't she?"

"I wouldn't know," said Jesse. "I don't faint much. Had whooping cough once when I was younger."

Edwin nodded, and the men traded an evil grin. "Somerset," said Edwin when his gardener came in. "Help your mistress; she is not feeling well."

Etta opened her eyes again. "No thanks to you, Edwin!" she said in a frosty tone. With a flawlessly manicured hand, she adjusted her hair and smoothed her skirts.

In the distant recesses of the vast mansion, the sound of a door opening rapidly and banging against a wall was heard, followed by the sound of running feet.

Jesse looked up just in time to see Katharine appear on the landing above, more beautiful even than he remembered. She was dressed in soft pink silk, and her hair, looking as though it could not be constrained by ribbons or lace, streamed about her face like tendrils of flame. Behind her, peeking out from Katharine's voluminous skirts, was Emily.

"Oh, Kat, Kat!" she said and quickly turned around to run the opposite way. There was a loud bang as a door slammed shut.

The smile on Jesse's face slowly evaporated as the heat in his loins increased.

"Jesse!" Katharine said excitedly. With handfuls of her rose-pink gown gathered in her hands and her crinolines showing, she ran down the steps; all thoughts of pretense and convention were gone. She was exuberant. He visited her in her dreams, and in that magical universe without walls they were always together. "Jesse, it's so good to see you!"

He stood his ground and stared coldly at her. His expression was like a bucket of ice water thrown in her face. It was a very embarrassing and awkward moment.

Her smile was replaced with uncertainty. "I'm pleased to see you again, Mr. McCallum."

"*Mr.* McCallum is it now?" His naturally arched eyebrow shot up sardonically, and his lips twisted into what had to be the coldest smile Katharine had ever seen. The result was inevitable. Her happiness at seeing him evaporated. "I'm impressed by your opinion of me." The pain he felt over their long separation and the love he had for her created an odd mixture of feelings. Her beauty and her sweetness captivated him, but his pride was hurt. "I look a fool," he admitted beneath his breath. He realized he was prisoner to a love so strong he was willing to risk everything for a chance to see her again, even humiliation; he didn't like it one bit.

"What *should* I call you?" Katharine said. The remembered intimacy, the eroticism of his touch and their shared passion made social pleasantries seem ridiculous.

"I've no idea," he said casually. "*Darling boy* seems out of the question, but I can think of a few choice words I might call *you*." His dark eyes glittered. The air was charged with electricity and tension, heating the room to an almost unbearable level.

Edwin looked uneasily from his daughter to Jesse. "I don't know your friend, Jesse. Whom," he said, turning to Isaiah, "do I have the pleasure of meeting?"

"Isaiah Briand," said Jesse. "My brother."

"Your brother?" asked Katharine, surprised.

"In spirit and heart," Jesse said proudly. He turned from Katharine to her father. Edwin grasped the black man's hand and shook it warmly.

"Good to meet you," he said. Isaiah nodded affably. "Now," Edwin went on, "what can I do for you men?"

"I've come to Boston for one reason," Jesse said. He lifted the pouch from his shoulder and dropped the bag of gold at Edwin's feet. There were twenty more packs just like it and a mine not fully developed in Colorado with his family's claim registered. "My pa came from Scotland. He was a scholarly man, a cleric. He had a dream. He wanted me to be a gentleman. To be educated."

Edwin nodded. "It is not an unreasonable ambition, Jesse. Most fathers feel that way."

Katharine was absolutely silent, holding her breath. She looked at Jesse standing in the pristine foyer filled with art, culture, sophistication and elegance. He was incredibly handsome, yet so rough-and-tumble, a wild man from the mountains in a world as alien as the mountains had been to her. *How hard it must be for you,* she thought, her heart touched.

"I can't read," he said softly beneath his breath.

"What did you say?" asked Edwin.

Jesse exhaled and said bitingly, "I can't read!" His eyes were hard, his face burning with shame. "But I have money," he said defiantly. "Enough, they tell me, to buy Boston and everything in it, and that's what I aim to do!" He had a chip on his shoulder for more than one reason.

"Buy Boston?" Edwin said, confused. Etta was standing with her hand on the rail, staring. Katharine had tears in her eyes, and Somerset was holding the garden rake poised, ready to strike at a moment's notice. The butler was nowhere in sight.

"No. Not exactly. I want . . ." he said and stopped. He

looked at Katharine and closed his eyes for a second before anyone could read the naked truth. "I want you to teach me to read." He lifted another pack of gold and dropped it at Edwin Dory's feet. "I'll pay you a million dollars to make a gentleman out of me. I'll keep up, I won't argue, and I'll do what you say."

"A million dollars?" said Etta. Her hand flew to her mouth as her eyes rested on the leather pouch.

Edwin was stunned. "You came all the way to Boston to learn to *read?*"

Jesse nodded and refused to look at Katharine. "Something like that," he said. His hands were balled into fists, his arms rigid at his sides.

Edwin's eyes softened. He saw the tears in his daughter's eyes and remembered the night by the campfire, her haunted look and the dreams. He knew there had been something between the two of them.

Nodding, he understood why Jesse was in Boston. It was nothing as hard as gold that had brought him so far; nothing as vainglorious as buying a concrete forest when he had lived within a kingdom grander than any man could form. What he sought was soft, small, sometimes weak and incredibly fragile.

"You don't have to pay me, Jesse, to teach you to read," Edwin said. "After what you did for my daughter, I'd consider it a privilege to help you in any way. You and Isaiah are welcome to stay with us for as long as you like."

"What?" snapped Etta. "Oh no, you don't, Edwin!" came her shrill voice. "These savages are not going to stay in our home! I don't care how much money he lays at your feet!"

Edwin turned calmly and looked at his wife. "Etta, this man saved your daughter's life and took care of her for more than a month."

"I realize that," said Etta, cowed for a second. "But surely, Edwin, you can find other accommodations for them, especially since he has enough money to . . . to *buy Boston.*"

She was reluctant to admit that her own family's declining fortunes were exactly what had prompted her to marry Edwin, whose family background was somewhat questionable, but whose father, Charles Dory, had struck it rich in the Klondike. True, the Dorys were considered nouveau riche, but Edwin was handsome, scholarly, a gentleman in every way. "There are fine hotels in the city . . ." she began.

Jesse stood silent, thoroughly humiliated.

"He'll do no such thing," said Edwin forcefully, but always softly, always diplomatically. "Mr. McCallum and Mr. Briand will stay with us."

"In the guest house?" Etta offered hopefully, her mind doing cartwheels as she mentally recited all the ways she could explain to her neighbors who these savages were.

"In our *home*, Etta. In this house. In a suite of rooms upstairs between your bedroom and mine." There was a pointed inflection to his words, an unconcealed displeasure in the separate sleeping arrangements he had with his wife.

Still standing on the landing, she began to blush, not from embarrassment but from anger.

"Truthfully, my dear, I don't know why you aren't compiling a list for a party to welcome our guests. After all, it isn't often we entertain gentlemen of such substance and integrity."

"Edwin, that is one remark I will not forgive," she warned. "Katharine, you have lessons and a fitting. The driver will be around at precisely eleven-thirty. You mustn't be late, and your hair looks a fright." With the coldness she was renowned for, she simply cut off the conversation, focusing her attention only on what she considered important.

Sadly, Edwin thought, *it has never been me.*

In an infantile attempt to wound her just a little, Edwin said, "You know, my dear, we are in need of funds. A million dollars is a lot of money. The railroad project has been suffering innumerable setbacks, and we have a schedule to meet with the federal government. If we don't show progress, we will forfeit the right-of-way. The money is a blessing, as is Mr. McCallum."

Etta blanched noticeably, turned with practiced dignity and went to her bedroom, making ready for her shopping expedition and tea. Katharine stood beside her father, feeling awkward and doing her best not to show it.

"If it's your wish to become one of us, Jesse," Edwin said wryly, "though only God knows why you would want to be, then I promise you I'll do my best to help you fulfill your father's dream. It wasn't so long ago that my father was skinning beaver and trapping in the Northern wilderness. Believe me, I do understand."

Jesse nodded silently and Isaiah grinned.

"We'll find you a tailor and begin your education," said Edwin brightly, trying to lighten the mood. "We'll use your money well, Jesse. We'll invest it in the railroad. I'll take you in as a partner. And I will personally see to it that you learn to read and write."

Jesse looked at him, suddenly feeling proud. A Bible he had wanted to read lay in his knapsack; the thought that he could read the words filled him with gratitude.

He turned his attention from Edwin to Katharine. The heat in his gaze would have struck fire to an iceberg. "Will you school me, Katharine?" he said. When he looked at her, he felt a hunger so raw that he could hardly breathe.

"Father said he would teach you, Jesse," she said helplessly. She felt such a desperate, breathless longing when she looked at him that she didn't know whether to laugh or cry. She knew that if they were in a room alone, she would succumb to her weakness for him. Heat rose to her cheeks as she remembered his powerful body, naked, glistening with sweat, covering her, and his face above her, so intimate and filled with such passion and heat, raining kisses on her lips, eyes, cheeks.

"You teach me, Katharine," Jesse said teasingly. "Make me into the man you want me to be." A vulnerable, defiant look of desire replaced his arrogance. "Whatever you want me to be, Katharine, I'll be," he said. The chemistry and the physical attraction between them was undeniable. "After all," he said smoothly, "I did teach you a thing or two on the mountain, if I recall."

Her eyes flew wide and she glared at him. "Nothing that I care to remember," she retorted defensively. If there had been an object within reach, she would have thrown it at his head and then asked herself later, after she had cooled off, why.

Her father stood nervously between the pair, eyeing them suspiciously. Isaiah just smiled.

"Oh, you will remember, Katharine," Jesse said easily. "All good things come to those who wait."

"Then you'll be waiting forever, Mr. McCallum!"

Jesse threw back his head and started to laugh, watching as Katharine marched indignantly up the stairs. His eyes were twinkling. He loved her.

"I've an eleven-thirty fitting, Father," she called down, trying to regain her composure. "And an afternoon walk in the park with Damien," she shot back at Jesse.

"Damien?" asked Isaiah.

Storm clouds suddenly reappeared on McCallum's face. "The fiancé."

"Fiancé?" Isaiah looked at him curiously.

"Little problem," admitted Jesse.

"You're her, uhm . . . and he's her . . . fiancé? How many men is a Boston women allowed to keep in her tepee?"

"One," Jesse said firmly. "Now I just gotta convince *her*."

"How?"

"I'm working on it," he said with a shrug.

Chapter Twenty-nine

*S*abotage, that's what it is," said John O'Sullivan. Brandy in hand, he stood next to the fireplace, his face set and angry. "That is the third shipment you've lost in the last two months, and I don't think anyone would believe that warehouse fire was a coincidence."

The study was masculine and solid. The impressively high walls were paneled in dark cherry wood with scrolled cornices and elaborate frieze work that was carried over into the beamed ceiling, giving the room an early Tudor feeling, in sharp contrast to the light, French style throughout the rest of the mansion. Bookshelves filled with books on every conceivable subject under the sun flanked a central fireplace formed of green marble.

Edwin Dory was silent. He sat in one of the twin wine-colored wingback chairs flanking the fireplace and stared thoughtfully into the flames. Across from him was Asa Whitney, and on the other side of the room, Jesse stood sullenly and somewhat defiantly, being measured by three tailors for a new wardrobe. Adam Dory, John O'Sullivan and Isaiah Briand and were also present.

"True," Edwin admitted tiredly. "Even with extra security guards posted, the warehouse and everything inside went up in smoke within hours. There was no containing the fire. And now this textile shipment is gone, too."

"You're thinking someone's trying to break you?" Jesse asked.

"Yes," Edwin replied flatly. He turned in his chair and looked at the young man draped in tapes and material of various lengths, smiling when the tailor laid a bright piece of green against his chest and Jesse knocked it to the ground with a flick of his finger. Jesse had been in Boston for over a month, but settling in had been no easy matter.

"I'm no peacock, man," Jesse said evenly. "Dress me like Edwin. I'll have none of that foppish look about me. I'm no dandy."

Heeding the warning, the tailor laid aside the bright colors and picked up rolls of classic fabrics, appropriate in any setting and utterly masculine and refined. O'Sullivan had to admit the young man with his beautifully muscled body would cut a dashing figure whatever he wore.

O'Sullivan grinned and stubbed out his cigar in the brass ashtray stationed on the thick mantel. "You would look a tad dandified in that lime green, boy-o," he said with a chuckle. His good humor, however, was fleeting. Within a matter of seconds, the storm clouds had reappeared in his twinkling, Irish eyes. "You know," he said with more than a touch of intuition, "I've a hunch Damien North has a hand in this, or at least knows who is behind it."

Jesse listened intently. "The fiancé?" he said. He didn't like North and not just because of his association with Katharine.

"That's nonsense, O'Sullivan," said Edwin. "Damien's money is invested in the railroad the same as our money. If I have to pull out of the consortium, it will affect him as well."

"Not necessarily," said Jesse. He had been briefed on

what Asa Whitney and Edwin Dory were trying to accomplish. He knew that Senator Benton had introduced the first Central Pacific Railroad bill last year and it had been accepted. "The laying of the tracks is time sensitive. If we don't meet our goal, we will lose our right to build. It may not effect North as much as you think."

"Why do you say that?" asked Adam. He was reading the paper and had already formed a tentative, wary friendship with Jesse. Certainly the money he planned to invest was coming in handy. On the other hand, he'd known Damien for years. He knew Damien played to win, but he didn't think of him as a cheat.

"Somebody is getting rich off those stolen shipments," Jesse said. "You're not finding them dumped in the harbor or burnt to a crisp in the warehouse. The goods have been stolen, then most likely sold. North would not be affected if he's getting all the profit from those sales."

There was a decided pause in the study as all the men considered that possibility.

"So my question is," said Jesse, "does North seem disturbed by the sabotage?"

O'Sullivan looked at the men assembled and said, "He is the only one of us who doesn't appear to be too worried. He has already offered to buy me out if we run out of time. And"—O'Sullivan locked eyes with the mountain man—"all of this started when you and Isaiah came to town."

"I've heard the rumors," Jesse said. "What do you think?"

"I know you," said O'Sullivan. "He's been talking against you since the moment he found out you were staying at the mansion."

Jesse narrowed his eyes and looked toward the window. He was beginning to hate Damien North. Fortunes could be repaired, but a man was only as good as his reputation.

Adam folded his newspaper and sat forward, frowning. "Come to think of it, North did ask how we were set financially, if we could weather the attacks on the yards. He said if we needed help, he would lend us some money to bail us out. When I told him collateral would be the problem since everything was mortgaged against the railroad project, he just shrugged and said he'd take shares or stock for collateral."

Jesse nodded. His growing suspicions about the man were right.

"He said he would try to help us out if we needed it. He doesn't know about you, though," Adam said to Jesse. "That you're going to invest as a silent partner."

Edwin smiled. "Our secret weapon. We are most grateful to you, Jesse."

The bullion would wipe out the loan, replace it with gold and give them a positive cash flow. Jesse preferred anonymity, and the partners had agreed. Yet he couldn't help feeling a surge of pride at Edwin's words.

"Almost every investor in the consortium has been approached at one time or another by North or one of his men," O'Sullivan said. "He told me that the project was only fit for risk capital and not really worth serious consideration. A few minutes later he said he'd be willing to take my shares, if I wanted to earn a little profit instead of waiting for a sure loss when the easement was forfeit."

"It is one possibility," Edwin admitted softly. "But I prefer to reserve judgment until we have absolute proof. I've known Damien and his family all of my life and I will admit he is an ambitious man, but I don't think he would stoop to a hostile takeover of his friends' fortunes. I'm sure he has some conscience."

It was at that moment that the tailor made the grievous mistake of measuring the inseam on Jesse's leg, touching him a little too intimately on the inner thigh.

"What the deuce are you doing, man?" Jesse said harshly. His burly hand reached down and hauled the tailor up by the collar of his shirt.

"Your inseam, M-master Jesse," he said quickly. His large,

owlish brown eyes widened in fright, and his glasses were skewed to one side. "I need to measure the length of your leg. That's all! I swear!"

Jesse glowered at him for a second, gauged his reaction and then set him carefully down. "Well, just have a care," he said, straightening his vest. "I'm a mite sensitive in that area."

"Oh, I understand completely," said the tailor as he straightened his shirt and knelt in a runner's position with one leg placed in front of the other. He lifted the measuring tape and said loudly, "Now I'm going to place the tape against the inside of your leg!"

Jesse looked at him disdainfully. "I said I was sensitive, not stupid. Don't speak to me like I'm an imbecile, you nitwit. Just keep your hands clear of my privates!"

"Sorry, sir," said the tailor, unable to stifle a grin. Jesse shook his head.

"I did get a little close," the tailor admitted. "I just wanted to make sure your trouser legs fit properly, sir."

"That's not my leg," Jesse said, irritated.

"Yes, sir," said the man, reddening. Isaiah snickered.

"Don't push me, Isaiah. The fool doesn't know the difference between a man's leg and his—"

"Jesse," warned Isaiah. "Mixed company." A blushing young maid was busy pouring tea for Mr. Dory.

"Sorry, miss," said Jesse. The girl curtsied and left the room. Isaiah peeked over his book and grinned. "Don't say a word," warned Jesse.

Isaiah lifted his book and covered half of his face as he read, laughing. He was enjoying this. "I've heard of three-legged milking stools, Jesse, but you are a first."

Jesse changed the subject as quickly as possible. "Edwin, what you need is a man on the wharves, someone who can trap a rat or two." He pointed at his own chest suggestively.

"Jesse, we've tried half of the men in town. No one has been able to prevent the fires or the thefts. It's exactly as O'Sullivan said; it's as if whoever is behind this knows exactly when the ships are coming in and where they are docking. I've already lost four good men; there have been beatings on the wharves, threats to my employees. No, I'm not going to risk you."

"I won't be the one at risk," Jesse said coolly. There was something lethal in his gaze as he looked from man to man. The mountains had schooled him to face the world on terms less than civilized. "When a man is being attacked, he has two choices. He can surrender, or he can go after whoever is attacking him. I won't wait to be picked off like a sitting duck. I want a fighting chance."

"I agree," said Adam. "Count me in."

Asa, Edwin, and O'Sullivan glanced at each other and nodded their heads.

"You're right," said O'Sullivan. "We have to do something."

"Going hunting," Jesse said quietly, looking over at Isaiah, who had placed his book aside. Jesse had more than one reason to go after North.

Isaiah nodded. "Even the score."

"No," said Jesse dangerously. "Wipe him out, whoever he may be. I'm not playing games here, Isaiah. I'm investing over a million dollars in this railroad and I'm not going to lose that money. There have been four more murders, and we are losing men because they are afraid of working the docks. I say enough is enough."

Every man present suspected North, yet he was the man walking with Edwin's daughter on the Boston Common that very evening.

"You can't hang a man on suspicion," said Edwin.

"No, but you can for murder," Jesse replied. "Now all we have to do is prove it."

Katharine and Damien walked quietly through the Common, taking the path that arched around the central fountain. The night was wonderfully warm and fragrant. The wisteria was still in bloom, and the grass had recently been cut so that the aroma in the air was as intoxicating as any wine.

"Have you decided on a date yet, Katharine?" Damien said. As always, he was impeccably dressed. This evening he wore a dashing suit of black and cream, accented by studs of winking yellow topaz, the color of a cat's eye.

"Truthfully, Damien," Katharine said, "I haven't given it much thought. Why do you ask?"

He was thoughtful for a moment, his fingers laced gently but deliberately around her arm as he led her through the park. The distance he felt whenever they were together was growing stronger by the day. He blamed it on his passivity, so he had decided to push her to set a date for their marriage. He didn't want to think that it could be McCallum's presence in the house that was drawing her away from him. Yet, unconsciously, he suspected it.

His fingers tightened perceptibly. It didn't matter. There were many ways to skin a man, or trap a thing of beauty, he thought somewhat dramatically. If there were nothing left of her father's fortune, nothing left for her to fall back on *except him*, wouldn't it be only natural that she would turn to him for help? Of course it would.

His calculating mind thought of killing three birds with one stone. He would acquire controlling shares in the Central Pacific, destroy McCallum and marry Katharine. It was an elaborate scenario, but one he enacted every day in his mind and was putting into practical application.

A few more "accidents" and he would be able to offer Edwin his help, lend him more money and acquire shares in the railroad as collateral. Fifty-one percent was all he needed, but he would rather have it all.

"Damien?" Katharine said, interrupting his musings. She had stopped walking and was standing under a gaslight, looking at him curiously. A few feet behind them, Emiline strolled, accompanied by Jacques, the butler. "Young persons must always be chaperoned," she had intoned gravely while donning her hat. Katharine was of the opinion that Emiline simply enjoyed strolling with the butler. Wisely, she kept these thoughts to herself. There were things she needed to tell Damien about Jesse and herself, things he deserved to know. But she was unable to tell him about the wedding ceremony on the mountain, doubting its validity, and her own strong feelings for the man. Jesse was not acceptable to her mother and never would be.

"Yes, Katharine?" Damien said. He was bored and disliked anyone disturbing him when he was thinking. Even her. Yet as he looked at her beneath the flickering light with the strands of her hair seeming to catch fire, he forgot his irritation and his nostrils flared slightly as he fought the desire to lift those strands and let them run through his fingers.

"Is there some reason we must set a date?

"Nothing in particular," he lied. "By the way, I haven't spoken to your father in days. How is everything going? Has his luck turned around?"

"No," she said. "As a matter of fact, it is much worse."

"How so?"

"Frankly, I don't know how to explain it. No matter what kinds of plans my father makes or how elaborate his warehouse security, something always happens and he ends up with a loss. He shoulders it all and rarely talks about it, Damien, but I know he is worried. We all are."

"I offered Edwin my help," Damien said. "I told him he could use my security guards. He shrugged my suggestion off. For instance, isn't he getting some silks from Indonesia in the next few weeks, and some spices from the Orient?"

"Yes," Katharine said. "But he's made plans to store the textiles in another warehouse further down the coast. He isn't docking in Boston harbor."

Damien stopped strolling and looked at her, staring.

"Hired an army of bully-boys, no doubt, too," he spat, furious. His reaction seemed totally out of proportion to her remark. Angrily he rubbed his temple, wishing he had laudanum, and realizing that it took more and more of the drug to ease his headaches.

"He does what he has to do, Damien! Besides, the 'bully-boys' that I've met seem like good, decent men. Last week some of them risked their lives to put out the warehouse fire. Four were killed when they were trapped inside. They had families, Damien!"

"Of course," he said with an indifferent wave of his hand, regaining control. "Let's change the subject. Let's talk of our wedding plans. Do you want to vacation in Europe for a few months? Take the grand tour?"

Katharine hesitated and didn't reply. She thought about Jesse and Father de Smet.

"South of France? The Caribbean?"

She thought of the kiss and the soft light in Jesse's eyes.

Damien was beginning to feel irritated. "India? An African safari?"

She thought of their wedding night and the stars and the full moon above their heads; his tenderness and her acceptance of him; the passion and the chemistry. She had to put an end to this hypocrisy.

"I need to talk to you about the wedding, Damien," she admitted. "I can't marry you."

He was stunned. "Why can't you marry me, Katharine? It is something we have been planning since childhood."

He was barely breathing.

"I love you, Damien," she said, because it was true.

He inhaled.

"But not the way one should love a husband. You are truly like a brother to me, and a friend."

He exhaled.

"Why?" he shouted. "Am I too much a gentleman for you?" His jealousy came bubbling to the surface with raging intensity. "Perhaps your tastes tend more toward border ruffians and mountain men?"

"Damien, that is unfair!"

"Is it?" He hated McCallum. "It's McCallum, isn't it?" He hated his presence in his fiancée's house. He watched him walk the grounds, groomed to perfection, laughing with Adam, Luke and Dan, playing cards with Nick and Edwin, and he hated him! He spoke to Emily and she responded, letting him carry her about, nestled in the curve of his arms.

"He saved my life," Katharine said firmly.

"Is that all he did?" demanded Damien. There was a mocking light in his eyes. The passion that existed beneath his well-bred facade bubbled to the surface. Not caring what Emiline or Jacques thought, he lost control. " 'Brother,' is it? Well, incest is best, is it not?" He grasped Katharine roughly by her shoulders and kissed her firmly on the lips. "I will wipe every thought of him out of your mind!" he vowed.

Startled, she struggled. "Damien, stop! You must stop!"

"Katharine," he said dangerously, his breath quick on her cheek, "you *must* marry me. I won't take no for an answer!"

"Stop, Damien! You're hurting me!"

"Not half as much as you've hurt me," he said bitterly. He hated her for a moment and he loved her desperately as well. He hated himself for loving her, but was unable to resist the attraction. "You will marry me," he said finally, not letting go of her arm. "I would rather see you dead than with another man."

"Damien!" Katharine cried, truly afraid. She had never seen this side of him. He had been her best friend and they had grown up together, but the hand that held her arm in a bruising grip and the eyes that glared at her so coldly were utterly alien to the Damien she had known.

"You, sir," said Jacques, "are out of bounds! Release that young lady at once!"

Emiline and Jacques moved closer, thinking that their positions as chaperones would give them authority. They were wrong.

"Don't you dare tell me what to do!" Damien said, his voice as frigid as ice water. And where another man's anger might have shown in ruddy skin and shouting, Damien's blood pressure appeared to have lowered, his breathing slow, becoming shallow. He didn't explode in rage but seemed to have cooled to an arctic chill. He was as menacing, dangerous and cold as death. He slapped Jacques open-handed. "I will not be talked to that way by a servant!"

Unprepared for his reaction, Jacques blanched and backed away. Emiline felt the storm and did what any motherly woman would do—she moved closer and batted Damien with her reticule, protecting her charge. Damien laughed quietly beneath his breath, his eyes glittering.

"We're going home now, miss," Emiline said firmly and took Katharine's arm. "And," she said as Damien turned the full force of his attention on her, "I'll brook no interference from you, sir! I may only be a servant, but I'll call the constable and *he'll* make short work of you!" Then she moved swiftly away with Katharine and Jacques in tow.

Damien didn't move. He watched them walk away, feeling betrayed again by Katharine, feeling enraged by her servants' loyalty and feeling powerless to do anything about it, *now*.

"It is the mountain man," he said quietly. He had known the minute he saw them together. "I won't forget this, Katharine. Ever."

Chapter Thirty

I need a word with you, Mr. McCallum."

With his arms outspread and draped with rolls of gray wool, Jesse looked up to see Etta Dory standing in the entrance to the study.

She was glowering, her face as rose-red as the gown she wore. At her right side was the gardener, Somerset.

Jesse looked quickly around the study, a prisoner of straight pins, an overzealous tailor and a million-dollar deal. "Now what have I done?" he asked uncomfortably.

"It's about rhododendrons, Mr. McCallum."

Jesse looked at Isaiah for help, but all he received was a shake of the head. "You are on your own, my friend," Isaiah said beneath his breath, looking down sheepishly.

"Rhododendrons?" Jesse said. "I can't recall meeting anyone by that name, ma'am."

"It's a *flower*, you imbecile," she said stiffly. The color drained out of McCallum's face. Another insult. He shook his head slowly as though warding off a blow and inhaled deeply.

"Well, thank you for that wee bit of wisdom, Mrs. Dory," he said. "But I still don't see what it has to do with me."

"This!" she said frostily.

Turning, she took a sack from Somerset and opened it wide enough for Jesse to see inside, then dropped it at his feet. Jesse looked questioningly at her.

"You'll have to do better than that, ma'am," he said. "I'm from the country and a tad bit slow by your standards. What do those weeds have to do with me?"

"Those *weeds,* Mr. McCallum, were rhododendrons! Healthy rhododendrons, I might add, before you . . . oh, before you . . . I can't say it!" She placed a palm to her forehead and closed her eyes.

Jesse looked at Edwin. "She's doing it again. The faint, I mean."

"Ignore," Edwin said with a tired wave of his hand.

"Somerset!" she shouted, opening one eye, her faint forgotten. "Tell him what he did to my pretty rhododendrons! I just can't bear it!"

"You peed on them!" said Somerset loudly. "That's what you did, you filthy heathen! And not only on my rhododendrons but on every other bush, plant and tree on the premises! You nearly caused the spinster, Miss Jeffrey, to faint dead away yesterday when she saw you watering the wisterias in plain view of everyone!"

Isaiah doubled over, laughing.

"Well, what's so shocking about that?" Jesse said. "What did the spinster think I had between my legs? A rose?"

"Mr. McCallum, you have habits that would disgust a dog!" said Etta.

"And women like you, Mrs. Dory, are the reason men cheat," he shot back.

"How dare you?" she said. "Edwin, you're supposed to support me!"

"I do," said Edwin quietly. "I have the receipts to prove it."

"He should be flogged!" shouted Somerset.

"Oh, I quite agree!" said Etta, her eyes gleaming. "And if someone will hold him, I'll help!"

"I wouldn't advise it," Jesse said acidly. He was standing in the middle of the study with his hands on his hips. There was a threat in his eyes. He was tired of being insulted.

The slamming of the front door and the sound of raised voices stopped further accusations from flying as everyone looked at each other questioningly. First, Jacques entered, his hazel eyes owlish and outraged. Edwin sat mute in his chair.

"Katharine," Etta said very softly when her daughter entered the study, holding tightly to her maid.

Jesse's anger instantly cooled. Katharine's head was downcast, and her maid Emiline looked absolutely livid. He suppressed the urge to go to Katharine, unsure what role he was to play in her life, if any. But he couldn't suppress his love for her and the physical pain he felt at seeing her head bowed.

"What's wrong?" he asked softly. His voice drifted to her, and when she looked up, the sight of her tears felt like a knife in his heart.

"Convention be damned," he whispered. He closed the distance between them and gently took the wrap from her shoulders. Her brothers were standing close by. He looked at her face and her wordless tears and noticed the bruise on her wrist. He didn't move or breathe.

"It was Damien North!" said Emiline in a rush of emotion. "He grabbed the young miss and kissed her full on the lips while walking on the Common! Bold as brass, and he wouldn't let loose until I pummeled him with my reticule!"

"What!" Etta said, truly shocked. "I can't believe what you're saying, Emiline."

"It's true, Mrs. Dory," said Jacques. "He slapped me when I told him to stop."

Katharine looked at Jesse, and something made her whisper, "I told him I couldn't marry him. I think it was more than he could stand. A momentary lapse in judgment." Loyalty and long years of friendship fought with her fear of what had happened. Guilt, shame and a need to please everyone overwhelmed and confused her. "He wouldn't hurt me," she said, unable to believe that he already had. "I'm sorry, Jacques," she said to the butler, apologizing. "Truly. Damien just had a bit too much to drink."

Jacques was silent.

"Stop making excuses for him," said Jesse quickly. He felt a surge of pride at the courage he knew it must have taken for her to tell Damien she wouldn't marry him. Her face was upturned, and when he looked down, he saw a child looking up at him with sad, tear-filled eyes. "Maybe," he said angrily, "Damien needs someone to speak to him about taking liberties with another man's . . ." Jesse stopped, leaving the rest of his thought unspoken. *Should I tell them, Katharine, or will you?* He gave her a threatening, covetous, proprietary and *husbandly* look. He shot daggers at her with his eyes.

"Stop! Just all of you, please stop! I can't take much more!" Katharine burst into tears and ran crying from the room.

"Katharine!" said Etta as she ran after her.

"Sweet child," clucked Emiline and she ran next.

"The cad," said Jacques and he followed. He would not forgive Damien for the slap, ever.

"I've a stronger word than *cad* for him," said Jesse. He walked to the oval table where the brandy decanter sat and filled a glass. His hand was trembling slightly as he lifted the fiery liquid to his lips and sipped. "The son of a bitch," he muttered beneath his breath. He had reached his limit. He turned and hurled the glass into the blazing hearth, shattering it. The liquid caught fire and flared brightly, turning the yellow-orange flames blue. "If he touches her again," he promised, looking straight at Edwin, "I'll kill him!"

"It's not your place," warned Edwin. "My sons will go and have a talk with Damien. And that is final!"

Chapter Thirty-one

Two weeks passed and it was the middle of June. Jesse and Isaiah slipped into the routine of prowling the wharves at night. John had gone back to Capitol Hill, lobbying for support for the railroad, and Dan would be starting his final year at Harvard, studying engineering. Adam was considering the seminary at Cambridge, and Nick enjoyed working in the family business. Luke wanted to accompany Jesse and Isaiah, joking that he could "throw down faster than greased lightning," and proving it when he pulled a pair of Colts from his pocket and fired both simultaneously, hitting his targets with deadly accuracy.

"Dead on," said Jesse.

Luke was hired to oversee the ships coming into port during the day, but at night it was McCallum and Briand who guarded the shipments. One dark man and one light, they blended into the shadows as easily as slipping into another skin. They found rats aplenty along the wharves, animal and otherwise. They worked together like two men sharing one mind, so used to each other that if one gave a single glance, a shrug, a subtle jerking of the hand, the other instinctively moved, ran or bled into a darkened alley, disappearing from sight within seconds.

The dirty little secrets kept coming to light. A shipment of spice from Malay was rerouted and confiscated down the coast, and the expensive cargo turned up in a shop run by an obscure owner. Crates of expensive liquor vanished. And men, once loyal, averting their gazes out of guilt, suddenly left, never to be heard from again.

A war was being fought that could not be ended with a handshake. Nothing could stop it except an equal or deadlier force.

One night as Jesse lay camouflaged beneath a fishing net, waiting for a ship to dock, he thought of Edwin, admitting that he couldn't stomach the older man's weakness. He liked the man, but he considered him weak and ineffectual. Edwin's ideals were high and his adherence to morality unimpeachable. But his Achilles' heel was his compassion, his inability to believe the worst about anyone. "There are always mitigating circumstances, Jesse," he would point out.

Damien had apologized, saying, "I'm sorry for my behavior in the park, Edwin. You know I would never do anything to hurt Katharine. I love her."

And Edwin had believed him. He had allowed the bastard back into their home and Katharine's life! *With her permission, of course!*

That was the part that rankled most, because Jesse recalled bitterly that it was probably his fault. He'd goaded her into it, standing behind her father in the library and baiting her into defying him. He'd shaken his head "No" when her father asked her if Damien had "permission to call once again, under supervision, of course."

Jesse had silently mouthed the words, *Don't you dare, Katharine!*

And just to spite him, she'd agreed.

"Can't Edwin see what a lying snake that man is?" Isaiah had asked Jesse when he heard that Damien was to be allowed to call on Katharine again. The distaste on Isaiah's face was obvious.

"He is a lying snake," agreed Jesse, glad to have someone on his side.

"What I still don't understand," said Isaiah, "is why she married you when she was engaged to him."

"I'd like to think that she married me because she loved me," Jesse had said quietly. "But you remember what happened at the Rendezvous. She felt like a prize bird, and my nest was the safest one around." He couldn't hold it against her. The mountains were a dangerous place for a woman.

"Why'd *you* marry *her?*" Isaiah had asked, laying down a pair of aces, beating Jesse's kings.

"I love her," he'd said simply, cleanly.

"You know, you can only hold on to your foolish pride for so long, Jesse. She is confused. Young. You need to tell her how you feel, court her."

"Court her?" he'd said incredulously. "I'm way past the courting stage. Is this a lecture now?"

Isaiah had shrugged. "Call it what you want. She is the child in you that never got to play because you were spending all your days taking care of your blind father and working a mine when you were barely able to walk. And you? You're the strength that she lacks, or more likely, keeps hidden. Opposites attract. For every taking there has to be a giving. You're the kind of man that makes a woman feel safe. The kind of man that keeps a loaded gun when the wolf comes calling at the door. You defend and protect what is yours, but you are a hell of a gentle, generous man."

Now, lying on the pier, watching the stars, Jesse remembered that moment just as the sound of approaching footsteps caused him to roll over on his side and reach for his knife.

Chapter Thirty-two

*D*amien was alone.

The study was large and cheerful, dominated by a beautiful portrait of his mother. Yet he was brooding; not even her soft blue eyes had the power tonight to exorcise his demons.

Stretched out in front of him were scores of maps with significant points sketched in graphic detail. Beside these were volumes written by surveyors showing the impossibility of placing the tracks through certain geological features—bedrock and granite that had been formed eons ago and would take more than one wagonful of dynamite to blast through. All that would take money.

Which was why he'd decided to let Edwin pay for the process of creating the railroad he intended to take over. His scheme, he thought smugly, was financially brilliant. He reflected quietly for a moment, staring at the burned cigars and half-empty brandy glasses littering the tables and floor. He'd never professed to be a saint and didn't care if anyone knew it now.

In three months the federal government would resume control of the Territory. Then the program would be out of his hands, and there were scores of people who now saw the potential in the railroad, and each one wanted a piece of the pie.

He dropped the maps to the floor.

Angrily he thought of the last few weeks and the sabotage he'd been hiding. Despite all his setbacks, Edwin had not offered him more shares in the railroad. He held a ledger before him and sat there mutely, never hearing the door slide open or the butler enter.

"Sir?"

Damien turned and faced the man, irritation evident on his face.

"So, Tom," he said brusquely, "what is it you want now?"

The butler looked at him calmly, accustomed to his mood swings. Damien had been in the study for the past six hours, undisturbed. "The courier is here with the packages you ordered, sir."

"Tell him I'll be out shortly."

"Yes, sir."

Tom left quietly, shutting the door with as little noise as possible, relieved to be out of the room.

Damien began to straighten his desk, stacking his papers and placing the sensitive ones in the desk drawer. Reaching inside his vest, he produced the cash from the sale of the latest shipload of stolen goods. It wouldn't be enough to keep up with the onslaught of expenses that he was enduring; one after another, the bills rolled in. He had to keep the source of this money quiet. So he kept two sets of books, one to be scrutinized by the board of directors, the other for his own benefit.

Bending over, he carefully rolled the tumblers on his safe. More of his real life was contained in this safe than anywhere else in the mansion. He was glad he was the only one who knew the combination.

What he kept hidden within the safe could send him to prison for the rest of his life—or worse.

With a last look into the mirror above the fireplace, he went to the door and opened it, hoping that tonight's shipment had come in as expected and that his men had no problems *borrowing* it from Edwin.

"You two go on down there to the edge of the pier and stay covered. I can see the boarding lights now. She's coming in through the channel."

The voice was gruff and quiet. The shadow the speaker cast across the planks was huge.

Jesse lay quietly, blending into the darkness, waiting for the man to step nearer. He saw two other men silhouetted against the backdrop of night, their shapes irregular against the flickering wharf lights as they walked toward the shore.

Without moving, he looked to the side of the warehouse, just barely able to make out Isaiah as he positioned himself to cut off all hope of escape for the men.

I don't want to kill you, thought Jesse. Then the calmness overtook him, the moment when no thought entered his mind except to win and survive . . . and to find out once and for all who was behind these raids.

One step.

One footfall and a scrape of heel, then the firm placing of a toe followed by the creak of a plank and the hiss of the night surf rolling in. One more move, closer, and then Jesse could reach out and pull the man down. But he waited, watching silently as Isaiah uncoiled from the side of the building, becoming liquid as the night, sleek and feline, slipping down on all fours, poised like a runner. Isaiah was ready to move and ready to fight.

The three men drew nearer. Jesse waited, sizing them up, intending to save the leader for last.

Then Jesse leapt out, a sinuous movement, quick and forceful. He grabbed the first man's leg.

"What the hell?" he shouted. "Lemme go!" The man struggled, reaching out.

One of Jesse's hands moved around the man's calf while the other grasped the tender skin on the inside of his thigh. With a swift, jerking movement, Jesse pulled him down, hard.

"Jesus!" the man shouted.

"Shut up, you fool!" Jesse hissed.

He slammed his hand over the man's mouth, while he brought his left elbow down like a hammer on his head. There was a moment of resistance, a breath-stealing thud. Then the man moaned, jerked convulsively and lay still.

One down.

Meanwhile Isaiah moved quickly toward the two remaining men as they came off the pier. They probably thought that because there were two of them they could easily overcome the big black man.

They were wrong.

Isaiah flung himself at the pair, caught and lifted and held them suspended like rag dolls, one in each of his large hands; then he laughed, his teeth glinting starkly white against the sheen of his black skin.

"You should have found another job," he said easily and then he shook them like a terrier shaking rats, finally bringing them together and cracking their skulls like ripe melons. They were dead.

Meanwhile, Jesse's opponent had regained consciousness and was on his feet, grappling with Jesse.

"You big devil!" Jesse swore at the leader of the thugs. Ducking his head, he threw his body toward the ground, bringing the man with him. The world went topsy-turvy as they rolled and changed places until finally Jesse was on top and the outlaw lay sprawled on his back beneath him. He was breathing hard and nearly unconscious from the blow to his head, but Jesse was so angry he didn't care; the only thing he wanted from him was a name.

He rolled to one side, sat up and straddled the man, placing his knees on the outlaw's arms. Unsheathing his knife, he held it against his throat in one fluid movement.

"Tell me," he said softly, his brogue pronounced, "who is paying you, man?"

"Go to hell," the man choked out.

"Been there, ain't going back," Jesse murmured and pressed his knees tighter. "Tell me!"

"Christ, let up, man!"

Jesse laughed quietly and pressed the knife tip against the outlaw's throat, drawing a thin bead of blood. "I know ways to make it last until you're weeping blood," he whispered. His eyes were brutal, cynical and determined. He had no pity for the thug. "Tell me," he said through gritted teeth. "Tell me what you know. If you don't use that tongue soon enough, I'll cut it out of your throat."

He pressed again. This time the pair was watched by Isaiah, who stood by to help if needed.

"Who pays you, man? Give me a name," Jesse persisted.

"What do I get out of it?" barked the man.

"You get to live," Jesse said quietly.

The man was silent, contemplating.

"I wonder what you're thinking. You're thinking you can strike a deal. You're thinking wrong. You have nothing to bargain with, so tell me what I want to know and I'll let you go."

"North," he growled sullenly.

Jesse sat back on his heels, nodding grimly, satisfied and not one bit surprised.

He moved, letting the man get up. He always kept his word.

"Look what you did," said the man, wiping blood from his neck.

"Don't whine," Jesse warned. "I don't like whiners. Besides, what's a little bit o' sore neck compared to getting your life back? I wouldn't waste a day of it, if I were you."

There was a reluctant look on the man's face, and Jesse knew he was wondering just how many days he did have left, considering his betrayal of Damien North. Jesse knew it was only a matter of time before the man bolted for high country on a very fast horse.

Without a backward glance, Jesse and Isaiah started the trek down the wharf together. Their silhouettes were evenly matched; large and imposing, both men moved with fluid, easy, athletic grace. They allowed themselves one triumphant look back at the ocean, seeing the prow lights of the frigate as she skimmed homeward, ready to unload her wares. It was merchandise from the East. There was a veritable fortune in her hull, and no one now to prevent the shipment from reaching its rightful destination, or the proceeds from going to the rightful owner.

"Now," Jesse said grimly, "let's see if we can roust that bastard Damien out of the house for good this time and away from my *wife*."

Chapter Thirty-three

*M*ore tea?"

Jesse heard the sweet, lilting voice as he walked down the stairs. *Katharine. Just who I want to see.* He had slept late and awoken to find the sun burning through the window. He was stiff and sore, and a dark purple bruise decorated his arm and wrapped itself neatly around his ribs. It hurt to breathe. But he would heal, and last night had been worth any amount of pain.

He turned the corner and stopped short.

"Thank you, Katharine."

The voice was undeniably masculine, undeniably North's.

"The bastard," Jesse muttered beneath his breath and entered the room.

Stark reality greeted him with the image of Katharine and Damien sitting companionably across from each other, enjoying tea and biscuits in the dining room. Perfect; they looked so perfect together, she with her pale skin and light eyes, dressed in lavender, and North, so impeccably dressed that it hurt Jesse's eyes to look at him. He surveyed him critically, searching for a flaw in his attire, his manners or composure, and couldn't find a thing. Suddenly self-conscious, he was aware of his dark mop of tousled hair, his plain white shirt open nearly to the waist and his dark trousers.

He glared at the pair. It was too late to turn around; she'd spotted him.

"Good morning, Jesse," Katharine said brightly.

"Morning," he said gruffly. He swung one long leg over the back of a chair and sat down, reaching for the platter of eggs with one hand and the rasher of bacon with the other. His forearm was within scant inches of Katherine's pert little nose.

Damien laughed, crossed his legs and looked at Jesse from beneath lowered lids, sipping his tea. But it didn't work this time, that superior look meant to put him in his place.

No amount of window dressing could change the fact that Damien was a criminal. Jesse smiled slowly, helped himself to eggs and bacon, winked at Damien and turned confidently to Katharine.

"I'm still in need," he said softly.

The double meaning of his words was not wasted on her. In the early morning light his heavy-lidded eyes and sexy hair awoke an ache deep within. Blushing, she looked down.

Damien's smug smile began to fade.

"My natural ways offend," Jesse went on. "Teach me, Katharine, how a gentleman should act."

Damien replaced his cup on his saucer and sat up straighter, clearing his throat. His eyes were glittering as he leaned forward. "*You* offend," he said bitingly. "No amount of teaching will change that."

All color drained from Katharine's face and her eyes flew wide in shock and embarrassment.

A cold smile replaced the casual warmth radiating from Jesse when he looked at Damien. With every ounce of self-control he possessed, he replied, "Tell me if your rudeness is arrogance or the mark of a scoundrel?"

Something like understanding leapt between the two men. "Touché," said Damien. Quickly he glanced at Katharine.

"I'm mortified by your behavior, Damien!" she scolded. He knew he was already skating on thin ice with her and her family after the episode in the park.

"You're quite right, Katharine," he conceded smoothly. "It was boorish behavior and a very bad example for your pupil there." He'd waited till four in the morning for his men to arrive; they never had. He'd heard about the altercation on the docks. The shipment had made it through. Luke Dory had caught a man replacing the lables on crates of goods from the Orient, rerouting them to a warehouse that Damien used as a front to store stolen goods. The Dorys still couldn't trace the warehouse's owner, and Damien would make damn certain they never would.

"I apologize, Mr. McCallum. You are being educated, aren't you?" His words held their own double meaning.

Jesse looked at him and nodded, taking a bite of toast. His powerful gaze spoke volumes. "I'm learning," he said. "I have to admit, though, I wasn't surprised."

Katharine looked from Damien to Jesse. The tension between the two was so thick it could have been cut with a knife. "He's doing well," she said in Jesse's defense. "Father has been teaching him math and accounting as well as reading. He says Jesse is a fine student and very good with numbers."

"Is that a fact?" said Damien.

"Yes," said Katharine. "Although Jesse and Isaiah had the whole household singing 'O Mistress Mine' yesterday. The children loved it."

Jesse nodded, laughing beneath his breath.

"Jesse," she said, "you do have a way of turning this house upside down."

"Does that mean you'll be my etiquette teacher?" Jesse asked innocently, spearing a piece of bacon with his fork.

"Of course I will," she conceded. "There is no time like the present, is there?"

"No, can't say there is," he said with a grin as he shoveled most of the remaining eggs and bacon onto his plate. Hungry this morning, he was alert to the possibilities of the day, taking great satisfaction in the expression on Damien's face, which was positively homicidal. "You drift through life in a fog, Katharine," he said, wishing she could see Damien clearly. "Especially where it concerns some people."

"Pardon?" she said, at a loss.

"Yes," Damien said acidly, looking like a snake scenting prey. "What did you say, boy?"

Jesse looked up quickly, spearing him with his sharp, intelligent eyes. "My name is McCallum," he said evenly. "I've been out of knee britches for a long time, and what I have to say"—he thought for a moment—"can wait." Revenge was a dish best served cold.

He chewed his bacon a little, placed his fork to the right of his plate, balancing it perfectly, and picked up his napkin, touching the corners of his mouth. Then he took the same napkin, snapped it open and placed it on his lap, sat up a little straighter, took his teacup, sipped, and replaced it with natural grace.

"Could you please pass the butter, Katharine?" he said. "I learn."

"Even an ape can imitate," said Damien bitingly, "and a parrot can mime words."

"True," said McCallum curtly. He kept his voice level, his thoughts and opinions to himself, biding his time. "But I'd still like the butter, Katharine."

"You have a thicker hide than an alligator," said Damien in disgust.

"And just as big a bite," Jesse admitted. "Seen one of them at the zoo. Butter, please?"

"Jesse!" It was Isaiah at the door. "They need us at the wharf." He glanced meaningfully at Damien and grew silent. Jesse picked up the signal and nodded.

"Let's go," he said, standing up. "Katharine, I'll see you later." He didn't say a word to Damien as he walked out of the dining room.

"Jesse?" Damien called.

Pausing to turn around, Jesse stared coldly at him. "You've got my attention," he said. "What do you want?"

Damien shook his head. "Nothing," he said. "Just wanted to let you know that I will be seeing you later, too."

"Count on it," said McCallum.

Amos Mott had ridden far and long until his future and Boston stretched before him, while behind him was the image of his dead brother, Josiah, tattooed forever on his mind. It was not the love of his brother he missed—he wouldn't have recognized that emotion—but the habit of companionship and familiarity. He'd become obsessed with taking revenge upon the black-haired man with the sharp eyes who had used the butt of a rifle like a sledge-hammer on Josiah's face.

He never thought to ask whether it had been a righteous act; he simply knew that he would do whatever he could to even the score. He'd heard that somewhere in the labyinth of Boston's wealth and poverty, Tom McCallum's son lived and breathed.

"Not for long," Amos muttered. He drove his heels into the horse and headed into town at a lively trot.

Chapter Thirty-four

*D*odge brought the maps but I haven't seen hide nor hair of them," grumbled O'Sullivan. His hand reclined on the mantel in Edwin's study, fingering a tiny gold griffin that Edwin prized. "You know, this whole business has set everyone on edge. They found two men dead near the wharf last night when the *Espiel* docked. Both with fractured skulls."

"I know," said Edwin softly.

"What are you talking about?" asked Jesse as he wandered into the room wearing a well-tailored pair of trousers, cut to show off every muscle in his well-proportioned legs. The white shirt he wore was clean, starched and meticulously pressed, and his hair was styled back in gentle waves. He looked every inch a gentleman, something that came as easily to him as breathing—the diamond showing beneath the rough-hewn mountain coal.

"The murders on the docks," said Edwin.

Jesse poured himself a glass of brandy and turned around to face the two. "Isaiah killed those men. I was with him."

"Good God, man! What are you admitting to?!"

"Nothing but the truth," said Jesse flatly. "They came to rob you and we stopped them. That's about as simple as it gets. If I could have done it without the killing, I would have. There were three of them, Edwin, and they were bought and paid for by your good friend, Damien North. The leader of the three told Isaiah and me."

"I knew it!" shouted O'Sullivan, slamming his fist down on the mantel. "I always knew he was a snake in the grass!"

"No," said Edwin, looking down. "I don't believe it. He is a partner in this business. It makes no sense for him to do this!"

Jesse snorted and tossed back his drink, relishing the fiery liquid as it burned its way down his throat.

"It makes perfect sense," he growled. "We talked about this a few weeks ago. It's the only thing that does. Why do you think he steals from you, Edwin? Diverts your goods? Do you think he tosses them into the ocean to rot? Of course not! He *sells* them! Think, man! You're spending the money to fund the building of a railroad, to pay for labor, supplies and guards. You are doing the work, risking money. All he is doing is waiting for you to go belly up so he can step in and help you right out of your fortune! Stealing your goods is only part of what he is capable of!"

"Piracy surely is a possibility," said Edwin hesitantly. "But he is already a shareholder in the enterprise. Why risk not only his reputation but his neck?"

"Because he doesn't want a share, Edwin, he wants it all," said Jesse firmly. "He's greedy and he has no conscience, and time is running out. The government contracts will be void in August, and he knows I have enough money to keep you going. I think he's been getting away with this for more than a year, judging by your books and the amount of theft and fraud."

"Before you showed up?" asked Edwin.

"I can't say that," said McCallum. "I don't know what would have happened if I hadn't come. My interest was more personal than property. I'm not like you, Edwin, I don't wear the veneer of civilization very well. I know what Damien is capable of and the choices he makes. I know how he thinks, because I'm like him in many ways."

Edwin was beginning to believe McCallum. "You're nothing like him."

"Yes," Jesse countered. "I'm a man who gets what he wants. So is Damien. The difference is, he doesn't care what he does to get what he wants. I do."

Jesse knew that Damien didn't just want control of the railroad, he wanted Katharine, too. "But it's gotten a lot more dangerous for him."

"Because now you and Isaiah know for certain?" said O'Sullivan.

"Yes," said Jesse. "But we can't accuse him publicly until we get more proof. That man we let go last night wouldn't have made it to trial. He'd have been killed, and he knew it. We have to get hard evidence and witnesses."

Jesse looked out the window. He was worried about Katharine. He had been living for two months in the same house with her, married to her in heart, mind and body and unable to act like her husband. He was strong. But this was worse than any torture he could remember.

Edwin looked at Jesse. "Alright," he said evenly. "I'm not convinced, but you have my permission to investigate. I'll do whatever I can to help."

Jesse exhaled in relief, watching in satisfaction as Edwin exited the study.

"You're pressing your luck," said O'Sullivan.

"I know," admitted McCallum. There was a lot at stake, fortunes and family reputations. "At least I have Edwin's support."

"Don't count on it," said a soft masculine voice.

Startled, Jesse turned toward the door. Damien stood framed in the muted candlelight and dark wood, smiling and oh, so chillingly cold!

Chapter Thirty-five

*J*esse! How could you even consider him, Katharine?" said Etta. "He may be making progress and a big splash in Boston with his showy ways, but he is of the wrong class. You have a social position, and that comes with certain responsibilities. I won't even consider a match between you!"

Katharine sat in the garden beside her mother and stared moodily at the nearly full moon drifting through the clouds. It was always the same: position, decorum and *"You must do this"* and *"You must do that"* and *"You must never, never do this!"*

"I won't have a daughter of mine acting like a fool over a man. Now, let's talk about Damien North or Jordan Summers. They are suitable partners for you."

"No, Mother!" Katharine said mutinously. "We won't talk about them! You won't tell me any longer who is or isn't right for me. I have done everything you and Father have asked—tried to be everything I could possibly be to please you, never once asking to be allowed to be myself. But on this, I will not be moved!"

"To be yourself?" her mother said. "What sort of nonsense are you talking? If you aren't yourself, then whoever are you?"

"What you want me to be," said Katharine seriously. "I feel like Pygmalion's statue, except someone has forgotten to breathe life into me. So here I've stood beneath your eyes, quiet and mute, watching your face for every indication of how to move, what to say and what to do. You've chosen my friends, my dress; you've appointed my room with the accoutrements of your taste."

Throwing up her hands in frustration, she cried, "I don't exist!"

"This is insane, Katharine," said Etta. "I only wanted the very best for you. I'm not about to listen to this nonsense."

"No! You *will* listen this time, Mother! You will!"

"This is about McCallum again, isn't it?" Etta said, arching one beautifully sculpted brow. "I never said I hated him. I *like* Jesse."

"I like Jesse, too!" said Katharine. "He may be a rebel, arrogant, opinionated and forceful, but he is a wonderful person! He works hard and tries his best to do what is right for everyone. Just because he doesn't conform to your standards, that doesn't mean he isn't socially acceptable!"

"He drinks straight from the brandy decanter, Katharine. I've seen him."

Glowering, Katharine stood up and walked to the serving cart where the sherry bottle sat. She picked it up and took a healthy swig.

"Like this, Mother?" she said icily. "And of course, he peed in your garden and destroyed your precious rhododendrons, and he wrestles like a bear on the lawn and eats in the kitchen, drinks from his finger bowl and squeezes the lemon into his tea and uses his teaspoon for his soup and everyone loves him, Mother! Everyone!"

"The escargot, Katharine," Etta said, shaking her head. "In front of all of our guests. I was mortified!"

"He was just being thoughtful! When he found out they were snails, he offered you money to buy beef so—"

"I know, so we wouldn't be forced 'to eat bugs.' Noble of him, wasn't it?"

"Yes, it was!" she said. "That is why everyone loves him. No artifice. He doesn't see himself as better than anyone else, though he is as rich as King Midas!"

"I never said your prince was a beggar. But he is not in the social register, Katharine."

"His nobility comes from putting others ahead of himself and his great capacity for compassion and his willingness to help and—"

"Katharine! How you go on! What's gotten into you?"

"Only some much-needed common sense, Mother," Katharine replied. "Father, if you will recall, was nouveau riche, yet you married him. There are eight healthy Dory children to attest that the relationship wasn't *in name only!*"

Etta sniffed. Outside of Beluga caviar, Dom Perignon champagne and *crêpes Suzette*, her favorite pleasure and pastime was whiling away the hours in bed with her husband. Passion was something women of her class rarely talked about but often keenly felt. Etta had married well, making a wise and loving decision. Her eyes would still grow wide and her heart skip a beat when Edwin stepped near, and it was more than social responsibility that caused her to shop for beautiful attire, spend hours in front of a mirror or rigorously censor her diet. She deeply loved her husband, and her goals in life were to be a good wife, mother and a social asset to her husband. She excelled in all three areas.

"Edwin is a good man," she said defensively. Her eyes grew soft.

"Yes, Mother. He is. And so is Jesse! I, like you, am more than a pedigree. I see Jesse as more than a pupil. He is my best friend, my knight in shining armor and my . . ."

She stopped herself in mid-sentence and her small, white hand flew to her mouth as she realized how she really thought of the incorrigible Scotsman.

Husband.

The feeling overwhelmed her like a tidal wave, as brutally forceful and awakening as a miniature tsunami. It was more than sexual heat and chemistry; it was admiration, respect and, yes, *love*, not just gratitude. He wasn't a character in a summer romance novel; he didn't fit the mold of proper or pedigreed. He was *real*. He couldn't be ignored. His presence was so dominating that wherever he went, he was noticed. For better or worse, Jesse made one hell of an impression.

And lover.

"Oh, my God," she whispered. "I'm not a virgin anymore!"

"What?" said her mother. "I didn't hear you. What did you say about McCallum?" Etta moved from the chaise lounge to stand within inches of her daughter. "Are you ill?"

"No, Mother," Katharine said. "Just incredibly confused." Her heart fought with her mind, and in the middle was her body, young and full of fire. "I'm going to my room, Mother." She suddenly felt naked, remembering Jesse's passion. His passion that made her fall desperately in love; fall desperately into his arms, diving deep and taking him with her just as far as she could go. The scent of the man's skin. His heat, his touch.

With a flourish of organdy skirts and silver ribbons, she turned and ran for the mansion, wondering how she was going to put out the flames—and not too optimistic that once she stood near him again that anything on earth could quench her passion and bank her fire.

"Incorrigible Scot," she whispered. "What have you done to me?"

Chapter Thirty-six

*T*he sky, which had been overcast for the better part of the day, sparked with heat lightning and a soft rain began to fall. The windows in the study were open and the drapes moved gently with the wind, now fragrant with salt spray and summer flowers. In the distance sounded the subdued rumbling of thunder, and occasional bursts of lightning scribed the darkened sky with fractured light.

Neither Isaiah nor Jesse spoke a word.

"Look what the cat dragged in," said O'Sullivan. He was done with pretense.

The only sound was the rain falling and the occasional crackling of a dry log. Damien looked at the three men in turn, trying to read their thoughts, which was an exercise in futility. Edwin had returned to the study when he heard Damien's voice.

"How long have you been standing there?" Jesse demanded.

"Does it matter?" Damien replied.

"Yes," he said, "it does."

Damien smiled thinly. "Long enough."

"I haven't the heart for this," Edwin murmured and sat down tiredly in his chair, folding his hands in his lap.

"Well, I do!" blustered O'Sullivan. His fortunes were nearly in ruin. His cash flow had dwindled while his debts had increased dangerously. If there was one chance in a million of proving who was behind the sabotage, then he would push with every bit of strength and money he had left. "I'll not be ruined by a thieving scoundrel!"

"Watch your tongue, O'Sullivan," said Damien dryly. "I just came by to let you know that my warehouse was torched this evening. I suspect it probably is the same thieves who have been plaguing your piers. Or possibly someone who wants to seek revenge for imagined slights?"

"Did you set the fire yourself?" asked Jesse. "Or did you pay one of your bully-boys? Don't insult me by suggesting otherwise. I'm an honest man, not a thief or assassin."

Jesse had reached his limit.

"You're a fool, McCallum. I lost over a quarter of a million in dry goods. Go down to the wharf and see for yourself! I'm not in business to lose money!"

Jesse was sick of the lies and the double-talk, sick of the feigned politeness. He knew Damien was behind everything, including the kidnapping of Katharine. He just wasn't sure why. There was something about that bit of the puzzle that didn't quite make sense to him; not yet anyway. Maybe it was another part of Damien's perfect plan that hadn't gone quite as he expected. A double-cross? By whom? His gaze narrowed, and he focused on Damien's face, trying to read the truth behind the mask.

"Well, hello, gentlemen!"

Jesse's concentration was interrupted by the appearance of the person he was beginning to feel was at the root of all the problems in the room. Katharine.

"Christ," he muttered beneath his breath. "Trouble on two legs."

Oblivious to the growing tension, she walked into the study, masking her irritation with her mother by wearing a bright smile and speaking with feigned cheerfulness. But in her heart, she felt confused and demoralized.

In answer to her greeting, Damien looked quickly at her and then at Jesse. Their expressions mirrored each other's perfectly, seeming to say, *It's not over! Not yet!*

Edwin broke the silence. Sighing, he rose from his chair. "How are you tonight, my dear?"

The stress of the last few months was telling on him; his eyes had deep purple rings beneath them that told of countless sleepless nights, and the lines on his face that used to be merely creases from frequent smiles had deepened into worry marks that moments of repose could not erase.

"Fine, Father," Katharine said. "I was just wondering how the preparations were coming for the dance welcoming Jesse to Boston. Mother has said scarcely a word about it."

Her voice, having started on a festive note, drifted away sadly, losing whatever momentum and energy she had endeavored to put into the words.

"As far as I know, everything is fine," her father said. "But frankly, I'm a little surprised that your mother hasn't been more involved. It isn't like her. Perhaps you can find out why that may be."

"I'll try," she said, secretly thinking that the guest of honor was the reason for her mother's less than enthusiastic participation.

Edwin placed his hands on her shoulders and kissed her forehead, turning her firmly toward the door. "Go on, now. Find that little Emily and go see about your mother. Tell her I've arranged for Jesse to be your escort that evening. It's appropriate since he is the one being honored."

Katharine was stunned. "You've done what, Father?" she said.

"I've made arrangements for Jesse to take you to the dance. Isn't that right, Jesse?"

McCallum played along. He knew what was going on. "All been arranged," he said quietly.

"I wasn't consulted," she objected.

"It isn't a choice, Katharine," Edwin said. "Trust me in this, will you?"

Sensing that there was more going on in the room than polite conversation, Katharine looked from her father to Jesse, then glanced quickly at Damien, who was glowering at them all. "I'll consider it part of his education," she said finally.

Jesse was piqued by her attitude. He was leaning against the bookshelves, gazing at her. His eyes were hard and flinty. "Consider it whatever you want, lady. I'll be ready to dance."

"So will I," said Damien smoothly. "Save room on your dance card for me, won't you, Katharine?"

"Of course I will," she said, bewildered.

Damien nodded, bowed and left, the sound of the slamming door echoing ominously in the mansion.

Jesse turned away from Katharine and stared into the fireplace. *That is one event you are going to wish you had missed, Damien,* he thought. *I promise.*

Chapter Thirty-seven

*A*sa Whitney stood on a washed-out brown granite precipice that jutted out from the side of a mountain a thousand feet above sea level. With him were Dodge and Fremont and Edwin's son Adam. July had come padding across the Southwestern desert like a tawny-eyed lion, devouring every blade of green or leafing plant in sight, leaving only bare pinion pines and thorny mesquite growing on the granite ledges of the Royal Gorge.

"How in the hell," Asa muttered, "are we going to build a track through *that?*"

The wind blew and shoved him gently back—a nudge to let him know who ruled the canyon.

"Narrow gauge," said G.M. Dodge. He had seen the schematics and knew it could work.

"If you say so," said Asa. He raked back his iron-gray hair, obviously not convinced, but open-minded enough to want to be. "But frankly, gentlemen, the best thing to do with this desolate hole would be to fill it in."

Fremont laughed and so did Dodge.

"There is a rich history here," Fremont said affably. "Legends left by the Utes and Blackfoot, even a rumor of a stolen government gold shipment of over seventy-five thousand dollars hidden in these rocks."

"Well, now, that we could use," mused Asa. He was worried about money. "What we need is a bridge across this span," he said, indicating the breadth of empty space over the gorge, beneath the rock formation known as the Three Chiefs, which was said to guard the gorge. "Going to have to fight the skunks, coyotes, bobcats, cougars and porcupines for space, though, I think."

"Don't forget the deer and the jackrabbits," added Fremont.

What we need is someone to help us find the buried treasure. Now, that would come in handy."

Dodge was silent. He stared at the gorge, thinking of a cable bridge and how to build it. He looked down the narrow canyon walls of granite, seeing the thin gauge line snaking across a path blown clean by dynamite. He saw the bridge as clearly as if it already existed. The transcontinental railroad was his dream. He would never have guessed that he would be the engineer who actually completed the project.

Fremont smiled. "Let's go get the men together and see if we can work out the schematics and find a mule path down this hole. That'll be a start."

A clattering of hooves caused the men to turn in surprise. Shielding his eyes with one hand, Asa looked south, watching as three riders approached, all wearing cavalry blue with their hats drawn down over their foreheads, riding hard.

"Now what?" he murmured.

It didn't take long for the riders to close the distance.

"Lieutenant McGuire!" said Asa in surprise when he recognized the leader. "What brings you out here?"

Asa reached forward and took the bridle in his hand, smoothing the forelock of the animal. McGuire was covered in sweat, and a powdery sheen of dust coated his face and caked his eyelashes and brows.

"News," said McGuire roughly. He reached for his canteen and took a healthy swig of water, replaced the cap and looped the leather thong over the saddle horn. "Now that I've washed the dirt out of my throat," he said tiredly, "I have some information that you might find interesting."

"Oh?" said Asa curiously. "What?"

"We think we know who killed Hugh de Angelucci," McGuire said. He reached into his saddlebags and pulled out a white cloth. Inside was a cuff link made of gold with a bright, shining topaz encased in the center. He tossed it to Asa. "Turn it over," he said.

Asa did. On the back was an engraved name that took his breath away. He looked twice to be sure he hadn't misread it. He hadn't.

"Where did you find this?" he asked hoarsely. The image of Hugh's handsome young face swam into his consciousness. He saw him working with block and tackle, hooking ropes and steel clips to the sides of the granite cliffs, ingeniously lifting pack animals over seemingly insurmountable obstacles, setting up equipment early in the morning and working long into the evening, playing cards until the wee hours, laughing, sitting in his library so absorbed in ancient volumes and out-of-print manuscripts that nothing short of a stick of well-placed dynamite could've moved him; sometimes so serious and absorbed, yet so caring and compassionate, so willing to help anyone around him.

"Hugh," Asa said softly. "A very good man." A flash of anger erupted in his eyes. He wrapped his fist around the cuff link and squeezed it tightly. His jaw worked slowly from side to side as he handed the cuff link to Adam. "Time to catch a rat," he said.

Adam looked at the cuff link, did a double take and then nodded his head in agreement. "The sooner the better."

Chapter Thirty-eight

*W*hat is it now, Tom?"

The irritation in Damien's voice at the appearance of his butler was unmistakable. He still couldn't believe his loss at the wharf. Nearly a quarter of a million in dry goods, gone up in flames, and he believed McCallum had had a hand in it.

"There is a man, sir—"

Before he could finish his sentence, the butler was shoved aside and the door was flung back. A huge man walked through. He was thick-jawed, heavily mustached with a star-shaped scar on his cheek, and a double set of crisscrossed bandoliers strapped across his brawny chest.

" 'Member me?" the man said softly. Turning, he grabbed the butler by his starched shirt and shoved him through the door, sending him sprawling across the marble foyer.

"We got us some talking to do," he said.

Then he closed the door.

* * *

Jesse haunted the docks, a hunter without prey. The rats had fled in fear and now he held sway in this misty kingdom by the sea. Restless, the water churned; restless, nightly he burned, filled with a longing he could not satisfy, for a woman who seemed to be slipping from his grasp.

He stood on the end of the pier and watched the surf rise and boil and twist around dark columns thrust deep beneath the water's surface.

"Makes you wonder what is on the other side," said Isaiah.

"Not me," said McCallum. "I'll take the mountains and prairie. That good earth is like a man's wife—you plant a seed and something grows. But the ocean, she's like no other. Plow a furrow and plant a seed, look behind and it's like you've never been there; she's indifferent to man and beast, with no past or future."

Like Katharine in a way, he thought, *oblivious to the undertows in her life threatening to destroy her roots and her future.*

"I can't quite get over Edwin Dory," said Isaiah. "It's been two days since we told him about Damien. What's it going to take before he throws the bastard out for good?"

"Proof," said Jesse. "Edwin told me he couldn't take a thief's words over a gentleman's. I almost asked him to show me the gentleman, because all I see when I look at North is a thief. And there's something else. Edwin told me it was Damien's man who knew where to look for Katharine in the Territories. Men go to the mountains to lose themselves; no one can find a man there unless he wants to be found, or someone knows where he is. Maybe North had a hand in the kidnapping too."

Across town that night as McCallum and Briand prowled the docks, safeguarding the shipments, a telegram arrived by special messenger from Adam addressed to his father. It contained seven simple words: *Raise money. Found the way! Coming home.*

"Thank God," said Edwin, visibly relaxing. "Finally some good news."

He walked over to his desk and flipped open the ledger. He ignored the redlined negative balance and went to the sheets filled with inventory, quickly assessing which items could be sold the fastest and with the greatest return.

O'Sullivan stood behind him and peered curiously first at the telegram and then at the ledger. "Why," he said quietly, "don't we just ask Jesse for some more money? He's offered more than once."

"I can't," Edwin said simply. "I just can't take advantage of that young man. He is already doing so much for us. The shipments are coming in again, and we finally have restocked our warehouses. There is actually a possibility of profit in the midst of this fiasco, all because of that young man and Briand. I just can't ask them for more help."

O'Sullivan smiled. "Whether you ask or not, I think you'll get his help regardless. McCallum has a score to settle. I have never seen a man look at another man the way he did Damien. He is just biding his time before he lowers the boom."

"For one reason . . . and one reason only," said Edwin quietly.

The men looked at each other and said simultaneously: "Katharine."

"The way I see it, mister," said Amos Mott, "you owe me."

He and Damien stood together in the darkness outside the mansion's library on a broad terrace that continued its Byzantine theme in stylishly tiled walkways, elaborate urns overflowing with ferns and ivy, scrolled motifs of dragons, and enticingly shaped maidens formed in marble and placed throughout the water garden.

There was a quietness about the place that Damien usually found soothing, but not tonight. Tonight he stood in front of a man he found curiously compelling—riveting and enigmatic in the strangest sort of way. He studied Mott in the muted light, looked at the eyes that held no emotion. Damien searched for a glimmer of something recognizable as human within their depths, something above instinct, and couldn't find a thing.

"I owe you nothing," he replied flatly, waiting for a reaction. "It was you who torched the warehouse, wasn't it?"

"Just a start," Mott replied. "I mean to see you pay."

Other men would have been afraid of Amos Mott, Damien knew. Other men would have needed a platoon of armed guards, or felt they did, but not Damien. He carried his weighted cane, ever ready . . . and the slight bulge beneath his jacket was caused by a pistol, loaded and within easy reach. If he needed to use it, he wouldn't waste time wounding Mott. He would kill this man without hesitation. Still, there was something fascinating about Mott's movements, as though he were a puppet whose actions were not guided by consciousness.

"Remarkable," Damien murmured, noting Mott's flat reaction to his statement. It was like hurling a brick into what you thought was a pool of water, waiting for the splash, and finding that you'd tossed it into quicksand. "I'm bored," he muttered. "You're wasting my time. What did you come to Boston for? You know you can't stay here! Your brother took matters into his own hands, double-crossed me. I repeat, I owe you nothing, you insect. As a matter of fact, I think it's you who owes me. That warehouse cost me a quarter of a million dollars. You owe me, you dirty bastard!"

Confident of his ability to bully everyone around him, Damien was unprepared for what happened next.

Mott's hands shot out and closed around Damien's throat, cutting off his air. Then he was lifted straight up until his feet were dangling above the terrace, flailing in midair.

"I want him," said Amos. Then he squeezed Damien's throat. "I mean to kill him. Then I might just kill you, too."

"Who?" Damien managed to choke out, baffled.

"Jesse McCallum."

Common ground.

"Put me down, you imbecile," Damien muttered as his fingers worked against the hands that held him. "Seems we're not so far apart after all."

A glimmer of a thought appeared like a phantom in Amos's dark eyes. He lowered Damien slowly to the ground and released him, stepping back.

With a perfunctory movement, Damien straightened his clothes and raked back a thick handful of hair, impaling Amos with a thoroughly brutal stare. Laughing softly, he shook his head at the irony of life. "Jesse McCallum. I want to kill him, too. Let's talk money here. How much do you want?"

The eyes that showed no emotion suddenly came to life at the mention of money.

"What'll you give me?"

"Whatever it takes. I want McCallum dead!"

Chapter Thirty-nine

*T*he end of July brought the festive dance held in Jesse's honor. The chaperones attended tables laden with gloves and fans for the women, which propriety demanded must be changed at the end of every dance set. The orchestra was in place. The candles and gaslights were ablaze, beckoning all to enter.

A subtle tension filled the air as everything was made ready inside and out for the grandest affair of the year. The servants stood smartly at attention, waiting outside as the first carriages rolled majestically down the street.

One by one, the carriages stopped in front of the mansion and the guests descended, elaborately and elegantly dressed, smiles touching the corners of their lips and anticipation brightening their eyes. The party was sure to be a success if measured only by the number of people in attendance. Inside, the maids were busy taking wraps and hats, while butlers and attendants led the way to the main ballroom.

Etta Stanford Dory stood beside her husband and cordially greeted their guests as they entered the foyer. Emily had taken a shine to Etta. The young girl was dressed in pale lavender and stood quietly beside her, gazing seriously at everyone who entered. Etta found herself doting on Emily, and had begun taking her to the best specialists in Boston. Katharine had been right: it was not difficult for Etta to find room in her heart for one more child.

In the candlelit ballroom festooned with flowers, the orchestra struck up a gay tune and the guests began to dance. Etta smiled fondly at Edwin as Emily danced with her pinecone doll, humming softly, turning in little circles beside them.

Near the garden door, Katharine watched Emily with amused eyes. Surrounded by eager-eyed young men wishing to be included on her dance card, she realized how changed she was since her mountain adventure.

"Pencil me in, won't you, Katharine?" said one young gentleman. She recognized him as a Newport, of good family and handsome. Once, she would have delighted in flirting with him; now she was uninterested.

"Of course," she said politely.

"Me as well," said his brother. "May I have the first dance?"

"She gave that to me," said the first brother.

"Don't be so sure!" argued the other. "I asked to be first. You simply supposed you were!"

"Now, gentlemen," Katharine began, seeing a potential argument coming. "Really, there is plenty—"

She stopped in mid-sentence and stared at the open door.

"I'll never ask permission or apologize for wanting to dance with you all night long. There should be only one name on your card, Katharine." The voice was pure silk, confident and masculine. *McCallum*. He came through the door and stopped in front of her with an amused and ironic smile on his face.

"Oh?" said the first Newport. "And just whose name should be crowding out ours?"

Jesse took out his handkerchief and dabbed like a dandy at his upper lip. Then he winked slowly at Katharine and grinned like the devil himself.

"Mine," he said. Taller than most men, he radiated animal magnetism, virility and pure sexuality.

"Jesse," she breathed.

"The very same," he said. Smiling, he pointed to his tuxedo, which was cut to fit every well-defined angle of his body. His starched white shirt was pulled taut over his well-muscled chest and broad shoulders; his hair was cut in the European style, slightly long around the top and sides and combed in sensuous waves, framing his face.

"Who?" said one of the brothers, bewildered.

"Who?" echoed the other.

"My escort and tonight's guest of honor," Katharine said. "My student, my nemesis, my knight and my secret sin, that incorrigible Scot, Jesse McCallum."

McCallum started to laugh. "Finally," he said. His dark eyes were smoldering as he looked at her. He had been denied for much too long what he believed was rightfully his. *Katharine.* "Giving in?" he asked.

"No," she replied, shaking her head with an uncomfortable laugh. He pretended a pout, and she noted the covetous glances bestowed on him by most of the women in the room. A new feeling competed with her desire: jealousy. She admitted to herself that she ached for him.

"Wait!" shouted the Newports in unison. "What about us?"

"Sorry, boys," said McCallum. "This woman's mine."

Then he took her dance card from her hand and tore it in half, tossing it over his shoulders. Their eyes met, and something like the feeling that had first overwhelmed her so long ago in the mountains—a peculiar sensation that she had looked into those very same eyes before—washed over her in familiar, aching waves.

"Dance?" she said somewhat breathlessly as he took her in his arms with a no-nonsense tug.

"Anything you want, lady," he replied. *Mirrors*. She saw her emotions mirrored in his. They were Adam and Eve in Eden, finding paradise within arm's reach.

A soft, radiant and knowing smile lifted the corners of his lips. His eyes were on fire, the lids half closed. *Fated*. He looked at her mouth and nearly growled.

"Christ," he said, made helpless and weak by the passion he felt for her. "I'm starving for you, girl." He reached up and touched one rough hand to the curved bow of her lips. Lightly he traced the edge of her chin, following the natural line of her graceful neck down her throat and across the smooth expanse of her bared shoulders and the mounds of her heaving breasts. The wealth of her red hair cascading over her shoulders made him close his eyes, captive to her charms. Without thinking, he reached instinctively for her. Transfixed, she didn't move. She let him touch her in full view of everyone at the dance, unaware and uncaring, enchanted by the man who held her so possessively against him.

His arm tightened around her narrow waist.

"Why," he said, "did you torture me for so long? You've made a beggar out of me. I'll never forgive you for that." He wanted to kiss her.

His hand moved softly, savoring the touch of her warm skin as it traced fiery trails across her chin, touching the cleft barely visible, gliding upward to feel the angle of her jaw, the basin beneath her small, shell ear, falling along the edge of her throat and the hollow ridge above her breasts. He turned her face upward to meet his touch.

"Stop," she whispered. Suddenly she placed her hand firmly over his, shaking her head. "Please." The music drifted like her frail words, fragile between them. Suddenly self-conscious as though coming out of a hypnotic dream, she became aware of all the eyes watching them. "I've made a beggar of you and a fool of myself," she said. A guilty blush heightened the color of her cheeks and an internal fever turned her eyes into the brightest green he had ever seen. Her breathing was ragged and quick. "Please, stop."

"Yes," said an icy voice, "do stop, please."

Katharine started at the sound of the familiar voice and turned to see Damien standing nearby. His eyes were narrow and hard, and the look on his face defied explanation. She gazed from one man to the other. Jesse's face was impassive as stone.

Everyone in the room pretended to be minding his or her own business. They were so well-bred that they knew it wasn't polite to interfere, yet they were human enough to strain to catch every exciting word and glance, all grist for teatime conversation and salacious observation.

McCallum was earning a reputation. They heard he hunted felons at night, while by day, he studied accounting. He could beat the boxers down on the wharves or sip from a demitasse in the finest drawing room. They knew he was as rich as King Midas, heard his origins were Scottish and that he fancied Katharine. But there was something uncommonly dangerous about the man. He was rather like a tiger on a short leash; the kind of man every woman warned her daughters about yet secretly admired and wished to admit to her bed.

"We had a dance tonight, Katharine," said Damien, reminding her. He would not be deterred by the presence of the Scotsman.

"*Had*," said McCallum.

"Gentlemen, please," said Katharine helplessly. She was caught in the middle of an impending firestorm and found it difficult to breathe or think. Every nerve in her body was on fire, and every place that Jesse had touched seemed to remember his warmth long after his hand was removed.

Dizzy and not one bit interested in the buzz of conversation around her, she looked at McCallum, realizing just how dangerous he truly was to her and her sanity, let alone her standing in the community.

At that moment, if she could have removed him from her presence, her memory and her mind, she would have. If she could have taken Damien into her arms and quenched the fire that McCallum had kindled, she would have. Ruefully, she admitted that it would be like trying to douse an inferno with a cup of tepid water.

"Jesse is my escort tonight, Damien," Katharine said evenly. "The first dance is ours." She started to reassure Damien that they would dance later that evening, but McCallum moved to stand directly in front of Katharine, barring Damien's view of her.

"The first dance and the last are mine," Jesse said with deadly calm. The look on his face was challenging. He wanted Damien to make the first move, to hit him; in fact, the Scot was praying North would give him a reason to take him down.

Damien read the look in his eyes and smiled dangerously.

"Of course," Damien said graciously, appearing to acquiesce. "Even bears and apes can be taught to dance." Then he smiled, bowed and drifted with elegance and grace into the crowd. "Teach, my darling Katharine," he said over his shoulder, "and one of these days I promise to give you a lesson you'll never forget." It was a veiled threat.

Instinctively Jesse moved forward, watching protectively with the eyes of a hawk as Damien nonchalantly began to dance with another young woman. "He'll not get near you again."

Shaking off his anger, he turned to Katharine and took her in his arms. Somehow he felt relieved; intuitively he sensed that he had rescued her again. He did not trust North at all. Yet he was aware that in Boston society, Damien was considered a more suitable match than he would ever be. He finally accepted society's opinion of him as he held his borrowed treasure in his arms, touching her as gently as possible.

"Let your ape dance with you tonight, Katharine," he whispered. "And in the morning, I'll remember you like a fallen angel remembers the light." Smiling ruefully as he wondered if he was losing her again, he moved elegantly to the music swelling through the room, a waltz as gracefully beautiful and seductive as the natural chemistry that existed between them. "You will haunt me all my life," he predicted, "this trained ape."

"Man," Katharine corrected. She heard the hurt beneath the word. His face, angled in the glowing lights, was shadowed by the sweep of dark hair falling over his forehead. His expression was closed and guarded against her.

"Grant me absolution," he said. He pulled her close until no space existed between them. The room flowed on the wave of music, which built and rippled through the scented air, a kaleidoscope of melting colors as the women moved and the petals of their gowns shimmered like pastel flowers attached to their gallant, dark-stemmed escorts. Johann Strauss was the unifying force that formed the dancers into a single, moving entity.

"Absolution," Katharine said. "If that is what you need."

"No," he said. "I need you. Absolution cannot save me from wanting you. It's too late."

"For both of us," she said. She knew every tongue was wagging. So she ignored the demands of society, free in his arms. She looked at no one except him. His hand was placed in the small of her back, a light, firm pressure that she enjoyed; the feel of each separate finger pressing against her skin evoked a feeling like chords of a trembling song. She remembered making love to him, his body above hers, dominating the night, eclipsing her world. She adored the feelings he evoked in her, opening to him trustingly. The sweetness of surrender blossomed as she wound her arms around his neck, pulling him to her. She had claimed him that night, chosen him and honestly admitted to wanting him. They'd made love.

As he sensed her mood, his eyes became heavy-lidded, languid as though he were drugged. She could feel his heart pounding against her breast. It had been so long since he had held her this close! Propriety demanded they dance, but not be too close; instinct pushed through the barriers that etiquette built. They passed the point of no return; they tumbled into the abyss, two angels falling.

His skin was hot to her touch.

"My borrowed darling," he said ruefully. He tried to look away but couldn't, damning himself beneath his breath.

"My secret sin," she taunted, teasing just a little. Her hand resting on his shoulder moved to his neck, caressing and gentle, moving upward, toying with the ends of his hair, moving around the outer edge of his ear. His eyes darkened in response, and he exhaled, losing control.

"Don't toy with what you can't control," he warned.

"I'm not playing," she said. Her lips were moist, and she laughed in her gentle, self-conscious way until her dimples appeared and she looked away, helpless in his arms. She placed her face against his chest, listening to the reassuring beat of his heart. She felt comforted and safe as he waltzed her into the garden.

Love.

She lifted her eyes and drank deeply.

He smiled as he looked down into her upturned face, and tightened his grip.

She plunged completely under his spell.

Dancing, they forgot the world, wagging tongues and the last few months. They forgot the pain of separation, angry words and the futility of trying to decide who was right and who was wrong. They knew this was a battle neither could win. Katharine heard Jesse laugh softly, and she felt his hand move a little lower, touching the deep curve of her back, poised above her bottom; the feeling sent a shudder through her so strong that her eyes closed in response.

"I need you now," he whispered into the wealth of her hair, into the shell of her delicate pink ear. "Reject me or love me, but decide." Their bodies moved to the rhythm of Strauss, dancing on the rippling currents that floated through the open door. They drifted helplessly together into the sheltered seclusion of the summer garden.

Instead of speaking her answer, she clasped her hands tightly around his neck, pulling him closer. Her feelings overwhelmed her, and she was swept away by a passion stronger than any words could describe. Under the artful pressure of his hands, her clothes melted from her skin like the petals of a summer flower in the heat of the midday sun. He kissed her throat, her breasts, and her open mouth. He lifted her and lay with her in a secluded gazebo, making love to her in slow, languid movements, savoring every touch. Falling, falling, falling . . .

"I love you," he whispered. "Believe me when I tell you that I can't live without you. I tried." Tears filled his eyes, and he touched her face with a trembling hand. "I tried."

"You came two thousand miles to tell me that?" she whispered against his cheek. Her bed had seemed empty every night, her pillow like a companion in her dreams that brought disappointment when she awoke. He was only a few doors from her room, but he could have been on the other side of the world.

"No," he said. "I came two thousand miles to hold you in my arms. I'll never let go." Searching her face, he was lost in her eyes. Burying his hands in her hair, he kissed her deeply. "Never."

On the perimeter of the dancers, Damien stood surrounded by beautiful women and snubbed, for the most part, by men. "News travels fast," he mused beneath his breath. Suspected, but not proved, a thief, a scoundrel, a murderer. His résumé of assumed crimes was impressive from a felon's point of view. However, he didn't consider himself one, believing that if he simply lay low for a while, the scandal would blow over and the gossip would turn to someone else. He almost thought it was funny. Almost.

Ironically, the women's opinions were not changed by the talk about him; indeed, their interest had been piqued. "Have I become a dangerous curiosity?" he wondered. A tide of beautiful ladies surrounded him, competing for his attention, wanting to prove, he supposed, that they were more desirable and more exciting than Katharine. Yet it was she his heart was set on marrying. There were moments when Damien wondered if it was the woman he craved, or the sport of acquiring what everyone else seemed to want.

He noticed with a stab of jealousy that she was not in the ballroom, and neither was McCallum. "Pity they banned public flogging."

He would see both of them on the block of public humiliation if he could. He had finally admitted to himself what everyone in Boston knew: Katharine Dory was in love with Jesse McCallum.

Pivoting on his well-shod heel, he headed for the door. There was no point in staying here any longer; if he did, someone was bound to be hurt. And causing a social scene was not something he would enjoy; it was too public, too revealing, and this was definitely not the time. Still, he would love to own Katharine, for a little while, use her like he felt she had used him, and then destroy her utterly. He would not be made sport of or insulted.

"They eat, they dance," he said coldly. "Well, I have an amusement of my own."

He thought of the huge, hulking man who now lived in his house. His presence was always looming, silent and threatening, over the mansion. No one would relish his leaving any more than Damien would.

He had hired Josiah and Amos Mott a few years ago to

handle any job that required strong-arming the competition, threats or intimidation. They were useful men whose lack of remorse had earned him a healthy profit until they double-crossed him. Now he had added Amos Mott to his list of victims; he was just waiting for the right time to extract a full measure of revenge.

"Damien? We need to talk to you."

He turned. Standing near the door to the library were Nick, Luke and Dan Dory. Shrugging indifferently, Damien walked to the room and looked inside. John O'Sullivan was there, and Edwin Dory was standing in front of the hearth, gazing into the fire. He turned to face the men.

"I have some interesting news," said Edwin. "There has been progress made by the surveyors and engineers regarding the best route for the transcontinental."

Damien nodded. "So I've been told." He had his spies working in strategic locations, informing him of courier activity, visitors, bills being pushed through Congress and any other information concerning the building of the railroad. After all, he had a great deal of money invested.

"The Cimarron Trail along the Arkansas River has been rejected; so now it's between the Oregon and Mormon Trails. Because of Benton's antislavery stance, he has been voted out of the Senate and is running for the House of Representatives. We didn't lose him, strategically; he has just been repositioned."

"Cut to the chase, Edwin," said Damien, tired and irritable. "Which route to the Pacific is the most viable? Central or southern?"

"Asa is for a central route. We've reached the Great Lakes, and he thinks the next logical jump is to Chicago and then onward to Oregon via the South Pass in Wyoming, across the Sierra Nevadas, then on to the West Coast. Jesse has traveled that route many times and says that the South Pass is open even in winter."

"Well, by all means, Jesse is the authority," said Damien

snidely. "It'll be a cold day in hell before I venture into that godforsaken territory again." He was suddenly alert and focused, wondering where Edwin was going with this. *Tread lightly*, he warned himself. "Would that change the terminus along the Missouri?" he asked. "Would it still be Saint Louis?"

"Possibly," Edwin replied. "There is some talk of Omaha, along the Mormon Trail. There is a cartel forming in Sacramento to build a railroad from west to east. I suppose the two lines could meet in the middle, in which case a port along the Missouri River makes sense. Asa thinks opening up the Territory to settlement will pay for the building of the railroad, or at least offset the cost. Personally, I think he is right. He has presented his plan to Congress and distributed brochures at his own expense, promoting the central route."

"Otherwise, Providence will provide, eh? Maybe it will rain pennies from heaven," Damien said sarcastically, taking a jab at O'Sullivan's belief in Manifest Destiny. "The settlers may pay for every other section of land, but they will not cover the cost of labor and supplies. The railroad needs us. Our money."

O'Sullivan looked at him angrily. "You're not the only investor, Damien." It was only money to Damien, but for John L. O'Sullivan and many of the men pushing the idea of the transcontinental, it was about building a nation out of a patchwork of states and territories littering the continent.

"You're right, I'm not the only investor," said Damien. "Just the largest, and the one with the majority of shares. I've been carrying Edwin for months, and he has been giving me what most consider junk collateral in those shares of stock. Are you going to suggest otherwise, O'Sullivan?"

Edwin shook his head. Damien was like a keg of dynamite with a short fuse. It was true. He owned the ruling shares in the company. No decision could be made without his consent. "I've ransomed my family's future," murmured Edwin beneath his breath, but not quietly enough to keep Damien from hearing him. Edwin didn't have the heart to ask McCallum for the funds to bail them out, even though his situation was dire.

He looked up to see Damien gazing at him with a smug gleam in his eyes. He hated that gloating appraisal almost as much as he hated the feeling of having to entrust him with decisions regarding his family's future.

"If I can be of any more assistance, Edwin," said Damien pleasantly, "just let me know. I'll have my banker draw up a note for any amount you need and deposit it in your account right away." The unspoken clause was there as well: *In exchange for more shares of your railroad stock.*

"You need money?" said Jesse. The smile on Damien's face faded. Turning, he watched as Katharine and Jesse walked into the library together, their arms linked securely around each other's waists.

"Did you enjoy your walk in the gardens?" Damien asked thinly. "Or was it something besides walking that you found so entertaining?" Katharine visibly paled, and Jesse took a threatening step forward. He wouldn't allow Katharine to be insulted. The flaring of Damien's crystal-blue eyes resembled twin blue flames. He was jealous, and thinly veiled aggression boiled off of him in waves.

"Excuse me, please," said Katharine. "I need to find Mother." She sensed the danger in the situation and thought it best if she left the room quickly.

"No, excuse me, Katharine," Damien said coldly. "I'm the one who is in the way. It's time for me to leave." With a curt, thin-lipped nod, he turned and walked toward the door, but stopped. He had the majority of shares in the railroad, but Katharine, he knew, was slipping out of his grasp. "I won't play the fool for anyone, even you."

Embarrassed, Katharine fled, glancing back at McCallum

like a child drowning and reaching for something safe to hold on to. "Absolution," Jesse whispered, smiling warmly.

"Absolution," echoed Katharine, smiling and taking courage from his strength and support. With a graceful turn of silvery blue skirts and a cascade of red hair, she left the men alone in the library.

Jesse was the first to break the tense silence. "What do you want, Damien? Katharine? The railroad? To break Edwin and his boys? Me?"

"No point in pleasantries between us now, is there?" said Damien.

"It's never been pleasant between us," Jesse said bitingly.

"There is a time for truth, isn't there?" Damien said. "*In heaven where all good angels dwell.*" He heard the echo of his voice as a child, drifting up chillingly from the well of his past. For a moment he imagined that his mother stood on the far side of the room, gazing at him with her warm, approving eyes. Another migraine sent white flecks of light dancing in midair.

"I know no time that isn't," said Jesse pointedly. "You don't need a good memory for the truth."

"Cards on the table?" Damien said. "You can't prove a damn thing!" Sweating, he shook his head, automatically reaching for the laudanum only to find it wasn't in his coat pocket.

"No," admitted McCallum. "But I'm working on it. I think you stole Edwin's shipments, then resold the goods, pocketing the profits while your partners suffered great losses.

"I think you're a murderer, not just hiring killers to do your dirty work, but killing with your own hands. I think you murdered Edwin's engineer, Hugh de Angelucci. I also think you had your own fiancée kidnapped. You took a hell of a risk."

"Oh? Why do you say that?" Damien was somewhat surprised at McCallum's accusations, and curious as to just how much he knew.

"Greed. You weren't content with a stockholder share;

you wanted it all. But that's what I don't understand, Damien. You are the richest man in Boston—what is the point?"

The artificial smile faded on Damien's face.

"The point? If someone did what you are accusing me of—and I'm not admitting that I did—it would be for one simple reason: *power*, you imbecile!" The mask of control vaporized in the heat of Damien's seething anger. Money would be the initial return on his investment, but control of the transcontinental railroad would also give the owner enormous power over agriculture, manufacturing and labor, as well as a powerful voice in politics and a legacy of wealth unheard of in the fledgling United States.

"The railroad," said McCallum, "and the rights to build are scheduled to revert back to government control in about a month, and we are in danger of breach of contract for failure to meet our goals. You had this planned from the beginning, long before I came into the picture. You've been lending Edwin money and taking shares of the railroad as collateral. You weren't helping Edwin. You were taking over his business."

A sly, shrewd look replaced Damien's fury. He looked like a cat on the prowl, ready to pounce.

Edwin was standing near his sons and turned to look incredulously at the two men talking.

"It's true," Damien admitted.

"You are a dangerous man, Damien," said Jesse, baiting him. "And I don't like you."

"Consider the feeling mutual," said Damien smoothly. He couldn't stop himself from thinking of McCallum's arm around Katharine's waist. "In fact, McCallum, I'd like to see you dead!"

"You'll have your chance," McCallum replied. "I'll make you an offer."

"You are in no position to offer me anything that I want."

"Wrong," said McCallum. "I'm offering you the rest of the shares in the railroad."

A protest of disapproval erupted in the library. "Wait a minute," Jesse said. "I'm not finished. As long as I'm alive, Damien, you'll never get the railroad or get near Katharine again! I promise you that!"

"Accidents happen," said Damien chillingly. His headache was worsening rapidly and his hands were trembling slightly. An image of his mother drifted into his consciousness; then he saw Katharine's face, like the last link to his humanity, hovering and just out of reach.

"All men bleed," said McCallum quietly, a deadly inflection in his voice. "You want a war with me? Then you'll have one, and I'll win."

"You think?"

"I know. But we'll fight this war like gentlemen, with a wager."

"What's your wager?" said Damien.

"We fight man to man. Down on the docks, bare-knuckle and no holds barred. Whoever is left standing gets the controlling shares in the Central and South Pacific."

Damien nodded. The two men stood facing each other barely six feet apart. The tension between them was so thick, it could have been cut with a knife.

"We both know only one man will walk out of the ring alive," Jesse said.

North nodded. "Yeah, me. I'll take good care of her, McCallum." Then he laughed and nodded to the others while muttering under his breath, "You damned ape."

"You won't get a chance," said McCallum. "Tomorrow night?"

"And all this time," said Damien mildly, covering his fury well, "I thought you'd simply been trying to frame me and send me to prison for things a good man like me simply would never do."

"No," McCallum said, shaking his head. Damien would never quit and he had no conscience. It was hard to say how many innocent people had died because of him. "I mean to kill you for what you've done."

"Good. Then we understand each other."

"Always did. It was just a matter of time."

"See you tomorrow night, McCallum."

"Plan on it."

Chapter Forty

*M*other," said Katharine. "If you have a moment, I need to talk to you."

Etta looked at her with a mixture of surprise and disapproval. "Can't the conversation wait until morning? As you see, I have guests to attend to." She did want to talk to her daughter, especially after her disgraceful behavior in the ballroom, but her guests came first.

"No, Mother," said Katharine seriously. "Frankly, I don't think it can wait." She was well aware that everyone in the room was gossiping about her relationship with McCallum, and speculation was running high. Perhaps by explaining their unique situation to her mother, some of the stigma could be rubbed off. Katharine was willing to try in order to preserve her family's good name.

"Alright," said Etta frostily. "I'll meet you in the, um, *garden?* By the *gazebo?*" One perfectly arched eyebrow lifted angrily over her pale eyes. "You do know where the gazebo is, don't you, darling girl?"

She knows! thought Katharine desperately. Which meant

that every wag in town either knew or would within the hour. Probably, thought Katharine, the news would make the local paper by morning and the church bulletin by the end of the week. She wasn't quite sure how it had happened. One minute her clothes were on and she was dancing with McCallum, and the next, no clothes and . . . well, the memory made her blush!

"Yes, Mother," Katharine said. "As a matter of fact, I was just there—"

"I am all too aware of that!" exclaimed Etta, managing to control her voice, but barely. "Garden," she said, pointing as she had when she sent Katharine to her room for naughty behavior.

"Now?" said Katharine, ready for a showdown.

"Now!" echoed her mother, snapping open her fan. Each woman attempted to stare the other down; it didn't work. They were like mirror images, perfectly matched.

Noticing the private battle, Edwin materialized at his wife's side. "Whatever you two need to discuss would better be done in private. People are starting to stare," he said sternly, then smiled nonchalantly when a couple passed close by, listening. "Lovely evening, isn't it?" he said charmingly.

"Indeed," said the gentleman. "Trifle hot in here, though, isn't it?"

"Yes, a bit," Edwin remarked and turned quickly to his wife and daughter. "Don't you two ladies have something to discuss?"

"Garden," said Etta firmly.

"Garden," Katharine agreed, but suddenly flared up in anger. "I've had enough of being under your thumb!" In fact, she felt like biting the hand that had fed her for so many years.

"Thumb! You're lucky I don't take a switch to you!" whispered Etta, feigning a smile for the benefit of her four hundred guests. Her jaw was beginning to ache with the effort.

"No absolution here!" Katharine said hotly.

She headed out the double doors and into the garden with all the grace of a soldier at war, head up, arms rigid at her sides, legs straight, marching along as her mother followed.

"Absolution?" Etta's eyes were narrowed, her fan open and working like a bellows at a forge press. "Oh, I'll give you absolution, my girl . . ." The rest was lost on Katharine, who didn't trust herself to turn around, afraid she would start shouting the instant she saw her mother's face. So she hurried along, reaching the deserted gazebo in record time.

A glance around the well-manicured lawn told Mrs. Dory that they were alone and well out of hearing range of the guests in the ballroom. Then she rounded on her daughter with the feline grace of a mother lion preparing to cuff her cub. *"Are you out of your mind, Katharine?"*

"I've done nothing wrong tonight, Mother," she replied evenly.

"Oh, that, my darling girl, is a matter of opinion, and the general consensus is that you have!"

"Then the consensus is wrong," she said. "And so are you."

"I saw you! As a matter of fact, half the gentlefolk in town saw you!"

"Saw me what, Mother?"

"Act like a common wanton, that's what! I was never so embarrassed! Letting that man touch you in public! He practically kissed you in front of the orchestra! And then you went off to the garden together!"

"Pity you didn't see what we did there," Katharine said brazenly. "Now, that was truly shocking."

Etta paled. "It is true. You are ruined. I don't know you anymore, my dear. I don't know what you did or why you are defending your actions, but that is no way for a young, unmarried lady to present herself in public! It is simply not acceptable!"

"Would my behavior be acceptable if I were a married woman?" Katharine demanded.

"Well, that would be different, Katharine." Etta noticed the tears in her daughter's eyes. "Married people are permitted such liberties."

"Then you needn't worry about my precious reputation. McCallum has every right to touch me! We're married!"

"You're *what?!*" Etta was stunned. The gloved hand replete with gemstone rings and dripping with gold bracelets rose dramatically to her forehead. This time it wasn't an act. "I think I'm going to faint!"

"No, Mother, please don't! I can't talk to you if you're unconscious!" Katharine moved to stand beside Etta, concern overwhelming her frustration.

"Unconscious! Here, you ungrateful girl, you might as well go to the study and take the letter opener and plunge it in my heart for all the pain and suffering you've caused me!" Etta pulled her shawl open, exposing her chest. "Right here, plunge the dagger! Death would be preferable to the humiliation of telling your father that . . . oh, my goodness!" She stopped short and grabbed her daughter's hands like a life preserver. "Your father! How am I going to tell him?"

"He suspects, I think."

"You *think*? Did you elope? Were you at the wrong end of a pistol during this affair, or did you simply wake up one morning and decide to send your future into obscurity and cast me into perdition along with the rest of this household?"

"No, Mother. We didn't elope. Not exactly. I did marry him, though," she said. "I think I did. Actually, I'm not sure." Bemused, as if she still couldn't quite believe it herself, she recalled the good-natured Jesuit priest in the clearing with his opened Bible, performing the ceremony.

"That's not possible," her mother blustered. "How could

you be married? There were no civil papers filed. Not even an engagement party, for heaven's sake. It's not legal! We'll have it annulled!"

"If it's not legal, then how can you annul it?"

"How did it happen?" asked her mother, pale beyond comparison.

"It was the Jesuit priest," said Katharine. She had to blame someone. "Or maybe it was the wine."

"You were drinking with a Jesuit priest?"

"No, with Jesse."

"You were drunk?"

"Very. My feet started to dissolve, or maybe it was the ground. I don't remember, except that the marriage was supposed to be pretend, Mother. Only it wasn't!"

"Pretend. A Jesuit priest married you and you thought it was pretend? Are you out of your Protestant mind? Those Jesuits play for keeps!

"What happened next?" Etta demanded.

"The same thing that happened in the gazebo. Every time he touches me, my clothes seem to fall off. He helps, of course."

"In other words, did you and McCallum, um . . . commingle?"

"Yes."

"No! No! No! Just shoot me now!" Etta's eyes closed. "But it was only a *little,* right?"

"No, Mother, we commingled a lot. All night long, in fact." Katharine wisely refrained from telling her distraught mother that she loved the commingling part; it was the promising to obey for life that made her shudder. "Maybe it was a dream," she said, bemused.

"A dream? I'm going to kill that McCallum! Kill him! Kill him! Kill him! First that hawk rocking on my Austrian chandelier, then the rhododendrons, and him drinking out of the finger bowl with the Turkish ambassador present, and then that mangy wolf howling by my window all night, and now you!" She strangled her fan, then ripped it to pieces. "Kill!"

"I think you'll have to take a number and stand in line, Mother."

"And I think you're taking some sadistic, adolescent pleasure in all of this, Katharine!" she retorted. "I'm having a heart attack right now! I just want you to know that when I drop dead at your feet! Then you can bury me next to my ruined rhododendrons, you ungrateful child!"

"Mother—"

"I can't believe this! You married a Catholic! A *Catholic*! Is McCallum Catholic?"

"No, the Pope is," said Katharine. "Jesse is Presbyterian or Baptist."

Defeated, Etta sank onto the garden's wrought-iron bench, looking helpless. "We need to investigate your situation further. You and McCallum—that incorrigible Scot," she said through gritted teeth. "You perhaps *petted* a little? A little hanky-panky, you know, touched just a little?" She made a box motion with her arms, bordering her anatomy from her neck to the tops of her thighs. "Nothing here? Correct?" she said sweetly, hopeful.

"No," said Katharine firmly. "We petted, kissed, fondled and—"

"Katharine!"

"We did, Mother, and I liked it," she admitted honestly. "Which, I may say, must run in the family since you have six miniature Dorys running around to prove that you don't find Father's touch unacceptable. We all know how you and Father spend your Sunday afternoons! Reading the newspaper indeed! No one ever sees you until Monday morning and the paper is still folded. We checked!"

"Stop!" said Etta, preparing to faint in earnest. "What your father and I do in the privacy of our suite is none of your business. What you do, however, is mine! So you admit that you are no longer a virgin."

"I do," she agreed. "So arrest me, disown me or send me to a convent. Frankly, I don't care!"

"Convent? Oh, just plunge that knife deeper, you ungrateful girl!" hissed Etta. "What you did with him in the gazebo and Colorado need never be mentioned again! There is no legal record of this marriage. We'll simply send you to the South of France until the scandal dies down. Poof! You're gone!" she said, snapping her fingers. It was settled. "Just like that!"

"Poof! I'm not! Just like that! Mother, there may not be a marriage license but there is physical proof! And I'm not going to France!"

"You, my dear, will do exactly what I say!" Etta balled her hands into fists and stomped on her broken fan. "Now, just keep your mouth shut and pretend."

"Pretend what?"

"That you're not married!"

"Pretending was what got me into this situation. I'm done pretending."

In the rear of the garden, ghostly white and clouded by a late evening mist, stood Jesse, silent and listening. Leaning against the bark of an elm tree with his hands crossed over his chest and his brooding eyes settled on his *wife*, he waited and heard . . .

"All I know is, McCallum isn't suitable! Not suitable at all! But time and silence will take care of this fiasco. All you need to do is forget about him! He'll be gone soon enough, I promise. I'll send *him* to the South of France!"

"Then send me with him, Mother," Katharine said, seeming to hear him whisper in her ear, telling her to *dive deep and take him with her*.

"Out of the question! Do you realize what you are throwing away for that illiterate man? He is a barbarian!"

"You don't like him at all, do you, Mother?"

"No. I don't like him at all and I never will! He is not good enough for you, Katharine! That man could graduate with top honors from Harvard and he would still be nothing more than the son of an ignorant man, unlettered, dressed in rags, begging in my foyer!"

"His father was educated in law, Mother, a preacher."

"Oh, so he says! Do you know how many gold diggers feign aristocracy or good backgrounds to worm their way into society?"

"A gold digger? He is the man who is loaning *us* money to invest in the railroad!"

"He is simply not suitable, Katharine! He was wearing rags when he came to the mansion's front door!"

"Buckskins, Mother, his very best. But you are right, he couldn't read because his father was blinded in a mining accident and was left to take care of Jesse when he was still a child. Jesse was practically an orphan with no mother, and he worked in a mine while still a boy."

"He is unsophisticated!" said Etta bitingly. "You could do so much better! I would never be proud to introduce him as my son-in-law, no matter how many tutors he has or how you try to gloss over the circumstances of his birth. I will always see McCallum as an illiterate, ignorant and ignoble man, Katharine."

In the shadow of the ancient elm, Jesse closed his eyes, barely breathing. "Will you exile me to the mountains, Katharine, and yourself to a frigid marriage of your mother's choosing?" he whispered to himself, shaking his head. "Borrowed. I'll never be good enough for you."

He let go.

Turning with a heavy heart, he walked to the house and through the open door. Numbly he climbed up the back stairs to his room. Within seconds he peeled the elegant new suit from his body, stripped off the starched white shirt and unlaced the shoes. Then he pulled the soft skins of mountain animals loosely over his form. He felt the first bitter salt tear slide down his cheek as he made his way outside.

The house was still lively and full of guests. He was in no mood for small talk, so he took the back stairs again. As he passed by the family's private parlor, he noticed a small miniature of Katharine on the mantel, smiling in that self-conscious, charming way with her dimples showing. Her image was enough to make him stop and stare.

Reaching inside his saddlebag, he pulled out a fistful of dollars, paper money equaling thousands, but worthless to him. The match with Damien was tomorrow night, but he didn't care about that. He didn't think about Edwin or the investors. Boston had been one insult and humiliation after another. The truth revealed by the woman who might be his mother-in-law had tipped the balance.

"I know what I am," he said bitterly and let the bills fall like a shower of leaves across the marble mantel. Then he picked up the miniature portrait and placed it next to his heart, looking around one last time. "And I'll never be good enough for Etta Dory's daughter. I've had enough."

Outside the mansion he made his way to the wolf's pen. "Ready to run, Sammy?" he said, roughing his fur. The wolf looked at him with his canny, sharp eyes, and Jesse knew that all he had to do was open the door. "They had us both in a cage, didn't they, boy?"

He released the latch and watched with growing anger as the wolf bounded free and the hawk, awakened by the noise, flew from his perch in the old pin oak tree and began to soar into the silken night sky. Jesse gazed up, noticing the progression of the hawk's flight as the giant wings eclipsed the diamond stars in soaring arcs and graceful geometric patterns.

"Never again," Jesse swore. "I'll never go near another cage no matter how pretty it looks!"

Grim-faced and determined, he saddled and mounted the big stallion by the garden gate. He could see them in the distance, Etta and Katharine, still exchanging words.

Ruefully he admitted that part of him wanted to charge forward, capture his wife and take her with him. The horse, sensing his mood, reared up, and Jesse pulled back on the reins, hard. He couldn't imagine living without her, but he was determined to try. "I can still feel you, kitten," he whispered. Then he laughed; it was a biting, hard sound.

"You win, Etta," he said, dark eyes glittering. "I'll leave you to trade your daughter to a lying, thieving, murdering scoundrel like North, who is good enough!"

He was determined to leave Boston for good. He knew Isaiah would be alright, would make his own decisions about staying or leaving, but as for himself, the mountains called. And this time, McCallum answered.

"I love him," Katharine said, throwing all caution to the wind.

Etta forgot to breathe. "You're quite insane," she said. "You would give up all of this"—her gloved hands moved in a conjurer's circle, describing riches and wealth beyond compare—"to live like a heathen?"

"I will live however he wants me to live, wherever he wants me to live. I will follow him to the ends of the earth or walk through fire for him. He has already done the same for me."

Etta shook her head, speechless. It was too late to put a lid on this scandal, which threatened to rock Boston society for more than a few days.

"I have lied so often to myself about Jesse that I was nearly convinced my feelings for him were nothing more than gratitude. I was wrong. It isn't he that is not good enough for me, Mother; it is I who am not good enough for him!" Katharine said. Her decision was made. "Good night."

The confrontation with her mother had cleared the cobwebs and helped Katharine understand her feelings for McCallum. She had sublimated and repressed her desire, rationalized her wishes by calling them *pretend*. She had hidden her feelings by acting hostile and aloof when all she really wanted to do was melt in his arms. Grasping the folds of her gown in both hands, she bolted at a very unladylike pace toward the mansion and up the main stairs in front of everyone.

"Jesse! Jesse!" she shouted as she ran, unmindful of the staring eyes of the servants and the guests. "Jesse!" she shouted again and burst through his bedroom door.

The room was empty.

His tailored clothes lay on the floor in a heap. His jewelry had been cast like Fortunato's dice on the bed. Gingerly she picked up his shirt in her trembling hands. The starched white fabric, softened by contact with his warm skin, moved gently in her hands. She lifted it to her face. His scent was clean, masculine, hinting at pipe smoke, brandy and a trace of cologne, overwhelming her senses. He was everywhere around her, present in his belongings, yet, like a ghost, gone.

A soft moan escaped her lips.

"Come back," she said, praying to whatever gods would listen. It was the second time she had lost him. "Please, Jesse, come back." She forgot about railroads and cotillions and counting shares and stocks; forgot about propriety and restraint, wishing only now that the shirt she held in her hands still clothed the man who wore it so well. She knew where he was going. West. To a land still capped in primitive snow, to trap and hunt and be free of a burden he hadn't wanted all along. Fragile in her youth, she was certain that her life was over. She was convinced that he was never coming back. Why would he? What had he received for his efforts but scorn and ridicule even though he had saved her life, her family's fortune and been willing to trade his world for hers?

Bowing her head, Katharine cried in the open doorway, not caring who saw her tears or whether everyone knew they were shed for a man rejected as *not quite good enough.* In her heart, she knew he was the best man she'd ever meet.

Chapter Forty-one

*D*amien stood silently in his Byzantine library, comforted by the soft lights. He stared thoughtfully into the last of the glowing embers in the fireplace and was suddenly drawn to gaze at his mother's portrait. Even in oil, her eyes were warm yet tragically sad, reaching out to him across the abyss of time. Without thinking, he moved closer to the portrait and stretched forth his hand, placing it gently on the folded hands captured within the frame. Perhaps he was hoping for a miracle, for his mother's hands to reach out and hold his, but the canvas was cool to the touch.

"How have I come to this, Mother?" he whispered aloud.

Sadness—that was what he felt. The emotion wasn't so easy to brush aside tonight or to ignore. Incredulous, he felt his power fading. The feeling of competence and dominance he'd always had was slipping away like a mantle falling from his shoulders, leaving him naked and vulnerable in the world. He was alone, with no family, hated and reviled by those who'd once respected him.

His father had taught him to control his feelings at all times. He had learned the art so effectively that he seldom showed any emotion at all. And with time, pretense became reality. He had a heart of stone, more dead than alive. But the statue was shattering. He was crumbling inside.

Starting over was out of the question. He couldn't step outside of himself and become someone else. This morning he envied the Dory household, lively, warm and filled with people. No one sang in his parlor, laughed on his terrace, or rushed to greet him at night. Desperately he tried to find the will to rebuild the walls of indifference that allowed him to feel little regret for the human lives he'd wrecked to reach the top.

"What is it now, Mother?" She was one anchor to the last vestiges of his humanity; Katharine was the other, but she was fast slipping from his grasp. "Will your gentle presence be the ghost that haunts me for the rest of my miserable life?"

In answer to his question, the door to the library opened and Josiah Mott's brother, Amos, walked through.

"So this, then," Damien said softly, "is what I've become?"

Black magic. His sins had come to greet him at his front door.

"You got a job for me?" said Mott.

"Yes. This is what I want you to do," said Damien. "Tonight McCallum is coming to the warehouse to box. He challenged me last night, and the stakes are higher than I can afford to lose. Though I know I can beat him, I cannot take the chance of losing control of the railroad."

Mott nodded. There was an expression nearly like a smirk on his face. He already knew what North wanted him to do.

"You want me to kill McCallum before he gets to the warehouse?"

"Exactly."

"You'll be there, waiting to avenge your good name, and McCallum will be shown for the coward that he is because he won't show up. The Dorys will lose control of the Central Pacific, not to mention their shipping lines, and be beholden to you for whatever scraps you decide to feed them, and that pretty little red-haired gal will be needing a shoulder to cry on. Am I right?"

Damien laughed dangerously beneath his breath. "You're smarter than you look. Sometimes it's not healthy to be that smart."

"Don't mess with me," snarled Mott. "I ain't your dog anymore, North! If it weren't for what I know about how you set up Dory's daughter—"

"Shut up! Shut up, you fool!" Damien was on him in a second. Though not as heavy as Mott, he was quick as lightning and knew holds that would make a man bleed tears. His white hand held Mott beneath the chin; his fingers pressed into the larger man's windpipe and his knee pressed against his chest. "One more word out of you and I'll rip your throat out!" It wasn't an idle threat.

The smirk was gone from Mott's face, replaced by a look of fear. Ice-blue rage stared back at him.

"You do what I say, Mott," said Damien evenly. "And no mistakes, got it? Nod your head up and down if you understand."

His fingers tightened their grip, and mechanically Mott nodded his head. As soon as he did, the pressure eased and Damien stood coldly beside him. "I could crush you in an instant, you insect. Now go do your job!"

"I get paid no matter what, right?" Mott said. He was rubbing his throat.

"Yes," Damien said, "you get paid no matter what. Now get out of my sight before I do the world a favor and put a bullet in you!"

Chapter Forty-two

W̱ho am I fooling?" said Jesse. He pulled back hard on the reins, staring at the indigo light spreading through the clouds. A rainbow arched over Boston, blooming from the milkweed belly of clouds that settled over the eastern horizon. "I can't leave her."

Jesse breathed softly. The air was chill and sweet, laden with blooming flowers and cut hay and spiced by the salt tang of the ocean miles away. Something akin to lightning burned quickly through him.

He could feel her.

He leaned against the saddle horn and looked at his wolf, who was watching him, tawny eyes glowing red in the early morning light. "Hell of a situation, ain't it? She's unclear as fog and about as sensitive as a porcupine." He couldn't escape her memory or outride it. Even if she didn't want him, he couldn't leave her to a man like Damien. There was no telling what North would do to her.

Sammy whined deep in his throat and Jesse searched

the sky, looking for his hawk. Nothing but a raven or two; nothing but mare-tail clouds brushing the sky.

"Night and day that woman haunts me." He shook his head, reached for his canteen and took a healthy swig, wiping his chin. *Not good enough.* Etta's words. *Even if he graduated from Harvard!* The stares and the ridicule. *You offend!* Damien's words. *Never good enough.*

He took one last glance toward the mountains that he knew would bring forgetfulness and maybe even peace. Then his attention was caught by his wolf, who nipped at his buckskin-clad ankle. Jesse looked down. Sammy yipped and loped east, circling, looking back at him and waiting for him to follow. "Borrowed or stolen," McCallum vowed, "I'll take you any way I can get you, Kat."

He turned his horse into the sun and kicked him in the flanks. Determined, McCallum headed back toward Boston, leaving the mountains behind. The ocean loomed ahead, challenging, and unpredictable. He didn't know the outcome of his decision, but he knew that his future was where sea met sky, in the arms of a woman he couldn't forget.

"The side door is usually open," Jesse whispered to himself as he wound his way through the dark, deserted streets toward the warehouse. He could see an American flag flying atop the warehouse on the pier some distance ahead. The flag was so threadbare that the dim light made it look transparent, yet somehow noble and stately in that dreary, deserted place.

Jesse wondered who had left that old flag barely hanging on in a place where no one would see it. Wiping a fist across his mouth, he remembered Katharine's words about "a great nation unlike any other," and Edwin's vision of a continent united by a steel horse and thousands of miles of rail lines. *The railroad.* He remembered a picture he'd seen in the newspaper of a gleaming black locomotive thundering into the Dunkirk depot at the Great Lakes with her colors flying, high and proud, and the banners decorating the podium where President Fillmore spoke to commemorate the great occasion. McCallum knew that some principles were more important than money and power and were worth fighting and dying for, and he felt a surge of pride and determination as he looked at the battered little flag.

"No one is going to walk on that flag," he said. "Or on me."

His thoughts turned to Damien—the lies, sabotage, and quite possibly, murder. "You're not getting the railroad or my wife." Instincts honed over two decades in primeval woods and glacial peaks came to the fore. Jesse reached for the hilt of the bowie knife lodged in the band of his tan leathers. Lifting his handsome face like an animal scenting prey, he peered down the alley off to the side with his head cocked, listening. The fine hairs along the base of his neck tingled, and he narrowed his eyes, adjusting his vision to the deepening gloom.

He was a man who valued his senses. They'd saved him more than once when logic and intellect fell short. Listening to his body, he knew something wasn't right. He sensed danger near, and adrenaline began to pour through him, sending his heartbeat into a staccato rhythm and causing his breathing to accelerate. He put down his pack and stood, poised on the edge of the alley, focusing. Oddly, he felt as if all the fragmented memories of the last few years had been threads woven together into a broader pattern that he'd been too close to see at the time. They came together now.

Some things were meant to be.

His apprehension proved right. A shape moved slightly near a box of crates piled alongside the warehouse ahead of him, next to the side door. The outline of a set of shoulders and neck was barely visible, lounging against the wall. The posture was too self-assured to be dangerous, too obvious to be smart.

You're a stupid man, thought McCallum. Automatically his hand tightened around the hilt of his knife. He heard a sound behind him, the measured meter of a footfall followed by another, stealthily creeping along behind him. He started to turn around.

"Not so fast, mate," said a voice thick with liquor and swagger. *A decoy!* The first man's positioning was obvious for a reason. He was intended to draw Jesse's attention while others circled around behind him. The decoy wasn't alone. Three other men closed the alley's entrance, blocking Jesse's escape, while the man near the door began to approach, slapping an iron pipe against his palm, grinning.

"Remember me?" asked one of the men behind him. Jesse turned. The speaker was standing between a sailor and another man dressed in city clothes. The speaker was taller than Jesse by nearly four inches, and three times as wide. A star-shaped scar ornamented his left cheek, testimony to an uninvited bullet and a considerable amount of luck.

Mott.

Jesse nodded. He remembered.

A strange moment occurred like a rip in the fabric of time, and he thought of Mott sprawled across the crates at the Dunes with a bottle of Taos Lightning at his feet.

"I thought I killed you once," said Jesse softly.

"You thought wrong."

"Sure there's enough of you guys?" said McCallum evenly. He watched as the other three men circled him like sharks smelling blood.

"We'll get the job done," said Mott.

"One thing," said Jesse. "Was it North who set me up? I mean, you're going to kill me anyway, so you might as well tell me who is paying you. Did he hire you to kidnap Dory's daughter, too?"

"He paid me to stop you," said Mott. "And I will!"

"How about Hugh? Did he murder the engineer, or did you?"

"Go to hell," snarled Mott.

"Uh-huh," agreed McCallum. "And I'm going to take you with me."

Then he laughed in a quiet, deadly way, dropped his right shoulder, jabbed twice with his left fist to gauge the distance to Mott's head and drove his right fist up and under his jaw, lifting the big man off his feet and sending him sprawling. The other three men looked at each other in surprise. Jesse wanted to disable the biggest threat first.

"C'mon!" shouted the sailor. He jumped on McCallum's back and threw his arm around his neck, pulling back his head by grabbing a handful of thick hair. He got head-butted for his efforts, and the big Scot drove an elbow into his ribs, while one arm reached up and pulled him over, slamming him to the ground.

The man in the city clothes threw a few wide punches and tried to kick. He was sloppy, his aim falling short of his mark, and smaller than the other three. Jesse turned all his fire and intensity on him, knowing that Mott was getting to his feet and his time was short. He wasn't just trying to defend himself or maim his foes; he meant to kill, because he had no choice. It was either him or them, and he had a debt to settle with North.

"Little man, you should have stayed at home," he said. Grabbing a forearm after a wide, useless punch fell on nothing but thin air, McCallum brought his knee up into the man's elbow, fracturing the arm. Then using the forward momentum of his punch, he flipped his opponent over on his back. Still holding the broken arm by the wrist, he aimed his booted heel at the man's throat and crushed his windpipe just as the decoy hit him on the side of the head with the pipe. Feeling blood pouring from his temple, Jesse shook off the dizzy sensation and turned around.

He noticed Mott getting to his feet and lunged toward him, knowing exactly what the decoy would do. He charged him with his iron pipe raised, and that was all Mc-

Callum needed. He waited until the last second, when the pipe started down and the man was nearly on top of him, and, keeping his legs wide and his center of gravity low, Jesse moved slightly to one side and threw the decoy off the pier and into the cold ocean below.

One man dead, one in the drink, one unconscious and the fourth stumbling to his feet.

"Cowards," Jesse said.

"I should have shot you!" shouted Mott, struggling to pull his Colt from his waistband.

"You should have thought about that ten minutes ago," Jesse said. He knew Mott was dangerous. He watched with a sense of slow motion as the pistol was pulled free and Mott's hand felt for the familiar notched grip, the thumb comfortable around the handle and the index finger reaching for the trigger. The only thing McCallum had on his side was that Mott was scared and his movements were hurried and careless. *He was afraid to die.* Jesse wasn't.

So he attacked. With his bowie knife in his right hand, he lunged forward. The sharp blade cut a thin line across Mott's cheek, causing the gunshot to go wide and the lead slug to bury itself harmlessly in the side of the building.

Before Mott had another chance to pull the hammer back, McCallum moved in. Mott's free hand grabbed Jesse's arm near the wrist and started to twist. His superior strength threw McCallum over, but he reached for Mott's shirt as he headed for the ground, taking the behemoth with him. The pistol lay forgotten on the pier and the knife rested a few inches away. The two men were locked in mortal combat, and both knew that one of them wouldn't walk away from this fight. Bred to war and living the life of gun and knife, McCallum had only one response when he was pushed. He pushed back harder.

Fighting lean, quick and agile, Jesse hit Mott with everything he had, driving his knee into the other man's groin with a powerful upward kick, followed by another. Every time he hit Mott, he saw the man who helped kill his father. The man who had kidnapped the woman he loved. The man who raped innocent girls and left them for dead in the desert sun. Jesse didn't pull a kick or punch, or regret the lethal effects of his well-aimed blows. He ignored his own pain and used it to fuel his anger until his foe was vanquished.

Like a dark avenging angel, his waves of jet-black hair moved in the night wind as he rolled away from Mott. "Straight to hell!" he said, keeping his promise. "Say hello to your brother." Then he pushed Mott's body into the swirling water, making sure he was dead this time. The whispering winds caught his words, and though it may have been a trick of light on water, the waves moved hard against the pier, rising spectrally high as Mott was laid in his watery grave.

"Let God sort your deeds," said McCallum. "I'm done with you!"

Breathing hard, he wiped his fist against his mouth, tasting blood. He looked at the warehouse. Savagery lay behind him, hell fast on his heels and a battle ahead. Colorado Territory was a haven in his thoughts, like a faraway dream; the warehouse was ahead with his nemesis inside, waiting.

"Crossroads," said McCallum. Dazed from the pipe blow, his temple still bleeding, he saw his wife's beautiful face. "I'm like a man bewitched. I can still taste her." He swore at himself for his weakness. Memories blossomed amidst the pain in his mind, her gentle laughter, her small moans of pleasure, her teasing touch, the raking of long, carefully tended fingernails across the skin of his broad back, the shadow of her hand placed against her face in a maidenly gesture. She beckoned him with emerald eyes, hypnotic, glowing and warm; he pictured her alabaster skin and ruby-red lips, her body willing and ripe, rising to meet each demanding, powerful thrust.

Less than a night ago, he'd held her body close, crushing soft, warm breasts against his chest, opening her before him in a garden perfumed by hibiscus and roses. Her beauty was like a drug, tantalizing, and his addiction to her sex was beyond redemption.

"I should have kept going," he said seriously. He knew it was already too late.

Fires blazed in metal barrels on either side of the warehouse door, giving a look to the place of Dante's *Inferno*. Jesse heaved a great, weary sigh and pulled his clan's tartan from the pack he'd carried to the pier. Blue, green and scarlet threads like the lifeblood of his ancestors, were woven into the design, connecting the present to the past and leading him toward an uncertain future. The tartan was over three hundred years old and was pinned with his family's broach from Scotland. Blood from his face trailed down his cheek, along his neck. It would mingle a new sacrifice with the old.

He walked unsteadily through the side door. He could hear the thunderous mob inside. He threw the tartan across his shoulder and wiped his hand across his bruised lips. Above his head, symbolic, solitary and untrammeled, waved Old Glory, triumphant. "I may look a fool," he said, "but a McCallum always goes down swinging. North won't get the railroad or my wife!"

Chapter Forty-three

*H*ow much longer must we wait?" said Katharine.

Edwin and O'Sullivan exchanged a brief glance.

"There is no point in staying any longer," said Edwin as they waited with the crowd of hopeful spectators for the fighters to arrive. "He is gone and he isn't coming back. That may be a brutal fact, but one that we are all going to have to deal with."

"But why?" Katharine asked.

"We expected too much of him, Katharine. He has been quietly shouldering the responsibility for our troubles, taking the fight to Damien's front door. Is it any wonder that it became too much? Still, there is a part of me that cannot understand why at this final moment he decided to leave."

"It may be my fault," admitted Katharine. She remembered last night in the garden with Jesse and then her talk with her mother. Her mother's words had been brutal. "Father, after Jesse challenged Damien to a boxing match, what did he say?"

"Nothing, really, he just left."

"Did he go toward the garden?"

"Yes. But why do you ask? It's already too late. The match is going to be forfeited unless Damien allows us to choose a stand-in for McCallum, and frankly, I doubt that he will."

Katharine was about to tell her father what she and her mother had been talking about when John O'Sullivan reached out and touched her arm.

"Here comes Damien now," said O'Sullivan. "It is too late." There was an angry gleam in his eyes as he watched North approach. Damien wasn't smiling—he was positively beaming—but his celebration was premature.

"My dear sweet Jesus," murmured O'Sullivan as he saw another man come in behind North. "I don't bloody believe it!"

"What?" said Edwin. He followed Sullivan's gaze and sucked in his breath. "What in the hell happened to that boy?"

Jesse was beaten and bleeding, standing in the open doorway with his hair matted with blood, a thin stream of scarlet trailing down his temple to his chin, his clan's tartan thrown over one shoulder and a look of absolute fury on his face.

"McCallum," said O'Sullivan, gratified to see him. He cast Damien a triumphant look. "I hate that bastard North," he muttered beneath his breath.

"So do I," said Isaiah. The two men flanked Katharine, whose expression went from shock to horror. She would have fainted or bolted to Jesse's side if it weren't for the strong arms holding her back. The men stood in front of her to block Jesse's view.

"Help him!" she said, holding tightly to Isaiah.

"Leave him be," cautioned Isaiah, who knew Jesse best. He saw the glitter in McCallum's dark eyes as he glared at Damien. "Just leave him be, Katharine."

McCallum stood braced in the doorway like Samson with wounded eyes and a battered body, chained by his word and the love of a woman he couldn't forget.

Hunting.

The smile on North's face began to fade. He stared in stunned silence at the ghost in the doorway. "I thought you were dead," Damien whispered, catching himself before his words could carry. Across the distance, McCallum smiled grimly, his gaze never leaving North's face; his eyes were filled with infernal fire, hellish in intensity and intent.

Isaiah, standing nearby, had heard North and he laughed. Turning toward him, he smiled. "There is a masculine power more than muscle, sinew or strength that keeps a man fighting even when there is nothing left inside of him to give. So, he gives it all—with only one goal in mind: to destroy his adversary even if it means destroying himself. It's too late to kill the dead, North," said Isaiah proudly as he watched McCallum stride down the aisle toward the ring. "I'm his second," he said to O'Sullivan, and he gave Katharine into the protective embrace of her father, who kissed her softly on the forehead.

"There is no man who loves you more than McCallum, or ever will be," Isaiah said. "He would die for you. Remember that when your mother tells you he isn't good enough." He had heard every detail from the kitchen staff. "You're a fool if you let that man go." Then he turned as the voice of the crowd, which had subsided to silence, began to build to a roar as hundreds of voices asked the same questions.

"What happened, McCallum?" "Hey, boy, what'd they do to you?" The words became louder and bolder, a tumultuous riptide of crashing sounds. "Who jumped you, McCallum? Who did the dirty deed?"

"Hey, boy-o!" shouted one burly man. "I got five dollars on you!"

"You should have bet ten," said McCallum as he casually reached over, grabbed the man's beer and took a long, cold pull. The man laughed and slapped his knees good-naturedly, and a roar of approval went up in the crowd as

Jesse drained the glass and wiped a bloodied fist across his lips.

"Well, maybe I will, then!"

"You'll get a good return," said McCallum. "I'm a good investment." Then he resumed his walk to the ring with his head held high, ignoring his pain.

"Jesse!" A high, sweet voice caught him like a knife to the midsection, riveting him on the spot. He turned and stared angrily at Katharine, who had freed herself from O'Sullivan and her father.

"What the hell are you doing here?" he said.

She was crying.

McCallum looked at her and shook his head. He couldn't stop himself from hearing her mother's voice in the garden—*Not good enough!*—and Damien's words—*Even a trained ape can be taught to dance! Never good enough*.

"I'm sorry!" she said. Her lion's mane of red hair spilled around her porcelain face. He remembered the silken feel of her tresses in his hands.

"Sorry?" he said. She was his obsession. He closed his eyes against her. "You made me an orphan, *twice!*" he accused hotly. "It'll never happen again!" He dismissed her in a rush of emotion driven by righteous wrath and masculine pride. "Never again," he vowed. He had come to save her from North. That was all. Without another word, he focused on his adversary, pushing the thought of her away even as he remembered: *Christ, she was sweet and so hot!*

"North!" he shouted, wanting to hit anything that moved. His voice with its Scottish brogue echoed through the room.

Damien looked at him coldly. His carefully choreographed show had one major flaw: *McCallum was not supposed to make it to the ring!* He started to laugh. "The best-laid plans of mice and men," he said beneath his breath. "What do you want, McCallum?"

"You," said Jesse. "I've already taken care of the men you hired to stop me."

"Well," said Damien, holding up his arms in mock surrender. "You have me, then! Don't add slander to your list of crimes," he warned.

"My only crime," McCallum said, "is not killing you when I had the chance."

"If at first you don't succeed . . ." said Damien carelessly as he strode toward the ring. The measure of laudanum he'd taken would minimize whatever pain Jesse would cause him; coca leaves mixed in tea had given him the energy and confidence he otherwise would have lacked.

A murmur went through the crowd as he passed within inches of Edwin and O'Sullivan. North was distracted by the sight of Katharine, his mock bravado fading and an expression of regret registering briefly in his eyes.

"Beautiful," he breathed. She was wearing a blue gown that contrasted with her light skin and red hair. He walked to her, lifted off his azure silk jacket and laid it gently over her shoulders. "Wear my colors, Katharine. You've already won my heart." With familiarity he pulled the coat gently around her shoulders, watching the expression on Jesse's face.

"Was she worth it, McCallum?" North said coolly, turning around. One arm was wrapped securely around her waist, preventing her from drawing away from him. He knew exactly what he was doing.

"Get your hands off of my wife," said McCallum. He was breathing hard.

"Your *wife*?" said North. "Not for long."

McCallum's eyes blazed.

"Get your filthy hands off of her!" Jesse shouted, pointing. "I'm warning you! I've had enough!" The big Scot started to push past Isaiah and several men blocking the aisle. "Get off me, Isaiah!"

"Calm down, Jesse!" said Isaiah. "Save it for the ring!"

"The hell I will!" said McCallum. "Now get out of my way! He's gone too far."

A wall of men prevented Jesse from crossing the last few feet separating them, pulling pistols from holsters and nightsticks from belts. Damien watched the events closely, grinning. He wanted to start a riot.

"You're doing exactly what he wants!" Briand said to Jesse. "He is baiting you so he doesn't have to fight you in the ring! You're letting him win!"

Jesse looked at Isaiah as his friend went on. "Get him in the ring, then I don't care what you do to the bastard."

Damien's smile evaporated. His ice-blue eyes glittered like a snake scenting prey. "Tell me, Katharine," he said cruelly, "was it a mercy wedding? Did you feel sorry for your trained ape? Well, that's too bad, because I'm going to kill him. And you're going to watch!" Damien knew he was losing his last link to his humanity when he saw the pained expression on her face. Turning from her, he peeled off his shirt, stripping down to his trousers as he started for the ring. "I'm going to kill you, McCallum."

"You can try," said Jesse. "But crippled or dead, you're never getting near Katharine again."

"We'll see about that," said North. Turning, he grabbed Katharine rudely and kissed her on the mouth. "Preview," he said. Her brothers moved closer, and Damien lifted his arms in mock surrender.

McCallum closed his eyes and turned away. *A time to live and a time . . .*

He knew.

. . . it was the shadow hour of death.

A time to die.

When he turned back to face the center of the ring, he was changed. *Ice*. His face was cold and without emotion. An eerie calmness settled across his features as he watched North climb between the ropes.

The ring was large enough to give a man space to move, yet small enough so that he couldn't move too far away. Each side was twelve feet long. There were three tiers of ropes, each looped through the corner posts. Two corners had been furnished with milking stools for each man and his second.

Towels were placed over the ropes and buckets of cold water beside the stools. Unguents, creams, bandages torn from clean cotton sheets and a surgeon's bag full of needles and sinew were lined up neatly beside a cart that doubled as a crude operating table.

Damien stood in the far corner like a shark, without conscience or remorse. He draped his scarf around the post as though laying claim to his territory, then turned around and leaned insolently against the ropes, staring as the Scot walked toward the ring.

He smiled. McCallum might know about the sabotage, the kidnapping, the murder, but he couldn't prove a thing. No one would speak out against him; anyone who did vanished. And Damien made a special effort to make sure that everyone who worked for him knew the consequence of a double-cross.

Isaiah pulled the ropes apart and Jesse stepped through. He looked around, held his arms up, and the crowd cheered. He could pick out the familiar faces around him—Edwin, John, Dan, Nick, Luke. O'Sullivan was seated near the ring, shaking his head every time he looked at him. Ruefully Jesse wondered just how bad he looked. Judging from the amount of blood on the tartan, he knew he hadn't fared well with the iron pipe. Then for some reason, he thought of the little battered flag and looked at Edwin Dory. Some had said he was an opportunist; others called him a mad dreamer, full of self-aggrandizement and illusions. Jesse knew that he was a man who lived his life for others; his vision was one of a land where everyone belonged, a New Atlantis, pulled together by an iron horse called a locomotive and a skein of steel railroad threads.

Maybe it was true. Maybe America was the Promised Land, a place where everyone belonged. Jesse looked at Edwin's sons, groomed to power since birth, filled with conscience and strength, leaders. Then he looked at Damien.

"You don't deserve her," he said with finality. He turned and noticed an old man with a tired little American flag, waving it brightly. "Hey, what'll you take for that?"

"Not money," said the man, standing up. "But I'd be proud to see it waving in your corner, McCallum."

"Me too," said the Scot. He took the flag and pegged it to his post. Then he tied his rough, woven tartan around it. "I may not be good enough," said McCallum to Isaiah, "but *that* is." And he pointed at Old Glory. Turning, he looked at Damien. "You don't deserve Katharine, the railroad or that beat-up old flag."

"What? A patriot now? Save it, McCallum!"

"If I don't make it," Jesse said to Isaiah, his vision blurring, "Keep him away from Katharine. Promise?"

"Promise," said Isaiah, grasping his forearm. "But you'll make it. I'm not going to let you die."

"I'll mediate!"came an authoritative shout. Edwin looked up, noticing a group of men entering together. His son Adam was walking beside Asa Whitney. Around them were burly men that Edwin had never seen before, grim-faced and determined.

"We aim to see justice done!" Whitney shouted. The determined look in his eyes punctuated the meaning of his words.

"Come ahead," said Edwin.

"There will be no cheating or dirty tricks!" said Asa. "When I say to a man, 'Break!' then he'd better do as I say or this peacekeeper I've got tucked into my vest will settle the match once and for all! And rest assured, I know how to use it!"

"Whitney, you're a fool," said Damien. "If you bring a gun in the ring you'll start a bloodbath!"

Asa threw him a contemptuous look. "Only," warned Asa, "if a man cheats!" His eyes narrowed. "There's evidence enough that cheating has been going on aplenty! Now, I want a fair fight, Damien, nothing less, and I aim to see that it happens that way. No more double-dealing." Asa's eyes were smoking. "I'd take a strap to you myself, if I could get away with it! I don't like you, North!"

Damien snorted and looked away. He sensed a change in the room. "Feeling's mutual, I assure you," North muttered beneath his breath. Glancing back, he saw the group of men who had come in with Asa, and also the cluster of his own paid bully boys. Damien knew a threat when he saw one, and he not only intended to walk out of the ring, he intended to win.

"Are you ready?" Asa said to the combatants. "Broughton's rules of London here. We've got the gloves ready to lace, and I want your seconds to know the rules, too. I won't have fighting over incidentals! Is that clear?"

Isaiah nodded. Each man was allowed a bottle holder, water and sponge. Each would affix his colors to the post near his corner. Damien pulled out an expensive silk scarf of azure edged in black and wrapped it around his post. Jesse displayed his tartan. Wherever he went, he brought Scotland with him, even into the ring.

Whitney addressed the seconds next.

"If your man goes down, it's up to you to bring him to his corner by the count of thirty. If you don't bring your man up after a fall, then it's a knockout and the other man wins!" A murmur of approval rippled through the audience. Both combatants approached the center, flanked by their seconds.

Asa continued to outline the rules, concluding with the exhortation, "No low blows! No eye gouging! I want a fair fight. Do I make myself understood?"

"Aye," replied Jesse. Some of the old power began to return to his eyes. Memories acted as a catalyst, fueling his movements and awakening a sense of righteous wrath. He remembered his father's battered body lying helpless and cold by the fire, the girls beaten and raped at the Dunes, sabotage and murder, all orchestrated by North.

Damien nodded. "You're dead," he whispered next to McCallum's ear as he touched his glove.

"Then I've nothing to lose," said McCallum, shoving back, hard.

Chapter Forty-four

*T*he kernel of what was to be America was represented in the warehouse that night. Rowdy Irish road gangs, Chinese workers, African-Americans, Anglo-Saxon Protestants, big German farmers, strong Poles, Italians, Russians, Swedes and the English who invested so heavily and exported the iron locomotives being used on American soil.

They all stood beside one another. Though they might once have been adversaries, at least for this one night they were cordial to one another.

At the front of the crowd, Jesse noticed Etta Dory. Surprisingly, she wasn't looking at him with her usual disdain. Her keen eyes kept traveling from her daughter, who was caught in the firm grip of her father's arms, still wearing Damien's colors, to the battered Scotsman in the ring beside his rough, woven tartan of blue, green and red. Etta's blue eyes miraculously softened when she looked at him, and the corner of her carefully rouged lower lip trembled with emotion. Somerset stood beside her, and she was leaning on him for support.

McCallum retreated to his corner, turned and looked across the ring at his opponent. The hunter's gleam had returned to his dark gaze. A coolness permeated his demeanor and a speculative light lit his eyes as he rested his elbows against the ropes. Isaiah was wiping the blood from Jesse's left temple. He had seen Jesse beaten to a pulp and rise again like a phoenix, fueled by an inner fire that the power in his eyes only hinted at. Isaiah refrained from telling him that the gash in his head should be stitched or that a sane man would forfeit the fight. He knew it would do no good anyway.

"Watch him," Briand said.

Jesse laughed and wiped his glove across his mouth. "He's the one in trouble," he said. Then he moved forward, matching his opponent's forward stride.

Speculating on the other's fighting style, reach, and looking for any weakness, the two men eyed each other as they moved cautiously together. Seasoned, they were nearly the same height and weight. Stripped bare to the waist, they wore loose-fitting trousers, their chests rising and falling with steady, unhurried breaths. Jesse knew from the way Damien moved that he was well trained. And North had one advantage: He knew his opponent was hurt; just how badly, he probably wasn't sure. The mocking gleam in his eyes told Jesse all he needed to know. Faces along the sidelines dissolved. McCallum saw only one face and watched it with focused attention as Damien came in, testing his reach to Jesse.

Jesse automatically dropped his right shoulder. His left fist was clenched and up, covering the lower half of his face, and his right was down, cocked back slightly as he moved in, careful to keep his weight distributed between his feet and his center of balance low. Instinctively he dropped his head down and drove his left fist forward in four rapid staccato jabs, keeping his eyes on Damien's face, watching him flinch from the lightning jabs even as he easily dodged the blows. They were meant as decoys, opening North up as he moved back away from McCallum's fists. The Scot saw an opening, and his movement was instantaneous; he had performed these movements so many times that thinking was not needed. The right hand with its powerful fist encased in leather drove up and under Damien's jaw, scraping the chin and cheek, while his left targeted North's eye. A shock rippled through North as flesh met flesh and his head rocketed backward; he stumbled, righted himself on the ropes and moved quickly, trying to avoid McCallum. But he was not quick enough! Another well-aimed right fist sent him flying backward into the ropes. A scream was torn from him as he stumbled to his knees. He had never been hit so hard in his life. Rubbing his chin, he looked up in surprise at the blood on his hands and face.

"All men bleed," said McCallum dangerously. "Get up and fight or I'll take you where you stand." He had been waiting to take North apart forever, it seemed, shrugging off his insults, suffering his attentions toward his wife, knowing what a scab he was. "Get up!" shouted the Scot, and Briand cheered as the crowd went wild.

North started to get up. The moment he was on his feet, Jesse was on him, using his body to pin him to the ropes. He wasn't about to wait for his opponent to recover. He used the rhythm of his jabs to coincide with the movements of the ropes, which threw North back at him each time he was hit. Determined, Damien ignored the wide, swinging roundhouse jabs opening the cut on his forehead. Blood flowed like a curtain across his cheek, mixing with the sweat and the salt; the sting and the burn of it reminded him that he was still alive. His breath became ragged as exhaustion set in and he struggled, ignoring the thin, whistling, knifelike pain that tore through his gut with every indrawn breath. This was revenge. Damien knew it. But he was too dangerous to be ignored.

McCallum was trying for a knockout. He hammered North with blows to his midsection and sternum, driving the air out of his lungs, ignoring Damien's stinging jabs to his head and face. Each time his fist connected, he felt the backlash of power as the blow vibrated the length of his body, lifting him off his feet, causing him to feel as if he were about to fall. He balanced himself by grabbing onto Damien's shoulders and tucking his head in a clinch. A moment of respite ended by the thunderous words, "Break, McCallum! Break!" And he did.

White lights danced at the periphery of his vision, and somewhere in the thundering roar filling his head he heard a warrior's drumbeat in the accelerated rhythm of his heart as the pounding rush of blood filled his ears. He was desperate to lay North out cold on the floor.

Then the sound of the bell. Three minutes of excruciating punishment and pain for both men. Three minutes that seemed an eternity to McCallum. Then he heard Whitney's disconnected shout of, "Break! McCallum, break! Let him loose! Round's over." *Was it an echo?* Jesse shook off the blows, focusing as Whitney shouted in his ear. Then he felt strong arms pull him back. Miraculously, he was still on his feet, mostly from dogged pride and stubbornness, swaying a little as he looked in North's direction. Sheer grit had carried him through the round. He had damaged Damien, too; drawn first blood. Shaking from exhaustion and pain, with sweat pouring from every pore in his body, he lifted a fist covered with North's blood. "Who's the dead man now?" he said grimly.

Stunned, Damien was slumped against the ropes. He stared hard at McCallum as he started back for his corner. There was a look of real fear in Damien's eyes. "You big bastard, you really don't care if you live or die." He was amazed.

McCallum nodded as he went to his chair. "You're right. I don't." His hands came down, resting at his sides. He looked quickly over at Katharine, then back at North. He motioned with one hand for Damien to come to him, baiting him. "Come on, North, you elegant, rich, panty-faced bastard! See how far your good manners will get you with my fist!"

Anger rekindled in Damien's eyes, and his infernal coldness coiled around him like smoke as he stood up. "It's Katharine you want," he said. "Katharine. Money means nothing to you." His eyes narrowed. He knew McCallum's net worth; he knew where the funds were coming from each time he had Dory and the other investors down on their knees. *McCallum was a silent partner.* "All of this because of a woman?"

Jesse nodded. His eyes flickered to the wealth of red hair and the emerald eyes; her fragile beauty, courage and sweet spirit had drawn him two thousand miles across the frontier; he'd staked his fortune and his life to save her.

"And now that you understand me," he said as the clock ticked away the minute between the rounds, "remember this: You're never going to get the Central Pacific and you're never going to get near Katharine again, even if I'm not around."

He felt Isaiah's rough hands on his forearm, turning him. Jesse complied and felt a wash of cold water on his head and stinging pain as ointment was applied to the gash. "You need stitches, McCallum," said Briand. "Can you see?" Jesse's left eye had swollen nearly shut.

"Well enough," he replied. The minute was over and the bell sounded. The sardonic expression Damien had worn was replaced by one of caution as he realized the fight would be no easy win. He kept his distance now, the wariness in his eyes betraying what he felt. His guard was up, and McCallum smiled grimly.

He understood.

"No one is above the law," he said softly and jabbed quickly, darting in and aiming straight for his opponent's face.

Damien dodged the blows easily. The moment McCallum was open, his right hand shot out, hitting the side of his head. McCallum stumbled backward and through experience and sheer determination, righted himself, turned with the agility of a mountain cat and circled back, on the prowl.

"I make my own laws," snarled Damien. Then he attacked. But whatever self-assurance he'd projected coming into the match was now gone. He was cut on his face; his stomach and ribs were bruised. His handsome face had begun to swell.

Both men were breathing hard from the physical toll the match was taking, and both knew that only one of them would walk out of the ring alive.

Furious, North went straight after Jesse this time. His skill at boxing was as good as McCallum's and his condition was much better. He knew McCallum was exhausted and he started to press his advantage, working him backward, hitting him where he was most vulnerable, aiming for the cuts above his eyes and the gash on the side of his head, hitting him until the Scot stumbled backward, struggling to shake off the blows. Then Jesse was against the ropes and North kept punching him until his body began to slump and he felt the edges of unconsciousness overtaking him. But North was just as tired. He held Jesse in a deadly embrace, his blows becoming weaker as the seconds ticked by.

"Dance away, Jesse!" shouted Isaiah. "Dance away!"

"More stumble than dance," muttered McCallum. Isaiah's voice was like a lifeline, reaching across the space, bringing him to his senses. The bell sounded, saving him.

"You," shouted North, "are dead!" Then he slammed one gloved hand into the other and raised his fists in the air, confident once again. Exuberant, he swaggered as he walked to his corner, jeering at the Scot. "You're an ape, McCallum! A trained ape!" He laughed as he sank onto his stool, swilling water and spitting blood into a bucket.

Across the ring, Jesse floated in and out of consciousness, leaning against his post. The fight and the ealier beating had taken a tremendous toll on him.

"Sit down!" shouted Isaiah, but McCallum shook his head stubbornly.

"I won't get up if I do," he said. He knew at least one rib was broken. He could barely see, and the roaring in his ears had increased to the point that he could feel every beat of his heart, reminding him he was only flesh and blood.

A sip of water and the bell sounded. Jesse moved again toward North, whose only evidence of the fight was a few cuts. Smirking, he moved in, jabbing, pushing the Scot back toward the ropes. *He knew he had him.* But his insurance was the salt he had concealed in his gloves. The moment he found an opening, he tossed it in McCallum's eyes.

A scream tore from McCallum. Blinded, he stood in the center of the ring, blinking as the stinging salt attacked the open cuts on his skin. Isaiah pushed through the ropes, bringing the water bucket.

"What the hell did you do to him, North?" Isaiah shouted. Quickly he poured water over McCallum's face. "Call the match, Jesse! You can't see!" He could hear Damien laughing in his corner, because Asa couldn't call foul what he didn't see.

"One . . ." counted Whitney.

"I win," Damien said with icy calm. Turning around, he looked at Edwin and Katharine. His coat was still around her shoulders. The laudanum stilled the rush of pain from the blows the Scot had landed; but the drug was wearing off and the pleasant euphoria had been replaced by a dull ache. He was sweating profusely, remembering his father's words at his mother's deathbed.

No one is keeping score . . .

"She's mine, McCallum. And so is the railroad."

"Two . . ." intoned Whitney, holding up his hand.

Jesse could barely hear as Asa continued the count.

"Three . . . four . . ."

There beside the ropes was a blur of red, a flash of skin, porcelain white. He heard his name and saw a small hand reach out for him.

"*Six* . . . "

"Jesse!" It was Katharine who reached for him. Katharine who was being held back by her father. Katharine who cried for him. It was her tears that touched his glove as she brought his hand to her face. She kissed his hand and shook her head. "Please," she whispered. "Stop." Somewhere deep inside he felt himself back on his mountain, surrounded by a world of white and cold, stars brilliant above his head, with a warm fire and her beside him.

She wouldn't let go.

"Seven . . ."

And the big Scot placed his hand on the lowest rope and remembered his father's body lying in a pool of blood; Katharine tied to a bed, beaten; the shipments stolen, men killed, and all of it tied to North in some way.

"He can't win," Jesse said quietly as he reached for the second rope, winding his fingers around it, pulling himself up. He could feel his legs beneath him once again. Clarity began to return to his mind where before oblivion had held court. He stood up, and the crowd roared.

Swaying slightly on his feet, he touched the tear-stained glove to his face, remembering the feel of her in his arms. Determined, he moved to the center of the ring. There was stunned silence, and then the crowd cheered. McCallum waited for North to make his move. His hands were down at his sides. He was wide open, like a sacrifice, waiting with his dark eyes glittering.

Asa stared at the man standing in the middle of the ring, his white skin smeared with blood and his body tattooed with bruises. The dark eyes were nearly shut, blinded.

"God help you," Whitney whispered, wondering where this man got his strength.

A hush settled over the warehouse. It was so quiet that not a man present missed what McCallum said.

"Come get me, you big bastard," Jesse said. "Now's the time."

And he was once again the man on the mountain, the man who didn't care if he lived or died. He knew he only had one chance. And he knew that North had only one weakness. He'd seen the way Damien protected his face. He had to stay away from the ropes and get as close as possible to his opponent. Chances were, he was going to die, but if he did, he was determined to take Damien with him!

North snorted and narrowed his eyes. "Call the match! He isn't even covering up," he said. "Call the match!" he shouted.

"Compassion, North, or fear?" Asa queried.

There was something eerie and implacable in the open stance of the mountain man.

"Fear? Don't make me laugh!" said North. He slammed one gloved hand against the other and headed toward his target with lethal intent, just as McCallum looked up, waiting and wide open with his big fists clenched at his sides.

"I'm going to enjoy this," said North. He meant to use a jackhammer blow, hit McCallum with everything he had and level him. "Your death wish is about to be answered." He came at Jesse like a juggernaut, sure in his strength, not wanting only to maim but to kill. He cocked his left arm back, bending at the elbow, and raised his right fist, meaning to strike a wide, roundhouse blow, putting all his weight and power in one lethal hit to McCallum's head.

Jesse could barely see. His eyes were swollen nearly shut. He saw Damien approach quickly, he knew he would use his speed and strength. He watched his left arm pull back and he saw the sweeping arc of the right, poised to strike like an ax and bring him down. He had to take the blow. He waited, putting every ounce of energy and power he had into his stance, waiting until North's energy was released.

Then Jesse was hit! The fist crashed against the left side of his face, rocketing his head backward, nearly knocking him over. And it was at that moment that his hand came up and under, putting all his weight and strength into one deadly blow. He hit North on his chin, feeling his fist connect and watching as Damien's head snapped back. North's eyes fluttered and closed as he slumped to the floor at Jesse's feet.

And McCallum was still standing!

"Glass jaw," said McCallum softly. "Count, Whitney. I think I'm dying." The noise in the auditorium was so deafening that no one could hear him. He saw a blur and recognized the doctor coming in his direction.

"One!" said Whitney.

He heard North groan.

"Oh, you big bastard," McCallum said, remembering the terms of the fight as he turned back and held his position. "Stay down."

"Two!" said Whitney.

Fighting broke out near the ring. Men who had been swindled by promises of access to shares of the railroad that North was never going to own were pouring down the makeshift stands, wanting a piece of him.

"Jesse!" The sweet, high soprano voice impaled him like a stake.

He could barely see, but, stubborn Scot that he was, he pretended he could. Everything was a blur. He knew it was Katharine, but he refused to give in to his weakness in front of most of Boston. He had his pride, and he would not drop to his knees in front of her! It was only the force of his will that kept him standing, trembling like an iron oak, swaying but refusing to fall.

A man had his pride!

"Three!" shouted Whitney, bearing witness to an event he would never forget.

"Four!"

"Hey," said North groggily, trying to rise. "Gi'me a hand up here."

"Put your foot on his neck," growled Jesse. "Or I will. I've had enough!" He closed his eyes as he felt a faint brush of silk against his exposed skin. He was being jostled by the crowd, but he could still sense the faint trace of remembered perfume. *He could feel her.* The doctor was saying something to him but he couldn't hear a word and he didn't care. *Another flash of blue. A blur. His hunter eyes were gleaming.* Dark silk, white skin and a cloud of fiery hair he wanted to tangle his hands in. Damn it to hell and back, she was still wearing Damien's silk coat!

"Jesse?" she said. *So soft, sweet and so hot!*

He felt her thin, fragile arms move around him and he exhaled slowly.

"Careful, there," he said. "You'll get your fine silks dirty and Damien's colors, too."

The rancor in his voice was thick.

"Five!" shouted Whitney.

A fight broke out between Asa's men and Damien's hired bully boys. Whistles and sirens were blowing, and shots like the quick popping of a dissonant drum began to echo in the warehouse. Guns were being fired in all directions.

"Bring a stretcher!" Jesse heard the doctor's voice and in a haze of confusion wondered who the stretcher was for. Was somebody sick? Still, amid the chaos he couldn't take his eyes off of Katharine or the coat covering her fair, beautiful, feminine shoulders.

"Six!" bellowed Whitney. "Get out of my bleeding way, you idiot!" he shouted. He pushed the doctor out of the way and apologized profusely when his foot accidentally landed on Damien's neck, pushing him to the floor with a thud. "Pardon me, Doctor! I didn't recognize you!"

"Oh, Lord, Whitney, wait until after the count before you

get into a row!" said O'Sullivan, his eyes bright with interest. Twinkling, he spit into his palms and rubbed them together. "There is plenty to go 'round," he said, bringing both fists up, poised and ready to jump into the fray.

"Seven!" said Whitney.

Jesse watched them and couldn't help it—he laughed. Then he shook his head as he looked at Katharine, his face becoming stormy once again. *That damned coat.*

"Eight!" shouted O'Sullivan when Asa forgot the count. "There is nothing a Celt likes better than a good fight or a woman, sometimes at the same time, right, Jesse?"

"Wouldn't know," said Jesse. His eyes were shining merrily.

"Here," said Whitney, jumping over the gurney. "They've brought a litter for you, McCallum. Lie down and let the louts carry you out. You earned it!"

"Count, Whitney," said Jesse, insulted. "I'm walking out of here. I'll not be carried like some panty-faced dandy!" He glared at Katharine meaningfully, who stared back at him, unsure of just what to do to tame the big beast. "I hate that damned coat," he finally admitted aloud to her.

"The coat?" she repeated softly, bewildered. "Why would you hate a coat?"

"How many reasons do you want?" said Jesse. "God, you're thick!"

"Nine!" shouted Whitney gleefully.

Someone shoved past Katharine and she landed squarely against Jesse's bare chest, making a little "Oh!" of surprise with her perfect red lips. "Done," he whispered.

She felt his hot breath on her face, and every ounce of his muscular body pressed against her so tight that not even a piece of paper would have fit between them.

"You're in trouble, Katharine," he warned quietly. He lifted the silken coat from her shoulders with distaste and let it fall to the floor, drop-kicking it out of the ring. Then he pulled the McCallums' blue, green and red tartan from his post and wrapped it around her silk skirt, jerking her to him with a no-nonsense tug. His one good eye appraised her with an earthy heat that would have set an iceberg on fire.

The tiger touched the flame.

"Trouble?" she said. "Whatever did *I* do?"

"You'll never know, will you?" he said, giving up. "Katharine, you live in a fog."

"Are we going to argue again?" she asked with a stamp of her little foot.

"No," he said in surrender. "I've got better things to do with you than fight." He lifted the tartan, covering her with his colors as he wound his arms tightly around her, holding her close.

"Do you want the silk scarf you won from North?" she asked breathlessly, watching in fascination as he lowered his face toward her. Her heart was thundering in her breast.

"No," he said possessively. "I have what I want." And he kissed her. It was a moment of exquisite relief—the sense of holding in his arms the one person he felt he could never live without. When his lips covered hers, he exhaled, and the sweetness and warmth of her touch felt like coming home.

"Ten!" shouted Whitney. "McCallum wins! Now get this bastard to the jail where he belongs for murder!"

"Murder?" Jesse's attention was riveted on Whitney. He knew about the sabotage, the kidnapping, the investment scam, but had never been sure of the murder. Asa must have known before the fight.

"Yes," said Adam Dory, who was among Whitney's men. He climbed into the ring and handed Jesse a small bit of cloth. "Open it," he said. There was a hard, bitter light in his eyes.

Jesse reluctantly let go of Katharine and unwound the cloth. Inside was an expensive gold cuff link embedded with an oval topaz. "It was found in the wagon of a murdered man," said Adam. "Hugh de Angelucci was killed last year, but we never knew who did it. Another surveyor took over his wagon and discovered the cuff link in a crack between the floorboards."

Jesse nodded his head. "How was he killed?"

"A blow to the head—several, as a matter of fact. There was enough blood in the wagon to indicate that whoever killed him wanted to make sure he wouldn't get up. I'm guessing that in the struggle, Hugh grabbed on to him."

"And pulled the cuff link out of his murderer's sleeve as he was falling?"

"Something like that. The cuff link," he said, pointing to it, "was Hugh's way to make certain that his killer wouldn't get away with it."

Jesse turned the gold cuff link over, and inside, etched in, elegant script, was a name. Katharine stepped forward when she saw the frown and the hesitancy on his face. Reassuringly, she placed her hand on his. "Read it, Jesse."

McCallum looked at her for a moment. A soft, vulnerable light lit his intelligent eyes. He recalled all the years of looking at his father's old Bible, staring at words he couldn't read but had understood and memorized; the painful admission in the mansion foyer; trading a lifetime of gold for an education and a woman he loved, who could look past the rough exterior and see the gentleman within.

The pregnant silence provoked a reaction from Asa, who looked in confusion from Adam to Jesse. "Can you see the words?" he asked.

"I can read," Jesse replied as he looked at Katharine. "Damien North the Third. I guess that is all the proof we need as to who killed Hugh."

"Right!" said Asa. Justice would be done!

"Constable!" shouted Adam, and the lawman made his way inside the ring. "We want you to arrest Damien North for the murder of Hugh de Angelucci!" A roar of approval went up from the crowd. North, nearly unconscious, was lifted onto the cart by Asa Whitney and John O'Sullivan. Unable to resist, Whitney looked at O'Sullivan, and with a nod of silent assent, each man gave the gurney a mighty shove.

"Ho!" they shouted in unison. "There he goes!" And North went head over heels into the crowd of men. "Here's your Barabas!" shouted Asa. "Let the constable deal with him!"

"Ready?" Asa said to O'Sullivan, putting up his dukes.

"What a question to ask a Celt. We're born ready!"

Both men laughed, looked at each other, then jumped into the throng of men, arms and legs flying. It was bedlam and they loved it. What little restraint was left in the warehouse was gone. Risers were being overturned and men were spilling across the seats, hitting anything or anyone that moved. Whistles sounded and policemen poured down the aisles. The pinging whine of gunshots and the staccato popping of buckshot flying overhead added to the chaos.

"Jesse!" said Katharine, alarmed. "Are they trying to hit us?"

"I'm not going to ask," Jesse said, laughing beneath his breath. Her face was upturned to his; the sense of absolute trust she placed in him was apparent in her wide-open expression. She was holding on to him for dear life!

"Too beautiful," he whispered as he brushed back the red hair from her face. Her small hand was pressed flat against his bared chest and she could feel the reassuring beat of his strong, faithful heart as she melted against him like butter on a hot knife. The dark eyes looking at her flared brightly and he claimed her lips. His mouth opened slightly until she could feel the trembling rush of his breath fill her mouth, the movement of his tongue and the hardness of his teeth. He cupped her chin and turned her face gently, his free arm moving down the length of her back, the tips of his fingers grazing her spine and causing a delicious, sensuous ache to build beneath her skin. It was as if they were the only two people in the world. His strong arms pulled her close and he grasped her hair with his rough hand and claimed her mouth in a kiss that was filled with need and want.

"Some people swim in a teaspoon of water and think they are wet. I prefer to dive deep," he said, remembering her sweetness and warmth as she'd opened to him like a night lily on a buffalo robe. Christ, she was so hot!

"And when I do," she said, remembering with a blush, "I'll take you with me." He overwhelmed her senses and eclipsed propriety and restraint. She had never wanted anyone so much. Breathless when he released her, she saw the expression on his face that said he would allow no interference between them again. His arms touched her familiarly, gently. Ahead lay an infinite universe to explore; lifetimes wouldn't be enough.

Her hands wound of their own accord around his neck, tangling in his dark hair. With a passion born of love, she grasped his hair and pulled him to her, kissing him until the walls dissolved and their breaths mingled. Once again they were in the mountains, lost in each other's embrace, making love under the stars beneath a buffalo robe.

"Am I good enough?" he asked. She saw the hurt in his eyes and wanted to erase it.

"Yes," she assured him. "There is no man better. You are what I want."

Restraint and decorum were gone. Nights of wanting were eclipsed by the reality of being in each other's arms. Her gentle hands toyed with the dark rain of his hair, and she laughed self-consciously at her wanton behavior until her dimples showed and he smiled.

"I need you," he admitted. She could feel the hard, hot length of him against her, and she knew where she belonged.

"What did you say your name was?" he asked testily. There was still one matter to be settled.

"Katharine," she answered dutifully with a pout.

He loved her pout.

"Katharine McCallum, Jesse McCallum's wife." She fully intended to have a proper Protestant wedding with four hundred close friends and family present, but she wisely decided to keep silent on that particular point. Then, of course, there was the matter of a marriage license.

"Do you realize we have no marriage license? Every time we make love, we're breaking the law! Legally, we're in sexual purgatory!"

"Call me a felon and sentence me to jail for life," he said huskily. He wondered if she had any idea what she did to him. He was getting dizzier by the second and it wasn't from boxing; his state of arousal was bordering on critical. "I fully intend to break the law on a regular basis.

"And we, wife," he said pointedly, "are going home. Now."

"Are you going to commit another misdemeanor?" she asked, fully aware of his arousal and the probability that they would not make it to the mansion for quite some time.

"I'm thinking felony tonight, Katharine," he said, hurrying her along. "They'd lock me up for what I want to do right now."

Katharine laughed, and the sound was like wind in his ears, making him smile. All prior sins and hurts were forgiven and forgotten in an instant as he wrapped his arm around her waist.

"Ahhh," he said. It was nearly a growl. "Misdemeanor in the morning."

"Only if you keep up," Katharine teased, "don't argue, and do exactly as I say."

Jesse winced in pain when she ran her hand down his bare chest. He could feel her manicured nails raking gently across his skin. "Anything you want, lady," he said helplessly. "Anything." He draped one arm across her fragile shoulders and looked at her, seriously doubting that they would make it back to the mansion for a week or more.

Then he did exactly what he'd said he would do. He

walked out of the ring a winner, with his prize on his arm
and a promise in his heart, because a McCallum refused to
take a fall for anyone and would never be carried!

> "The
> Question is this: is man
> An ape or angel?
> Now, I am on the side of angels!"
> Disraeli

With special thanks to my friend,
Yozan Dirk Mosig,
Fireflies and simultaneous strikes.
The children are still laughing. . . .
Vicki